Abou

Lynne Graham live
a keen romance re
married, Lynne has f
natural child. Her ot
dear to her heart, are a... The family has a variety of pets, and Lynne loves gardening, cooking, collecting all sorts and is crazy about every aspect of Christmas.

Diana Hamilton's first stories were written for the amusement of her children. They were never published, but the writing bug had bitten. Over the next ten years she combined writing novels with bringing up her children, gardening and cooking for the restaurant of a local inn – a wonderful excuse to avoid housework! In 1987 Diana realised her dearest ambition – the publication of her first Mills & Boon romance. Diana lives in Shropshire, England, with her husband.

Fiona Hood-Stewart credits her mother with putting her on the path to becoming a writer, who encouraged her to read avidly! Fiona has led a somewhat cosmopolitan life – schooled in Switzerland and fluent in seven languages, she draws on her own experiences in the world of old money, big business and the international jet set for inspiration in creating her books. Fiona lives on a stud ranch in Brazil with her two sons. Readers can visit her at: www.fiona-hood-stewart.com

Latin Lovers

December 2020
The Billionaire's Persuasion

January 2021
Under the Latin Sun

February 2021
Duty and Desire

March 2021
Claiming the Heiress

April 2021
Spanish Sunsets

May 2021
Dusk 'til Dawn

Latin Lovers: Claiming the Heiress

LYNNE GRAHAM

DIANA HAMILTON

FIONA HOOD-STEWART

MILLS & BOON

All rights reserved including the right of reproduction in whole or in part in any form. This edition is published by arrangement with Harlequin Books S.A.

This is a work of fiction. Names, characters, places, locations and incidents are purely fictional and bear no relationship to any real life individuals, living or dead, or to any actual places, business establishments, locations, events or incidents. Any resemblance is entirely coincidental.

This book is sold subject to the condition that it shall not, by way of trade or otherwise, be lent, resold, hired out or otherwise circulated without the prior consent of the publisher in any form of binding or cover other than that in which it is published and without a similar condition including this condition being imposed on the subsequent purchaser.

® and TM are trademarks owned and used by the trademark owner and/or its licensee. Trademarks marked with ® are registered with the United Kingdom Patent Office and/or the Office for Harmonisation in the Internal Market and in other countries.

First Published in Great Britain 2021
by Mills & Boon, an imprint of HarperCollins*Publishers* Ltd,
1 London Bridge Street, London, SE1 9GF

www.harpercollins.co.uk

HarperCollins*Publishers*
1st Floor, Watermarque Building,
Ringsend Road, Dublin 4, Ireland

LATIN LOVERS: CLAIMING THE HEIRESS
© 2021 Harlequin Books S.A.

Claimed for the Leonelli Legacy © 2017 Lynne Graham
Claiming His Wife © 2001 Diana Hamilton
The Society Bride © 2004 Fiona Hood-Stewart

ISBN: 978-0-263-29942-7

MIX
Paper from responsible sources
FSC™ C007454

This book is produced from independently certified FSC™ paper to ensure responsible forest management.

For more information visit: www.harpercollins.co.uk/green

Printed and bound in Spain
by CPI, Barcelona

CLAIMED FOR THE LEONELLI LEGACY

LYNNE GRAHAM

In memory of all the great Mills & Boon authors who went before me and inspired my stories.

CHAPTER ONE

'It's a very big favour and I have no right to ask it of you,' Andrew Grayson admitted ruefully, angling his wheelchair closer to the fire, his pale worn face taut.

Max Leonelli, a multimillionaire financier at the age of twenty-eight, who had known Andrew since he first entered his household at the age of twelve, frowned. 'Anything,' he declared, without hesitation in making that pledge.

Andrew surveyed the younger man with quiet pride. It was way too late to admit that he should have married Max's aunt and adopted him. His housekeeper's nephew had come into his life as a homeless adolescent, traumatised, frightened and distrustful. No sign of those traits was to be seen in the powerful and sophisticated businessman Max had become.

Women, furthermore, were mad for Max. The beautiful boy with wounded eyes had grown into a striking man with olive-toned skin sheathing spectacular bone structure and a hard, challenging gaze. Max was tough and his humble beginnings and horrible childhood had merely made him tougher but he was also fiercely loyal. And since Andrew's failing health had removed him from the daily stresses of his international business empire, Max had been at the helm of it in firm control. While it had been Max's baptism of fire he had proved to be more than equal to the challenge.

'This goes *beyond* anything and you won't like it,' Andrew warned him.

Max was confused because Andrew usually came straight to the point. 'OK…'

Andrew breathed in, his breath rasping in his struggling lungs. 'I want you to marry my granddaughter.'

Black-lashed dark eyes flaring bright as topaz in the firelight, Max stared back at the older man in sheer bewildered disbelief. 'Your granddaughter lives in a convent in Brazil.'

'Yes and I want you to marry her. It's the only way I can protect her when I'm gone,' Andrew declared with conviction. 'I should have fought her father when he refused to let her visit me but up until last year I still hoped that Paul would come home and step into my shoes and I didn't want to alienate him. After all, she was *his* daughter, not mine. It was his right to decide how he wanted her raised.'

Max released his pent-up breath slowly. Marry a girl he had never met? A convent-bred female oddity who had not returned to the UK since she was born? It was an utterly extraordinary request but it was also the only serious sacrifice Andrew had ever asked of him and would inevitably be a *last* request because Andrew was dying. At that thought, Max's eyes burned as though he had got too close to the fire, his sleek, strong, bone structure tightening into disciplined rigidity because Andrew's quiet dignity demanded that restraint.

'Tia is all I have left, my only surviving blood relative,' Andrew reminded him heavily, his shadowed eyes veiling at the acknowledgement as he turned his greying head away, momentarily sidetracked by the grief of having lost both his sons.

Three years had passed since his elder son, Steven, had died childless, but it was only two months since Andrew had received word that his younger son, Paul, had succumbed to a sudden heart attack in Africa where he had been buried without fanfare and without ever properly mending fences with his estranged father. Tia was Paul's daughter, the result of his short lived marriage to a Brazilian fashion model.

'She should have been made a part of our lives long ago,' Andrew sighed.

'Yes,' Max agreed, reflecting on what little he had learned about Tia's father, Paul. A generation younger than both of Andrew's sons, Max had only ever known Steven. Steven had worked for his father for years, a conscientious plodder who lacked initiative. Paul, so Max had been told, had been far brighter and more promising, but he had walked out of his job in his mid-thirties and gone off to become a missionary, severing his ties with his father and the business world and ultimately losing his wife in the process. On Paul's first posting to Brazil, his wife had gone off with another man, leaving her husband and her infant daughter behind her. Paul had dealt neatly with that unwelcome responsibility by placing the little girl in the care of the local nuns and continuing his travels to work with and preach to the poor in the world's most troubled places.

'Why would you want me to marry her?' Max asked gently.

Andrew groaned. 'Think about it, Max. She knows nothing about our world and she'll be a substantial heiress. It would be like throwing a newborn baby into a shark tank. She will desperately need someone to look after her and guide her until she finds her own feet.'

'She's not a child, Andrew,' Max pointed out wryly. 'She's…what? Twenty-one?'

'Almost twenty-two,' the older man conceded grudgingly. 'But she still needs a safe harbour until she can learn her way in this cut-throat world.'

'She may have grown up in the Amazon Basin but she may also be a great deal more current than you think,' Max argued.

'I doubt it and, while thousands of my employees depend on the stability of my companies, I'm not prepared to take that risk. I have a duty of care towards them as well. Tia will be a sitting duck for fortune hunters. I've been in contact with the Mother Superior at the convent. My biggest concern was that Tia ultimately intended to become a nun but apparently she has never expressed that wish.'

'So why is she still living in a convent in her twenties?' Max enquired with a faint edge of derision.

'I understand that she works there now. Don't judge her, Max. She's never known anything else. Paul was a very rigid man and frankly more than a little sexist in his outlook. He wanted a son. On his terms a daughter was simply a worry and a disappointment. He seemed obsessed with the idea of keeping her pure and safe from modern influences. I believe he hoped that with his encouragement she would eventually enter the novitiate.'

'But she hasn't.' Raking a long-fingered hand through his black tousled hair, Max strode restively across the room to help himself to a malt whiskey while wishing that he could not see Andrew's point of view.

As the Grayson heiress, Tia *would* be a target and Max knew what that felt like because he had been a target since he made his first million. He knew more than most about being wanted primarily for his wealth and the richer he became, the more he was stalked, pursued and flattered by women who would have been equally keen to catch him were he ugly and old.

'And I'm very fortunate that she hasn't because everything I worked all my life to achieve would be sold up and given to the convent if she were one of the sisters there,' Andrew pointed out ruefully. 'I owe my employees more than that. I would also like to meet her…'

'Of course you do.' Max compressed his wide sensual mouth. 'But I don't need to marry her to fulfil that wish.'

'It's unlike you to be so slow on the uptake,' Andrew murmured wryly as he frowned at the younger man with shadowed blue eyes. 'Obviously I want to leave everything to you and Tia together.'

'Together?' Max repeated in a stunned undertone.

'As a couple. If you marry Tia you become family and my empire will become absolutely yours. I know that, no matter what happens between you, when I am gone you will continue to look after her interests as well as your own. I *trust* you to do that,' Andrew completed with satisfaction. 'That's what's on the table, Max. This arrangement would greatly benefit you as well.'

Max stared back at him in shock for it had never once occurred to him that he would inherit anything from Andrew. 'You can't be serious…'

'I'm very serious,' Andrew assured him. 'I have already had my will redrafted to allow for that development.'

'You're prepared to try and bribe me into marrying her?' Max breathed in consternation.

'It's not a bribe. I prefer to call it a realistic incentive. After all, giving up your freedom would be a big sacrifice for you. I know that. I also appreciate that you have no current plans to marry and settle down,' Andrew stated grimly. 'And goodness knows what Tia will be like after the strange cloistered upbringing she's had. She certainly won't be like the sort of women you usually take out and about.'

Max stared down into his glass, reluctant to comment because he didn't usually take his women out and about, he simply took them to bed. He didn't do girlfriends and dates. He kept his affairs much looser than that, never offering flowers or explanations or exclusivity. That way there were no misunderstandings, no expectations and no dangerous routines or suggestion of permanency established. There was nothing complex about his attitude. He liked sex and he didn't need or want to commit to any woman to enjoy it.

'On the other hand, I can say upfront right now that I understand that this may be simply a starter marriage for you both. Isn't that what they call it these days? A *starter* marriage? You and Tia may not get on and one of you may eventually want your freedom. I'm not unreasonable. I have faith that you would do right by Tia even if you separate. That said, what do you have to lose?'

'You've given me a lot to think about. I can see you've considered this from every angle,' Max conceded, the smooth planes of his lean, strong face tight and unrevealing.

'And you haven't outright refused,' Andrew pointed out with satisfaction.

'You're assuming that Tia would be *willing* to marry me. That's a pretty big assumption.'

'Max, you've been romancing women since you were fourteen years old.'

Max winced. 'I don't do the romantic stuff and I'm not prepared to lie to her. I'll consider the idea. I can't promise more than that.'

'Time's ticking on,' Andrew reminded him heavily. 'I've told the Mother Superior that I'm ill and that you'll be flying out there to collect Tia and bring her back here. She was very protective of Tia, demanded a lot of details from me and a character reference for you.'

'Right,' Max sighed, a steel band of tension tightening round his head, that and the occasional nightmare the only hangover from his dysfunctional childhood. He got nasty migraines and he could feel the approach of an oncoming attack.

'Tia *could* be the love of your life,' Andrew remarked in an upbeat tone. 'Stop being such a pessimist.'

Having notified Andrew's live-in nurse that he was leaving his patient alone, Max mounted the stairs of the big house. *Love,* he thought with rampant incredulity. Only Andrew, the veteran of a long and happy marriage and a wife who had died long before Max's arrival, could talk so knowledgeably and confidently about love.

Max had never experienced love. His parents hadn't loved him and his Aunt Carina, Andrew's former housekeeper, who had given Max a home when he'd needed one, hadn't loved him either. Neither a sentimental nor child-hungry woman, Carina had done her duty by her dead sister's son, nothing more, nothing less. And bearing in mind his sordid childhood, Max didn't blame his aunt for her coldness. If he too struggled with memories of his dark past to the extent that he had never yet discussed it with anyone and hated even to think about it, how much harder must it have been for his mother's sister to feel any genuine warmth towards him? After all, nothing could ever change the reality that he would always be his father's son.

Even more pertinently, Max had good reason to distrust love and the damage it could do. He had become wildly infatuated with a girl in his teens and it had been a disaster. His supposed best friend at the time and the girl Max had loved had schemed against him, hoping to destroy him and cover their own sins. He had seen first-hand the harm that trusting and loving the wrong person could unleash.

So, no, Max didn't seek love in his life. Even so, he had dimly assumed that it would sneak up on him again some day and catch him when he wasn't protecting himself from its treacherous influence. But that hadn't happened either. He was entirely heart whole and rather ashamed that the women in his life were all but interchangeable, not one more memorable than the last. He went for identikit brunettes with a sexual confidence to equal his own. He didn't daydream about them, didn't miss them when they were absent, indeed he reckoned that they were purely a selfish means to an end. He gave them jewellery and they gave him sex and if he stopped to think about that exchange it left a nasty aftertaste in his mouth.

A wife, however, was something else entirely and the very concept of a wife brought Max out in a cold sweat. A wife would be around *all* the time, particularly a clingy, dependent one, who needed support.

Of course, he could say no...*couldn't* he?

Unfortunately, Max was ruled by two very strong drives. One was loyalty, the other an equally fierce streak of ambition. Andrew had presented him with the perfect package deal calculated to tempt. Andrew had been his mentor and the closest thing Max had ever had to a father. Everything that he had achieved he owed to Andrew, who had paid for the expensive education that had propelled Max and his razor-sharp wits straight into the heady realms of meteoric business success. Yes, Andrew had had motives of his own for that generosity, he conceded wryly, but that did not change the fact that Max had profited greatly from his support and advice. How could he possibly refuse to offer that same support to Andrew's last living relative?

In addition, Andrew had mentioned that all-encompassing word, *family*. Max would become family if he married Tia. The word, the very connotations of the word harboured a mysterious allure for Max that increased his discomfiture. All his life in one way or another Max had been an outsider. He had wanted to *belong* and he never really had—not within any group—because he was very much a self-made man. His dirt-poor repugnant background, which Max himself could never forget, kept him isolated in many ways. At his exclusive school the other pupils had been from privileged backgrounds and he had naturally kept his childhood miseries a secret for fear of being pitied. His birth family had not been a family in the normal sense of the word and Andrew's careless reference to Max becoming one of *his* small family had made much more of an impression on Max than the older man could ever have guessed.

* * *

The rain was torrential and like no rain Max had ever seen in his life. The downpour that had already reduced the road to a dangerous mud bath still bounced in shimmering noisy sheets off the windscreen and bonnet of the heavy-duty four-by-four he had hired to convey him from Belém to the Convent of Santa Josepha.

Through the flickering vehicle lights ahead he saw, not the established mining settlement he had dimly expected to see, but something more akin to a shanty town. On both sides of the road tumbledown buildings, shabby cabins and even tents stretched off in every direction. The view put him strongly in mind of a refugee camp. Meanwhile his driver continued to chatter in voluble streams, possibly explaining why so many people were braving such primitive conditions to live in the back of beyond, but Max understood only one word in ten because although he was fluent in several languages, sadly Portuguese was not one of them.

An ornamental bell tower loomed ahead and he sat forward, noting the dark outline of the extensive buildings rising behind a tall manicured hedge.

'*Estamos aquí*… We are here!' his driver proclaimed with an expansive wave of his hand as he stopped at a gated archway, shouting out of the window until an elderly man appeared and moved very slowly, his narrow shoulders bowed against the wind and rain to open the heavy wooden gates.

Max suppressed a sigh but, while he was weary after the unexpectedly onerous journey and his delayed arrival, he was far from bored. In fact Max's adrenalin was running at an all-time high and he sincerely hoped that a hot shower and a meal awaited him in the accommodation the Mother Superior had offered him for the night. Above all though he was incredibly impatient to meet Constancia Grayson and discover if Andrew's last wish was in any way viable.

Unaware of Max's arrival, Tia was swathed in a plastic rain poncho to deliver food on a battered tin lid to the mournful little dog sitting patiently waiting for her below the shrubs outside the doors of the chapel.

'Teddy,' Tia whispered guiltily, hurriedly looking around herself to check that she was unobserved before bending down to pet the little animal as he eagerly gobbled up the food she had brought.

Pets of any kind were forbidden at the convent. When human beings were going hungry, using precious resources to feed an animal that did not itself provide food was unacceptable. Tia told herself that she was using her own food and not taking from anyone else but Teddy's existence and her encouragement of his attachment to her weighed heavily on her conscience. For Teddy's sake she had done things that shamed her. She had *bribed* Bento, the old man who kept the gate, not to close the hole in the fence that Teddy used to enter the convent grounds. She had lied when Teddy had been seen in the playground and she had been questioned, and she was lying every time she smuggled food off her own plate to take outside and feed to him.

But Tia *loved* Teddy to distraction. Teddy was the only living thing who had ever felt like hers and just a glimpse of his little pointy tri-coloured face lifted her spirits and made her smile. Only what was going to happen to Teddy now that she was supposed to be travelling to England? But *would* that actually happen? After more than twenty years at the Convent of Santa Josepha, Tia couldn't imagine *ever* getting the opportunity to live another life in a different place. That seemed like a silly fantasy.

Why, after all, would her English grandfather suddenly decide he wanted her when he had ignored her existence for so many years? And now, worryingly, Andrew Grayson's representative had failed to turn up to meet her. Mother Sancha had said the man's non-arrival was probably due to the bad weather but Tia remained unconvinced. Tia, after all, was very much accustomed to broken promises and dreams that didn't come true. How many times, after all, had her father visited and suggested that she might eventually be able to leave the convent to work with him? Only it had never happened. And over two years ago he had paid his last visit and had declared that it was time she became independent because he could no longer afford to contribute to her care. Once again he had suggested that she become a nun and when she had asked why she couldn't live with him and support him in his ministry he had bluntly told her that a young attractive girl would only be a hindrance to his work, and her safety a source of worry.

After her father's death the solicitor had explained that there was no money for her to inherit. Paul Grayson had gifted her his bible and left his savings to the missionary team he worked with.

Tia hadn't been the smallest bit surprised to be left out of her father's will. It had always been obvious to her that her father had no great fondness for her or even interest in her. Indeed, nobody knew better than Tia how it felt to be rejected and abandoned. Her mother had done it first and then her father had done it when he left her at the convent. He had then cut off her options by refusing to help her to pursue the further education that could have enabled her to become properly independent of both him and the convent. So, how could she possibly abandon Teddy?

Teddy *depended* on her. Her heart clenched at the image of Teddy trustingly continuing to visit long after she had gone only to find that there was no more food for him. How could she have been so selfish as to encourage his devotion? What had she been thinking of? What were the chances that he would miraculously find someone to give him a home? In two long years nobody had cared enough to do that while Tia had slowly transformed Teddy from a living skeleton to a bouncy little dog. Teddy had been abandoned too, probably by one of the miners chasing the gold rush, who had left again in disappointment when he failed to make a notable find and his money ran out. The prospectors regularly left women, children and animals behind them.

Hurrying back to her room in the convent guest quarters, Tia peeled off her poncho and hung it up. Her hair was damp and she undid her braids, brushing out her thick honey-blonde hair to let it dry loose. There was nothing for her to do now but go to bed and listen to the little radio one of the girls at the convent school had given her. Occasionally she came across magazines and books in the bins when she cleaned the school building and that helped her to stay in touch with the outside world. Although she earned a wage for her work, there was nothing much to buy within reach and she had been slowly accumulating savings at one stage, only that hadn't lasted in the face of women struggling to feed hungry children. She was a soft touch and unashamed of the fact, confident that she knew which women were the decent mothers, whom she could rely on to use her money to buy food rather than alcohol or drugs.

A knock sounded on her door and she opened it to find one of the sisters, there to tell her that Reverend Mother Sancha was waiting for her in her office.

'Your visitor has arrived,' Sister Mariana told her with a smile.

Tia hurriedly straightened her hair but there wasn't time to braid it again. Smoothing down her rumpled clothing, she breathed in deep and headed downstairs into the main convent building. Her grandfather's representative had arrived, she registered in genuine surprise. Did that mean that she was truly going to travel to England and the grandfather who hadn't seen her since she was a newborn baby?

'Tia is a very kind, affectionate and generous girl and she may impress you as being quiet,' the Mother Superior informed Max levelly. 'However, she can be stubborn, volatile in her emotions and rebellious. You will need to watch over her carefully. She will break rules that she disagrees with. At the moment she is feeding a dog she has adopted, which is not allowed, and she has no idea that I am aware of her behaviour.'

Max studied the calm, clear-eyed nun and reckoned that very little escaped her notice. 'She is not a child,' he asserted in gentle reproach.

'No, she is not,' the Reverend Mother agreed. 'But although she badly wants her independence I'm not sure that she could handle too much of it too soon.'

'I'll keep that in mind,' Max fielded, relieved to hear that Tia was imperfect and desired her independence. Somehow Andrew had given him a disturbing image of a pious young girl with high ideals, who would do no wrong, and he found the elderly nun's opinion of her character reassuring rather than off-putting.

And then the door opened and Max's mind went momentarily blank as a young woman of quite extraordinary beauty tumbled through the door spilling breathless apologies. A great mass of honey-blonde hair tumbled round a heart-shaped face, distinguished by high cheekbones, cornflower-blue eyes and a perfect pouty little mouth. Her skin was flawless. He breathed in deep and long, disconcerted and temporarily stuck for words, which was a quite unfamiliar experience for Max with a woman.

Tia stopped dead a few feet inside the door. In the lamplight, one glance at Max literally took her breath away. He had one of those almost Renaissance faces she had seen in illuminated manuscripts. Smooth bronze skin encased a sleek, stunning bone structure that framed a straight masculine nose, a wide sensual mouth and eyes as dark and rich as chocolate, fringed by dense black lashes. He. Was. Gorgeous. That reaction thrummed through Tia like a bolt of lightning and suddenly all she was conscious of was what she herself lacked. She had no make-up, no decent clothes. Her hands smoothed down over her skirt in a nervous, awkward gesture.

'Tia. This is Maximiliano Leonelli, whom your grandfather has sent in his stead,' Mother Sancha announced.

'You can call me Max.' Max relocated his tongue as he sprang upright and extended a lean brown hand in greeting.

'Tia…' Tia muttered almost inaudibly, barely touching his fingers and gazing up at him in surprise, for she was quite astonished by his height. He had to be well over six feet tall and she only passed five feet by two inches. The few men she met were usually smaller, much older and of stockier build and few of them were clean. Max in comparison was all lean, muscular power and energy, towering over her in a beautifully cut suit of fine dark grey cloth.

She had her grandfather's eyes, Max recognised while trying to fathom what she was wearing and what sort of shape was concealed beneath the frumpy long, gathered skirt and the worn peasant blouse with its faded decorative stitching. She was small in stature and either very thin or very tiny in proportion, her breasts barely visible in the loose smocked top, her slender hips no more prominent below the skirt. She wore stained espadrilles on her feet and for an instant Max was incensed by her poverty-stricken appearance, but he didn't know who to blame. Paul for being a lousy, neglectful father or Andrew for not trying harder to make his son put his daughter's needs first.

'You can show Mr Leonelli to his room and ensure he receives the meal I have ordered for him,' Mother Sancha suggested. 'You'll be leaving us tomorrow, Tia.'

Tia whirled back, her blue eyes very wide. 'Will I?'

'Yes,' Max confirmed.

The Compline bell for prayers peeled and Tia tensed.

'You are excused for this evening,' Mother Sancha told her. 'Mr Leonelli is not a practising Catholic.'

'But what about your soul?' Tia shot at Max in patent dismay.

'My soul gets by very well without attending mass,' Max told her smoothly. 'You'll have to accustom yourself to living a secular life.'

Catching the Mother Superior's warning shake of her head, Tia folded her lips, taken aback by the prospect of a grandfather who never attended mass either. Her father had said his father, her grandfather, lived in a godless world and it seemed on that score, at least, he had spoken the truth.

'I expect prayers are an inescapable part of life in a convent,' Max remarked as he accompanied her down the corridor.

'Yes.'

'Nobody will prevent you from attending services in England,' Max assured her thoughtfully. 'You will be free to make your own choices there.'

Tia nodded, a little breathless about the prospect of *having* such choices.

'What exactly does your job here entail?' Max asked as they mounted the stairs, noting that her golden hair tumbled as low as her waist, or to where he guessed her waist had to be since the tremendous amount of fabric she wore prevented any body definition from showing.

'Lots of different things. Every day I go where I'm needed. I bake, I clean, I work in the orphanage with the young children. I give English lessons to the girls in the school. Sometimes I go out in the community to work with the sisters.'

'The community looks like a refugee camp,' Max commented.

'There's been another gold rush. Someone found a tiny bit of gold and because of that miners flooded in from everywhere. Nothing's been found since, of course, so the fuss will die down and most of the prospectors will give up and move on somewhere more promising. Right now it's like the Wild West out there,' she told him with a rueful smile.

Max studied the perfect bow of her upper lip and the soft inviting fullness below, his body stirring, sexual imagery awakening that for the first time ever embarrassed him. He tensed defensively. And then argued with himself. To marry her he *had* to want her. He could not marry a woman he didn't find attractive. Why was he trying to stifle a natural physical reaction? Andrew's granddaughter was a classic, unspoilt, utterly natural beauty. Of course he was reacting.

Tia showed him into the room at the other end of the corridor from hers. 'There's only you, me and Sister Mariana up here, so it'll be quiet enough.'

Max elevated a fine ebony brow. 'Are nuns noisy?'

Tia cast down her eyes but not before he had seen the brightening leap of amusement in them. 'That would be telling…'

Max was entranced and he forced himself to study the room instead, unsurprised to see that it was as bare as a cell with an iron bedstead set below a large wooden crucifix and the absolute minimum of furniture, while cracked linoleum snapped beneath the soles of his hand-stitched leather shoes.

'The bathroom is opposite. Do you want to eat first?' she prompted, staring up at him, wondering how often he had to shave because black stubble already covered his strong jaw line. Her curiosity about him was intense. In fact dragging her attention from him was proving to be an incredible challenge.

'Yes…feed me,' Max teased, black lashes semi-screening his dark golden eyes as he gazed down at her, marvelling at the glow of her skin even below the stark unflattering light shed by the bare bulb above them. 'I'm hungry.'

'I'll take you down to the refectory.'

'And tell me about the dog,' Max suggested. 'I understand there *is* a dog.'

'Who told you about Teddy?' Tia gasped in horror. 'Oh, my goodness, Mother Sancha *knows*, doesn't she?'

'I would say that very little gets past that woman and of course she mentioned the dog. If you want to bring him back to England with you I will have to make arrangements to allow him to travel,' Max pointed out levelly.

Her heart-shaped face lit up with instantaneous joy. 'I can bring Teddy with me?' she cried in wonder. 'Are you sure?'

'Of course you can bring him, but he will probably have to spend some time in quarantine kennels before you can take him home with you again,' Max warned, mesmerised by the sheer brimming emotion that had flooded her formally still little face and glittered in her beautiful eyes. 'I'll have to check out the rules and regulations and organise it.'

'I can't believe I can just bring him like that,' Tia confided in amazement. 'Won't it cost a lot of money?'

'Your grandfather is a wealthy man and he wants you to be happy in England.'

'Oh, thank you, thank you...*thank you*!' Tia wrapped her arms round Max with enthusiasm and gave him a fierce hug of gratitude without even thinking about what she was doing.

For a split second, Max froze because he wasn't accustomed to being hugged, in fact could not recall *ever* being hugged by anybody, and that acknowledgement in the face of her enthusiasm made him feel uncomfortable and think about the kind of stuff he had always thought it best to repress. He very slowly lifted his arms and placed his hands rather stiffly on her slight shoulders. 'Don't thank me, thank Andrew when you see him. I'm only acting for him.'

Buoyant with happiness, Tia took Max down to the refectory, chattering away in answer to his questions, her earlier unease forgotten. 'Do you like dogs?' she asked.

'I've never had one but I believe your grandfather kept dogs when he was a younger man.' And an astute little voice was warning Max not to hand all the bouquets to Andrew when he was supposed to be trying to impress Tia.

Unhappily Max had not a clue how to impress a woman because he had never had to try before and a pair of sparkly diamond earrings was highly unlikely to cut the mustard with Tia. But had he but known it, he had done the one thing calculated to open the gates to Tia's heart and trust.

That Max was willing to arrange for a very ordinary little mongrel to travel to another country simply to please her overwhelmed Tia's every expectation of him and filled her with appreciation and gratitude. He had to be a kind, sensitive man, she decided happily.

Max and Tia were not left alone at the table in the refectory for long. Visitors to the convent rather than the school or orphanage were rare and various nuns arrived to make his acquaintance. Max withstood the onslaught with admirable cool and the inherent courtesy engrained in him by his education. English was in short supply but Max contrived to speak in French,

German and Spanish to facilitate the dialogue and Tia was even more impressed. Sister Mariana managed to extract the fact that Max was single and even the explanation that he had not yet married because he had still to meet 'the right woman'.

Once the pleasantries were at an end and Max had regretfully declined an invitation to watch a DVD of the Pope's most recent message in the common room, Tia was spellbound by him, convinced she would never meet a more self-assured and refined, sophisticated male in her lifetime. Not that she had much experience of such men, she was willing to admit. Max smiled at her, dark eyes mesmerising below the thick veil of his lashes, and butterflies danced in her stomach while her heart beat so fast that she felt weirdly dizzy.

Sister Mariana accompanied them back upstairs and showed Max the small seating area on the landing. 'You must have so much to discuss,' she said cheerfully before she headed for her own room.

'Does she think I'm about to jump you or something if you come into my room?' Max asked, shocking Tia.

Paling at the crack, she looked up at him wide-eyed. 'No, she meant to be kind,' she replied stiltedly. 'She knows I would not go into your bedroom.'

As a deep rose flush flowered to chase Tia's pallor, Max recognised his mistake but could not even explain to his own satisfaction why he was so on edge. 'I apologise. I thought the rules were restricting us, which would be a little ridiculous when you are leaving this place tomorrow.'

'It's not "this place",' Tia murmured a shade drily. 'It's been my home.'

'I do understand that but this...all this.' Max shifted

a brown hand expressively. 'I'm a complete fish out of water here.'

Tia absorbed the fluid elegance of that physical gesture and marvelled that even his movements could be so graceful. Recognising his discomfiture, she forced a smile. 'Yes. I can understand that. I can only hope I won't feel the same way in my grandfather's home.'

Max gazed down at her, recognising that the laughing, relaxed Tia had gone into retreat as soon as he'd spoken earlier. 'Not while I'm around,' he swore instinctively, feeling ridiculously protective for no reason that he could comprehend.

'Do you live with my grandfather?' Tia asked hopefully.

Having stumbled again, Max almost swore out loud. 'No, but I'm a frequent visitor.'

'I'm glad to hear that,' Tia told him.

Her sincerity mocked all that Max was concealing from her. His strong jaw line clenched. Rain lashed against the window beside them as they stood there. A sexual tension so strong it almost unnerved him gripped Max, tightening his every muscle into immediate self-disciplined restraint. He connected with translucent cornflower-blue eyes. He lifted his hand and brushed a stray strand of gold hair back from her cheek to tuck it behind a small ear.

That intimate little motion, the brush of his fingers against her ear lobe, seemed to burn a fiery trail across her skin and the breath caught in Tia's throat, the noise of the rain outside suddenly mirroring the tempest inside her. She could feel a tightness in her breasts and a sudden embarrassing surge of warmth between her legs. Still as a statue she stayed where she was, foolishly wanting him to do it again, wanting him to *touch* her. As an adult she wasn't used to being touched except by the younger children. Oh, she had been shown plenty of affection by the nuns while she was still a child but as she'd matured the sisters had naturally become less demonstrative and affectionate and the kind of touching that could remind you that you were not alone in the world was what Tia had missed the most in recent years…only she hadn't realised that until Max broke the ice and showed her that reality.

Max forced his hand to drop back to his side and breathed in slow and deep. He was incredibly aroused and incredibly frustrated but her sheer innocence overpowered and haltered his lust. 'I must phone Andrew. He'll be waiting to hear all about you,' he explained, the Italian accent that had faded over his years in England fracturing every word.

Tia nodded. 'I'll catch Teddy before breakfast so that he can't wander away and lose his big chance to travel,' she joked and, turning on her heel without another word, she left, evidently quite unaware that he had wanted to grab her in the most inappropriate way and kiss her.

Still breathing like a man who had climbed a mountain only to discover another mountain awaiting him at the summit, Max went for a shower to cool off. It was the absolute worst and coldest shower he had ever had but Max, who now took luxury and comfort for granted, genuinely didn't notice, so preoccupied was he with his own thoughts.

CHAPTER TWO

MORNING DAWNED—but not before Max, who had slept fitfully on his lumpy mattress on a frame that creaked with every slight movement of his body.

He had risen early, craved his usual black coffee and had had to start his day without it. He had immediately contacted his PA to plan for the dog and organise various other bookings.

'Take her to Rio and kit her out,' Andrew had urged effusively on the phone the night before. 'She's a woman. Never met one that didn't like clothes.'

Max's eloquent sensual mouth hardened. He doubted that Andrew would have been quite so chirpy on the subject had he seen for himself how very poorly his grandchild was dressed. Yet her father had visited his daughter and must not have cared. Max marvelled at the hypocrisy of a man who had apparently done much genuine good in the world and yet had utterly neglected his own child. That was at an end though, he reminded himself grimly. Tia's new chapter was only beginning, and a few months down the road she would in all likelihood cringe at what she remembered of her current lifestyle and it would no longer be mentioned because it would become a source of embarrassment to her.

Max was disconcerted at the faint stab of regret he experienced at the prospect of Tia changing radically and losing that innocent openness. She had not learnt guile or the feminine skill to tease and flirt yet.

And that was what had probably knocked him for six the night before, Max judged with a strong sense of relief at that explanation. How did he relate to a woman so different from any he had ever met before? Or slept with? Max's experience lay solely in the field of highly sexualised flirtations that led straight to the bedroom in which there was no before and after to be considered and very little adult conversation.

He had *tried* to tell Andrew that his plan wasn't going to work because Tia was far too 'nice' for him and he didn't have anything in common with nice girls. Virgins were not his style. He had few inhibitions but, coming awake several times during the night, he had acknowledged that seducing a virgin would never feature on any bucket list of his.

Of course, there was a slight chance that she might not be quite that naïve, he reasoned, and then he discarded the suspicion, recalling that moment on the landing when she had looked up at him with a complete lack of any awareness.

Other men would target her and bed her without a thought, Max acknowledged grimly, anger filling him at the realisation. What the hell was the matter with him? Why was he so conflicted about this situation? He was usually very decisive. *Dio mio!* He could marry her or he could stand back and watch her get her heart stamped on and kicked by some bastard who only wanted her for her inheritance. He could not have it both ways. It would either be him or someone else.

He walked out of the bedroom and was surprised to see Tia seated on the landing with something on her lap. It was the dog. As he moved towards her the dog began to growl. It bared its teeth and would have leapt off her lap into attack had she not restrained the animal.

'Good morning,' Tia said with the most radiant smile that lit up her whole face. 'I've never been able to pet Teddy properly before because I didn't dare smuggle him in here and I fed him secretly…well, not secretly enough it seems.'

Teddy began to bark and she scolded him but Teddy had neither discipline nor manners and he strained forward, snarling at Max as he approached. He had not the slightest doubt that he would be bitten could Teddy have only got free of the piece of twine lead and the makeshift collar he now wore.

'He's not a friendly dog,' Max remarked tactfully.

'He was probably abused. He only trusts me. It's sad,' Tia reflected, still sunny.

'Have you packed?' Max prompted.

'I didn't have much to pack,' she admitted. 'But one of the sisters gave me a bag last night and I used it. I went back downstairs to say my goodbyes then to everyone…'

As her voice thickened and trailed away, tears glistening in her eyes, Max hunkered down at a safe distance from Teddy's snappy jaws. For a tiny dog, he was ridiculously aggressive. 'It's all right to be upset at leaving. As you said, this has been your home for a long time,' he murmured soothingly.

The dark rich tenor of his voice shimmied up and down Tia's spine like a caress and she scolded herself, for she had lain awake more than she had slept the night before. She was attracted to him, of course she was, because he was young and gorgeous and kind. But she had sworn she would not make a fool of herself over him by staring and acting foolishly as she had often seen some of the teenage schoolgirls doing over a handsome young gardener who had worked at the convent for several months. Tia told herself that she was old enough and mature enough to know better.

But meeting Max's glorious black-lashed dark eyes only a couple of feet away convulsed her throat and unleashed the butterflies in her tummy again. She could feel the colour and the heat of a blush building in her cheeks, and as his gaze lowered to her mouth even her lips seemed to tingle with responsiveness. Never had Tia felt so out of her depth as she did at that moment or more aware of her own deficiencies. The teenagers she had once felt superior to had known much more about how to talk and behave with a man than *she* did. When Max got close and she looked at him, she felt almost choked by shyness and awkwardness and every feeling, every sensation she felt was magnified to quite absurd proportions.

For a very experienced man, Max was strangely exhilarated by that blush and he studied her with a weird sense of achievement. She was *not* indifferent, *not* unaware of him. And she was doing what women had done decades before equality transformed the dating scene and waiting for him to make the moves. Flowers, Max thought for the first time in his life in a woman's radius. She would like flowers, being old-fashioned and all that, he decided vaguely.

'We're being picked up in an hour.'

'Mother Sancha has asked us to join her for coffee before we leave but I'll get you breakfast first.'

Max gritted his teeth as Teddy glowered at him over Tia's shoulder and bared his own in a silent snarl of warning. Hate at first sight, Max conceded with sardonic amusement. 'If you could have one special thing, Tia...*anything*, what would it be? There must be things you want—'

'A mobile phone,' Tia told him with a haste that embarrassed her, worried that she sounded greedy.

'You don't have one?' Max queried in disbelief.

'Mother Sancha banned them. She won't allow the girls in the school to have them here. I should explain...' Tia hesitated. 'When I was at school here it was a normal boarding school but that changed as the number of boarders went down. The girls who stay here now are more transient and don't stay for as long. Their parents send them here because they're...troubled,' she selected uncomfortably. 'The sisters have a good record for straightening out troubled teenagers.'

His mouth quirked at that information. 'Yes, I imagine being sent out here to the back end of nowhere and being deprived of even a phone would have a sobering effect on most adolescents.'

'The school fees keep the orphanage going and fund the community work the sisters do!' Tia exclaimed repressively.

'I wasn't mocking the system. I was merely making an observation,' Max challenged.

'You sounded sarcastic,' Tia countered.

'I often am,' Max admitted equably. 'You'll have to get used to nuances like that with people. People don't all think and speak and act the same.'

Tia rounded on him at the foot of the stairs, her ready temper roused at being patronised as if she were still a young girl when she was a grown woman and proud of the fact. 'Do you think I don't know that?' she questioned fierily, an angry tightness marking her small face.

'I think you live in an institution where being different is frowned on and probably have little experience of what life is really like beyond the convent gate.'

'Well, then you'd be wrong because I have often seen the consequences of alcoholism and addiction, domestic abuse and prostitution. There can be few evils that I have not some knowledge of,' Tia argued furiously, hotly dismissing his apparent conviction that she was some naïve little flower. 'Maybe you thought you'd find me on a hill somewhere singing among the wild flowers? Yes, I *am* acquainted with sarcasm, Max!'

Max was taken aback by the display: she had gone from zero to ninety in seconds and lost her temper. 'Does that also mean you need to start shouting at me?' he shot back at her.

Recalled to her wits but still trembling with annoyance, Tia stilled and sucked in a steadying breath, appalled at the rude way she had attacked him. 'I'm sorry. You didn't deserve that rant. I suppose I'm worrying about how I will appear to you and to my grandfather and that I won't suit.'

'You needn't worry about that. If you had horns and a tail, Andrew would welcome you. You're his only relative,' he responded wryly.

'I have a terrible temper. I'm supposed to go for a walk and practise breathing exercises when I get mad, so that I don't lash out at people,' Tia confided guiltily.

'I'm pretty tough, Tia. I can take hard words,' Max countered.

Shame engulfed Tia because this was the person trusted by her grandfather to take her to England, the man who had already ensured Teddy's continuing health. 'I'm sorry,' she said again gruffly.

Max closed a hand on her arm to prevent her from walking away. 'It's OK,' he breathed more forcefully. 'You're right in the middle of a huge upheaval in your life.'

Tia blinked back the tears that had been gathering in hot, prickly discomfort behind her eyes. 'Don't make excuses for me. I was horribly rude.'

'You have fire. I like that, *bella mia*,' Max admitted huskily, his dark deep intonation somehow rousing a curl of heat low in her pelvis. 'I was being patronising and you were right to call me on it.'

'You're very...understanding,' Tia breathed soft and low, locked into his stunning dark eyes as he bent towards her, Teddy's feisty warning growls at her feet ignored by both of them.

And for a split second she actually thought he was going to kiss her and she craved that kiss as she craved water on a hot day, needing somehow to know if that soft, full lower lip of his would be hard or gentle on hers. *Hard,* she decided, lost in a sensual daydream for the first time in her life.

'I have Mr Leonelli's breakfast waiting,' Sister Mariana called down the corridor, and Max jerked back, releasing her wrist, lifting his head again, a telling gleam of feverish colour accentuating his high cheekbones.

Nearly forgot yourself in a convent, Max derided for his own benefit, fighting his arousal with all his might while wondering how she would react if she noticed. He was discovering that when Tia looked at him as though he could walk on water, he liked it, and that astonished him.

Tia was in a daze over breakfast. She knew all the facts about sex and had always thought the actual mechanics of the act sounded fairly disgusting: what the man did, what the woman had to allow. But Max had walked into her life the night before and even her outlook on that had changed because she was now putting Max into that couple equation and found that she was madly curious and shockingly excited by the concept. What startled her the most was the deep current of desire rippling through her whenever she looked at him, whenever she even *thought* about him. In his radius her body no longer felt like her own and was certainly no longer fully under her control.

'So, where do we fly from?' she asked as she settled into the four-wheel drive. Teddy was not impressed to be confined in the pet carrier inside it and whined in complaint but his new official owner didn't want him biting Max and she was rather afraid that he might if given even the smallest chance. The little dog she had quietly adored for so long was revealing unexpected traits now that he was being forced to mix with other people.

As for Tia, her eyes still damp from parting from Mother Sancha who featured in her earliest childhood memories, she felt like someone at the start of an adventure and was working hard at concealing that less than cool reality.

'Rio,' Max told her, lifting his darkly handsome head from the tablet he had been using. 'Sorry I'm distracted but I have work email to answer.'

'We're going to Rio? I thought we were going to Belém.'

'We are, but we are flying to Rio before we head for the UK.'

'I love Belém. It's so big and busy,' Tia chattered and told him about the annual boat trip the sisters took along the River Guama to see the Círio of Nazaré procession, which was the biggest and most important religious event in Brazil.

She talked a lot, Max reflected, and culture shock was likely to hit her when she saw the size of Rio de Janeiro because the city of Belém was tiny in comparison. He also wondered what he would do with her in Rio because he had work to do. It was all very well for Andrew to send him halfway across the world for Tia, but Grayson Industries did not run itself and fast decisions had to be made every day to keep Andrew's companies running smoothly. In addition, Max worked very long hours to convince himself and anyone else who cared to quibble that he was fully capable of being CEO of Grayson Industries despite his comparative youth.

'If we're really going to Rio,' Tia said breathlessly, 'I have a school friend there whom I would love to visit. I haven't seen Madalena since we were eighteen and she left school to go home to her family. We write to each other…well, she writes occasionally. She's very busy.'

'Is she one of those *troubled* girls you mentioned?' Max enquired almost lazily.

'Of course not. Madalena was Head Girl in our last year,' Tia told him cheerfully.

'You should spend an evening with her,' Max suggested.

'Yes. It would be wonderful to have the chance to

catch up with what she's been doing,' Tia remarked, thinking that she would be listening rather than contributing at any such reunion because Madalena's family was well-off and her former schoolmate seemed to enjoy a dynamic social life. But even so she would very much enjoy seeing the bubbly brunette again. Madalena was a lot of fun and fun was something that had been in very short supply in Tia's life since her school days had ended.

At the airport, they boarded a private jet. Tia was astonished when Max pointed out the Grayson logo on the tail fin and explained that her grandfather owned it. When he had said 'wealthy' it had not occurred to her that he could mean quite *that* level of wealth. She sat quietly in her upholstered leather seat while she was served a delicious lunch. Max pretty much worked and she wondered if that was the norm for him or if rather, and which she felt was very likely, she simply *bored* him. Their lives were very different. They had nothing in common, she conceded unhappily. What could an international businessman of Max Leonelli's stature possibly find worthy of interest in a girl who had spent her entire restricted life in a convent?

Thoroughly depressed by that thought and scolding herself for the reality, Tia petted Teddy, who had quietened down considerably after his spell in the carrier. Teddy went to sleep and Tia eventually dozed off too.

As the jet landed at Rio, Max reflected with satisfaction on his morning of work. He only belatedly recalled his passengers and the whole point of the trip to Rio de Janeiro. He was supposed to be using the opportunity to get to *know* Tia. Yet unlike most women he knew she had not uttered a word of complaint at being ignored.

His conscience twanged as he studied her, her beautiful face tranquil in sleep, that exquisite pillowy mouth more tempting than ever in repose. Teddy's little beady eyes snapped open as if he could sense Max's proximity even when asleep and he bared his teeth in a silent snarl.

'Get used to me,' Max murmured drily. 'I'm not going away.'

He would marry her. It was true that he hadn't even thought of marriage before Andrew cornered him but Tia was beautiful and kind and undemanding. How could any man possibly do better than that winning combination in a woman? He had had a lot of partners in his bed over the years, had revelled in all the variety that imbued such freedom; however, Tia ticked all the right boxes. And came with a massive inheritance, the other side of his brain reminded him. But that wasn't a box he had sought to tick because, even before he'd accepted Andrew's offer to step temporarily into the CEO job to free Andrew up for his unsuccessful treatment, Max had been rich enough in his own right to be satisfied with his lifestyle. At the same time though he relished the daily challenge of controlling Grayson Industries. Power, he acknowledged wryly, was definitely an aphrodisiac.

Tia whooped in delight when she saw the massive Christ the Redeemer statue, Rio's most striking landmark. Max was quick to realise that he was unlikely to escape that tourist pilgrimage and he breathed in deep. Well, at least someone was likely to appreciate the private chapel at Andrew's country house which the older man had had meticulously restored in the hope of encouraging his devout son's, Paul's, return to England.

When the limousine that had collected them at the

airport drew up outside the giant opulent hotel where they were to stay, Tia was momentarily overpowered. '*This* is the hotel? But it's famous.'

'Yes.' A dancing smile slashed Max's beautifully shaped mouth, his dark as night eyes gleaming. 'I thought you would enjoy it.'

Tia felt overwhelmed. That smile engulfed her like a tidal wave, washing away clear thought, igniting afresh all the physical reactions that both thrilled and unnerved her at one and the same time. She smoothed her fingers down over her best skirt, made of cotton cloth that had once been a pristine white but which now had a creamy tinge. 'I'm not dressed for a place like this, Max,' she pointed out uneasily.

'But you will be soon,' Max told her. 'I've organised a new wardrobe for you. Someone is coming to our suite to measure you and someone else will then arrive with a selection of clothing for you to choose from.'

'Are you joking?' Tia whispered in astonishment.

'No. Your grandfather wants you to have whatever you want.'

'But I didn't ask for clothes.' Tia reddened. 'Well, I know I need them.'

'Let's not make a big deal of it, then. Andrew is a generous man,' Max told her, nodding to the driver to open the passenger door beside her.

Flustered, Tia climbed out, smoothing her skirt again, her palms sweating as she scanned the ornate front entrance and the even more opulent interior she could see through the open doors. Inside she could see elegantly dressed people moving around and her courage almost tanked at that point because she knew how shabby and poor she had to look in comparison. What had passed muster at the convent could not even compare to the smartly uniformed staff surging towards them to pick up their luggage. Teddy was checked in to the equivalent of a luxury kennel and Tia parted with her pet with reluctance.

The dog settled, Max planted a controlling hand to the base of her spine and swept Tia back into the lift, ignoring her resistance. 'Stop acting so nervous,' he breathed in her ear. 'You're a Grayson and your grandfather has made that name something to be proud of. Clothes aren't important.'

It was all right for him, Tia reflected on a surge of brief resentment, for Max exuded the sophisticated, exclusive lustre of a male who had only just stepped off a glossy magazine cover. Every inch of him was groomed and sleek. He reeked of money and self-assurance, neither trait being one she had ever enjoyed, but she knew that Mother Sancha would have agreed with his outlook rather than her own and she gritted her teeth. Within minutes they were ensconced in the lift with their luggage.

The magnificent suite reminded Tia of rooms she had seen on a popular Brazilian soap opera based on a very rich family. The views were stupendous, on one side looking out over the huge city and on the other out over a vast beach and the sea. Every window opened out onto a balcony and the furniture was beautifully upholstered in colours that struck her as wildly impractical for daily use. She followed the porter into a glorious bedroom, walked into an attached bathroom resplendent with marble and mirrors and gold taps. Her fingertips brushed a white fleecy towel and then trailed over the shot silk spread on the bed before withdrawing again.

'Tia,' Max called. 'I have something for you.'

Tia moved forward on uncertain legs, already overcome by her luxurious surroundings and the bewildering suspicion that she had accidentally strayed into someone else's dream. She gazed up at Max, colliding unwarily with his stunning, heavily lashed dark as night eyes. Her breath feathered in her throat and her heart slammed with sudden force against her breastbone as he extended his hand. 'For you from me,' he intoned. 'It's all charged up and ready to use.'

It was a mobile phone with a sparkly cover, the sort of cover a teenager might have admired but Tia was not fussy. With a whoop of pleasure at finally receiving what she had long wanted, Tia whirled breathlessly round the room. Madalena had kept on sending her phone number as if Tia could somehow magically conjure a phone out of thin air but she had kept her friend's letters. 'Thank you, Max,' she said.

Max was a little disconcerted not to receive another hug, had indeed braced himself for one, but Tia, did he but know it, knew she had to be more circumspect around him once she had understood how much he attracted her. She didn't want to behave like an infatuated schoolgirl and make a fool of herself.

The flowers were the next delivery, a gorgeous display of white lilies and foliage arranged by a maid in a crystal vase. 'For...*me*?' Tia whispered breathlessly, a fingertip stroking a velvety petal in appreciation.

'Of course for you...'

Tia could not imagine why Max was giving her flowers when they were already in each other's company and he had nothing to thank her for. The romantic angle, she discarded entirely as an explanation, having decided during the flight that allowing foolish fancies to take over her brain was likely only to lead to her humiliation.

Max got the message that he was not making his interest obvious enough and that was when he regretted not paying more attention to her while they were airborne. He studied her glowing face as she caressed the lily and imagined that small work-roughened hand gliding over a far more responsive part of his body and anticipation leapt through him like a sudden flame ready to burst out of control. The stirring of enthusiasm at his groin was unmistakeable and made him ache. He didn't know why she had that instantaneous effect on him. Indeed, his lack of control around Tia annoyed him because he hadn't suffered from the affliction of involuntary arousal since he was at school.

'You like the flowers?'

'Yes,' she whispered distractedly. 'I love flowers. I always dreamt of having a real garden of my own.'

'I thought you wanted to be a teacher,' Max remarked, because the Reverend Mother had shared that with him.

'I was willing to be one to get the training and the education. In my life it's always been a question of *not* what you want but what is possible,' Tia explained. 'There's a teacher training college in Belém and I thought that studying there would be achievable but my father wasn't willing to pay for it and that was that.'

'Andrew's country house has beautiful gardens,' Max told her, watching the tip of her tongue steal out to moisten her full lower lip as she looked up at him and almost groaning with the force of his arousal.

His dark eyes were gleaming like gold ingots and Tia couldn't drag her gaze from his lean, darkly beautiful face. Without even knowing what she was doing she took an infinitesimal step closer and Max reached for her almost simultaneously, hands sliding round her back and yanking her into contact with his lean, powerful body with a sexual insistence and impatience that should have shocked her but which instead thrilled her.

It was Tia's first kiss—first *everything*, really—and the hard, hungry pressure of his beautiful masculine mouth crashing down on hers unleashed so many sensations in her body that she felt dizzy. The tips of her breasts tingled and stiffened, pushing against the coarse cotton material of her top. A sliding warmth prickled between her thighs and made her press them together tightly. Suddenly she was insanely conscious of a part of her body she never thought about, of the sensitivity and the shocking level of physical awareness she had never known before.

His tongue licked along the fullness of her lower lip and then nibbled at the tender swollen flesh before his tongue plunged into her mouth and withdrew. At that point her legs would have folded under her had he not literally been holding her upright with his hands because the sexual vibrations assailing her only intensified. A choked gasp was dragged from her as he spread his fingers across her narrow shoulder and held her there to kiss her breathless.

Max was fiercely fighting an insane urge to carry her into his bedroom when the knocking at the door finally penetrated the fog of his passion. What the hell was he doing? he asked himself furiously as he jerked back from her, almost overwhelmed by the passionate response he had won from her. He wanted more, he wanted *so* much more that it took a lot longer than the few seconds he had to get a grip on himself before he opened the door.

Four women greeted him with wide smiles and swiftly identified themselves as the team engaged to provide Tia with a new wardrobe. Shooting her a cloaked glance to note that she was very flushed and dazed in appearance, he urged her to take them into her bedroom.

Diavolo, he castigated himself as soon as the bedroom door closed. He had jumped the gun, offered too much too soon and probably shocked her, but going slowly with a woman, much like talking in a normal way, was something Max had never done before. And he had utilised all the finesse of a bull in a china shop, an awareness that infuriated him as he stomped off to change and have a cold shower to chill the fever still burning through him. It was not as though he were sex-starved, he reasoned angrily with himself, so why that lack of control? That mad grab and hold making-out session, which was not his style at all?

Relieved to escape the immediate aftermath of that embrace with Max, Tia was happy to be distracted by measurements and catalogues depicting various styles. She had only wanted jeans and tee shirts and some decent shoes but there was, she discovered in amazement, a vast area of choice from which to make selections. The little girl and disappointed teenager who had never got to have pretty clothes triumphed in the adult she had become and she went a little crazy before panicking and surging back into the other room to find Max.

'What's my budget…? I mean, how much can I spend?' she pressed anxiously.

'There is no budget. Order anything that takes your

fancy…handbags, shoes, *everything*,' Max stressed. 'You'll need it all in England and it's better to arrive prepared.'

Tia surveyed his darkly handsome features with wondering appreciation. Had ever a young woman been so blessed as she was at that moment? she marvelled, smiling widely at him. She could buy anything she liked and Max, the man of her dreams, had kissed her, which meant that he was attracted to her as well, even if she suspected that he hadn't quite intended to kiss her when he had.

Was Max struggling with the same feelings she was struggling with? Feeling buoyant at that suspicion and walking on air in the belief that the growing strength of her feelings was being reciprocated, Tia vanished back into the bedroom.

CHAPTER THREE

'I DON'T WANT TO,' Tia said simply as Afonso, one of Madalena's male friends, tried to pull her into the bedroom that had just been vacated by another couple.

'Thought you wanted to lose that V-card…' In the face of her refusal, Afonso managed to both smile and sneer simultaneously. He was good-looking and he knew it, his lack of familiarity with rejection obvious to her.

'Maddie was joking, for goodness' sake,' Tia declared, wishing that that were true of her former best friend but no longer quite sure because she felt as if she was learning the hard way that four years could change a friend into someone she barely recognised.

'No, she wasn't,' Afonso insisted, still unwilling to accept that no meant no in Tia's case as he pulled her against him with a possessive and determined hand.

He was drenched in cologne and she could hardly breathe that close to him. She gave him a dispassionate glance, hating the swimming sensation in her head from the alcohol she had already told Madalena she didn't want to drink. Not because she was stuffy and prim, as Maddie had insisted she was. She had refused more alcohol as soon as she'd felt her body overreacting to that second large drink. No, indeed: the very last thing Tia wanted to risk was getting drunk at a wild party full of strangers, none of whom she felt she could rely on.

It was ironic that she wasn't having anything like the fun she had once assumed such social events delivered when she was younger. Fun, she rather thought now, depended on the company you were in and she knew she was in the *wrong* company. Losing her virginity with some stranger on a night out had no appeal for her. Maddie, however, had decided it was a terrific idea, pointing out that the first time was always 'rubbish' for a woman. Tia had said nothing because that conversation had taken place in a group setting and she had been embarrassed at having her sexual ignorance talked about in public as if it were solely a subject for amusement.

Nothing with Maddie had gone as Tia had planned and hoped. When she had phoned Maddie that afternoon, the brunette had invited her over that very evening and Tia had naively pictured a chatty session of catching up. When she'd arrived, though, Maddie had already been entertaining a bunch of friends and the first thing she had done was insist that Tia borrow some of her party clothes to go out with them. Stripped of her jeans and tee, Tia had found herself being crammed into tight satin shorts and a backless top, both garments exposing far more of her body than she was comfortable with. But the other women had been wearing similar outfits and she had wanted so desperately to try to fit in and not be the party pooper Maddie had suggested she was that she had kept her reservations to herself.

Maddie was engaged to a handsome young businessman. Unhappily the couple had vanished within minutes of arriving at the party, lumbering Tia with Afonso and his sidekicks, whose only topic of conversation appeared to be dirty, rather infantile jokes. Before Maddie had finally abandoned her, however, Tia had seen a scattering of powder below her school friend's nose and had suspected that she was using drugs, which probably explained her unfamiliar highly extroverted and bad-tempered behaviour.

'So where exactly are we here?' Tia asked again.

'Why do you keep on asking me that? I don't know the address. It belongs to Domingos Paredes. We're in Jardim Botânico. It's an exclusive residential area.' Afonso trailed a suggestive hand down her bare back, making her shudder. 'Play your cards right and you could end up swanning around a house like this. I bet there's nothing you want more than to be a wife and a mother. Some guys go for that. Come on…stop being such a prude.'

'I'm not a prude,' Tia argued as Afonso backed her up against the wall. 'I don't feel that way about you.'

'But you haven't even given me a try,' Afonso protested, hands roving all over her and trying to go in for a kiss but stymied by the manner in which Tia hastily jerked her head away.

'Let go of me!' she told him with sudden loud, angry emphasis. 'I don't have to put up with this if I don't want to!'

Afonso backed away a step and swore viciously at her. 'You're a freak,' he told her nastily. 'Nothing but a damned freak!'

As the young Brazilian stalked back into the crowded main room of the party in a rage of wounded vanity, Tia was trembling and tears were burning the backs of her eyes, making them throb. She walked towards the back of the big house, stepping over prone bodies and entwined couples to escape the worst of the noise. On the terrace she dug out her new mobile phone with a shaking hand and rang Max, who had programmed his number in.

'I want to come back to the hotel,' she told him chokily.

'What's the address?' Max queried. 'Has something happened?'

'I'm at a party and someone called me a freak. It's probably the truth,' she told him in a shaky rush. 'I don't know the address but I know who the house belongs to and the area. I can't get a taxi because I have no money.'

'I'll find out where you are and pick you up as soon as I can.'

'I'll wait outside.'

'No, stay indoors where it's safe,' Max instructed. 'And calm down.'

Ashamed of the tears blurring her vision and what felt like her general uselessness as the strong independent woman she was determined to be, Tia approached a female in the bathroom queue and finally asked for the address, which she duly passed on to Max.

'Where the hell have you been?' Maddie demanded of her in the hall. 'And what did you do to poor Afonso? When I last saw him, he was really into you.'

'I wasn't into him.'

'Well, it doesn't matter. We're all moving on now to this great club.'

'I'm going back to the hotel, but thanks for bringing me out,' Tia said very politely.

'Mother Sancha did a real number on you, didn't

she? You really don't know how to enjoy yourself at all,' Maddie declared pityingly. 'If I'm honest I always thought you'd join the flock.'

'I never had a vocation,' Tia admitted, wondering how long it would take for Max to arrive and sitting down on a chair by the wall because she was light-headed. 'But I'll admit that I don't know how to enjoy myself the way you do. I'll return these clothes back to you tomorrow.'

'Oh, don't be silly. I won't wear them again after *you've* worn them,' Maddie confessed with a little moue of distaste at the idea. 'I'd only be dumping them.'

Tia reddened and nodded, more uncomfortable than ever. In the convent, they had utilised and recycled everything possible. 'I'll collect my jeans,' she said stubbornly. 'They're my very first pair.'

'And that says it all really, doesn't it?' Maddie said almost sadly as she walked on by.

Her colour fluctuating, Tia thought about Max and admitted that what she had felt in his arms had also told her all she needed to know. After all, once he had kissed her she had immediately known that she didn't want anyone else kissing her. But what if on *his* terms it had merely been a casual kiss? Of the same sort that Afonso had offered? How did she tell the difference? How did she *know*?

All that she knew was that Max's mouth on hers had been the most glorious and exhilarating feeling she had ever experienced and she literally couldn't wait for him to do it again. But would he *want* to do it again? And how did a woman encourage a man to make that kind of advance without being brazen about it? She was mortified to acknowledge that she would have gone into a bedroom with Max without a word of protest. What did that mean about her? That the convent teaching of purity before marriage had hit stony ground when it came to her? Or that while she was aware of that moral ideal, it was *only* an ideal and she was equally well aware that many people experimented with sex before marriage?

Max was in the back of a limousine speeding through the Jardim Botânico area and he felt like the biggest bastard in the world. He was supposed to be taking care of Tia but he had no experience of looking after anyone and, clearly, he'd fallen at the first hurdle. Instead of accompanying her to her friend's house, he had let her go alone and he had not even ensured that she had money with her. Admittedly he had first established that Madalena Perez was the daughter of a respected diplomat and seemed a safe companion. Although it hadn't occurred to him that Tia could be going out on the social scene, it should have done and he *should* have been there. *Shoulda, coulda, woulda*, a minatory voice sneered in his hind brain. He had ducked his responsibility because he'd wanted to work.

What did that say about him?

After all, Tia was infinitely more precious to Andrew Grayson than his empire and Max knew it. As Max's future bride, she should be equally precious to Max and deserving of special attention, but he had let her down. He had organised a spa grooming appointment for her the next day, not to mention a trip to see the giant religious statue on top of Corcovado Mountain, but those were superficial treats and would be of little consolation to her when she was as hurt and upset as she had sounded on the phone.

Max helped himself to a second drink, his inbuilt alcohol monitor screaming reproach at him for the choice. As the son of a violent alcoholic, Max usually only had one drink at a time, never more, fearful that he could have inherited a gene that could make him more likely to fall into his father's addiction. Not that there was anything good to be said for *any* of the genes Max had inherited, he conceded with grim self-loathing. Not for the first time, he reminded himself that his mother's sister, Carina, his aunt, had been a perfectly normal woman in decent employment and respected by all who knew her, but it didn't remove the sting of shame that any recollection of his own seedy beginnings invariably unleashed.

Even in the surge of arrivals and departures that saw cars constantly moving up and down the driveway to the big villa, Tia was primed to recognise the one that contained Max and she had bounced up off her chair even before he appeared at the door, head and shoulders wider and taller than the two younger men who arrived there before him. When someone dragged open the door and her expectant gaze landed on his darkly beautiful features she felt ridiculously tearful and had to restrain herself from throwing herself at him like a child.

Max, for his part, was frankly shocked rigid by the vision of Tia in skin-tight red satin shorts, a silky, glittery, barely there top and Perspex stripper heels. He had relished the shape of her in the jeans she had worn earlier that afternoon, almost painfully aware of her long slender legs and her delicate but highly feminine curves at hip and chest. But braless and in shorts, *everything* was on view and he had an outrageous urge to yank his jacket off and drape it round her because the blatant sexuality of what she brandished in such an outfit was a very poor frame for the young woman she actually was.

'Max...' she breathed, hurrying towards him, her eagerness to leave the party unconcealed in the huge cornflower-blue eyes pinned to him.

Max herded her outside towards the limo, striving honourably to ignore the little bounce of her small firm breasts as she went down the steps and the flash of long creamy inner thigh that led up to her scarlet-defined crotch. But he was still a man and he got painfully hard just picturing that first full-frontal view of her again, his brain quick to conjure up the definition of thin satin over a woman's most intimate area. And then the rage took a hold of him like a rejuvenating bolt of lightning that burned out all sexual response, which in the strangest sense was a relief for him.

As soon as the driver closed the passenger door on them, Max rounded on Tia, dark eyes flaming gold with instinctive fury. 'You don't *ever* go out dressed like that again!' he thundered across the car at her.

Taken aback by that sudden attack, Tia bridled and her eyes flared a darker blue in angry confusion. 'What on earth are you talking about?'

'You look like a pole dancer or a stripper. You're showing too much skin. Where did you get those clothes? I can't believe the stylist authorised those shorts.'

'What's a pole dancer?' Tia enquired icily, her spine very stiff in her corner of the car because who did *he* think he was to tell *her* what he thought she should be wearing? He was a man and what she wore was none of his business.

'Not the sort of woman you want to be mistaken for.'

'Madalena loaned me these clothes and I wasn't comfortable in them,' Tia admitted grudgingly. 'But her friends were wearing the same sort of thing. And the stylist didn't *authorise* me to choose clothes today, I made my *own* choices and they were probably pretty boring choices because I didn't pick any party stuff like this.'

'People...men in particular will judge you by what you wear,' Max bit out with a raw edge, his anger compressed but still burning like a solar flare inside his chest because every time he thought of the men who had enjoyed the same view of Tia that he had had, he got furious all over again.

'That's very old-fashioned,' Tia replied without hesitation. 'Anyway Maddie made sure our companions knew I wasn't as sexy as I looked because she told them all that I was a virgin,' she confessed boldly, far less embarrassed by that reality than she had been earlier that evening after Maddie had forced her to deal with that topic in public.

'She *told* them?' His nostrils flared with distaste, an ebony brow flying up in frowning query. 'What the hell was she playing at?'

'She tried to persuade me to lose my "V-card", as she called it, by going into a bedroom with one of the men,' Tia confided. 'I refused and that's why I got called a freak.'

'She's *not* a friend,' Max pronounced, helplessly cast back to his own experience of betrayal by a friend he had trusted when he had been a teenager. 'Definitely not a friend. Friends don't try to harm or humiliate you.'

Tia winced. 'Think I've kind of worked that out for myself, Max. I even suspect that dressing me up like this was part of the joke for her. She wasn't the girl I remembered from school.'

Max closed a hand over hers where her small fingers were curling defensively against the leather upholstery. 'Not your fault. It was mine. I shouldn't have let you go alone. I didn't even make sure you were carrying money.'

'No, Max…' Tia yanked her hand from beneath the comforting warmth of his although it took effort to voluntarily break that contact. 'Don't treat me like a child you have to take care of. I have to learn how to handle myself and not depend on others. I'll find my way. I won't be a freak for ever.'

'You're *not* a freak,' Max growled, forcibly closing his hand over hers, all the more tense because he knew he had utilised that same word in his head when he'd first learned about her unusual background. 'You're only a little out of step with the modern world and given time that will quickly fade. Your father should've been shot for leaving you at the convent even after you finished school.'

'He didn't want to be bothered with me and out of sight was out of mind for him. My mother wasn't much different,' Tia sighed. 'I think they were both a bit shallow and selfish when it came to personal relationships. With Dad, all his passion went into his missionary zeal and he didn't really have room for anything that interfered with that. My mother, I think, is more driven by money and social position.'

His brows had drawn together. 'You've *met* your mother? I assumed you hadn't seen her since she left your father when you were a baby.'

Tia compressed her generous mouth and looked

steadily back at him, for the first time striking him as being more mature than her age on paper. 'Curiosity brought her to the convent. She visited me when I was thirteen to explain why she'd left me behind.'

'Che diavolo...!' Max exclaimed in surprise. 'That must've been some explanation that long after the event.'

'No, it was quite simple.' Tia's luscious soft mouth compressed. 'She broke up with the man she originally left my father for and then she met another man, a rich man, and they married. Although her second husband knew she had been married before, he didn't know she had left a baby behind her. They went on to have children together, two boys and another girl, I seem to remember.'

'Your half-brothers and half-sister,' Max commented.

Tia shrugged a slight shoulder in dismissal of that familial label. 'But they don't know I exist and my mother doesn't want them to know because she's afraid she would lose her husband and her wonderful life here in Rio after keeping me a secret for so long. *He* was more important to her than I could ever be. It was really that simple.'

For some reason that non-judgemental tone of acceptance made a kind of murderous rage swell up inside Max's broad chest. His own parents had been appalling in terms of family affection and Tia had not done that much better, yet her parents had not even had the excuse of ignorance, poverty or addiction. He breathed in deep in the silence and swallowed hard, for there was really nothing he could say to her that she hadn't already worked out for herself. She was shrewder than he had given her credit for, convent-bred or not. He was both disconcerted by that acknowledgement and relieved, for the more intelligent and wary she was, the quicker she would adapt to life as Andrew's heiress. And as his *wife*?

Max stiffened, squaring his wide shoulders, his handsome mouth flattening. He refused to even think about that aspect this early in the day. If he did marry Tia as Andrew had urged him to do, no actual wedding would take place for months. Max refused to rush into anything. Max liked structure, order, strategic planning. He didn't do impulse or invite disruption in any field and would never have scaled the heights he had without serious self-discipline. With Andrew expecting to survive another six months at least, Max planned to utilise a good part of that time to move in unthreatening, measured steps with Tia while she got to know her grandfather.

The limo drew up outside the brightly lit hotel. Max sprang out first and then disconcerted her by peeling off his suit jacket and draping it round her shoulders as she emerged from the car.

'Is that really necessary?' Tia enquired, reeling a little and struggling to find her balance in the ridiculous heels as the fresh air engulfed her.

'*Sì*...if you can turn *me* on this hard and fast when I'm striving to stay cool, I imagine other men will stare too, and I am assuming you would prefer not to be stared at and lusted after,' Max murmured in a raw undertone, astonishing her with that abrupt and unexpected admission. 'On the other hand, if you enjoy being the centre of male attention, give me my jacket back...it's entirely your decision.'

She turned him on. Tia was exhilarated by that grated

confession and clutched protectively at his jacket, which fell past her knees, revelling in the intimacy of the silk lining still warm from his skin and the faint evocative fragrance of his cologne that still clung to the fabric. She breathed that fragrance in like an addict. Unlike Afonso, Max didn't drench himself in scent. The attraction *was* mutual. Of course, she had suspected that after the kiss but Max had been very businesslike and detached when they had been alone after the stylists had departed and she had felt discouraged. Now standing in the lift, wrapped in Max's jacket, struggling not to study him with lustful eyes lest he instantly recognise her shamelessness, Tia felt transformed, shedding the sense of failure and mortification that events at the party had wakened in her.

If Max wanted her too, *could* anything else matter to her? In that instant nothing mattered to Tia but the way she was feeling. For so long she had been locked away from all the normal experiences she should have begun enjoying in her teen years. That was when she should've enjoyed her first kiss, falling in and out of love, dating, gossiping, learning all the many things that a young woman had to learn as she grew up. But Tia had been denied that adult education and now that she had met Max, she was greedy to catch up with everything she had missed out on.

Butterflies were whipping up a storm in her tummy and her heart was beating very fast. Max glanced down at her and swiftly looked away again, his strong jaw line pulling tight to define his superb bone structure even more cleanly.

'You'll want to go to bed now. You have an early start in the morning,' he informed her briskly as he opened the door of their suite and stood back for her to precede him, the courtesy making her feel delightfully feminine.

'I'm not a child, Max,' Tia reminded him afresh.

Max gritted his teeth together, for he had not been impervious to the way she had studied him in the lift. But that kind of early intimacy wasn't on his schedule and he refused to deviate from what his logic told him was the right and proper way to embark on any sort of relationship with Tia Grayson. That one kiss had been dynamite and he didn't play with dynamite and he didn't lust uncontrollably after virgins like the creepy little loser who had already tried to lure her into bed that night, he reasoned.

'I'm twenty-two in three months' time,' she reminded him, wriggling her slight shoulders to remove his jacket and settle it on the arm of his chair.

Her golden mane tumbled round her lush little face and that was when he finally nailed her startling resemblance to a poster of a film star his mother had much cherished as a feminine ideal. It was those wide perfect cheekbones, those bright cornflower-blue eyes, that delicate little nose and that wickedly sultry mouth. He was transfixed as she settled down on top of his jacket, long graceful legs stretched out. She angled her head back, the elegant pale line of her throat revealed, and as her spine arched her firm little breasts thrust out below the fine material of the draped top and Max's rigid controlling schedule went out of his mind so fast she might as well have flipped a switch.

'Your grandfather expects me to look after you,' Max reminded her tautly, uneasily conscious of the throbbing ache at his groin while idly wondering whether it would disgust or intrigue her before hastily suppressing the thought as unwise.

'And you're doing a terrific job,' Tia told him sunnily.

Max frowned at that undeserved accolade. 'Not tonight, I didn't.'

'That's nonsense,' Tia denied, leaping upright to walk closer to him and reinforce her conviction. 'You calmed me down and came to pick me up. I feel safe with you—'

Max expelled his breath in a pent-up hiss. 'But you're *not* safe with me. I'm not qualified to be playing a big brother role around a gorgeous woman—'

Tia stood her ground, a slight giggle at his terminology escaping the ripe pink parted lips that were his sole focus while she wondered if he really meant that flattering word he had ascribed to her. 'I don't want you as a big brother, Max, and I'm glad you can be so honest because *I* want to be honest too…' she began.

Max made a last-ditch effort to save her from him and from herself and disconcerted her by suddenly bending down to scoop her up into his arms and stride at speed towards her bedroom, where he intended to stow her safely out of reach. He burned for her but it wasn't that simple. He would not allow himself to be tempted beyond the boundaries he had set. He didn't want her to be honest with him when he couldn't *be* honest with her. Andrew had forbidden Max to even tell his granddaughter that he was terminally ill because he wanted to handle that information personally. Andrew wanted Tia kept in the dark about everything: his business empire and her inheritance, his fears, his fiercely protective desire for her to marry Max. Regrettably, Andrew's rules simply made Max's role more difficult.

For a heady split second, Tia assumed that Max was taking her into her bedroom for immoral purposes and in the mood she was in she was fully on board with that idea, but when he laid her down on the wide bed he started to straighten and pull back. It occurred to her then that he was actually physically putting her to bed like a misbehaving child and, outraged by that suspicion, she shot out a hand to grab his sleeve and pull him back to her.

'Max!' she censured sharply.

Max jerked back another step and hit his head, a crushing blow on the ornate wooden strut of the four-poster bed frame. For an instant he literally saw stars and swayed and, seeing that, Tia succumbed to guilt and regret.

Scrambling up on her knees, she grabbed his hand worriedly. 'That was my fault. Are you all right? That was quite a thump you got.'

'*Sì...*' Max conceded, blinking rapidly in an effort to clear his fuzzy head and dismiss the pain while slowly turning to look down at her. Her blue eyes were so honest and anxious and the luscious mouth below them so perfectly plump and inviting that the ache at his groin almost made him groan out loud.

'Sit down for a minute. You've gone very pale,' Tia told him.

'I don't need to sit down.' A shred of sanity remained in Max's bemused brain and in it the bed loomed large as a trap of catastrophic proportions.

'Sit down, for goodness' sake.' Wondering if he had concussion because he seemed dazed, Tia used her hand on his to yank him down on the mattress beside her. Rising to her knees, she reached up to feather her fingers gently through his tousled black hair to feel the faint swelling beneath. 'We should go to the hospital.'

'It's only a bump, Tia,' Max groaned, turning his head to look at her in wonderment because after the childhood he had endured bumps and bruises, including broken bones, were nothing new to him.

'If I hadn't been…messing around…' Tia selected her wording with care, her conscience still twanging as she marvelled at her own misplaced and mistimed boldness '…it wouldn't have happened.'

And what was about to happen wouldn't happen either, Max continued inwardly, absolutely enthralled by the upturned pink swell of her tantalising mouth and discovering too late that that was the true trap, not the bed, after all, because he leant down as if being drawn by invisible strings to touch his mouth to hers.

And holy hell, she tasted like sweet juicy strawberries and the hot, spicy night air. Max fisted a hank of golden hair in one hand and he crushed her soft pillowy lips beneath his own with fervour, hunger leaping through him with unstoppable force.

His tongue flicked against the sensitive roof of her mouth and delved deep and a massive ripple of seductive sensation slivered right through to Tia. Unlike Max earlier she had no doubts about what she was doing or what she was inviting. Max was, basically, the man of her dreams and when Tia wanted anything she threw her heart and her soul into getting it with a stubborn, steady-minded resolve that her grandfather would have recognised as his own. Max was kissing her again, which meant he wanted her as much as she wanted him. Of course, he had tried to put the breakers on this exact development, she acknowledged absently, loving that he hadn't wanted to rush her into anything too soon, recognising what she saw as being an honourable streak in his character.

But Tia made her mind up fast and she was eager to live the life she had been denied for so long, in fact, grab it with two greedy hands and run as fast as she could with it…

CHAPTER FOUR

TIA SUCKED IN a great lungful of air as Max temporarily released her mouth. There was a golden glow of what she fully recognised as lust in his stunning eyes. It didn't have to be love, she told herself, she wasn't looking for love yet, was content with a dose of healthy normal lust. In the future, there would be plenty of time and opportunity for her to fall in love. But even so, nothing had ever felt so necessary as Max's sensual mouth plundering hers and the sweet, sliding invasion of his tongue.

Her body was all pulled taut and needy with responses that were new to her. Her breasts felt ridiculously sensitive, the tightly beaded tips pushing against the scratchy fabric of her top.

'You should make me wait for this,' Max growled soft and low, conflict in his hungry gaze as he perused her.

Already flushed, Tia's face burned at that unsought advice. 'I can't believe you're saying that to me. I thought you wanted me.'

'Doubt there's a man in Rio who wouldn't want you, *bella mia*,' Max assured her helplessly. 'But I also don't want you to have any regrets.'

'Why on earth would I regret this?' Tia questioned, sitting lithely up to reclaim his drugging mouth again for herself, hands settling on his warm, wide shoulders, fingers flirting with the silky tips of his black hair. The buzz in her body wouldn't let her stay still or act compliant.

Max loosed the halter tie at the nape of her neck and found the soft pouting swell of her breasts with his hands, catching her nipples between thumb and finger to pluck at the swollen buds, pushing her back against the banked-up pillows as she writhed.

The liquid heat at the heart of her went into a frenzy when he touched her breasts. She pressed her thighs together, head rolling back and shifting restively against the pillow as he released her reddened lips to close his to her straining nipples. The light was burning and her lashes flickered on a sudden view of Max's dark head over her bare breasts. For an instant she went rigid, mortification threatening to claim her because she wasn't accustomed to being even partially naked in front of anyone and the shock of that glimpse was extreme. *Are you a woman or a mouse?* a little voice asked at the back of her head, and the words bubbling on her tongue died there. She knew what she was doing, she *did*, she told herself, trembling as the heat between her thighs mounted with every tug of his mouth. How could anything that felt so good be wrong?

Max rearranged her petite body on the bed the better to enjoy her. Her nipples were a delicate tea-rose pink, darkened by his attentions, and her breasts exquisitely shaped but bare handfuls to a man used to better-endowed women. Even so, Max was enthralled by her porcelain-pale skin and the satiny softness of it, even while he was deciding that while Teddy the dog might be a little on the porky side his owner was a little too thin and needed feeding up. He wrenched at the shorts and the thin material ripped, startling her, troubled blue eyes opening to belatedly recognise that he was still fully clothed.

'Take your shirt off,' she whispered.

Charmed by that instruction, Max dealt her a slanting grin. 'You wouldn't think you were a first timer at this.'

Forcing herself to keep her hands loose on the bedspread when self-consciousness prompted her to cover her breasts from his view, Tia watched him strip off his shirt.

'I'm a quick learner,' she told him, her mouth watering as he exposed the coiled lines of muscle across his abdomen and flat stomach. The dampness at her core increased and she couldn't drag her gaze from his lean, powerful body. His bronzed skin sheathed rippling muscles, a broad chest and narrow hips stretching down into long, hair-roughened thighs and around there her scrutiny bounced hurriedly upward again, noting the trail of dark hair that ran from his navel to disappear below the band of his boxers and, the whole time, striving not to think nervously about his obvious arousal.

Was she stupid? She was annoyed with herself for that schoolgirlish embarrassment. He was aroused, of course he was, just as she was. She wasn't about to let the horror stories told by Maddie and her potty-mouthed friends of their first sexual experiences to unnerve her… *was she*? She was a grown woman, not an adolescent playing with forces she didn't understand.

Max came down on the bed, kneeling over her, caging her with his big body and a rush of excitement snaked through her, every nerve ending jangling with anticipation. He had done this before, hadn't he? Of course he had, she told herself instantly. But it didn't always pay to make assumptions about people, she conceded.

'You've done this before…haven't you?' Tia pressed awkwardly.

And Max, who didn't embarrass easily, in fact who would have said he was impervious to embarrassment, could feel his face heating up. 'Yes,' he pronounced flatly, reasoning that, as she had waited, it was not impossible that he could have been the sort of rare male who waited too for that one special experience. And unfortunately, that set off a whole train of conjecture in his head about what Tia might want from a man. An innocence that matched her own? A guy who went to mass? A perfect shining angel of a male, who was honest and decent and religious? He didn't think he was any of those things.

'A lot?' Tia could not resist prompting uneasily. 'I mean…er, have you had a lot of women in your life?'

Wide, sensual lips compressing, Max simply jerked his head in acknowledgement, wishing that the heat in his face would subside.

Her own face warming, Tia closed her eyes but still saw the troubled dark gold of his gleaming eyes below the black fringe of his lashes. She had embarrassed him and she shouldn't have done that. At least he had been honest, though; at least he hadn't lied about it, she reflected ruefully.

'I think this would be a lot more challenging if we were both virgins,' Max breathed curtly while thinking he had never thought to share such a conversation in his life with a woman. Then again, he hadn't bargained on a Constancia Grayson figuring in his future, had he? And Tia was very much one of a kind.

'You're probably right,' Tia conceded.

'But you're also probably disappointed,' Max breathed and gritted his teeth, suddenly feeling furiously out of his depth, wondering where he was planning to go with the dialogue and finally registering just how off his game he was that he didn't actually know.

'No. I don't think I am,' Tia murmured, huge blue eyes opening to dreamily survey him, pale fingers smoothing from his shoulder down over his chest in a considering caress that blanked his mind and locked his tongue, because the one thing Max did know at that precise moment was that he wanted her hands *all* over him.

Max lowered his dark head, drawn by forces he didn't even understand. She might want some ideal, perfect male but guess what? She was getting *him* and she could learn to deal, he thought, with the kind of raw aggression that powered him through the business world. He focused on that soft, pouty mouth and went back hungrily for more, smiling into the kiss as her spine arched and her whole body reached up to him, responding to *his* expertise, wanting *him*.

Long brown fingers smoothed along her thigh and when she emerged from that kiss he was working his sensual path down over her squirming length and at some stage of the proceedings her knickers had gone and she felt shockingly, wickedly naked. But before she could even process that discovery, Max parted her thighs and began to do something she had read about but had never dreamt she would actually experience.

The wave of heat and mortification that pulsed through her shaken body was intense. In an abrupt move, she reached down and snarled her fingers into the black luxuriance of his hair and then he licked her, *there*, where she had never dreamt she would be so intimately touched, and such a pulse of shattering excitement gripped her that she fell back helpless against the pillows.

He did it again and she gasped, neck lifting, breasts straining, suddenly in the hold of something seemingly much stronger than she was. Her body writhed of its own volition, a crazy pressure building at her aching core, and her nails dug into his shoulders. He was ravishing her, *tormenting* her with pleasure, she thought wildly, in thrall to pure sensation. She trembled, shook, emitted muffled cries, utterly out of control, her entire being locked to the feeling of his fingers entering her previously unbreached body. His tongue flicked across the tiny bundle of nerves he had exposed and it was as though her body detonated, the pressure peaking and the aftershocks passing outward, sending a coiling energy blast of delight to pull at her. Sated, dazed, she fell back against the pillows in wonderment at what sex was all about.

'No, you do not get to go to sleep now, *bella mia*,' Max warned her thickly, sliding up her relaxed body to gaze down at her with molten golden eyes awash with hunger and need.

And Tia realised for possibly the first time that it wasn't all about her and guilty colour washed her face, a new tenderness sliding in its wake as she noticed the tension etching his lean, darkly handsome features. As he lifted her legs and tilted her up to him, she only just restrained herself from wrapping her arms round him and hugging him for giving her a superlative introduction to the physical that bore no resemblance to the sexual horror stories she had been subjected to earlier that evening.

'I hope this doesn't hurt much but it might,' Max breathed in a driven undertone. 'I haven't been with a virgin before.'

'That's all right,' Tia framed in a rush, stretching up her head and claiming a kiss from that wide, sensual mouth that had taught her the meaning of pleasure.

As Max kissed her back, doing that flick of the tongue thing again that enthralled her and reanimated the heat in her pelvis, she felt him push against her tender flesh, inch by inch pushing for entry into her untested body. She was insanely conscious of his every tiny movement, equally aware that he had prepared her as well as he could. And it seemed to work until he drove deeper and there was a sharp pinch of pain that forced an involuntary gasp from between her parted lips. And he stopped.

'No…go on,' Tia urged, gritting her teeth, her body even more primed than she was for the great reveal, indeed the churning liquid heat in her pelvis craving exactly that development.

Max thrust home, crazily aware of her lush inner walls clenching round him. *'So good,'* he ground out helplessly, revelling in every tight, hot, wet atom of her welcome and somewhere around then he lost himself as he had never lost himself in a woman before.

Hands clenched on her hips, he pulled back and then plunged into her again, hard and fast. The shock of it thrilled through her tender body like a storm warning.

It was the most extraordinary pleasure she had ever experienced. As he pounded into her, her hands clawed in his hair and then into his shoulders and then down his back, the excitement and the pressure rising and rising until she could no longer contain it. Her heart thundering in her ears, her head jerking back and forth on the pillows, she felt that mighty surge of sensation gripping her womb and throwing her high as outer space again. She thrashed beneath him, unable to contain the ecstasy as convulsions quaked through her satiated body.

In the aftermath she felt so heavy, so languorous, she was bemused. 'That was...don't have the words...'

In bed or out of bed, Max rarely had words with women, preferring to escape intimacy with silence on the sensible grounds that what wasn't said couldn't be misinterpreted. But Tia had both arms and both legs wrapped around him and he was trapped. 'That was the best sex I've ever had,' he mumbled thickly, his head now aching so badly he couldn't think straight.

In consternation at that awareness, Max reeled out of bed, as dizzy and disorientated as a drunk, and he finally appreciated that there was something badly amiss with him, something worse even than his usual punishing migraines. 'Sorry, feeling weird,' he framed with difficulty. 'Think I must be overtired...'

Tia leapt out of bed as he sank down on the rug. 'You need a doctor,' she gasped.

'Don't want a doctor,' Max told her predictably.

Fortunately, Tia discovered that a doctor was easily obtained by the helpful hotel staff. The minutes that followed her call were frantic. Between fetching Max a glass of water and finding and getting some clothes on her naked body before registering that Max was naturally equally naked, she felt harassed and anxious and very guilty. It was concussion, she knew it was, having seen the effects before in the convent infirmary. Max rambled on about his susceptibility to migraines and the medication he wanted her to get from his room but Tia only grabbed clothes from the built-in units in his room.

Persuading him to get back into the bed was a challenge but he didn't appear to own pyjamas or a dressing gown and the only item of clothing she managed to get him into was a pair of boxers. By that stage the doctor was at the door and she had to answer it flustered and barefoot, but such was her apprehension for Max that she wasn't concerned.

The young, chatty doctor wanted Max to have a hospital scan but Max was as immovable on that score as concrete laced with steel. For some reason, he didn't like hospitals and he didn't like scans. After considerable pressure from the worried doctor, who was equally convinced that Max had concussion from the blue-black bruising and the swelling that was visible when his hair was parted, Max agreed to attend the hospital the following morning. Discussing the treatment Max required, Tia saw the doctor out of the suite.

'Tia…' Max called almost as soon as she was out of his sight.

Breathless, Tia sped back and studied him, wondering what was normal for Max because the doctor had asked her that question when telling her to look out for abnormal behaviour. But how much did she know about the man she had just slept with? Next to nothing, came the answer. Ashamed of that reality, Tia reddened.

'I can't simply lie here in bed like I'm ill!' Max bit out in frustration.

'You have to. You're very dizzy and if you fall I couldn't get you up on my own,' Tia pointed out sensibly, her practical nature taking charge. 'It's midnight anyway and it's only for a few hours.'

'I don't go to bed at midnight like your grandfather. In fact I'm used to late hours and little sleep,' Max murmured drily, studying her from below the lush black fringe of his lashes, barely contriving not to flinch. There she was: his beautiful downfall, the film-star beauty ruffled but no less appealing, golden hair tumbled round her heart-shaped face, blue eyes sparkling. She had a sort of effervescent glow about her. Knowing that he was about to douse that glow didn't improve his mood.

'Tia...I didn't use protection,' he divulged in a harsh undertone of self-blame.

'What do you mean?' she prompted uncertainly.

Max groaned out loud, for that naïve question said it all as far as he was concerned. He had taken cruel advantage of her innocence, he conceded grimly. 'I assume that thump on the head left me disorientated. I didn't use contraception with you.'

Belated comprehension striking her, Tia froze and her complexion turned pale and clammy. 'Oh,' she framed in dismay.

'As I'm regularly tested there is no risk of disease,' Max assured her, his intonation brusque. 'Believe it or not, I have never before had sex without using protection. Obviously one doesn't want consequences...'

'Consequences...you mean, me getting pregnant,' Tia gathered, her brain still struggling to handle the deeply unwelcome surprise he had dealt her.

How could she have been so foolish? She had got so

carried away that she hadn't even considered the risk of pregnancy and the acknowledgement that she could *be* that irresponsible was even more of a shock.

'Clearly that's a risk,' Max spelt out flatly, having watched her pale and flinch from that reality. 'We're both young and healthy. There could definitely be consequences.'

Only that morning, Tia had wakened in the convent, still naïve and ignorant about matters that other young women took for granted at her age. Now all of a sudden it felt as though she was being subjected to a frightening crash course on what adulthood demanded and she was appalled by her carelessness. She had forgotten all common sense, everything she had been taught about how to look after herself and stay safe. She couldn't even recall how many years it was since she had been assured that purity was the only certain way to avoid an unplanned pregnancy. So informed, her classmates had giggled and exchanged superior glances while whispering remarks about modern birth control. But, Tia told herself unhappily, her hindsight and regret came a little too late to the table to be helpful. It was done; wrongly or rightly, it was done.

'We'll have to get married,' Max informed her without hesitation. 'Immediately. In this situation where I was entrusted with your care, it's the only possible remedy. Your grandfather trusts me. If there's the smallest chance that you could be pregnant I need to marry you now.'

In silent disbelief, Tia stared back at him. Perspiration beaded her brow. That was the moment that Tia registered that, not only did she not want to be pregnant, but she also didn't want to be married either. No, not even if Max resembled a Renaissance prince and took her to heavenly heights in bed. What Tia had dreamt of for so many years, what she had always craved was… *freedom* and independence. And nobody needed to warn her that there was little wriggle room for freedom in either matrimony or motherhood.

CHAPTER FIVE

BENEATH MAX'S INTENT, measuring gaze, Tia had lost all her natural colour and her bright eyes veiled as she studied the highly polished wooden floor instead of him. He realised instantly that Tia was not receptive to the idea of marrying him and it was a shocking wake-up call for a man who had spent years on the social scene being relentlessly pursued by ambitious young women in search of a rich husband. Tia had slept with him but she didn't want to *marry* him.

It was a revelation and it hit Max's ego hard because, he realised angrily, he had placed too much importance on her obvious attraction to him. Very possibly right now she did not feel much different than he did after a one-night stand. She might have enjoyed herself but that didn't mean she was eager for a repeat.

'You have a very expressive face,' Max murmured grimly.

'That's why I'm *trying* not to look at you!' Tia protested with emphasis. 'Mother Sancha always knew what I was thinking almost before I did. It's just…what you said about getting married startled me. I wasn't expecting that.'

'As I see it, we don't have much of a choice,' Max inned, his delivery bordering on curt in tone. 'Bringing you home to Andrew unmarried and pregnant would be a disaster, possibly more for *me* than you I'll admit. I fully believe that your grandfather would forgive you for anything but he has higher expectations of me...and I'm not a member of his family.'

The gruff note on which he completed that very honest little speech unexpectedly touched Tia's heart. For possibly the first time she appreciated that, while he might not be a relative, Max was undeniably fond of Andrew Grayson.

'I have no idea how you even know my grandfather or what your relationship with him is,' Tia reminded him uncomfortably. 'Do you work for him? Are you a neighbour? A friend?'

Max breathed in deep, already inwardly monitoring what he was willing to tell her and all the many things that he planned to take to the grave with him. 'I was born in a small Italian village. My background is poor and rather sleazy,' he admitted starkly. 'When, for reasons I won't go into, my parents were no longer able to look after me, my mother's sister, Carina, who worked in England for Andrew, agreed to give me a home. She became my guardian when I was twelve. Your grandfather generously paid for my education. I lived under his roof during the holidays, not as a guest, though, but as the housekeeper's nephew in the housekeeper's apartment.'

Tia was taken aback by all that he revealed, having assumed that Max came from much the same sort of privileged and financially comfortable background as her father. Her lashes fluttered rapidly as she absorbed that new information, for it *did* put a different complexion on their situation. Clearly, Max felt he owed Andrew Grayson a debt for his kindness and did not feel that he could afford to rely on the older man to forgive or overlook any mistakes he made. Did Max think that getting entangled with Tia counted as a mistake? Suddenly, she was very much afraid that that was exactly how he viewed their passionate encounter.

'Everything that I am today I owe to Andrew's generosity,' Max confessed harshly. 'I don't want to do anything that distresses him. He's eighty and he's…' unusually he hesitated '…frail.'

'Our getting married could distress him,' Tia suggested.

'No. Don't forget that Andrew is from an earlier generation of men. He still sees marriage as the best source of happiness and security for a woman,' Max told her flatly.

'So, you're willing to marry me simply on the off chance that I could conceive,' Tia recapped. 'I understand that but I would prefer a husband who wanted to marry me for a more conventional reason like love.'

'I won't lie to you,' Max murmured in a tone of frustration. 'I can't offer you love. I was only in love once in my life when I was very young and I hated the effect it had on me. But I *can* promise to be caring and supportive…and, assuming it's a normal marriage, faithful.'

Inwardly reeling from that declaration, Tia plonked herself down in a corner armchair and gazed back at him. Her body still ached from his possession and that spur of recollection sent a snaking coil of heat down into her pelvis when she studied his lean, strong face. She respected his honesty even if she didn't like his embargo on love because she strongly suspected that, given sufficient time, she could fall for Maximiliano Leonelli like a ton of bricks. After all, he was offering her almost everything that she would eventually want…only she hadn't wanted to find it quite so soon after leaving the convent.

She should have thought of that reality before she'd shared her body with him, she reflected guiltily, should have thought of who he was and who she was and how her grandfather might react to that intimate connection. But she hadn't thought one sensible thought since Max had exploded into her safe little world, she conceded. He was lean and dark and beautiful and his sophistication and charisma had stolen her wits. She suspected that from the outset she had been behaving rather like an infatuated teenager, all overexcited and encouraging, wildly impulsive while never counting the cost. Or even considering the question of repercussions. What if she *were* to conceive a child?

Wasn't that the real bottom line? Wasn't she being horribly short-sighted and selfish when she thought regretfully of the freedom she had planned to embrace in England? The putative career choices and socialising she had dreamily envisaged? In their own way, weren't such aspirations rather similar to the single-minded selfishness that had persuaded her own parents to abandon her? A dependent baby hadn't fitted in with either her father or her mother's plans. Once their marriage had broken down, Tia had become an unwelcome inconvenience to Paul and Inez Grayson. Was she to take the same attitude to her own baby, were there to be one?

Everything strong and ethical in Tia cried out against that attitude. If there was to be a baby, that baby's needs should be placed central and first, not sacrificed to her self-interest. She would behave better than her parents had, she told herself urgently. She could make sacrifices if necessary and rearrange her own priorities if she became a mother. But naturally all of that would be easier to do if she had the father of her child by her side to help. Whether she liked to admit it or not, Max's proposal *could* be a lifeline and one that she would very much need if she had a baby.

'Can't we wait and see if we have anything to worry about first?' Tia asked, her colour high.

'I don't think we should risk your new life in England starting out under a cloud,' Max admitted truthfully. 'Your grandfather would be upset if we had to suddenly confess all and get married in a hurry. We could get married here in Rio and return to England as a couple. It would be easier.'

'But it could also be quite unnecessary. I may not be pregnant,' Tia pointed out uncomfortably.

'And if that proves to be the case, we can reconsider our situation at a later date, free of all other concerns,' Max stated with an almost imperceptible wince, thick lashes dropping down on his eyes to shield them from the strong light, his chiselled jaw line clenching at even the prospect of her conceiving.

Scolding herself for her preoccupation, Tia rose to switch off the lamps, so that the only light entering the bedroom was shared from the reception room next door in a wide triangle that plunged the bed and Max into semi-darkness.

'Thanks,' he sighed.

Tia drew in a decisive breath. 'I'll marry you if you honestly believe that that's the best option we have. I don't want to do anything to upset my grandfather either. After all, without his intervention, I would still be at the convent.'

Relieved by her assent, Max relaxed his wide naked shoulders and rested back on the pillows. 'Use my room and go to bed now. It's ridiculous that the doctor told you to sit here and keep me awake all night. Believe me, without my migraine medication I'm in too much discomfort to fall asleep.'

'I'm not leaving you alone,' Tia answered stiffly. 'If I'm going to be your wife, it's my duty to look after you.'

'Don't kill me with enthusiasm,' Max quipped, cringing behind that humour at the label of 'wife' but far more unnerved by the prospect of a pregnancy.

After all, Max had never planned to have a child. *Ever.* He didn't want to pass on what he saw as his murky genes. He didn't want to face the challenge of being a father when his own had been such a monster. All he had ever wanted was a reasonably peaceful, solitary and successful life. But between them Andrew and Tia had tripped him up, thrusting a giant spoke into his structured and controlled existence, throwing up worries and vulnerabilities he had never had to face before. He didn't want to brood about that misfortune though. Life was always challenging, he reminded himself impatiently. And most men would not consider a very beautiful, very sexy wife a burden…

Why did *he* have to be different? But he knew the answer, didn't he? Born of violence, he didn't want to take the risk of forming a permanent relationship with a woman or having a child of his own because he could never quite trust himself, could he?

As his ever vigilant and distrustful aunt had often reminded him, 'Who knows what you'll be like when you grow up? I can only do my best with you but blood can tell in the next generation, and I'm sure you don't need me to tell you that your father was a brute and your mother was delusional.' It had been one of Carina's favourite speeches and it had ensured that Max never once forgot his sordid start in life.

Unaware of her future husband's bleak thoughts and falling far short of her duty of care as a potential wife, Tia dozed off, exhausted by the day she had had. When she wakened it was late into the morning and she was no longer in the chair, she was lying on the bed with a cover thrown over her, and Max was nowhere to be seen. Assuming he had returned to his own room, she went for a shower, revelling in the refreshing beat of the water against her skin, so very different from the weak lukewarm trickle that had purported to be a shower at the convent. Reluctant to put on her crumpled clothing again, she made use of the fleecy robe on the back of the door and emerged, stilling when she saw Max, fully dressed and apparently restored to normality, in the bedroom doorway.

'Can you get dressed quickly? I've ordered breakfast for you but we're running late for your appointment.'

'I have an appointment? Where?' Tia walked barefoot over the polished floor, fighting to keep her voice level and her expressive face still because her mouth had run dry and her heart was pounding. Clothed in a light grey suit that exuded the exclusive expense of personal tailoring, Max, from the smooth olive planes of his exquisite bone structure to the deep-set drama of his black-fringed golden eyes, was simply breathtaking.

'One of those women's grooming places,' Max proffered. 'I had my PA organise it for you yesterday because I thought you would enjoy the experience. They'll do your nails and stuff like that.'

Tia nodded, a jolt of happy anticipation bringing a sudden smile to her tense mouth. At the party the night before in the company of much better groomed women she had been mortifyingly conscious of her unstyled hair, the ugly callouses on her hands and her short nails. Although she had been raised to believe that vanity was a sin, when she had still been at school with Maddie she had experimented with make-up just like every other girl there. Once Maddie had moved on with her life beyond school, however, Tia had had nobody to share those little vanities with.

'I will enjoy it. Have you been out?'

'I went for the hospital scan first thing,' Max admitted, surprising her. 'I have concussion, which will heal on its own. I feel fine.'

Tia wanted to slap him for not waking her and allowing her to accompany him. Concussion and he just shook the injury off as though it were nothing? Wasn't that taking macho male denial of weakness too far?

'I'm relieved that you got checked out but surprised because you seemed so against it last night.'

'I don't like hospitals but I'm not stupid. I've had concussion before and it was more serious on that occasion.' Max shrugged a dismissive shoulder while watching her pull various garments to consider from the wardrobe. 'Wear the blue dress. It'll highlight your eyes,' he advised, striding back into the other room.

Clad in the blue dress, Tia slid her feet into light sandals. She rubbed her pale cheeks to lend her wan reflection a little colour. She looked tired, not her best and she marvelled at Max's undeniable energy after his accident the night before. He'd had concussion *before*? Had he got into a fight with someone or been involved in a car accident? Frustratingly there was so much she didn't know about Max Leonelli and she wanted to know more.

An astonishing array of dishes greeted her in the room next door. Teddy had been released from his kennel for an hour and he was standing guard below the table, growling every time Max moved, but when he saw Tia he raced to greet her in a tail-wagging, doggy-licking surge of happiness.

Wryly watching the delighted reunion taking place a few feet from him, Max waved an eloquent hand over the food. 'I didn't know what you liked so I ordered a selection.'

'But this is so wasteful,' Tia whispered instinctively. 'I won't eat half of this.'

'This is your life now,' Max countered with level assurance. 'You have the luxury of choices. You don't have to make do any more.'

With a guilty sigh, Tia lifted a plate and served herself. 'It'll take a lot of getting used to.'

'It does,' he agreed. 'It was like that for me when I first arrived in England. But you'll soon adapt. We're getting married in forty-eight hours.'

Tia almost dropped the plate, cornflower-blue eyes huge. 'How is that even possible?'

'You can thank your Mother Sancha for organising it for us. Fortunately you hold dual citizenship, which simplifies matters, but the Reverend Mother certainly knows how to get things done quickly and sidestep any awkward rules,' Max declared with visible appreciation. 'Father Francisco will conduct the ceremony in the convent chapel and the ceremony will be screened live on social media for Andrew's benefit.'

Tia stared back at him wide-eyed, the *pão de queijo* baked cheese roll in her hand forgotten. 'My goodness, how have you arranged all that this early in the day?'

'It's almost noon. My work days usually kick off at dawn,' Max told her gently.

I'm getting married, Tia thought dizzily. Married to Max. But only because she might be pregnant, she reminded herself darkly and her face heated as that visceral surge low in her belly made her mortifyingly aware of the dulled ache that still lingered between her legs. Nothing to be proud of there, she reflected tightly, bitterly aware that she had grabbed at her first chance of freedom without properly weighing up the advantages and the disadvantages. And yet when she looked at Max across the table, her mind was blank of disadvantages and she was more conscious of the swollen sensitivity of her nipples and the audible hitch in her breathing. She seemed to be as susceptible to Max as Teddy was to all forms of food.

Tia [illegible]ed her trip to the beauty salon. She had never had her hair professionally trimmed or styled before and could barely credit that her very thick hair could be subdued into a flourishing silky mass that tumbled quite naturally round her face. Her hands were softened and her nails transformed into pearly pink elegance. Every inch of her was moisturised and polished and shaped and after a light lunch she sat entranced while she was expertly made up, watching every move the cosmetic artist made because she wanted to be able to copy the look for herself. For the very first time ever she revelled in being a woman.

Max went rigid the minute he saw her walk out to the limousine. Without the smallest enhancement, Tia was naturally beautiful, but fresh from a professional salon she became eye-catching enough to stop the traffic. Rich swathes of honey-blonde hair bounced round her narrow shoulders, framing that wide cheekboned, heart-shaped face to perfection.

'You look incredible, *bella mia*,' he murmured, dark deep-set eyes raking over her flushed face. 'I had planned to take you on the tourist trail this afternoon but I'm afraid you have a more pressing need to pick your wedding dress. A selection is being brought to the hotel.'

Tia blinked. 'I was wondering what I'd wear.'

'All the trappings. Your grandfather will expect it.'

But *nothing* was happening as Tia had once expected it and events were moving far too fast for her to handle with calm. Inside herself she was a massive heap of nerves and insecurities and doubts. She was marrying the first man she had ever slept with, marrying practically the first attractive man she had ever met, to move to a new country and meet a wealthy grandfather, who was a stranger but to whom she owed her opportunity to make a new life. But it wouldn't be the new life of freedom that she had once naively envisaged; it would be a different life built round a husband and even—potentially—a child. How could she possibly be a good or effective mother when she barely knew how to survive in the modern world?

CHAPTER SIX

SISTER MARIANA CRIED when she saw Tia in her wedding dress, insisting, however, that her tears were happy tears. The older woman had explained that now that Tia was getting married the nuns believed they could feel secure about Tia's future and stop worrying about her welfare. Max, it seemed, now occupied a starring role as Tia's protector in the dangerous new life she was embarking on.

Tia was misty-eyed too as she absorbed her reflection in the glorious confection of lace and tulle that shaped her figure and fell to her feet. She was willing to admit that it was a gorgeous dress even if it was far from being her dream dress. The demands of a convent wedding had made the more fashionable gowns she had been offered inappropriate and Tia had settled for traditional and modest, ruefully aware that that combination would best meet fond hopes. Having to please other people rather than herself had become so much a part of Tia's character that it had come naturally to look away from the short flirty dress she would have preferred and choose the one that swept the floor instead. It wouldn't always be like that for her, she told herself soothingly. Somewhere in her future there would be a time and a place when she could put herself first and stop worrying about pleasing other people...wouldn't there be?

It was an anxious inner question and Tia had struggled with it many times over the past forty-eight hours. Max had made no attempt to be intimate with her again and his restraint had only heightened her insecurity. How much did Max genuinely want her? How did he *really* feel about her? Was he truthfully only marrying her because there was a chance that she could conceive? In short had her body been her only real attraction? And if he could so easily resist her now, what would their marriage be like? Lukewarm? Practical? Unhappily for Tia, she was hot-blooded and passionate and she needed and wanted more.

The day before she had met her grandfather for the first time during a video call. His warm interest in her had been reassuring but his gaunt features and the fact that he was seated in a wheelchair had driven home the reality that Andrew Grayson was every bit as frail as Max had implied. That reality had saddened Tia, making her wonder for how long she would have the great gift of an actual caring relative in her life. Although Andrew had urged Max to take her away on a honeymoon before bringing her home to England, Tia had agreed with Max that they should return as soon as possible.

Tia saw Max waiting for her in the chapel, very tall and dark in his formal suit beside the small, rotund figure of Father Francisco. His likeness to a Renaissance prince in a medieval painting was intense, from the high smooth planes of his stunning cheekbones to the fullness of his sensual mouth. Beneath the black fringe of his spiky lashes, the dark aggressive glitter of his eyes entrapped her and the butterflies in her tummy broke loose again. But in their wake came a deeper, more visceral reaction that was anything but innocent, a tight clenching at the heart of her that she recognised as sexual desire, and her cheeks burned as if she was wearing that need on her face for all to see.

Max watched Tia walk down the short aisle towards him. Her slender figure enhanced by fragile lace and floaty layers, she looked as delicate and beautiful as a spun-glass ornament. One glimpse of that exquisite face and that captivating smile and her grandfather had been totally enchanted. Max's reaction was infinitely more physical, his muscles tightening as he tensed, scorchingly aware of his arousal. He had had to fight himself to stay out of her bed before the wedding but he had won that battle. Max needed to be in control of every aspect of his life; anything less struck him as weakness and he refused to be weak, particularly with a woman. He had made that mistake once in his life and paid dearly for it; he would not make the same mistake again.

'You're a lucky devil, Max,' Andrew had pronounced feelingly on the phone after his first glimpse of Tia. 'She must get her looks from that Brazilian mother of hers, certainly not from my side of the family tree. We were all homely and plain. When you saw her you must have felt like a lottery winner.'

Not so as you would notice, Max affixed wryly to that assurance. He was about to be married at the age of twenty-eight when he had once assumed he would be a single man all his days. In some ways, he was still in shock from the fallout of that sudden life change. But the rush marriage and the possibility of consequences were entirely his own fault, he conceded grimly. Blindsided by his bride's extraordinary beauty, he had succumbed to temptation and he had lost control like an overexcited teenager. Why was he worrying? How did he even know he *could* father a child? Maybe he shot blanks, he thought hopefully, and his anxiety at the prospect of fatherhood might yet prove to be a waste of energy.

As for being a married man, he thought as they knelt, a bride that looked like an earthbound angel had to be a huge encouragement for any male wary of settling down. Tia gripped his fingers as though she were in fear of drowning when he eased the gold ring into place. She needn't have worried. A lot of change was coming her way but Max would look after her in every way and to the very best of his ability. He hadn't needed a wedding ring to accept that responsibility though; he would have cared for her simply out of respect for Andrew Grayson. And sliding his own ring on when Tia struggled to get it over his knuckle, he smiled with satisfaction, knowing that as Tia's husband he was also becoming a member of Andrew's family and finally a recognised part of someone's cherished family circle. In all his life Andrew had been the only person willing to overlook Max's frightful background and have faith in him as an individual in his own right.

Boarding the Grayson private jet at Belém, Tia fingered the delicate gold crucifix Mother Sancha had given her and breathed in deep. She was a married woman but she didn't feel the slightest bit married when her bridegroom had yet to even kiss her. As he took his seat, Tia glanced at Max from below her lashes, more and more convinced that he was no longer as attracted to her as he had once been. Why else would he be so distant?

'I'd like to change into something more comfortable,' Tia confided soon after take-off.

Max showed her into the sleeping compartment. She wanted to slap him for his air of courteous detachment. It was their wedding night, after all. Tia had a quick shower and, smothering a yawn that had crept up on her out of nowhere, she donned the filmy turquoise shorts and thin top she had chosen for the occasion. The *occasion*, she mocked herself, her soft mouth down-curving. Was she supposed to go out there and throw herself at him when he was probably working? March down the aisle stripping as she went? Laughter shook her slight frame and another yawn pulled at her lips. She lay back against the pillows, just for a moment to relax and regain her energy, and that was the last thing she knew.

Max swore under his breath when he found his bride fast asleep: a siren in turquoise silk, deliciously pert nipples visible through the fabric, long, pale, slender legs bare. His earthy visions of orgasmic sex were grounded. He wanted to fall on her like a starving man at a banquet because he was so hard he ached, but it had been a very long day and her rapturous reception in England would last even longer. In any case, he *needed* to learn control around Tia, Max reminded himself resolutely, still slightly unnerved by the way in which she had broken through his defences from the outset.

Sheathed in a hot-pink dress, jacket and perilously high heels, Tia joined Max for breakfast. 'Where did you sleep last night?' she asked him bluntly.

'Right here. The seat reclines. I didn't want to disturb you,' Max responded smoothly.

'A normal bridegroom would have shaken me awake,' Tia murmured only half under her breath.

His dark golden eyes flared in surprise. 'I beg your pardon?'

'So you should,' Tia told him roundly, refusing to back down. 'It was our wedding night and we spent it apart.'

'Perhaps I was trying to be considerate.'

'The next time you get the urge to be considerate, run it by me first,' Tia advised waspishly.

Sardonic amusement flashed across Max's lean, strong face. 'I'm not the most democratic guy you'll meet. I tend to take unilateral decisions.'

Tia frowned. 'That won't work for me. I believe that marriage should be an equal partnership.'

'Duly noted, *bella mia*,' Max drawled, more amused by that fiery note in her nature than persuaded to change either his outlook, in which marriage would make very little difference to his life, or his strategy in how best to integrate a wife into his daily schedule.

Teddy was parcelled off to a quarantine kennel to fulfil UK pet regulations. He would stay there for a few months until he had passed a final rabies test. Misty-eyed at that enforced parting, Tia clambered awkwardly into the limousine that collected them from the airport, displaying a long, slender stretch of creamy thigh.

'You have fabulous legs,' Max heard himself say, his attention riveted to that shapely expanse of pearly skin.

Tia smiled at him, honey-blonde hair falling across her cheek, because his phone had been ringing since they landed and he was finally ignoring it and paying heed to her instead. She had every respect for a man with a strong work ethic but not when it came between her and what she wanted. And what she wanted was a man who acted like a new husband. Circumstances might have dictated that they shelve any prospect of a honeymoon, but that didn't mean it was all right for Max to behave as though they had been married for twenty years. She stretched out her legs, encouraging the hem of her dress to shimmy higher up over her thighs. It was hugely important for her to feel wanted by Max because nobody had ever really wanted or needed her before.

'Are you trying to tempt me?' Max intoned thickly.

Tia rested innocent blue eyes on him. 'Why would I try to do that?'

And Max forgot his ringing phone and his strategy and how considerate he ought to be and simply grabbed her, tugging her across the car and down onto his lap. Long brown fingers darted below the hem to stroke up a satin-smooth inner thigh and rake across the taut stretch of her knickers, skimming her most tender flesh with his nails.

Thoroughly disconcerted, Tia gasped into the mouth that plunged hungrily down on hers. It was as if fireworks were detonating inside her. Her whole being was locked into the provocative exploration of his fingers. She was hot and damp and tender and she had never craved touch the way she did at that moment, her body pushing up into his hand, her thighs splayed, her nipples hard little buds that tingled.

'As you see, I don't need that much encouragement,' Max growled into her ear as he yanked at the garment preventing him from reaching his objective. He traced the heart of her, finding her as aroused as he was. He eased his finger in while his thumb brushed back and forth across her most sensitive spot and before she knew where she was or what she was doing, Tia yelped and bucked. Her excitement peaked so fast she was electrified and she arched and sobbed with intoxicated pleasure as the thunderous waves of release crashed through her entire body.

'And neither, it seems, do you,' Max declared, treating her to a wickedly appreciative appraisal that shot even more colour into her flustered face.

Tia was stunned by what had just happened between them. Within minutes excitement had sent her body racing from zero to sixty. With a trembling hand she retrieved her underwear but dug it into her bag, intensely aware that while she was satisfied, *he* was not. She slid closer, small fingers smoothing uncertainly over a lean, muscular thigh, awesomely conscious of what was concealed below his trousers.

Max caught her hand in his. 'Not here,' he breathed in a roughened undertone, a little taken aback by her readiness to experiment but very much excited by the unexpected promise of that adventurous vibe. 'Later, *bella mia.* I shouldn't have touched you here in the car. We need more privacy.'

A giant blush of self-reproach engulfed Tia in what felt like a head-to-toe flood. She didn't have the sexual confidence to argue with him but she didn't like the fact that he had contrived to do what he wanted but was now denying her the same freedom. She felt controlled and that annoyed her. Perhaps she would have done it wrong, she told herself in consolation; perhaps she would have humiliated herself had she continued. Or perhaps her boldness had turned Max off. She stole a glance at him and discovered, with a faint little smile of feminine satisfaction tilting her full mouth, that that was not the problem.

Tia spoke little until the limo turned off the road down a long driveway edged by mature woodland.

'Redbridge Hall, your grandfather's country house. He grew up here,' Max explained. 'His father bought the place before the First World War. Andrew has a town house in London as well but he rarely uses it. I live in a city apartment.'

Tia stared as a rambling Tudor mansion surrounded by lush trees appeared in front of them. The patterned red-brick walls were matched by tall arched and mullioned windows that reflected the sunlight. 'My goodness,' she whispered. 'It's huge.'

'I believe there are twelve bedrooms,' Max remarked.

'There are a lot of cars here,' Tia noted, because at least ten luxury vehicles were parked on the gravelled frontage. 'Are there people staying?'

'I doubt it. It looks more as though Andrew has given way to his need to show you off.' Max bit back a frustrated exclamation because he had advised the older man to allow Tia a little time to adapt to her new surroundings before plunging her into a social whirl.

'Who on earth would he want to show me off to?'

'Friends and family.'

'Family?' she queried with greater interest.

'Although you're Andrew's only blood relative, his late wife, your grandmother, had several siblings, so you do have a bunch of cousins on that side of the family,' Max told her, his lean, darkly handsome features stiffening because most of her cousins resented his very existence, not to mention his business connections with and his closeness to Andrew.

'Cousins. That should be interesting,' Tia commented, stepping out with care in her high heels, already missing Teddy's reassuring presence.

Her grandfather awaited her in a big crowded drawing room. Andrew Grayson beamed and opened both his arms. 'Come here, my dear, and let me have a closer look at you,' he urged.

While she sat beside the old man, the guests drifted over to meet her. 'I'm Ronnie…' A pretty brunette with adorable twin girl toddlers clinging to her legs gave Tia a harassed but very friendly smile.

There were too many names and faces for Tia to absorb all at once. She got mixed up about which were siblings and which were couples, but she was overwhelmed to finally have relatives eager to make her acquaintance. Throughout the session, Max stayed anchored nearby and Andrew frequently consulted him. Tia noticed that most of the visitors were daunted by Max and that in company he seemed much more aloof and remote than he was with her in private. But she was grateful for Max's support when she was faced with more searching questions about her years in Brazil, her mother and her father's activities, for he parried the more challenging queries with an unblemished cool that she could never have matched.

'So, you only married Max yesterday?' Ronnie shook her head in wonder as she poured tea for Tia, her warm brown eyes brimming with curiosity. 'A whirlwind romance, I gather, and I must admit that *that* was a shock. Max always strikes one as a very controlled, cold-blooded businessman, not the type to do anything madly impulsive, but then the rule book goes out the window when a beautiful woman is involved. And you are, if you don't mind me saying so, remarkably beautiful and probably very photogenic. The press will go mad for pictures of you when they find out you exist.'

Unable to relate to the concept of Max being in any way cold-blooded, Tia had gone pink. 'Why would the press be interested in me?'

'Are you serious?' Ronnie rolled amused eyes in emphasis. 'Andrew's long-lost granddaughter from Brazil gets married to the CEO of Grayson Industries? Andrew is a very rich and important man and Max is renowned in the business world and on the social scene.'

'I haven't grown up with that background the way you have,' Tia said uncomfortably.

'Oh, neither did I. I grew up on a farm. Your grandmother may have married a tycoon but the rest of the family is reasonably ordinary in terms of wealth and status,' Ronnie explained.

Tia was relaxed by Ronnie's warm, open manner. 'I believe Max is very successful.'

'You know that legendary king who could turn anything to gold with a touch?' Ronnie interposed and nodded solemnly. 'When Max was in banking, he was a total whiz-kid. Doug was always very jealous of him.'

'Who's Doug?'

'A cousin who doesn't visit. He and Max went to the same school but they don't get on,' Ronnie muttered, her face rather flushed as she looked apologetically at Tia. 'Please don't mention to Max that I brought up Doug. I would hate him to think that I was pot-stirring.'

'But why would he think that?' Tia asked in surprise, glancing across the room only to encounter Max's dark observant gaze and experience a snaking shivery little frisson somewhere in the region of her pelvis. She remembered the heat of his mouth and his wickedly skilled hands and was honestly afraid that she could spontaneously combust.

Ronnie winced at the question. 'I'm not getting into old scandals. The truth is we've always been rather intimidated by Max. When he was younger some of the cousins were quite rude to him because he was related to Andrew's housekeeper. It must've been tough for him. I've never had much time for that kind of snobbery.'

Some of the other guests joined them. Unused to a crowd of strangers, Tia was relieved when Max rescued her to bring her back to her grandfather's side. Seated quietly with the older man, she began to relax again.

Dinner was served in a big dining room at a table almost groaning beneath its weight of crystal, elaborate porcelain and burnished silver.

'It's like another world,' she muttered to Max.

'This lifestyle *does* belong to a bygone age,' Max agreed. 'Andrew lives as his father lived.'

'In incredible comfort,' Tia whispered back. 'But I'd really like to see the housekeeper's flat where you grew up.'

A rueful and surprised smile at that declaration tilted Max's expressive mouth but he had tensed. 'I'm afraid it doesn't exist any more. Andrew renovated the servants' accommodation after my aunt died and upgraded it all.'

'When she did pass away?' Tia asked.

'What was that that you were saying?' her grandfather demanded from her other side.

'I was asking Max how long it is since his aunt died,' Tia explained, looking up.

'Eight years,' Andrew supplied, his thin face tightening. 'It was a complete shock. Carina caught the flu and it turned into pneumonia. She was gone by the time Max managed to get to the hospital.'

'I was a student on a work placement in New York at the time,' Max explained.

'She was a good woman, Max,' the older man pronounced, his voice quavering slightly, his sorrow visible.

And Tia noticed that the table had fallen silent and that the rest of the diners seemed disproportionately interested in the subject being discussed. She wished she had kept quiet and refrained from mentioning Max's aunt, but she could not imagine why the passing of the old man's former housekeeper should rouse such curiosity.

'Tomorrow, I'll show you round the house,' Max murmured lazily, apparently impervious to the tension in the atmosphere. 'Then you'll feel more at home here.'

Tia did not think she could ever feel at home with servants and fancy clothes and even fancier furniture, but then she glanced at Max and a kind of peace entered her soul. He made her feel safe and, while he was present, he made her feel as if she belonged. Yet ironically, if she was to believe Ronnie, as a boy Max had been looked down on at Redbridge for being related to the housekeeper. Was that why he still seemed unapproachable in the company of Andrew's relations and friends? Did he think that old snobbish outlook still existed? Or was it simply that Max was a loner?

After the coffee was served, guests began to leave

and a welter of invitations came Tia's way. Her phone was soon crammed with new numbers and names.

'Who's Doug?' Tia pressed Max, recalling Ronnie's nervous backtracking and that evocative word, 'scandal', which had only roused her intense curiosity. 'And why doesn't he visit?'

'One of your cousins. Someone mention him?' Max's strong jaw line squared. 'He doesn't visit because of something that happened a long time ago when we were teenagers,' he admitted grittily. 'It was supposed to destroy my reputation but instead it destroyed Doug's family and made Andrew angry with him.'

Andrew's housekeeper, Janette, a slim, no-nonsense brunette, escorted them upstairs and Tia was forced to swallow back the dozen nosy questions brimming on her lips.

'Mr Grayson asked me to prepare the master suite for you,' the housekeeper informed them.

Max frowned in surprise. 'But that's—' He bit off what he had almost said and compressed his lips. The master suite had once been Andrew's, but since his illness had been diagnosed Andrew had been using a specially adapted room on the ground floor and, given that he needed a wheelchair, it was far more suitable for him. But putting both Max and Tia into the principal room at the hall was making a very public statement about how the owner of the house viewed the status of his newly married granddaughter and her husband.

'I hope you'll be comfortable here, madam,' Janette declared warmly, closing the door on them.

'It's beautiful…' Tia whispered, her bright eyes skimming appreciatively from the welcome log fire burning in the grate to the silk-clad bed and the arrangement of glorious white roses sited in front of the elegantly draped windows. Kicking off her high heels, she moved closer to the fire because the spring chill of an English evening was downright cold compared with the hot, humid climate she was used to.

Turning her head, she focused on Max. 'Now tell me about what happened between you and this Doug,' she urged.

'Later,' Max breathed, his faint accent fracturing the word as his hands came down on her narrow shoulders to slowly turn her round and ease her out of her jacket. The fire cast a reddish glow over her blonde hair, darkening the glossy strands while accentuating the creamy perfection of her skin.

Her breath fluttered in her dry throat. 'Later?' she queried, the evocative scent of him, heat and masculinity with a faint hint of something citrusy, flaring her nostrils.

'Right now I only have time for you,' Max confided, tiny flames reflected from the fire dancing in his dark eyes, transforming them to liquid bronze. 'I let you sleep last night because you were very tired. It was the unselfish thing to do. I also thought you might be... *sore...*'

Her face flamed. 'Not any more.'

'And I need you to be at full strength,' Max imparted, 'because I'm not sure I could be that gentle again, *bella mia*. In your radius I'm in an almost continual state of arousal.'

'Is that so?' Tia almost whispered, all woman, all appreciation of the compliment being paid.

'I'm naturally a selfish bastard but I'm trying very hard to put your needs first.'

Tia lifted her hands and let them skim down over his warm torso, revelling in the strength of the muscular body beneath his shirt. Her fingers drifted lower, discovering the bold outline of him, stroking and caressing with newfound assurance. 'I think you're going to be a terrific husband,' she told him, smiling as he arched his hips into her hand. 'But if we're going to be true equals I've got a lot to learn too.'

'You can practise on me whenever you like,' Max admitted, peeling off his jacket and wrenching at his shirt with flattering impatience.

As the ropes of muscle across his abdomen flexed, Tia unbuckled his belt and unzipped him. Max breathed in starkly, savouring the fact that she constantly took him by surprise. Her hand stroked the length of him and she bent her head, her tongue flicking out to taste him. By the time the warm, wet heat of her mouth engulfed him, Max was almost unbearably full and hard, the grinding pulse of driving hunger gripping him in a vice. Watching her pleasure him excited him beyond bearing and, long before she could tease him to a climax, he reached down and forcefully pulled her up to him, lifting her to plunge his tongue deep into her sweet, intoxicating mouth and feel the answering leap of response vibrate through both of them.

'Max…I—' Tia began.

'Another time,' Max growled, settling her down on the edge of the table by the window, pushing up her skirt and stepping between her spread thighs. '*This* is what I've been dreaming of all day.'

And with that grated confession, Max tilted her back, hurriedly donned a condom and thrust into her hard and deep and strong. The table creaked in complaint but Tia's body was hot and slick with arousal and her tender flesh yielded to him.

'Dannazione,' he groaned feverishly. 'You are so tight.'

Tia jerked, her head falling back, blue eyes shaken by his fire as she jerked under him with a helpless moan of sensual pleasure. He was aggressive, dominating in a way he had not been the first time, and the welling of sensation deep within her throbbed with a wild hunger that thrilled her, excitement climbing as his movements became rougher and more demanding. Little internal tremors shimmied through her, bands of tension tightening within her pelvis until her body clenched convulsively around him at the height of her excitement. Wave after glorious wave washed over her as orgasmic aftershocks took her by storm. A low guttural sound was wrenched from him as he too reached completion.

In the aftermath, her body was weighted and limp. Max carried her over to the bed and laid her down, tilting her to unzip her dress and pull it off, unclipping her bra as an afterthought. As he vanished into what was obviously a bathroom, Tia released a happy sigh of contentment. Max had just shown her the hunger, passion and impatience that revealed his need for her. No, there had been nothing lukewarm about that encounter, she reflected with satisfaction, struggling to muster the energy to get up and go and wash.

'Have to take off my make-up,' she mumbled as he stepped out of the shower naked and dripping to reach for a towel.

Tia showered, her feminine core still pulsing from the intensity of the release he had given her and the no less energising discovery that sex could take place on a table as well as a bed and be fast and glorious as well as slow and wonderful.

She padded back to the bed and climbed in, snuggling up to Max without hesitation, one arm wrapping round his broad chest. 'So tell me why this Doug would have wanted to destroy your reputation,' she murmured, curiosity flickering afresh. 'I need to learn all the ins and outs of this family…and the secrets if there are any.'

Max tensed and released his breath in a hiss as he sat up and, in so doing, freed himself from her hold. 'All families have secrets.'

'But this relates to you and we're married,' Tia reminded him unnecessarily.

Max gritted his teeth, belatedly recalling why he never stayed the night with a woman, never risked getting cosy with one, never shared late-night chat sessions. Unfortunately, he acknowledged grimly, there was no escape from a wife occupying the same bed…

CHAPTER SEVEN

'DOUG AND I attended the same boarding school as teenagers,' Max divulged reluctantly. 'I didn't know him then the way I do now. I trusted him as a friend. It didn't occur to me that he already saw me as competition and thought Andrew took too much interest in me. In my own eyes I was the housekeeper's nephew and I didn't ever expect to be anything more. I was staff, Doug was *family*.'

Tia rested her tousled head back on the pillows and reached for a bronzed masculine hand, lacing her fingers into his without any help from him. 'Go on...'

Max retrieved his hand. 'Doug's family lived nearby and he was a frequent visitor. His mother was on her second marriage and he had a stepsister, a very pretty redhead called Alice. We were only seventeen. Doug brought Alice here repeatedly that summer and I fell in love with her. Only a few weeks after I began seeing her she announced that she was pregnant and that I was the father of her child,' he revealed grittily. 'I was surprised because I had only slept with her on one occasion and I had been...*careful*.'

Tia sat up to study him in consternation. *'And?'* she pressed.

'There was a huge family row. Doug's stepfather stormed over here and tried to beat me up, and then in the midst of all that, with Alice's mother and my aunt screaming in the background and Andrew calling for order, Alice took fright and finally told the truth. The baby was Doug's. She and Doug had been having sex for months and when she realised she was pregnant she panicked because they had been expressly warned by their parents that they were expected to think of each other as brother and sister. Together, she and Doug decided that *I* should be set up to take the blame, which is why she slept with me in the first place…'

'And you loved her,' Tia muttered unevenly, her nails digging into the palms of her hands to enable her to listen to the tawdry tale without making tactless comments. Max had been the fall guy in a nasty set-up, his conviction betrayed by a boy he had believed to be his friend and a girl whom he had learned to care about.

'Yes, but I got over it,' Max completed with a brisk lack of sentiment that did not impress her in the slightest. 'However, Doug's mother and stepfather's marriage broke down because of that pregnancy and, sadly, Alice miscarried a few weeks later, so everyone lost out.'

'At least she told the truth in the end,' Tia sighed.

'Can we please drop the subject now?' Max murmured, his stunning heavily lashed dark eyes welded to her troubled gaze. 'I was a boy and now I'm a man but I still don't like remembering that hellish affair.'

Inside her chest, Tia's heart ached for him and she reached for his hand again.

Max snaked his fingers free a second time. 'You asked me and I told you. I don't need or want your sympathy. It hit me hard at the time because Alice loving me felt special but afterwards I realised it had all been a giant fake. And afterwards, in front of everyone when she was trying to save face and impress Doug, she asked me how I could ever have thought that she could have had feelings for someone like me…'

'Someone like you,' Tia repeated with a frown, rolling over and curving another arm round him, needing to retain some kind of physical contact with him. She was outraged that, not only had the wretched girl tried to set him up, but she had also struck out at his pride with a nasty comment. 'What was that supposed to mean?'

'You don't want to know.'

'No, you don't *want* to tell me,' Tia translated flatly.

'Surely I'm allowed to retain a few secrets,' Max said very drily as he slid free yet again and sprang out of bed. 'If Andrew is still awake I have some business to discuss with him. It slipped my mind earlier.'

'I'm not stupid, Max. If you come back to bed I won't ask any more questions and I won't touch you either,' Tia countered fierily. 'There are only so many times I will allow you to push me away.'

Max set his teeth together, his lean, darkly handsome features clenched hard. 'I know it's a cliché but…it's not you, it's me. I'm not good with demonstrative people. I'm not accustomed to physical affection. The only kind of touching I have ever experienced was sexual and anything else…it feels uncomfortable.'

At least he got back into bed, Tia consoled herself, watching him below her lashes, the strong line of his darkly shadowed jaw line revealing his lingering tension. She stayed on her side of the bed, lying straight, all limbs in alignment like a tomb adornment sculpted out of stone. 'You didn't have affection even when you were a child?' she could not help asking.

'No, and my aunt wasn't the touchy-feely type either.'

'My grandfather?'

'My relationship with Andrew has always been formal.'

And Tia lay there, feeling so sad for him because he had never known normal affection and was now so inhibited that that kind of touch made him uneasy. What must his parents have been like? And why did he never ever mention them? Why had he been left in need of his aunt's care in the first place? That was the crux of the matter, she sensed, but not something she intended to pursue at that moment.

In the morning she woke in Max's arms and she came sleepily awake, moaning involuntarily as expert fingers slid between her parted thighs and played there, sending little ripples of mounting delight filtering through her. Response came as naturally to her as breathing and she arched up as he shifted lithely over her and plunged into her, stretching her with his girth. An almost shocking tide of pleasure engulfed Tia in a blinding surge and she whimpered, eyes fluttering open on his lean dark face and the ravenous dark golden eyes locked to her. And she recognised that in that moment Max was hers, absolutely, unequivocally hers, wanting her, needing her, craving her and that knowledge satisfied the hollow feeling that had spread within her the night before over his disinclination to even hold her close.

He brought her knees up and rocked back into her hard and fast and a fevered gasp escaped her. She couldn't lie still, she couldn't get enough of him and when the voluptuous release of orgasm claimed her she cried out his name. Max rolled over, carrying Tia with him, and slumped back against the pillows. He couldn't keep his hands off her and that bothered him. What about showing a little restraint? A little cool? When he had woken with Tia's shapely little body next to his and the smell of her coconut shampoo surrounding him, he had *had* to have her. It was that simple, that basic, and no sooner did he reach climax than he was wondering how soon he could have her again. The strength of that lustful craving chilled him to the marrow because it was outside his parameters and like nothing he had ever experienced before.

'Thanks,' Max framed, pausing to drop a kiss on the top of her head and then shifting free of her with alacrity to leave the bed.

Thanks? Tia ruminated, savouring the split-second, casual kiss but disappointed by the cut and run that followed. Why had he thanked her? Hadn't she enjoyed herself as much as him? Next time *she* would thank him, she resolved. She could be polite too. In fact she would outpolite him in spades and see how he liked being thanked as if he had provided a service with his body! But what wonderful service he gave, she reflected helplessly.

'What are we doing today?' she asked.

'Apparently you're seeing the family lawyer after breakfast. And no, I don't know what it's about. Andrew doesn't tell me everything,' Max admitted.

A couple of hours later, a little man with an egg-shaped bald head and wire-framed spectacles studied her across Andrew's desk in the library. 'All you have to do is sign these papers,' he told her, fanning out a selection of documents in front of her.

'But what is this about?'

'Your inheritance, of course,' he said in surprise. 'Your grandmother became a wealthy woman during the course of her marriage to Andrew and she left her estate in trust for her grandchildren. You are the *only* grandchild and I am now releasing those funds to you.'

Tia blinked in bewilderment. 'I have an inheritance?' she gulped.

'Now that you're resident in the UK, you do. Your grandmother stipulated that any grandchild had to be resident in this country to qualify, which is why you haven't heard of this bequest before,' he explained patiently.

'How much money is involved in this?' she asked incredulously.

'I haven't had a recent valuation for the jewellery that's included, and of course her bequest is modest in comparison to your grandfather's holdings,' he warned her, 'but I would estimate that her estate is currently worth, well, almost four hundred thousand pounds...'

In shock, Tia froze with the pen in her hand. 'And it's...*mine*?' she exclaimed in disbelief.

'Unconditionally yours,' the older man declared.

Tia signed, stumbling out of the door minutes later to track down Max and tell him that the grandmother she had never met had been kind enough to make her a wealthy woman. Max was infuriatingly unimpressed by that revelation.

'It's *ours* now...that money,' Tia pointed out, trying to win a more enthusiastic response from him. 'Don't you understand that?'

'I have plenty of money of my own,' Max divulged gently, amusement tugging at his beautiful mouth. 'Now thanks to your grandmother you have a nest egg and I'm happy for you.'

Tia calmed down. 'I'd like to make a substantial donation to the convent to help the sisters with their work.'

Max nodded. 'Of course.'

'You don't mind?'

'You can do whatever you like with your inheritance, *bella mia*. While you are with me, however, you will never need to use it,' Max told her smoothly.

'So, what's mine is yours doesn't cut *both* ways?' Tia gathered stiffly.

'I have a visceral need to keep my own wife. Call it the caveman in me,' Max advised

Tia breathed in deep and slow. They were not going to argue about money. He didn't want what he saw as hers...*fine*! Seemingly he was well enough off to consider her inheritance as a cosy little nest egg barely worthy of excitement. 'And what about when I find a job?'

Max looked at her in astonishment and an eyebrow elevated. 'A *job*?'

'Yes. I haven't decided what I want to do yet but I do want to work. I'm not sure I want to do any more studying though,' she admitted ruefully.

'Take your time and think it over. Andrew supports several charities. Volunteer work could be a practical option for you to begin with,' he suggested.

That night Tia came awake with a start when Max made a sound and she switched on the bedside light, only then registering that he was still asleep and clearly dreaming. The bedding was in a tangle round his long, powerful body, perspiration gleaming on his bronzed skin as he cried out again in Italian and in obvious distress. In dismay she shook his shoulder and voiced his name to waken him.

'You were having a bad dream.'

Max threw himself back against the pillow, breathing rapidly and raking his fingers through his tousled black hair. 'I don't get bad dreams,' he countered defensively.

'You *could* talk to me about it,' Tia told him ruefully, not believing that he didn't get bad dreams for even a second. 'I wouldn't tell anyone else. You can trust me.'

'Leave it, Tia,' Max urged, thinking she would be booking him onto a psychiatric couch if he wasn't careful. 'There will always be stuff in my life that I don't want to discuss.'

Cornflower-blue eyes rested on him with unnerving directness. 'I don't like secrets,' she said simply. 'I want to know everything about you.'

'Good luck with that because I'm not a talker,' Max derided, punching the pillow back into shape and lying back down, making it clear that the conversation was at an end.

Tia lay awake almost until dawn, wondering if she could settle for a husband with secrets. She didn't think she could. She hadn't been joking or exaggerating when she had admitted to wanting to know all that there was to know about him. On her terms, that kind of fearless honesty was the backbone of a strong relationship, but Max didn't seem to crave that kind of closeness and it worried her.

'And *this* is what you're wearing tonight?' Ronnie gasped in admiration as Tia brought the long ice-blue gown out to show her friend. The fabric shimmered as if it were sprinkled with diamonds. 'Tia…it's gorgeous!'

Grayson Industries had started out fifty years earlier and a half-century party was being staged in a luxury London hotel as a celebration. Tia was accompanying Andrew and Max and finally stepping out in public as a Grayson.

'And it's blue because Max likes me in blue,' Tia muttered shamefacedly as Teddy capered round her feet, getting in the way.

The little terrier had been much quieter since he'd emerged from quarantine and was no longer so aggressive. He behaved like Tia's shadow now though, as if he was afraid that she might disappear again.

Ronnie shook her dark head. 'You are *such* a newlywed. And Max isn't missing the single life, is he? There he is with an apartment in London and he still flies back here every night to be with you.'

Tia was more inclined to put Max's frequent flying down to his fondness for her grandfather. Unfortunately, she was still feeling very guilty about the discreet visit she had made to the doctor first thing that morning, because she hadn't been able to bring herself to admit that she believed she needed a pregnancy test to Max or to anyone else. Somehow that little worry had become her secret. And now that little worry had grown into a *massive* worry…

But, she didn't have to share *everything* with Max, did she? It nagged at her conscience that only a few months ago she had thought less of Max for his unwillingness to share everything and now here she was doing the exact same thing. But then, no doubt like Max, she had her reasons.

And now that she knew that she *was* pregnant she felt stupid for having been so blind because she had always assumed that a woman ought to somehow know such a thing even if the signs beforehand were misleading. They had been married for three months and she had twice had what she believed to be periods. Admittedly both had been unusually irregular and brief, but when she'd told Max that she was out of commission he had smiled and laughed, pointing out that they now had the proof that she wasn't pregnant. And fool that she was, she had believed that Max must know the symptoms of pregnancy better than she did. When her appetite had failed, when her breasts had become swollen and she had suffered strange moments of dizziness, she had ignored those sensations until she became worried enough to consult a doctor.

Consequently, Tia had been shattered when the doctor had told her that there was nothing actually wrong with her and she was merely suffering the common side effects of early pregnancy. Apparently her experience of partial periods was not quite as unusual as she had assumed, nor was it a sign that her pregnancy was unstable. But how was she supposed to tell Max that she was pregnant now when he was totally unprepared for that reality? His relief at the seeming proof that she was not pregnant some weeks after their wedding loomed large in her memory. Max had been relieved that she had not conceived and had felt free to reveal that reality.

Was it any wonder that she had not even told him that she'd intended to visit a doctor? Unsure of how he would react to her secret fear, she had refused to admit her apprehension. In truth, things had been so good between them that she hadn't wanted to risk tipping the scales by sharing a worry that had seemed groundless.

Yet in spite of her concern, being married to Max did

make her incredibly happy. Oh, nothing was perfect, Tia conceded. He worked too many hours and he could be so preoccupied with business matters that he didn't always hear what she said. He commuted daily by helicopter between the London headquarters of Grayson Industries and Redbridge Hall. Max hadn't dared say it but she knew that he didn't want her to find a job and for the moment she had put that ambition on hold because learning that her grandfather was living on borrowed time had changed her outlook.

Andrew had only months, not years, ahead of him and she was keen to make the most of what time he had left. She had been devastated when he'd finally confessed that he was terminally ill and initially angry with Max for not telling her sooner, but she had gradually come to understand that Andrew had wanted her homecoming to be a joyous occasion unclouded by anything distressing.

Tia also understood that it was the very strength of her feelings for Max that had enabled her to adapt to the awareness that her grandfather would not be in her life for much longer. Without Max's support she would have been far more devastated at the prospect of that coming loss. In truth, she didn't know when she had fallen for Max because he had been so very important to her from the first moment she had laid eyes on him. His first look, his first smile, his first kiss? It was as if he had cast a spell on her and bound her to him bone and sinew.

At the same time, Tia was painfully aware that Max didn't love her back. Maybe she wasn't the sort of woman who appealed to him on that higher level, she sometimes thought ruefully. In any case, Max kept his own emotions in check as if he feared them and she could hardly credit that he had decided love was not for him based on a distraught teenage girl's betrayal. Didn't he realise that everyone got hurt at some stage when it came to love?

Tia had loved her father long and undeservedly despite his cutting criticisms and lack of interest in her. She loved Max because he made her feel as though everything he did was for her benefit, whether it was asking Andrew's cook to surprise her with a Brazilian meal or coming home with random little gifts for her that he just so happened to have stumbled on. A handbag the same colour as her eyes? A book he thought she might enjoy? A pendant with ninety-odd sparkling diamonds denoting the number of days they had been married? Max did nothing by halves and he took being a husband seriously. How could she fairly ask for more than that? How could she reasonably expect more from a man who had only proposed to her in the first place because there was a risk he could have got her pregnant?

And yet, unreasonable or not, Tia recognised that she had a very strong need to be loved. And for a husband whom she could confide anything in at any time. But Max's very unwillingness to commit himself to that level of frankness had put barriers up between them and made Tia less open to sharing her own private insecurities and worries. Her parents' lack of love had left her vulnerable and she suspected that Max had had a similar experience with his parents. Unfortunately, that same lack had left Tia craving love to feel secure while it had left Max denying his need for it and shutting the possibility out as being too risky.

Tia knew that she should not allow Max's lack of

enthusiasm for having a child to influence her thinking. But that was impossible, she thought unhappily. She knew she would prefer to have a family while she was still young but still wondered if being older would make her a *better* parent. Reminding herself that she could not do worse than her own parents had done with her, Tia swallowed hard. What sort of a mother would she be? Hopefully a better one than her own had been. But what if Inez's inability to love Tia enough to keep her had been passed on to Tia? She shivered at that fear and prayed that she would be able to love her child like any normal mother.

But most daunting of all, what was she going to do if the man she loved genuinely didn't *want* their baby? Fearful of that pessimistic worry taking control of her before she even had the chance to break that news to Max, Tia thrust it to the back of her mind and suppressed it hard.

She was hopelessly excited about the baby she carried, she conceded ruefully, daring to hope that, once Max got over the shock of her condition, he would feel the same. But starting a family *was* a life-altering event, she conceded afresh, and anxiety gripped her. She was only just learning how to live in the modern world and soon she would be responsible for guiding an innocent child through the same process. But she would have Max with her, she told herself urgently. Max had been everywhere, done everything. Max was her fail-safe go-to whenever she needed help. But that made her dependent on him and she hated that reality because she didn't think it was healthy for her to be forced to continually look to him for advice. It made her feel more like a child than an adult and she badly wanted to stand on her own feet. And sadly, she appreciated, a pregnancy was only going to make independence even more of an impossible challenge.

'You look stunning,' her grandfather told her warmly that evening as she climbed out of the limousine, hovering in spite of his objections while he was assisted from the vehicle at the side entrance to the big hotel.

Max had opted to stay in the city and change at his apartment before meeting them. He emerged to greet them, wonderfully tall, sleek and sophisticated in a dinner jacket and narrow black trousers that provided the ultimate presentation for his wide-shouldered, narrow-hipped, long-legged frame. Her breath snarled in her throat, familiar damp heat licking at the heart of her, as always her body and her senses clamouring on every level for Max's attention. Sometimes she suspected that she was a shamelessly sexual woman and her colour rose as her eyes met the dark allure of his, her spine tingling as though he had touched her.

And then the moment was gone as one of the paparazzi who had been waiting in a clump at the front entrance came running to snatch a photo and, with Andrew's nurse taking charge of the wheelchair, they hurried into the hotel.

'That dress is sensational on you,' Max husked, gazing down at her with hot dark eyes, the pulse at his groin a deeply unwelcome reminder of his susceptibility to his bride.

He needed to pull back from Tia; he knew that. He knew that he needed to pull back and give her space. In a few months' time without Andrew around Tia might decide she wanted her freedom and there would be little point him craving then what he could no longer have. Was that why he had to have her every night? Why going one night without her felt like deprivation of the worst kind? Her hunger matched his though, he reminded himself stubbornly. The need was mutual. And being hooked on sex wasn't that dangerous a weakness, was it?

Tia caught at his sleeve. 'I have something to tell you,' she whispered, needing to share, wanting him to demonstrate the same joy that had been growing in her since she'd first learned that she was carrying their first child.

She had wasted so much energy tormenting herself with doubts and insecurities while all the time her deep abiding pleasure at the prospect of becoming a mother was quietly building on another level. She was going to have Max's baby and she was happy about that development and, now that the opportunity had come, she suddenly couldn't wait to share her news.

'We've got official photos first,' Max warned her.

So, they posed and smiled with Andrew to mark the occasion and then, Andrew safely stowed in the company of old friends, Max began to introduce her to what felt like hundreds of people. She set her champagne glass down and quietly asked the waiter for a soft drink while she waited for her moment to tell Max about their child.

The moment came during a lull in the music when everybody was standing around chatting and, for the first time, they were miraculously alone. 'Remember I said I had something to tell you?' Tia whispered.

Lashes as dark and lustrous as black lace lifted on level dark golden eyes and he lifted his chin in casual acknowledgment. 'I'm listening.'

'I'm pregnant,' Tia told him baldly.

And beneath her gaze Max turned paper pale below his bronzed skin, his facial muscles jerking taut to throw his hard bone structure into shocking prominence. 'Are you serious?' he pressed in disbelief. 'How can you be? You were clear—'

'No. We thought I was and we were wrong.'

Max was shattered and struggling to hide the fact. She had conceived? Although his brain knew better, he had always subconsciously supposed that a pregnancy was unlikely after a single sexual encounter. He had simply assumed it wasn't going to happen, had been convinced by the evidence that they were safe from that threat and he had relaxed. And now that she was cheerfully assuring him that it *had* happened he had no prepared strategy of how to behave to fall back on in his hour of need. And it *was* his hour of need, Max registered sickly as an image of his thuggish father's face swam before his eyes and momentarily bereft him of breath. Like a punch in the gut, he had once seen his father's hated image every time he closed his eyes to go to sleep, his father, his bogeyman, the memory of brutality that had haunted him since the dreadful night his mother had died.

'But you can't be sure yet,' Max assumed, grasping hopefully at straws. 'Surely it's too soon to be sure? You'll have to see a doctor.'

'I saw a doctor this morning. It's official. I'm pregnant. For goodness' sake, it seems I've been pregnant all along,' she divulged shakily. 'We'll be parents in six months' time.'

Tia felt so sick because Max wasn't a very good actor. He was appalled by the idea of her being pregnant and he couldn't hide it. A tight band of pain seized her chest and she could hardly breathe for hurt and disillusionment. How could she have been so naïve as to credit that Max would welcome a baby that would undoubtedly disrupt his life even more than she had done? Max had given up his freedom to marry her and possibly he had hoped that he would eventually regain that freedom, but the birth of a child would make that process a great deal more complicated.

Max released his breath in a rush. 'You took me by surprise.'

'Obviously,' Tia pronounced tightly, focusing fixedly on his scarlet silk tie, refusing to meet his eyes and see anything else she didn't want to see because it hurt too much.

Yes, she had accepted that he wasn't in love with her, but she had trustingly believed that he would welcome fatherhood even if the planning or the timing weren't quite ideal. But that had been a false hope because she had judged Max all wrong. Max just didn't *want* a child, which was a much more basic issue. Suddenly she was in a situation she had never ever envisaged and flinching in horror from the ramifications of what she was discovering. How could she possibly stay married to a man who didn't want their child?

Even her own parents had not been that set against becoming parents. Her father would have been quite content to be a father if her mother had stuck around to take care of her, while her mother had been content to be a mother as long as her husband was a wealthy businessman based in London. When Paul Grayson had announced his plans to become a missionary and work in some of the poorest places on earth, Tia's mother had been aghast and the baby she'd carried had simply become an inconvenient burden tying her down to a life she had very quickly learned to loathe.

'We'll discuss this later,' Max breathed in a driven undertone. 'Discuss how to handle it.'

Handle it? What did he mean by that? And what was there to discuss? A pregnancy didn't come with choices as far as Tia was concerned. A cold shiver snaked down her spine as Max turned to address a man who had hailed him. Was he hinting at the possibility of a termination? Surely he could not credit that she would even consider such an option?

The evening wore on with Tia seeking out her grandfather's company and sitting with a group of much older men. But she remained hyper-aware of Max's every move and glance in her direction. He looked forbidding, his high cheekbones taut, his beautiful mouth compressed. It struck her as a savage irony that Max should seem as unhappy as she was and that that reality could only drive them further apart. He should have been more honest with her when he proposed, she thought bitterly. He should have admitted then that he didn't want a child in his life. He had been prepared to marry her to throw a mantle of respectability over the possibility that she might be pregnant, but evidently even then he must have been hoping that she would fail to conceive.

Shortly before they left because Andrew was grey with exhaustion, her grandfather gripped her hand firmly in his. 'Do you have any idea how much I regret not standing up to my son when he put you into that convent?'

'It was his decision, not yours,' she responded gently.

'I should've fought him, offered him money for his

good works in return for you,' Andrew sighed wearily. 'But he was my son and I wanted him to come home and I was afraid to take the risk of arguing with him.'

'I was fine at the convent. I *am* fine,' Tia pointed out quietly.

'You're a wonderful girl,' Andrew assured her as they waited indoors for the limousine to arrive.

'And I have a little secret to tell you,' Tia whispered, suddenly desperate to give her news to someone who would appreciate it.

Her grandfather responded to her little announcement with a huge smile and he squeezed her hand with tears glistening in his blue eyes. 'Wonderful,' was all he could say. *'Wonderful.'*

'Congratulations,' Andrew told Max when he swung into the car with them. 'Our family will continue into another generation.'

For once Max experienced no inner warmth at being included in Andrew's family and his lean, strong face remained taut, his hard jaw line clenched. He was furious with himself. He knew his lack of enthusiasm had hurt and distressed Tia. He had allowed his emotions to control him, filling him with a fearful sense of insecurity. *Man up,* his intelligence urged him with derision. *Be an optimist, not a pessimist.* If he put his mind to it, surely he was capable of being a good father?

'I'm very tired,' Tia admitted at the foot of the stairs. 'Perhaps we could talk tomorrow.'

'You go on up to bed,' her grandfather urged cheerfully. 'Max and I will have a nightcap to celebrate.'

'You're not supposed—' she began.

'One drink,' Andrew specified with a wry grin.

'Surely even the doctor would not deny me that on a special occasion?'

Tia mounted the stairs, striving not to relive Max's reaction to her pregnancy. She fingered her pendant with its ninety-odd diamonds as she removed her jewellery. A diamond for every day she and Max had been together. She had thought that that was so romantic but obviously it had just been a gesture, the sort of gesture a man made when he wanted to look like a devoted new husband. That newly acquired cynicism shocked her, but what else was she to think?

Tia clambered into bed and, in spite of her unhappy thoughts, discovered that she was much too tired to lie awake. She slept, waking as dawn light broke through the curtains to find Max shaking her shoulder.

Max gripped her hand, which struck her as strange and she frowned up at him. 'What's wrong?' she framed.

'You have to be very brave,' he breathed with a ragged edge to his dark deep voice.

Tears were shimmering in his liquid dark eyes and that fast, she knew. *'Andrew?'* she exclaimed.

'He passed away in his sleep during the night. A fatal heart attack. I'm sorry, Tia...'

A sob formed in Tia's tight throat. She didn't think she could bear the pain. Max and Andrew together had been her support system but Max had let her down the night before and now Andrew was gone as well. In a world that now seemed grey, she wondered how she could go on and then she remembered her baby and knew that she had more strength than she had ever given herself credit for.

CHAPTER EIGHT

TIA SAW HER MOTHER, Inez, seated inside the church and almost stumbled on the way to the front pew.

'What is it?' Max murmured.

'My mother's here,' she framed, dry-mouthed.

'Well, Andrew was her father-in-law for a while,' Max conceded. 'Perhaps she felt a need to pay her respects.'

But the former Inez Grayson, now Inez Santos, was not a religious, respectful nor, for that matter, a sentimental woman. And her presence at Andrew's funeral shook her daughter, who had not seen her parent in almost ten years. The past few days had turned into a roller coaster of grief, disbelief and anger for Tia. Max had kept his distance, using another bedroom after telling her that he didn't want to 'disturb' her. Tia had run the gamut of frightening insecurities. Was her pregnancy such a turn-off that he didn't want to be physically close to her any longer? Or did Max need privacy to come to terms with his own grief at the loss of the man who had done so much to support him when he was young and vulnerable? And, moreover, who had expressed his confidence in Max to the extent of making him CEO of one of the largest business concerns in the UK.

It would be typical of Max to choose not to *share* that grief with her. He was much more likely than she was to wall up his feelings and hide them, particularly when he was already very much aware that he was not actually related to his former mentor except by marriage. It hurt her that yet another event that she felt should have brought them closer had in fact driven them further apart. They had both fondly trusted that Andrew would be spared to them for another few months and unhappily they had learned that no timer could be set on death. Her grandfather's heart had given out under the strain of his illness and that was God's will, Tia reminded herself, and she would not question that.

'The minute I heard I dropped everything to come to you!' Inez gushed as she intercepted Tia on the church steps. 'You need your *mamae* now more than ever.'

'Your maternal concern comes a little late in the day,' Max murmured with lethal cool.

As a muscle pulled tight on Inez's perfectly made up and undeniably exquisite face, guilt assailed Tia because, for the first time, her mother looked her almost fifty years. 'You're welcome back at the house,' she forced herself to declare.

'Why did you invite her?' Max asked drily as soon as they were back in the limousine. 'You know Cable's waiting to read Andrew's will and she can't be present for that.'

'Inez can mingle with the other guests,' Tia retorted. 'Whatever else she is, she's still my mother. I should respect that.'

And not for the first time, Tia resented the reality that the funeral had been rushed to facilitate the will reading because the stability of her grandfather's business empire depended on smooth continuity being re-established as soon as was humanly possible. It was all to do with stocks and shares, she recalled numbly, the weariness of stress and early pregnancy tugging at her again.

She took her seat in the library with Andrew's other relatives for the reading of the will. The lawyer read out bequests to long-serving staff first before moving on to the children of Tia's grandmother's siblings. Disappointment then flashed across a lot of faces and Tia stopped looking, thinking that people probably always hoped for more than they received in such cases and, mindful of her own inheritance, she was determined not to be judgemental. Silence fell as Mr Cable moved on to the main body of the will and the disposition of Andrew's great wealth.

Redbridge Hall and its contents were left in perpetuity to Tia and any children she might have, along with sufficient funds to ensure its maintenance and a sizeable private income for her support, but the bulk of Andrew's money and his business holdings were left exclusively to Max. Only if Tia and Max divorced would there be any change in that status quo and, even then, Max would have the final word on every decision taken in that situation.

A shocked muttering burst out amongst Tia's companions as a wave of dissension ran around the room. Tia was disconcerted by the will but not surprised, having long since recognised that her grandfather's strongest desire had always been to ensure that Grayson Industries survived for future generations. Building Grayson Industries into an international empire had been Andrew's life's work, after all, and, as far as Tia could see, how he chose to dispose of his life's work and earnings had been entirely his business.

As threats to take the will to court and distasteful insinuations and accusations about Andrew's state of mind and undue influence being used on him were uttered, the lawyer mentioned that Andrew had taken the precaution of having a psychiatric report done a couple of months earlier to make bringing a court case on such grounds virtually impossible. He also intimated that his employer had for several years been very frank about his hope that Max would marry his granddaughter and take permanent charge of his empire. Amidst much vocal bad feeling, Tia rose from her seat and quite deliberately closed her hand round Max's, for as far as she was concerned Andrew's last wishes were sacrosanct and she did not want anyone to think that she stood anywhere but on Max's side of the fence.

Not that Max, his dark head held high as they left the library, seemed to be in need of her support, particularly not when those also present at the will reading spread amongst the other guests. A low, intent murmur of chatter soon sounded around them and Tia could tell that she and Max were the centre of attention. Her face went pink at that acknowledgement but Max seemed gloriously impervious to the interest of other people.

'How do you feel about all this?' Max enquired almost lazily.

'Andrew *wanted* you to inherit,' Tia murmured with quiet emphasis. 'It was his business and it was his right to dispose of it as he saw fit.'

His lean, strong profile taut, Max dealt her a frowning appraisal from glittering dark deep-set eyes as if questioning that she could really feel like that. Tia evaded his direct gaze because what had happened between them in Brazil was playing heavily on her mind and she knew she had questions to ask her husband before she was willing to bury the subject.

'We'll talk in here.' Max flung open a door off the crowded drawing room. 'By the way, don't feel sorry for your cousins. Andrew made generous settlements on all of them *before* he died.'

'Good to know.' Tia preceded him into a small sitting room. Faded curtains and rather outmoded furniture attested to the fact that it had once been her grandmother's favourite room. It had stayed unchanged for over a quarter of a century and the sight of it and the beautiful view out over the colourful rose garden never failed to touch Tia's heart. Her grandfather had mentioned how he still liked to picture her grandmother sitting writing letters at her bureau and of how in the initial stages of his grief he had liked to sit there to feel close to her again.

'How do you feel?' Max prompted again, standing with wide shoulders angled back and legs braced as if he expected her to attack. 'You can be honest...tell me.'

'Did you know?' Tia asked hesitantly, her luminous gaze welded to his devastatingly handsome, lean dark features.

'What would be in the will? Andrew filled me in on the details only *after* we had married,' Max admitted flatly, raking a frustrated hand through his tousled black hair. 'Prior to that I assumed he would leave it all jointly to both of us.'

The will had shaken Max and it was ironic that, while the disposal of Andrew's assets had made Andrew's other relatives jealous, it had almost made Max groan. He didn't need the ownership of Grayson Industries to feel good about himself or the future. As far as Max was concerned, Grayson Industries would always rightfully belong to Tia, who was a Grayson by birth. He was not sorry, though, to be left with complete autonomy over the business because he would not have enjoyed interference from any other source.

But what Max disliked most of all was the suspicion that Andrew's will had muddied the water in his marriage and no matter what Tia said, she had to have serious doubts about how much she could trust him now. Did she secretly suspect that he had married her for her money? He needed to be more frank with her about *why* he was with her and why he had been willing to marry her, he acknowledged grudgingly.

The worst of Tia's tension had already dissipated. 'It would never occur to me to think of you as a fortune hunter, Max,' she confided ruefully. 'I would never think that of you.'

'Then possibly you should think again. I have to tell you the truth because I won't lie about it. Before I came out to Brazil to collect you, Andrew told me how worried he was about bringing you home here when he was dying. He was worried sick about how you would cope as his heiress in a world so far removed from that of the convent and he *asked* me to marry you to protect you.'

All her natural colour draining away in the face of that unwelcome revelation, Tia fell back a step from him in consternation: Max had not freely chosen to be with her. It was as though her whole world lurched and spun around her because she suddenly felt sick and dizzy and disorientated. Her legs like woolly supports, she dropped down heavily into an armchair and stared back up at him, her cornflower-blue eyes huge in the white triangle of her face.

'That is the one secret I won't keep from you, *bella mia*,' Max declared harshly. 'Andrew came up with the original idea. You heard the family lawyer refer to it. It was news to me, however, that he was considering the idea years before he mentioned it to me. I said I'd consider it after I had met you but the minute I saw you, I stopped considering anything. I wanted you and I didn't want any other man to have you.'

Tia gazed back at him in shock, never having associated such strong emotions with Max.

'Right there and then, I became determined that you would be mine,' Max continued in a harsh undertone. 'I didn't think about the business or the money. That didn't come into it for me. I'm an ambitious man but prior to meeting you I had built up enough wealth to satisfy me and anything more was icing on the cake. Somehow in a very short space of time you became both the icing *and* the cake. Even so, I was intolerably greedy and selfish. I didn't want any other man to have an excuse to come near you.'

'Intolerably?' Tia queried his choice of words shakily.

'A more honourable man would have wanted you to come home and have the freedom to explore the dating scene. My blood ran cold at that prospect. I'm possessive. I didn't want to run the risk of losing you to someone else. I didn't want anyone to have the chance to take you from me. I knew I would meet Andrew's expectations and look after you and, whatever happens, I will continue to do so. When I give my word, I stand by it, and you are my wife and I will always stand by that.'

And she recognised that stubborn strength and resolution in him and it cut her and made her bleed where it didn't show, made her bleed for what she couldn't have and what she would have given anything to possess. Had he loved her she would have forgiven him anything but he didn't *love* her. He desired her. Yes, she understood that perfectly, for she had desired him with equal fervour when they had first met. But desire had steadily transformed into love where she was concerned, only it hadn't happened that way for Max. She understood that he would do only right by her; that she could rely on him and that he had not married her only for the riches that that marriage would bring him.

But, that didn't change the reality that she was married to Max now because *Andrew* had wanted Max to be with her, giving her the protection that Andrew had known he would not be around for long to give. Their sexual chemistry had persuaded Max that such a marriage could work but without the pressure of her grandfather's emotional blackmail would it have ever occurred to Max to marry her?

Tia thought not. Furthermore, there was a huge unacknowledged elephant in the room—the baby Max had yet to mention in any shape or form. He had had three days to brood. Surely that was time enough for a man to deal with an unexpected and unwelcome development? And as Tia rested troubled eyes on Max, her heart was sinking because she knew they did not have a future together. He didn't want their child. He would do what he had to do, say what he had to say but without the spur of love and genuine interest he would be a poor parent. Much as her own father had been, Tia decided wretchedly, bad memories pulling at her. She had spent a lifetime trying to please a man who could not be pleased. She had struggled endlessly to win his love and approval, writing him weekly letters to which he never responded and passing every exam that came her way. And her efforts had only been a thankless and heartbreaking learning experience and she would never impose that burden on her baby. Sometimes, she thought sadly, *no* father could be better than an uncaring, indifferent one.

'Now isn't the time for this,' she breathed, rising with sudden decisiveness. 'We have a house full of visitors.'

And Max thought, so much for the much-vaunted tactic of telling the truth and baring your heart. It hadn't got him anywhere. Tia's face was shuttered, eyes on lockdown, her lush mouth closed. *Madonna diavolo!* He wasn't going to lose her—no way was he prepared to let her go! Particularly not now when she was carrying his child. *His* child, he reminded himself doggedly, striving valiantly to accustom himself to that astonishing idea. Some time soon when her grief was not so fresh he would tell her the whole story of his childhood and then she would understand his apprehension, wouldn't she?

Right now he didn't want to weigh her down with any more stress and worry. She looked fragile as a bird in her elegant black dress and he knew she was eating little more than a sparrow's ration at mealtimes. The tension of anxiety settled into Max's bones. So far he was dismayed by what pregnancy appeared to be doing to his wife. He knew that a pregnancy wasn't an illness but Tia looked wan, thin and drained and her once buoyant spirits were at basement level.

Tia quickly discovered that gossiping tongues had been busy in the drawing room because her mother wasted no time in tracking her down to draw her into a quiet corner and say angrily, 'We'll take Andrew's will to court. It's a disgrace. Your inheritance has been stolen by your husband. He's a fortune hunter! No wonder he doesn't want me around!'

'I'm not taking anyone to court, Inez,' Tia countered in a firm undertone.

'Can't you call me Mamae like my other children?' the blonde woman asked plaintively.

Tia breathed in deep. 'I don't want to be unkind but you were never my mother in the way you were a mother to them...and it's too late now. We're strangers. I needed a mother when I was a little girl. I've got used to not having one now.'

'But it could be different...if I stayed here, if I *lived* with you,' Inez argued vehemently, 'then we could get to know each other.'

'*Lived* with me? Why would you want to live with me when your home and your husband are in Brazil?' Tia queried in genuine astonishment.

'Francisco has replaced me with a younger woman,' Inez admitted with a dismissive toss of her head and a shrug. 'We're currently going through a divorce and my children have elected to stay with their father and their future stepmother.'

Tia had a scornful urge to ask her mother what it felt like to be abandoned and was immediately deeply ashamed of that spiteful prompting. 'I'm sorry. It must be very hard for you right now.'

'But if I could move in with you, everything would be much easier,' Inez confessed. 'I would have no financial worries and I could live in comfort.'

And comprehension set in then with Tia. Her mother

had only come to the funeral because she had decided that Tia might finally be useful to her, and of course she wanted Tia to take Max to court and fight Andrew's will because the wealthier Tia was, the more useful she could be to her mother. Bitterness threatened to claim Tia. For an instant, she recalled the loneliness of convent life for a little girl who never got to go home to a family during the holidays like her classmates. Inez's self-interest was not a surprise but what did surprise Tia was that her mother's selfishness could still hurt and disappoint her.

'That's not possible,' Tia responded deflatingly.

'But this is *your* house now,' Inez protested, making it clear that she had received that confidential information from someone present at the reading of the will. 'You can have whoever you like to stay and who better than your mother?'

'Her husband,' another voice interposed and Tia glanced up in dismay to find Max towering over them, his lean, strong face formidable in its hard resolve. 'Tia has me and right now she doesn't need anyone else.'

Inez's mouth took on a venomous twist but before she could say anything more, Tia stepped away. 'It was good to see you today, Inez,' she said politely as she walked away.

'I feel awful,' she whispered to Max. 'I don't feel anything for her. Well, actually, that's another lie. At one point I felt angry, bitter and nasty and I hate feeling like that.'

Max shrugged a broad shoulder. 'She made it that way when she walked out on you and never came back, *bella mia*. Don't blame yourself for being human.'

And instantly, Tia felt soothed, gazing up into lustrous dark golden eyes, her tummy flipping a somersault in sudden excitement as that sliding sensation thrummed between her legs and she ached down deep inside. Every response seemed heightened by the rawness of her turbulent emotions. For a heady split second she craved his mouth with every fibre of her being, hunger threatening to roar up inside her like a raging fire. She sucked in a shuddering breath to calm her fevered body, wondering where she would focus that passion when she no longer had Max. On her baby? On some other interest?

Max swallowed with difficulty, his hand clenching into a fist and digging into his pocket. It was neither the time nor the place and her fine-boned face was etched with strain and fatigue. He didn't want her to have to play hostess any longer; he wanted to scoop her up in his arms and lay her down to rest somewhere quiet and peaceful. Knowing she would do her duty, however, he stayed by her side, handling the more difficult conversations that roused her grief and brought tears to her eyes. He urged her to sit down whenever possible and was barely able to conceal his relief when people began leaving.

'I think I'll have an early night,' Tia told him over a dinner in which she merely rearranged her food on her plate.

'Good idea. It's been a very long day.'

'I miss him,' Tia confessed gruffly.

'I've never been in this house before when he wasn't here. It feels strange.'

Tia lay in the bath, composing herself while she made plans for her future. Max didn't want their child and he didn't want her except in the most basic sexual way. She deserved better and she wasn't about to settle for less, she told herself urgently. She had to be strong and decisive. She would leave and use her grandmother's inheritance to build a new independent life, possibly the life she would have enjoyed had she not met Max. What else could she do?

Max had married her primarily to please Andrew and Andrew was no longer alive to be hurt and disappointed by her decision to abandon her hasty marriage. Max wouldn't miss her. He would be far too busy with Grayson Industries. He didn't want their child, couldn't even bring himself to talk about the baby she carried. No, the best he could seem to do was ignore the subject in its entirety. Leaving was her only option.

Max would not feel he had lost out when he had no contact with the child he had accidentally fathered. Their child would lose out on having a father but if Max wasn't keen on being a father, wouldn't his absence be less damaging in the long run? Perhaps years from now Max would succumb to curiosity as her own mother once had and he would find that he could communicate more easily with their child when he or she was more mature. Tia knew she could not expect to stay hidden for ever.

Tears dampened her cheeks in the hothouse temperature of the opulent bathroom. How could she walk away from the man she loved? Even if it was the best thing for them both? Eventually they would have to get a divorce, which would leave them free to seek another relationship. Just then Tia didn't think she would ever again be attracted to anyone and the thought of Max with anyone else absolutely destroyed her. Indeed, all she could think of at that instant was Max, his hair-roughened bronzed skin hot and a mixture of rough and smooth against her, the intoxicating taste of him, the burning need he excited…

Irritated with herself, Tia clambered out of the bath, her body tingling and pulsing, and wrapped herself in a towel. In the bedroom, she hovered. One last night, she thought crazily, one last night with Max…why not? Why the heck not? She loved him, she wanted him. Afterwards she would write him a letter explaining how she felt but she wouldn't tell him everything. If she told him she loved him he would feel guilty that he had hurt her. No, she would tell him that she needed her freedom; that life was too short to waste, that setting out to make her own life and live alone was what she had always dreamt of…and it would be the truth with just a few salient facts withheld.

Swathed in a towelling robe, she walked out into the corridor and down to the bedroom that she knew Max was using. She didn't knock on the door because she felt that would be silly. No, she walked straight in and caught Max lying in his boxers on the bed watching the business news. Against the backdrop of the white linen sheets, he was a breathtaking vision of masculine perfection.

'I don't want to be alone tonight,' she told him honestly.

Max was very much taken aback. He sat up, brilliant dark eyes widening as Tia untied the sash of the robe and let the robe tumble in a heap to the floor. He couldn't believe what he was witnessing because Tia was usually endearingly modest and now here she was naked under the lights. Yet light was a good friend to that porcelain skin with its pearlised glow, that honey-blonde hair as glossy as polished silk and the full, pouting, pink-tipped breasts that shifted with her every movement. Max had never liked surprises but just then he felt as if he had died and gone to heaven and the television went silent as soon as he had made a successful fumbling attempt to locate the remote.

'I'm all yours, *bella mia*,' he breathed thickly, the pulse at his groin responding with alarming rapidity to his appreciation of her.

Tia got on the bed and slid over him like a siren, leaning down, pink-tipped breasts brushing his chest as she planted her succulent pink lips against his. Max put his hands up and dragged her down to him, his urgency thrilling her. Bossy as always, he rearranged her to his satisfaction on the bed and worked his sensual passage down over her squirming body from her delicate collarbone to her straining nipples and then all the way down to the tender flesh between her thighs.

'I wanted to torture you,' she complained. 'This was supposed to be *my* show.'

'Some other time,' Max growled, fighting to stay in control as he teased her damp receptive core and she made little gasping sounds that went straight to his groin and made him as rigid and hard as steel.

'When's it going to be my turn?' she complained, running a desperate hand down over his strong muscular shoulders and clawing her fingers through his hair because those were the only parts of him she could reach.

'I'm in no condition to argue right now.'

He turned her firmly over onto her knees and plunged with erotic force into her. She cried out because he felt so impossibly good and she was only just realising in sudden dismay that if everything went to plan she would never experience such intimacy with Max again. That conviction panicked her and his next surge only intensified her body's reaction. She arched as the tingling waves of excitement threatened to consume her, her whole body hot and liquid with uncontrollable craving.

'Don't you dare stop!' she moaned, barely knowing what she was saying, unable to think and too frightened by what she had thought to even want to think.

And Max didn't. The long dreadful day of sadness faded with every voluptuously satisfying penetration of her receptive body. Tia's need for him had startled him because her muted response to his earlier explanation about how he felt about her had disappointed him. Their all-consuming passion sparked and flamed into a frantic blaze of hunger neither of them could restrain. As release claimed them both into the trembling, perspiring aftermath, Max groaned out something ragged in Italian.

When Tia rolled away, Max stretched out an arm and brought her back to him, knowing she needed that closeness, fighting his own awkwardness to give her what she deserved. He had not enjoyed sleeping apart from her, but it had been a necessary sacrifice when Andrew's death had brought her so low, when he couldn't trust himself to share a bed with her and not reach for her in the night.

'Thank you,' she said softly. 'That was amazing.'

'You don't ever need to thank me for something that gives me so much pleasure.'

'You thanked me once,' she reminded him.

Max didn't remember. '*Did* I?'

'You did,' she whispered, quietly pulling free to slip out of the bed, knowing she had that letter to write and plans to make.

'I got it wrong,' Max husked softly. 'Sometimes I'm going to get it wrong without meaning to.'

Tia's eyes prickled with tears because there was just no room for getting it wrong with a baby. It had gone wrong for her and she suspected it had gone wrong for Max as well, because why else would he be so reluctant to talk about his childhood? But she was determined not to let it go wrong for her child even if that entailed walking out on the man she loved. Her child was not going to pay either now or in the future because she had foolishly picked the wrong man to love and marry. That was her mistake and she would not allow her little boy or girl to pay the price of that mistake because it was a mistake that would reverberate down through the childhood years and leave a scar that wouldn't heal.

CHAPTER NINE

NINE MONTHS AFTER Tia's disappearance, Max finished the last phone call and stared at his desk. The Reverend Mother had promised him she would get in touch if she heard anything from Tia and she had not. Inez Santos had snarled down the phone that she had still not heard from her daughter and had no desire to hear from her. Ronnie had never been in a position to offer him any helpful leads. Tia had not confided in anyone.

The trail, such as it was, was dead. Tia had departed in a taxi with one suitcase and Teddy. The taxi had taken her to the railway station from where she had travelled to London. A couple of weeks later there had been a possible sighting of her on a train heading to Devon. He supposed that he should at least be grateful that she had inherited her grandmother's money and was presumably making use of it. At least it meant that she was not destitute. But she had not once used the credit cards that he had given her or attempted to access the substantial private income that Andrew had set up for her. No, she had rejected everything Max and Andrew had given her and walked away.

Every line of the letter she had left behind haunted Max. It had been so blunt, so honest. *You don't really want me.* That said all that needed to be said in terms of his performance as a husband, didn't it? He had been married to Tia for over three months and that was the impression she had taken away from the experience. *You married me to please Andrew.* No, he hadn't but he needed to find her to tell her that. *You don't want to be a father.* Well, she had got that right. *You don't want our baby.* She had got that wrong. He had climbed aboard that man train where you acted strong rather than admit fear and ambiguity and he had shot himself in the foot. Tia didn't understand because he hadn't told her what she needed to know to understand. And now it was too late.

Max lifted his chin, his formidable bone structure grim. It would never be too late because he would not give up. When something truly mattered to him, he refused to accept defeat. Somehow, sooner or later, he would find some small piece of information that would lead him to his runaway bride and he would then face his biggest challenge—persuading her to come home. Her and Teddy and hopefully their child. Had she had a safe delivery?

But he reckoned bringing his little family home to Redbridge—if all had gone well—would be the toughest challenge he had ever faced. Tia, after all, had never truly wanted to marry him. She hadn't wanted to be tied down to a husband and if she had made the best of it for a few months he should be grateful for small mercies. She had wanted her freedom and now she had taken it. What nagged at Max most of all was the insidious suspicion that, had he moved more slowly with Tia, she would have wanted to stay married to him.

* * *

Tia tenderly zipped Sancha Mariana Leonelli back into her sleeping bag and tucked her back into her cot where she would sleep while her mother baked.

Motherhood was very different from what Tia had expected. She had not been remotely prepared for the intense joy that flooded her when she initially saw her infant daughter's little face or for the anxiety that rocked her when Sancha got her first cold. After three months of being a mum, however, she had become a little more laid-back but she could still get emotional. When Sancha opened the dark liquid eyes that she had inherited from her father along with his blue-black hair, Tia's heart clenched and her eyes sometimes stung because she was learning that time did not heal every pain.

Even nine months away from Max had failed to cure her heartache. Yet during those months of independence she had discovered so many enjoyable things and she had worked hard to make the days go past more quickly. But neither the satisfaction of a walk in sunlit frosted fields nor hard work had made her miss Max one atom less.

She had missed him worst of all when she gave birth to Sancha. Having attended a pre-natal class and made some friends, she had not been entirely alone at the hospital, but the absence of the man she loved had made her feel painfully isolated. Yet she knew that was ironic when Max had wanted neither her nor their child and would, had he but known it, have been very grateful to avoid the hullabaloo of childbirth and the chaotic aftermath of learning how to live with a newborn.

She had made friends when she moved to the picturesque village with the ancient church. In summer the village was busy with tourists. She had bought a little corner terraced house that came with an attached tea room, which she planned to open as a business in the spring. During the winter, she had baked traditional Brazilian cakes to offer at a church sale, and when the requests had come in for birthday cakes and fancy desserts she had fulfilled them and had ended up taking orders and eventually charging for the service. Before she knew where she was she was selling them like proverbial hotcakes and barely able to keep up with the demand.

Tia marvelled that a talent she had not even recognised as a talent was now providing her with a good living. She had learned to bake at Sister Mariana's side and the fabulous cakes she produced had once provided an evening treat at the convent. Her repertoire ran from coconut cake to passion fruit mousse cake and back to peach pound cake, which could be sliced and toasted for breakfast and served with fruit and cream. She planned to make her cakes the mainstay of her offerings at the tea room when it opened and, that in mind, she had hired a local woman to work with her.

Hilary was an energetic brunette and a terrific baker. Experienced in catering, she had helped Tia deal with suppliers and customers and had helped her work through the stringent health and safety regulations that had to be passed before the reopening of the tea shop could be achieved.

'Sancha is already sleeping through the night for you,' Hilary remarked enviously, the mother of a rumbustious boy, who was still disturbing her nights at three years old.

'And I am transformed,' Tia responded with a roll

of her eyes. 'I was run pretty ragged the first couple of months. Just getting myself up in the morning was a challenge. I couldn't have done all this without you.'

'No, you couldn't have done it without your incredible cakes,' Hilary countered with a wry smile. 'Not many women could have achieved as much as you have in a few short months. Certainly not as a preggers mum-to-be on her own. Do you think your husband will eventually want to come and visit?'

'I don't know,' Tia said awkwardly, wishing that she had found it possible to lie to Hilary and pretend that Sancha was the result of a one-night stand. Instead she had found herself admitting that her marriage had broken down when she had revealed her pregnancy to a man who was less than keen on fatherhood. 'Tea?'

'Even if he wasn't that keen on being a dad, he's bound to be curious. I think you should consider giving him a chance,' Hilary reasoned, settling at the table with her tea and some paperwork. 'But then what do I know? I didn't do so well with my own marriage.'

Tia stared out of the window while she drank her own tea and brooded over the unsettling thoughts that Hilary had awakened. Sancha *was* Max's daughter as well. Had she given Max a fair chance in the parenting stakes? She knew she hadn't given him a chance at all. Despite his lack of enthusiasm over her pregnancy, wasn't there at least a possibility that his reservations would have melted away once he saw his baby daughter in the flesh? And just when was she planning to give him that chance?

Why was it that she hadn't thought about what was fair to Max nine months ago? She had made her deductions and acted on them in the heat of emotion, which was never wise. Everything had happened so fast: her marriage and her pregnancy, Andrew's death and his will and her unsettling encounter with her mother, when once again she had been forced to recognise that she was the child of a woman who chilled her. Would she still have walked out on Max if she had taken the time to think through events more calmly? Might she not have decided that talking to Max and giving him a fair hearing would be a more reasonable approach? More and more, Tia's conscience warned her that she had not so much walked out as run away from a situation that had made her feel trapped and powerless.

And whether she liked it or not, Sancha was Max's baby too. She had ignored his rights, favouring her own. And what about the divorce he probably wanted now? He would want his freedom back and the opportunity to move on with his life, but the vanishing act she had pulled would make that process even more difficult.

Tia was ashamed of the truth that she didn't want to give Max a divorce and see him move on to another woman. How could she be that selfish? Hadn't she walked away? He was entitled to his freedom if he wanted it. Not that he so far seemed to have taken much advantage of their separation, she conceded. Max had led quite an active life on the social scene before he met her, for she had checked him out on the Internet and, from what she had been able to establish since then, if Max *had* returned to his former lifestyle he was being very discreet about it. Of course, she had made that awkward for him too because he was neither single nor even officially separated from her.

And just as Tia had taken charge of her life nine months earlier she recognised that she had to come out of hiding now and face the music. It was time for her to stand up and deal with the challenges she had been avoiding. The very first step of that process, she acknowledged ruefully, would be contacting Max.

While Hilary was enjoying her tea, Tia pulled out her phone and before she could lose her nerve she accessed Max's phone number on her phone, attached a photo of Sancha to it and texted him her address as well as the name she had been using to avoid detection. For the sake of anonymity, she was known as Tia Ramos locally. Ramos had been her mother's maiden name.

Max received that text in the middle of a business meeting and his rage knew no bounds as he scrutinised his first blurry picture of his daughter, Sancha. She looked at the camera with big dark eyes, her tiny face astonishingly serious for a baby. Sancha Leonelli, Max was thinking in wonderment, until he read the full text message from his runaway wife and registered on a fresh tide of threatening fury that Tia had cast off the Leonelli name as entirely as she had cast off her husband. A blasted text! Not even a phone call. Was that all he rated after a nine-month silence? Nine months of unceasing worry that would have slaughtered a lesser man? A text… Max gritted his even white teeth, launched upright and strode out without even an apology for his departure. He had a wife to deal with.

Tia was slightly surprised when Max did not respond to her message. Had he changed his number? Moved on from their marriage to the extent that he did not feel her text required an immediate response? Common sense kicked in, reminding her that Max had only just received his first glimpse of his baby daughter. More probably Max was furious with her. Anxiously mulling over those possibilities, Tia kept herself busy once she had put Sancha down for the night. The tea-room kitchen where she did all her baking was linked by a door to her house and, as long as she set up the baby monitor while she worked, she could hear her daughter if she wakened, but during the day she kept Sancha tucked in her travel cot and within easy reach.

She was busy packing an Anthill cake, which was stuffed with chocolate chips, when she heard her house doorbell ring and she sped back next door before the noise could waken Sancha. When she opened the door to Max she was knocked for six because the very last response she had expected from him was an instant unannounced visit.

'Oh, it's the kitchen fairy,' Max derided, running gleaming dark eyes down over her flour-smudged nose to her full ripe mouth and the shapeless chef's overall she wore. He had checked her out before his arrival and he knew all about the cakes she was baking. It irritated him that, not only had he not known that she could bake, but she had also not once made the effort to bake anything for him.

Tia went red, grateful she had removed her kitchen hat before she answered the door, but her fingers lifted to self-consciously smooth the hair braided neatly round her head. Poised below the porch light, Max looked amazing, blue-black hair glossy, his lean dark angel features smooth over his high cheekbones while a shadow of dark stubble roughened and accentuated the contrast between his angular jaw line and his wide, full modelled mouth. Her mouth ran dry.

'Or maybe it's Heidi and you're about to start yodelling,' Max breathed between gritted teeth.

'Heidi?' Tia frowned, not having come across that book as a child, staring up at him, frantically wishing she were dressed and wearing proper shoes with heels instead of clad for comfort and warmth in jeans, a winter sweater and flatties.

'It must be the cute little-girl braids,' Max extended sardonically, moving forward to force her to move back, a waft of cold air eddying into the house with him. 'Makes you look about ten years old.'

Tia backed several steps and thrust the door shut behind him. 'You should've told me you were coming,' she protested defensively, feeling menaced by the intimidating size of Max in the confined area of her small hallway.

'My apologies,' Max intoned softly. 'Your nine months of silence killed any manners I ever had stone dead.'

Tia's colour flared again because there wasn't much she could say to that in her own defence. She had speculated so many times about what seeing Max again would be like and now she was appreciating that she had got it wrong every time. She was all flustered, every sense on overdrive. She had forgotten his sheer physical impact on her, the heightened heart rate that dampened her skin, the challenge to breathe evenly, the surge of helpless excitement when she collided with his brilliant dark golden eyes. Feeling weak and uneasy with that least allowable sensation, she hastily thrust open the lounge door.

'I'm sorry I didn't get in touch sooner,' Tia murmured tautly. 'I didn't know what to say. I know that's no excuse but—'

'You're right. It's not an excuse. If it was I'd have

first call on it,' Max sliced in without warning. 'I didn't know what to say when you told me that you were pregnant…and, *Dio mio*, haven't you made me pay for that lack of verbal dexterity?'

Wrong-footed once again, Tia clasped her hands together tightly in front of her. 'I didn't want my child to have an uncaring father.'

'On what grounds did you assume that I would be uncaring?' Max shot back at her. 'And where is my daughter? I want to see her.'

'She's asleep.' Tia swallowed hard, unaccustomed to being under attack by Max, feeling the novelty of that unexpected experience like a sudden blow, her skin turning clammy and cold.

Max planted himself expectantly back by the door into the hall. 'I can be very quiet,' he told her.

'Max, I—'

'I've waited months. I won't wait any longer,' Max informed her impatiently. 'When was she born?'

Tia gave him the date of their daughter's birth.

'Naturally I've been worried sick about you all this time,' Max pointed out curtly. 'I wondered if you were ill, whether you were in hospital, seeing a doctor regularly for check-ups…I even wondered if you could have lost the baby.'

'I'm sorry, I didn't think my silence through,' Tia countered stiltedly, mounting the narrow stairs and then stepping back from the doorway of Sancha's little bedroom to let him precede her, if anything grateful for the distraction from the hard questions he was shooting at her and the guilt he had awakened.

Max had believed his rage would ebb once he entered the house but being greeted by his wife as though everything were normal when it was as far from normal as it was possible to be had grated on him. Being forced to *ask* to see his own daughter didn't help and the suffocatingly small bedroom sent another biting surge of fury through him. As a child he had had so little. Now that he had a child of his own he wanted his child to have everything, and everything encompassed space and comfort and every material advantage he could provide. Now he stood in a small slot of a room only just big enough for a cot and a chest of drawers. It was clean, adequate but not sufficient to satisfy him.

'The courts take a very dim view of mothers who deny fathers all right of access to their children,' he heard himself impart grimly.

The blood chilled in Tia's veins because what she heard was a threat. 'I thought I was doing the best thing for all of us when I left. I thought you didn't want her, didn't want the responsibility.'

'But I never said that, did I? Nor did I ever suggest that you terminate the pregnancy or indeed anything of that nature,' Max reminded her fiercely, finally approaching the cot with somewhat hesitant steps and looking down to see what he could of the sleeping baby. The light from the landing illuminated her little face, the sweet sweep of lashes on her flushed baby cheeks, the fullness of the little rosebud mouth she had definitely inherited from her mother. The sudden tightness in his chest forced Max to drag in a long, deep, steadying breath. Sancha was very small and the short tufts of her tousled dark hair stuck up comically in all directions while her tiny starfish hand lay relaxed against the mattress.

'She's...gorgeous.' Max almost whispered the word,

what he had planned to say next flying back out of his head while he drank in his first glimpse of his daughter.

'She looks just like you,' Tia framed nervously, still reeling from that reference to the courts and parental rights because she knew what she had done and was bright enough to fear the consequences.

'What does it say on her birth certificate?' Max prompted tautly.

'Sancha Mariana Leonelli. I didn't know any of your family names so I couldn't include any,' Tia told him. 'And the sisters were the only family I ever knew.'

'I wouldn't have wanted my family names included,' Max admitted in a raw undertone, striding back to the door. 'There are no good memories there that I would want carried on into the next generation.'

Tia chewed uncertainly at her lower lip and then glanced at him at the top of the stairs, clashing involuntarily with glittering dark eyes of challenge. 'I kind of suspected that,' she confided.

'That's why I found it so challenging to imagine becoming a father,' Max revealed, clattering down the stairs, using the activity as cover to make himself force out that lowering admission of vulnerability. 'Actually I couldn't imagine it... I found the concept too frightening.'

'Oh... Max,' Tia whispered, her eyes burning with a sudden rush of moisture and regret. 'Why didn't you tell me that? I was nervous of becoming a mother too. I worried that I wouldn't be able to cope or that I wouldn't be able to feel attached to my baby because...for whatever reasons... Inez never got properly attached to me.'

'Even so, my background is considerably less presentable than yours,' Max volunteered diffidently. 'I have never discussed that reality with anyone, which only makes it more difficult for me to talk about it. But my aunt didn't *want* to know and Andrew said my past was better left decently buried, so I kept my experiences to myself.'

Tia was aghast that a clearly damaged child had been forced to keep his ordeal a secret that decent people needed to be protected from. 'I don't think that was the right approach.'

'I don't know,' Max conceded with a grim shake of his arrogant dark head. 'Perhaps if I'd been encouraged to talk and think about what happened I would have wallowed in it, which would have been worse. I had nightmares at first and they still come occasionally.'

'I remember you dreaming,' Tia remarked uncomfortably.

Max nodded confirmation. 'But aside of that I did manage to move on without looking back, but my own experiences ensured that I had no plans to ever have kids. There's bad blood in me and I didn't want to pass it on—'

'There's no such thing as "bad blood",' Tia interrupted, angry on his behalf. 'Who used that expression?'

'My aunt. Carina was always waiting for me to reveal some violent, criminal tendency that I had inherited from my father. She never trusted me and never let me forget the fact.'

Seeing no point in sharing her poor opinion of his aunt's attitude towards the child in her care, Tia breathed in slow and deep. 'Your father was violent?'

'Very violent. An alcoholic tyrant. He didn't start out that way though. He was from a decent family and the son of a well-respected businessman but he became a drug-dealing thug at a young age. His family threw him out and he took up with my mother, who was equally wayward in her youth. She once told me that I was the child of his rape,' Max breathed curtly. 'But I suspect that that was her excuse for getting involved with a vicious loser. I'll never know because they are both dead now and the truth died with them.'

'Oh, Max,' Tia muttered, tormented on his behalf. 'What a truly awful thing to tell an innocent child.'

Max froze by the window, bold bronzed profile set, wide shoulders rigid. 'He killed her when I was twelve years old, during one of their frequent rows about money. I was there when it happened. He went to prison for life, which is why I ended up in England with my aunt. He died in prison a few years ago.'

And there was so much revealed in those few clipped sentences that Tia reeled, her every expectation trounced by his brutal honesty. She was very much shocked. He had seen his father murder his mother and had then become his aunt's responsibility. 'You must've been traumatised,' she framed shakily.

'Completely but I got over that and learned how to function in my new life,' Max countered briskly to discourage her sympathy. 'To be frank, that new life was one hell of a lot better than my old life. Plenty of food, a comfortable bed, no beatings, no police harassment, no bullying at school. It was a cakewalk compared with what I had been used to.'

'I'm so sorry, Max,' Tia breathed tautly. 'I had no idea.'

'How could you have had? It's not information I share and it's my past, not my present, Tia,' he declared with forbidding finality. 'I've only trailed all this out now so that I can try to explain to you why I was less than enthusiastic about the idea of becoming a father. There are no male role models in my background. My only role model came when I was older and it was Andrew, and even he turned out to be not quite the man I believed him to be. I was afraid that I'd be a useless father.'

'But you're not your father. You have none of his violence in you. Even tonight when you're so angry with me I have not once felt physically threatened by you,' she pointed out, wanting to ask him how her grandfather had disappointed him, but reluctant to demand too much at once from a man who was only telling what he had so far told her because he felt he had no other choice. 'You're also honourable and honest, responsible and law-abiding.'

'Yet my wife walked out on that honest, honourable, non-violent man and hid herself from me and stayed away as long as she could,' Max retorted with crushing dismissal. 'So, where does that leave us?'

Tia flinched from that sardonic reminder. 'That's a whole different story,' she argued in consternation. 'The leaving was about me, not you. I was so unsure and confused about everything in my life. Everything changed so fast and then Andrew died and you freaked out about me being pregnant—'

'I didn't freak out,' Max broke in angrily.

'In silence, you freaked out,' Tia rephrased. 'A first baby is a huge life change for a woman. I needed you to want our baby as much as I did because neither of us were wanted children and that didn't turn out well for us. I wanted our baby to have everything we didn't have, starting with caring, involved parents.'

'But you didn't give me a chance,' Max argued vehemently, dark eyes shimmering pure gold condemnation in the lamp light. 'Andrew had just died. I didn't want to lay my sordid background on you on top of everything else you were already going through. You were pregnant and I tried to deal with that as best I could without involving you.'

'Which meant you acted like it hadn't happened,' Tia slotted in ruefully. 'I couldn't handle that. We'd got married in a hurry. I'd got pregnant in a hurry. I had to put my child first and I knew I needed to be stronger. I couldn't get stronger *with* you because you were too busy looking after me to let me learn how to do things for myself. And I thought of Inez, who's spent her whole life needing a man to lean on and provide for her…and I was determined that *I* wasn't going to be that kind of weak woman.'

'Leaning on me isn't a weakness,' Max growled as the door bell sounded. 'Who's that?'

'Probably my customer wanting to pick up his party order,' Tia recalled belatedly. 'You stay here and I'll sort him out.'

But Max was too curious about the life that Tia had built away from him to keep his distance. He watched her greet a man in his thirties and walk through to a spacious catering kitchen to lift a set of cake boxes. Max's lean, strong face clenched as he listened to them banter like two old friends and he stepped back into the lounge while she showed her customer out again.

'Who is he?' he asked baldly when she reappeared. 'He was flirting with you.'

'Was he? I don't think so,' Tia responded with amusement to that suggestion because she had learned a thing or two over the past months. Now she knew when a man was flirting with her and when it was better to ignore an off-colour joke or call a halt to any overfamiliarity before someone got the wrong idea. 'He's a married man with five children and this is their third birthday party in as many months, so I've got to know him well.'

'How many other men have you got to know well?' Max enquired with lethal cool.

Tia glanced at him in open shock.

'Obviously I'm going to ask. I'd prefer honesty,' he admitted stonily.

Tia went pink. 'There hasn't been anyone…*anything*,' she breathed tightly. 'I'm very aware that I'm still married.'

'Ditto,' Max traded flatly. 'We've both been living in limbo since you walked out. If you wanted your freedom, Tia, you only had to say so. We could have separated with a lot less drama and stress.'

Tia lost colour. 'Is that what you want? A separation?'

Max settled glittering dark eyes on her. 'I'm still so angry with you that I don't know what I want.'

'Angry?' she queried uncertainly.

'Very angry,' Max qualified without hesitation. 'Perhaps you've forgotten that last night… I haven't.'

Tia's face flamed. In fact she felt as though her whole body were burning with mortification below her clothes.

'The last thing I was expecting the following morning was that letter. Why the goodbye sex?'

'I don't want to discuss that.'

Max planted himself in the doorway to prevent her from leaving the room. 'I'm afraid you're going to have to talk about a lot of stuff you don't want to talk about before I leave you alone. I deserve the truth, Tia. I have always tried to be straight with you.'

Tia spun away from him, embarrassment claiming her, for she had often squirmed when she looked back to the way she had wantonly thrown herself at him that night after the funeral. 'Oh, for goodness' sake, I wanted you… *OK?*' she exclaimed.

'The wanting was more than OK but the walking out on our marriage afterwards wasn't,' Max delivered icily. 'Not giving me the opportunity to answer your concerns was very unfair as well. There are no polite words to cover what I went through over the following months worrying about you. The press speculated that you'd left me because I screwed you over with your inheritance and they had a field day with your convent upbringing in comparison to my freewheeling days of sexual freedom.'

'I had no idea!' Tia exclaimed in dismay. 'I don't read many newspapers but I've kept a very low profile here. There was only that one photo of me that appeared in the papers, the one taken the night of the Grayson party and nobody would associate that designer-clad young woman with the woman I am now. I don't try to draw attention to myself here with my clothes or hair or anything.'

Max didn't know whether he should tell her that nothing could detract from the pure symmetry of her delicate features, the clarity of her skin or the slender suppleness of her body. 'But that simply means that you're living a lie here with Sancha,' he condemned.

Tia bridled, eyes widening, head flipping back. 'What's that supposed to mean?'

'That no matter what you do, you're a very wealthy heiress and my wife. You can't escape what you are, short of returning to Brazil and joining the good sisters again. This is your life and mine.'

An irritable burst of barking from outside made Tia unfreeze. 'Oh, I forgot about Teddy! I let him out into the garden while I was packing those cakes.'

Brushing past him, Tia sped out and seconds later Teddy surged into the room, freezing with a growl the instant he settled his eyes on the unexpected visitor and then moving closer to sniff at Max's trouser legs.

'You've met up with worse than me since we last were together?' Max conjectured, daring to reach down and pat Teddy's head. The terrier made no attempt to growl or bite.

'He's got much more used to other people, living here. I take him for regular walks.' Tia paced restlessly round the room, her full attention welded to Max's lean, powerful figure. 'Where do we go from here, Max?'

'You want an upfront list of demands?' Max queried. 'I want you to come home so that I can get to know my daughter.'

'Redbridge Hall is not my home,' Tia parried in disbelief.

'I may have been paying your staff for you for the past nine months but, legally and every other way, Redbridge is yours until you either sell it or dispose of it in some other way. And the will probably restricts what you *can* do because Andrew wanted the property kept in the family,' Max reminded her.

'*You've* been paying the staff?' Tia gasped.

'Well, someone had to take responsibility for them,' Max pointed out very drily. 'Your grandfather employed a lot of people and several businesses operate on the estate. I think eventually you will decide to scale down the household staff to a more appropriate level.'

Tia had lost all her natural colour. 'I didn't think.'

'No, of course you didn't. You've never had staff before but now that you do, you do have to take care of them. And there are decisions waiting that I was unable to deal with because I am *not* the legal owner of the estate,' he pointed out.

Tia reddened. 'I'm so sorry, Max. I should've thought of all that.'

'On the good news front, Grayson Industries is flourishing as never before and the profits will be astronomical this year because I've had little else but work to occupy me,' he proclaimed with sardonic bite.

Tia sank weakly down on an armchair. Of course, he wanted her back at Redbridge to release him from the added burden of what had never been his responsibility in the first place. She was ashamed that it had not even occurred to her that in her absence life had had to continue at Redbridge. Wages had to be paid, maintenance decisions made and probably requests had had to be answered because the estate land was often used for local events.

'I don't care about the profits,' she declared woodenly.

Max crouched down in front of her to study her with scorchingly furious dark golden eyes. 'Well, I and thousands of other people employed by Grayson's *do* care,' he countered with lethal derision. 'And it's *all* yours. I may be in charge, I may be the figurehead but at the end of the day all those profits are yours, *not* mine.'

Taken aback by his vehemence, Tia flinched back a few inches. 'But that's not what Andrew intended.'

Max swore long and low in Italian, literal sparks dancing in his stunning dark eyes. 'I don't care what Andrew intended. I will only take the salary and the bonus package that was agreed when I first took over. I will not live off my wife's wealth, or my ex-wife's... or whatever you are planning to become.'

Tia was more shaken still by that aggressive statement. Max vaulted upright again, long, lean muscles flexing in his thighs, the fabric of his trousers pulling taut. She recognised that he had run out of patience and that he wanted decisions now. But she was taken aback by his attitude to the Grayson wealth. He didn't want what he saw as *her* money.

'What do you want now, Max?' she murmured tautly. 'You haven't told me that yet.'

Max froze. The anger she had sent soaring through him ebbed and he thought about what *he* wanted. He looked at her and what he wanted was very, very basic. 'I want you to untangle your hair from those ties and strip. I want sex. It's been nine months and I've never gone through a dry spell this long since I grew up.'

Shock rocked Tia where she sat, transfixed like a deer in headlights. Slow colour rose in a tide below her fair skin, heat curling at the heart of her, touching and warming places she had stopped thinking about when she left him. She had suppressed that part of herself, her sensual side, meeting with it only in dreams that she could not control. Now she gazed back at Max, marvelling that he was so bold, so unapologetic about what he wanted and oddly excited by the forceful sexual energy he saw no reason to hide.

CHAPTER TEN

'AND NOW THAT I've begun being honest, I'll continue in the same vein,' Max gritted in a driven undertone, working off a 'might as well be hung for a sheep as a lamb' soapbox. 'I also want my daughter with me under the same roof. I will not negotiate on that demand. I've missed out on an entire three months of her life and I'm a stranger to her through no fault of my own. That has to change—and fast. We'll return to Redbridge Hall tomorrow.'

'That's absolutely impossible!' Tia exclaimed, leaping upright in emphasis, guilt, shock and consternation flooding her in a heady tide. 'I'm about to open the tea room for the Easter visitors and I have loads of orders to fulfil.'

'You also have a very competent co-worker and you can afford to hire another employee to take your place. Oh, yes, I did my homework before I came here,' Max intoned with sizzling cool.

'But you don't understand… Salsa Cakes is *my* business.'

'No, your business is Grayson Industries,' Max contradicted without hesitation. 'Not what you have here. It's time to join the real world again, Tia. You were born into one of the richest families in the UK and you can't run away from your heritage.'

'I didn't run away!' Tia seethed back at him, her hands clenched into fists by her sides, her colour high.

'Your choice, your decision. I'm sorry but you're rich and you're married to a bastard who will take you any way he can get you. Deal with it, *bella mia…I have.*'

The thready wail of a hungry baby pierced the smouldering silence and very quickly grew into a much louder demonstration of baby impatience. 'I'd better feed Sancha,' Tia mumbled, bereft of breath and protest, indeed barely able to think or vocalise, too shaken by the change in Max, who certainly could not be accused of soft-coating his message.

She ran upstairs to scoop her daughter out of her cot and returned to the lounge at a slower pace. As Max moved forward, his lean, darkly handsome features unexpectedly softened, she disconcerted him by literally stuffing her sobbing child into his surprised arms. 'Max, meet Sancha… Sancha, this is Daddy and he is at the very foot of a learning curve when it comes to babies.'

'But I'm a quick study,' Max asserted, bundling up Sancha and resting her against his shoulder, a big hand smoothing her back in a soothing motion.

'I have to heat her bottle…and…er…change her…'

'You don't breastfeed?'

'I did initially but I had problems so we ended up with the bottle and she's thriving,' Tia explained, leaving him to go and take care of necessities.

Max sat down and surveyed his angry-eyed daughter, who was struggling to catch her breath between sobs. He extracted her from the sleeping bag with great care and was amazed by how wriggly her fragile, light little body was. He was surprised to realise that much of his own anger had dissipated. Telling Tia how he felt had helped. Holding his daughter helped even more. All of a sudden he realised that he had moved on from the past that had once haunted him. Sharing that background story had been like curing an illness he had kept locked up inside him. And now he was looking forward and not back on a successful adult life, a stunning wife and an equally beautiful daughter.

My *daughter,* Max thought in wonderment, studying the little being snug in his arms. Her eyes and hair might be dark like his own but the shape of her eyes, her mouth and possibly her little button nose were all her mother's. Her very beautiful mother. Max breathed in deep, fighting the reaction of his body with all his strength. He had been crude but the truth was the truth. All the months without Tia had suddenly just piled up in the back of his brain like a giant rock crushing him. Life without Tia was dull, predictable and barely worth living.

A bastard who will take you any way he can get you.

Tia had been shaken by that statement but strangely fired up by his raw conviction as well. Max *was* very likely illegitimate, she acknowledged, for the background he had described seemed unlikely to have contained legally wedded parents. Why on earth was she thinking about something so irrelevant when Max had laid down what he wanted and it was *all*—from the sex to the immediate relocation—unacceptable?

The trouble was…life without Max was equally unacceptable because she wasn't happy. That was a huge admission for Tia to make to herself when she had worked so hard to achieve independence. She adored her baby, she loved her little house and her embryo business, but existing deprived of Max's presence was like eating curry every day without the spice. Nothing else could compare to the joy of knowing Max was in the room next door, within reach and with their daughter. Even though he was angry, knowing Max was near her again was like her every fantasy come true, she acknowledged shamefacedly. She still loved him. She hadn't got over him. She looked at him and the wanting kicked in again within seconds and it was like coming alive after a long stretch of being denied sunshine and stimulation. Could she settle for the wanting? It did seem to be *all* Max had to give her.

'I'll show you how to feed her.' Tia slotted the bottle into his lean brown hand and showed him the angle. 'She guzzles it down quickly at this time of night.'

And Max settled back into a more relaxed pose and fed their child and the sight of them together warmed the cold space inside Tia, because she had feared that her baby would never have a proper father and that that was entirely her fault. Max followed her upstairs and watched her settle Sancha again.

'You said something about my grandfather not being the man you thought he was,' she reminded him softly. 'What was that about?'

Max groaned. 'I shouldn't have mentioned it.'

'Whatever it is, tell me. I'm sure Andrew wasn't a saint all his life. Nobody is,' she said wryly.

'Did you notice the interest at the dining table on the night you first arrived when you mentioned my aunt's death?' Max prompted.

'Yes, I did,' Tia admitted.

'When I was in my teens, I came back to Redbridge from school unannounced one day and saw Andrew and my aunt kissing. I was shocked,' Max confided. 'Shocked and embarrassed. It was never discussed but I picked up on the evidence after that and realised they'd been having an affair for years.'

'Never...discussed...I mean, even after she died?' Tia pressed in disbelief.

'Never,' Max confirmed. 'I don't think it was any great love affair. I think it was two lonely people finding comfort in each other. Andrew was depressed for a long time after his wife passed away and, although he and my aunt were very discreet, a lot of the family knew about their relationship and regarded her as his mistress.'

Tia wrinkled her nose with distaste. 'That must have been awkward for you.'

Max shrugged. 'I was used to stuff that is whispered behind backs and never openly declared. When I lived in Italy my parents were despised for their lifestyle and I was despised too. Secrets were familiar to me as well. I was also intelligent enough to realise that Andrew probably paid for my fancy boarding school education because an adolescent hanging around on a daily basis would have cramped their style. But I can't complain because I benefitted from that education.'

'I'm surprised he didn't marry her.'

'Marrying his housekeeper wouldn't have been Andrew's style,' Max opined wryly.

On the landing, Tia turned in an unsettled half-circle. 'I assume you're planning to stay here tonight.'

'Yes. I have an overnight bag in my car. I'll bring it in.'

As it was a two-bedroom house with only one small double bed in her room, an involuntary tingle that was far removed from panic shimmied through Tia. What was she playing at? What was she planning to do? Obviously she had to return to Redbridge Hall and deal with matters there, whether she was making arrangements for the house in the short term or more lasting plans for the future. That was, undeniably, her responsibility.

More importantly, Max was demanding full access to Sancha and she could hardly criticise him for that. Their daughter would benefit from a normal relationship with her father. And Tia, who didn't want to picture a future empty of Max, wanted that as well.

'Is there a shower I can use?' Returned to the present, Tia showed Max the bathroom, which was perfectly presentable because she had had to have it replaced soon after moving in.

He had *arrived* with an overnight bag. The significance of that when there was little accommodation to rent in the village outside the tourist season made Tia's lips quirk. Max had never planned to take no for an answer. Max had come prepared with an ultimatum.

He would take her any way he could get her.

Which was pretty much the same as he had said the day of the funeral.

Somehow in a very short space of time you became both the icing and *the cake... I'm possessive.*

Caveman-speak for love? Whatever he felt for her, time hadn't changed him in the essentials and she was suddenly awesomely grateful for that reality. He didn't have a collection of sweet words or compliments to offer her but he was very honest and she loved him for that quality.

As Max emerged from the bathroom, his shirt loose and unbuttoned to display a slice of bronzed chest, Tia slid past him, clad in a robe, and stepped straight into the shower. He was right: she *had* run away from Redbridge, using the belief that he didn't want their child as an excuse. But she had needed that breathing space, that time alone to be independent and self-sufficient so that she could think for herself and finish growing up. She knew now that she *could* live her dream but that her dream would not be perfect in the starry way she had imagined it. And in truth she no longer wanted that original dream if it didn't contain Max. Most probably she did not figure in any of Max's dreams, but perhaps she would have to settle for that because half a loaf was better than no bread at all, particularly when it meant she could live with the man she loved and give her daughter the father she deserved.

Tia brushed her hair. It rippled in snaking waves across her shoulders, volumised by the braiding she used to confine it every day. Her heart beating very fast, Tia walked back into the bedroom.

'You're not allowed in the bed,' Max was telling Teddy grimly as he tried to stop the terrier from tunnelling under the duvet to take up his favourite position.

'He's a great foot warmer on a cold night.'

'No,' Max told her forcefully as he straightened, a lithe bronzed figure clad only in silk boxers, his muscular abs rippling with his movement.

Tia's breath escaped in a faint hiss as she averted her eyes and scooped Teddy off the bed to stow him in his basket. 'He can be very pushy. He'll just wait until we're asleep and sneak back in,' she warned him.

Max slid back into the bed while she watched dry-mouthed, as impressionable as a teenager with a first crush. His biceps flexed as he tossed the duvet back out of her way and looked expectantly at her. One glance and he froze. Honey-blonde swathes of hair foamed round her heart-shaped face, framing her mesmerising blue eyes and soft, full mouth. She shed the robe to reveal a vest top and shorts with a cutesy dog print. He breathed in slow and deep to restrain himself but he still wanted to grab her and fall on her like a hungry, sex-starved wolf.

'Why did you pack an overnight bag?' Tia murmured. 'How did you know you'd be staying?'

'I knew I couldn't risk leaving you once I actually found you. It would be too easy for you to disappear again,' Max breathed curtly.

Tia looked at him in astonishment. 'But I bought this place. I couldn't just pull up sticks and walk out of here on a whim.'

'You did before and you have the resources to stage a vanishing act any time you want,' he reminded her. 'I won't risk losing you and my daughter again.'

Shame gripped Tia as she scrambled below the duvet. 'I wouldn't do that to you again.'

Blonde hair brushed his arm and she turned over to look at him, cornflower-blue eyes full of regret. 'I promise I won't leave like that ever again.'

Max's gaze dropped to her soft, full mouth and he tensed, dense black lashes lifting on burning golden eyes, fierce sexual energy leaping through him in a stormy surge. The chemistry got in the way of his brain, he finally acknowledged. That intense pull had clouded his judgement from the first moment he saw her. He was determined not to let it happen again.

Tia lifted a hand that felt detached from her control and stroked her forefinger very gently along the sensual curve of his lower lip and she shivered, hips squirming, the heat at the heart of her making her press her thighs together for relief. Max stared down at her and the silence throbbed and pulsed, the atmosphere so tense it screamed at her.

And then he took the bait that she had only dimly recognised was bait and his mouth came down so hard on hers she couldn't breathe. His lips pushed hers apart and his tongue delved and her spine arched and all of a sudden she couldn't speak because her body was doing the talking for her, lifting up into the hard, muscular strength of his, legs splaying, breasts peaking. A powerful hunger was unleashed in both of them and it swept them away. He came down on her, flattening her to the bed, crushing her breasts, and he kissed her until her mouth was swollen and reddened.

'You want this…?' he husked, giving her that choice at the last possible moment.

'Want…*you*,' Tia protested, her back bowing and her legs rising and locking round his lean hips as he pushed into her yielding flesh with a hungry groan of need.

And it was wild and rough and passionate and exactly what they both needed, a release from the shocking tension that had built throughout the evening. Afterwards, Tia lay slumped in Max's arms, utterly drained but happy.

Max was already wondering if he had got it wrong again, feeling like a man who had a very delicate glass ornament in his hand and who had accidentally damaged it. He never knew what to do with Tia; he never knew what to say to her. What he did say when he was striving to be honest tended to come out wrong, so he knew that his silence was a necessary precaution. Even so, the knowledge that he would wake up with her in the morning brought a flashing smile of relief to his lips. She had both arms wrapped around him and he decided he liked it. Teddy regarded him balefully from his basket but nothing could dull Max's mood.

Max knew nothing about love. He hadn't grown up with that example to follow, Tia was musing, and the one time he had surrendered to that attachment he had been deceived and hurt. But she knew as sure as God made little apples that the look in Max's eyes when he'd first held Sancha had been the onset of love. If he could love their daughter, he could learn how to love Tia. Baby steps, she told herself soothingly, baby steps.

Max woke up in the morning with his wife and a terrier. Said terrier had sneaked into the bed during the night and, far from settling in the location of a foot-warmer, had instead imposed himself between Max and Tia like a doggy chastity belt. Max's phone was buzzing like an angry bee and his daughter was crying and he eased out of bed, leaving Tia soundly asleep.

He was thrilled with his achievement when he contrived to make up a bottle for Sancha by following the very precise instructions. He gave Teddy a large slice of cake, which hugely boosted his standing in the dog's eyes, and Teddy stationed himself protectively at his feet while he fed his daughter. That done, he carried the little girl back upstairs to find clean clothes for her. Changing her and dressing her was the biggest challenge he had ever met because she wouldn't stay still and her legs and arms got lost in the all-in-one garment he finally got her dressed in. But she was clean and warm and that was all that mattered, he told himself while he made arrangements on his phone to have Tia's possessions moved to Redbridge Hall.

Tia came racing downstairs in a panic when she found Sancha missing from her cot, and Max looked forgivably smug when she stared in surprise at her daughter slumbering peacefully in her travel cot, utterly lost in an outfit at least two sizes too large for her.

'You should've wakened me,' she told him in discomfiture.

'No. I want to be involved whenever I can be.' Gleaming dark golden eyes locked to her, Max slid upright and stretched indolently, long sleek muscles flexing below his shirt as he reached for his jacket. 'You need to see that we can do this better together and that I can be as committed to Sancha as you are. I don't plan to work eighteen-hour days any more, not now I have both of you back in my life. That is a fair assumption, isn't it?' he pressed tautly. 'You are...*back*?'

'Yes, I'm back,' Tia murmured, torn up inside by the sudden flash of insecurity she read in his strained gaze. He wasn't sure of her yet, didn't quite trust that she would go the distance, and she didn't think she could blame him for that.

It was two days before they got away from her house, two days of frantic packing and planning with Hilary, who would manage Salsa Cakes and in due course open the tea room with Tia's financial backing. Max made himself very useful thrashing out the business details.

Late season snow was falling softly as they drew up outside Redbridge Hall. The trees were frosted white and the air was icy cold. When Tia walked into the spacious hall where a fire was burning merrily in the grate, she felt as if she was coming home for the first time.

'It's our first wedding anniversary,' Max reminded her with satisfaction.

'My goodness, is it?' Tia exclaimed, mortified that she had forgotten.

'I'm afraid that because I didn't know you would be here I haven't made any special preparations.'

'That's OK. Just us being here together is enough,' Tia whispered as they went upstairs with Janette, the housekeeper, to see the room that had been prepared for their daughter.

'It'll need decorating,' Max grumbled.

'It's perfect,' Tia insisted, able to see how much work the staff had put in trying to make an adult bedroom look suitable for a baby. A very large and handsome antique cot had been refurbished with a new mattress and, laid on it, Sancha looked little bigger than a doll. Tia rummaged through her bags of baby essentials until she had located everything she needed to make her daughter feel comfortable.

'We should hire a nanny to help out,' Max suggested. 'We stayed home every evening while Andrew was ill because we didn't want to leave him alone but I'd like to get back to having a social life and sometimes you'll be staying in my London apartment. We need that extra flexibility.'

Tia nodded thoughtfully. While she couldn't imagine having a nanny, she did want to spend as much time as possible with Max. The life they had led during the first months of their marriage had been limited by her grandfather's infirmity and they had rarely gone out.

Max dropped a hand to her spine and walked her

into their bedroom. 'I had this room updated. It was dark and dreary before.'

'But very grand,' she conceded, scanning the lighter colour scheme with approval. 'This is an improvement.'

'I do have one gift for you,' Max murmured, indicating the wrapped package on the bed.

Tia smiled and began to rip the fancy paper off to expose an exceptionally pretty framed picture.

'It's the Grayson family tree,' Max murmured. 'I thought you would enjoy seeing exactly where you come from and who your forebears were.'

The names had been done in exquisite calligraphy, and hand-painted flowers decorated the borders. It was a thoughtful, meaningful gift and her heart turned over inside her because the information on her own family tree was exactly the kind of information she had been denied all her life when her father had insisted that her curiosity was foolish because she would never even travel to England.

'It's really beautiful, Max. Thank you,' she whispered sincerely. 'This means a lot to me. I like what you've had done to this room as well.'

'I haven't used it since you left. I came back here every weekend. It gave the staff a reason for being here.'

Tia studied his lean, strong face. 'I haven't thanked you for that yet…for looking after things for me.'

'That's my job. That's what I do. All my working life I have taken care of stuff for other people…their money, their businesses. But when it's for you, it's a little bit more special and it doesn't feel like work,' Max volunteered.

'Why is that…do you think?' Tia prompted hopefully.

Max glanced at her in surprise. 'You're my wife and this is your home.'

'This is *your* home too,' Tia reminded him. 'When we got married I had nothing and you're not the housekeeper's nephew any more. You're the man Andrew chose to run Grayson Industries and the man he asked to marry me.'

'No regrets there,' Max breathed. 'Not now I've got you back again.'

'You honestly don't regret marrying me?'

'How could I regret it? There is some stuff I regret,' Max admitted reluctantly, his lean, darkly handsome face grave. 'Mainly that I had to rush you into marriage, but I hate that I missed out on you being pregnant and that I wasn't by your side when you had Sancha.'

'I thought you'd be very uncomfortable with all that,' she confided.

'Why would I be when you were carrying our child?' Max asked simply. 'Maybe some day you'll consider having another baby and we'll share everything then right from the start.'

'Maybe in a year or so…I think I would find it all a lot less scary with you by my side,' Tia admitted, touched by the source of his regret and his evident hope that they would have another child. 'You know, it may not seem like it but…I love you very much, Max.'

'You already know how I feel about you and it didn't keep you *with* me, *amata mia*,' Max murmured in a roughened undertone.

'What do you mean, I already know?' Tia asked in bewilderment.

'I told you the day of the funeral that there would

never be another woman for me, that you were "it" for me, as it were,' he completed very awkwardly.

'You said I was the icing and the cake,' Tia recalled abstractedly, totally thrown by what he was saying. 'Did you mean that you had fallen in love with me?'

'What else would I mean by that?' Max demanded, as if she were the one with faulty understanding. '*Dio mio*, I admitted that I couldn't stand the thought of losing you, that I didn't want any other man to have even a chance to take you from me. What else would I have meant?'

Tia gave him a tearful appraisal. 'I didn't get it… don't you understand? If I'd known you loved me, I would never have left. I thought you were talking about sex.'

'The sex is spectacular but nothing is as spectacular as just having you in my life, having you to come home to and having you smile at me. Are you sincerely saying that you wouldn't have left if I'd used the word "love"? I gave you a pendant with a diamond for every day we'd been married. Didn't that say it for me? Surely it was obvious how I felt?' Max was studying her with rampant incredulity. 'I could feel you slipping away from me that week. I was panicking and then the will was read and Andrew had stabbed me in the back and made everything impossible.'

A sob convulsed Tia's throat. 'Oh, Max, I don't care about the money. I *never* cared about the money. I don't even know what to do with it or how to take care of Grayson Industries. All I ever wanted was you and I've spent months breaking my heart for you and trying to have a life without you…and I hated my life without you! But I wouldn't admit that even to myself.'

'Tia… Tia…' Max framed her distressed face with trembling hands. 'It was love at first sight for me. I had no control over my feelings. I wanted you at any cost but I felt like a bastard for taking you to bed so quickly and then pushing you into a marriage you weren't really ready for. There is nothing I wouldn't do to make you happy and persuade you to stay with me. I need you.'

'I need you too,' Tia said chokily and flung herself into his arms. 'Love at first sight and you never even mentioned it!'

'I don't talk about stuff like that. You'd have thought I was mentally unstable if I'd told you at the time because we hardly knew each other,' Max argued vehemently.

'Then I was mentally unstable too!' Tia told him, covering his disconcerted face with kisses. 'I felt the same. Max… Max, I love you to the moon and back.'

'Loved you through all nine miserable months of your absence,' Max confessed grittily. 'Thought…just my luck to fall for a bolter.'

'I swear that I will never leave you again!' Tia told him passionately as he settled her down on the bed while Teddy scratched unavailingly at the door.

'You love me…and yet you *still* left me,' Max marvelled in bewilderment. 'How is that possible?'

'I wanted our baby to have a loving father and I didn't think you wanted to be one. I also thought that possibly you felt trapped, getting married at Andrew's instigation and then me falling pregnant immediately.'

'I wouldn't have married you if I hadn't fallen for you like a ton of bricks. I knew what Andrew wanted but I'm my own man and I make my own decisions… and then I met this incredible Brazilian angel…well, angel-like,' Max adjusted as she wrestled him out of his jacket. 'And the writing was on the wall from that moment. One look and you owned me body and soul. One look and I knew I'd never want another woman again.'

'But you didn't show it and you didn't say it either,' Tia lamented. 'You've got to say the words for a woman to hear.'

Max said it in Italian because she startled him by ripping his shirt open.

'No, I don't know Italian. Say it in English,' she urged.

'You've come over all bossy,' Max commented warily.

'Please say it…' Tia urged, stroking a long muscular thigh encouragingly.

'I love you.' Max kept on saying it because the reward was Tia's full attention and her desire to incessantly touch him where he was very keen to be touched. 'But I didn't recognise that what I felt was love until it was too late.'

Teddy slept outside their bedroom door that night because his humans didn't emerge. The next night he sneaked in and slept under the bed until his snoring alerted Max to his presence and he got thrown out in the early hours. The third night he sat outside the door crying and gained entry by taxing Max's patience. He was satisfied with that advance in his campaign but his ambition was set on regaining his rightful place back in the bed and he was a very determined little dog.

Two and a half years later, Tia studied the traditional Brazilian Christmas cake she had baked for Max. It was his favourite and that was saying something because he liked all her cakes. She had started up another branch of Salsa Cakes at Redbridge and it was thriving and providing more employment on the estate. Her cousin, Ronnie, had become her closest friend and, keen to have a job now that her children were all at school, she did the accounts for Salsa Cakes.

Tia was always very busy, but then she liked to be busy if she could take time off when she needed it to be with Max. And now that they had a wonderful nanny, time off was no longer a problem. She had done a part-time course on estate management to help her to run Redbridge but she had taken up other interests as well. She raised funds for the convent orphanage and did community work at various charitable events and, with Max as an advisor, had set up a workshop at the settlement for handicrafts and toiletries made from Amazonian plants. The convent was thriving and she made regular visits back to her former home. As a rule, she and Max ended those trips with a self-indulgent few days relaxing in Rio.

In a few weeks, her mother, Inez, was marrying for the third time and Tia was attending the wedding. She was looking forward to spending some time with her two half-brothers and her half-sister. Inez had finally agreed to tell her children about Tia's existence and that had considerably enhanced Tia's attitude to her mother. Since then she had met her mother's second family on several occasions and they all got on well. As for her mother, well, she knew she was never going to be close to the older woman for they had nothing in common but at least they were now on relaxed and friendly terms.

Of course, Tia already had her own snug little family with Max and Sancha. Sancha was a lively toddler on the brink of starting nursery school and Tia had decided that it was finally time to think of having another child. A baby was now on the way, the well-defined bump of her pregnancy reminding Tia of that fact every time she bent over a table and found her stomach was in the way. The new addition to the family would arrive in the new year. Max was very excited. He said there was more of her to hold and he seemed to like that. In fact, Tia thought cheerfully, Max seemed to relish every change that signified her advancing pregnancy. Where she saw fat, Max saw voluptuousness and he couldn't keep his hands off her.

Not that that was anything new in their marriage, Tia reflected with a heightening of colour in her cheeks. Sometimes she wondered if it was because they had come so close to losing each other that they never dared to forget how lucky they were to be together. And these days she could think without the smallest resentment that her grandfather had picked a very fine husband for her. Max was a terrific father, a great husband and a real family man, which was a wonderful trait to find in a male who had never enjoyed a proper family of his own.

The past no longer bothered Max. He had moved on from his sense of secret shame, learning that he could be whatever he wanted to be if he worked hard enough at it. He had set up an executive team to help him run Grayson Industries and was no longer so constantly on call. Unlike his mentor, Andrew, who had never spent much time with his two sons and whose relationship with them had suffered accordingly, Max put family first and work second.

It was Christmas Eve and Tia twitched the nativity

scene in the hall into place with care. She had incorporated some Brazilian traditions into their Christmases. Now she sat down by the fire to await Max's return, Teddy at her feet and Sancha pretending to read very importantly from one of her picture books.

Max breezed through the front door festooned with packages. Sancha dived at him, telling him about her day while Teddy bounced at his feet, joining in the excitement but not actually greeting Max. Max smiled at her, his wide charismatic smile that never failed to light her up like a firework inside. Her beautiful Max.

'You look…amazing,' Max told her truthfully, because she did and he could never quite believe that she was his, his to hold and keep. In a black stretchy dress that hugged her shapely form, blonde hair bouncing on her slim shoulders, cornflower eyes sparkling, she took his breath away.

There was no end to the advantages of being married to Tia, Max thought complacently. There were the cakes, cakes to die for. There was Sancha and a second child on the way. There was the sheer joy of living with Tia's sunny, positive nature and her boundless energy. Sometimes he couldn't credit that one woman could transform his life as much as she had and he was tempted to pinch himself to be certain he hadn't dreamt his perfect woman up. There was something wonderfully reassuring about the arms Tia wrapped round him while the enthusiasm of her response to his kiss travelled straight to another spot.

Max surfaced abstractedly from that kiss to see their nanny taking Sancha off for her tea and Tia clasped her hand in his and led him up the stairs. 'I thought we were having Christmas cake,' he said weakly.

'After supper,' his wife told him repressively. 'We're on a timetable. We're going to Midnight Mass later.'

'And after…?' Max ran glittering dark golden eyes over her lovely face and exhaled with pleasurable anticipation. 'I love you, Mrs Leonelli…even when you dictate when I can eat cake.'

'The rules are for Sancha. You can eat cake whenever you like.'

'Only if I can bring it up to the bedroom with us. Teddy will take care of any crumbs,' Max bargained.

But Teddy wasn't falling for that unlikely offer. He knew Max wasn't a messy eater. Teddy's beady eyes were locked to the currently untended cake on the low coffee table.

Tia laughed and tasted Max's mouth again, sinuously, sensually, revelling in the knowledge of his arousal. He scooped her up into his arms on the landing, pretended to stagger at her increased weight, got mock-slapped for his teasing and totally forgot about his craving for cake. Tia told him how much she loved him and it all got very soppy, and then sexy, and then soppy again.

Teddy got the cake.

Tia got more diamonds for Christmas.

And a couple of months later a little boy was born and christened Andrew.

* * * * *

CLAIMING HIS WIFE

DIANA HAMILTON

CHAPTER ONE

IT WAS warm and airless in the room, but not unbearably so. Outside on the bleached rolling miles of the *campos*, the heat of this July afternoon would be almost intolerable.

Cassie waited. Her body felt damp with perspiration beneath the grey and cream linen suit she had worn for the journey from London to the vast Las Colinas Verdes estates in Andalusia.

The suit, understatedly elegant and deliberately so, had survived the flight and the taxi ride out here well, she thought thankfully. No way had she wanted to present herself looking less than businesslike and in control.

She lifted a hand to check that her rich chestnut hair was tamed, severely anchored into the nape of her neck. And her heartbeats were steady—that was another consolation. There was no reason for them to be otherwise, of course; she was no longer a nervous, besotted bride of just twenty-one. She was three years older and a whole lot wiser.

Satisfied that her appearance was as good as it could get—given her average kind of looks—she glanced at her watch and wondered how much longer she would have to wait. The taxi that had brought her from Jerez airport had deposited her here at the farmhouse over half an hour ago. The atmosphere in the heavily furnished, sombre room was beginning to stifle her, the louvres closed to keep out the merciless white heat of the sun.

'I will send someone to tell your husband that you are here,' her mother-in-law had stated. Doña Elvira had spoken politely; she always had, Cassie remembered, even when offering up her barbed insults, insults unfailingly echoed by her two older sisters, Roman's aunts—Tía Agueda and Tía Carmela.

'Is my son expecting you?' A faint pinching of patrician nostrils had denoted that that lady had known Roman was not, that he had long since lost whatever interest he might once have had in his unsuitable, estranged wife.

No longer as frighteningly squashable as she once had been, Cassie had ignored the question and coolly stated, 'I'll wait. In the meantime, I'd like to see Roy. Perhaps you could send him to me.'

And so she waited. Her disgraced twin brother, Roy, it transpired, was not available. He had been put to work erecting fences out on the estate, under the blistering sun, a part of the punishment that was only just beginning.

'I'm under house arrest at Las Colinas Verdes, while Roman decides what to do with me,' he'd complained during his distraught phone call of a couple of days ago. 'I can't face ten years in a Spanish jail, sis—I'd rather top myself!' he'd added, his voice beginning to rise with panic. 'You could persuade

Roman not to bring charges. He won't listen to me. You know what he's like—he's got a tongue like a whip and a mind like a maze; you never know what he's thinking! It makes it impossible to get through to him!'

'I'll phone him this evening,' Cassie had reluctantly promised. She'd felt sick with disappointment over what her brother had done, the way he was dragging her into the mess he had made. 'I'll call him from the flat, the boutique's busy right now.' In fact, it was buzzing with bargain-hunters on the first day of their summer sale. Her boss and best friend, Cindy Corfield, had already gestured frantically to her to end this call and come up front to help out. 'Though Roman isn't likely to listen to me, either,' she'd warned Roy, her voice tight. 'If I ask him not to bring charges against you, he'll probably do just the opposite to spite me. You shouldn't have been such a damn fool in the first place!'

'I know, and I'm sorry—but for pity's sake, sis, phoning him won't help me! He'd just hang up on you—he's rigid with pride, you know that! Come out here. He won't be able to blank you then. He'll listen to you—well, he'll have to, won't he? Damn it all, Cass, the guy's still in love with you, even if you did walk out on him!'

Which was absurd. Roman Fernandez had *never* loved her. He'd married her because it had been, for him, a matter of expediency at the time. And for her? She didn't think about that, not ever. Three years ago she'd been naive and terribly vulnerable. Roman had taken the tears from her eyes and replaced them with the stars that hadn't lasted much longer than the actual wedding ceremony.

But she was a mature adult now and refused to dwell on past mistakes. And because she'd looked out for her volatile twin for most of her life she'd agreed to do as he'd begged. Roy probably didn't deserve it, but she knew how frightened and alone he'd be feeling, so she'd give it her best shot and hope it would be good enough.

And so now she waited and refused to let herself fidget. During the forty-eight hours or so since she'd received her brother's cry for help she'd worked out what she would offer in return for Roy's freedom.

Offers only a hard-hearted brute could dismiss. She tried not to remind herself that that was exactly what Roman was, and against all her hopes and expectations her stomach flipped over when he finally walked into the room and closed the heavy panelled door behind him.

He was wearing a straight-brimmed black hat tipped forward over his eyes and the black denim of his shirt and jeans was covered in the dust of the *campos*. He brought the evocative scent of leather and maleness and white heat into the musty room that she knew from her long, lonely months spent here was never used, except as a repository for unwanted furniture.

She had never tried to pretend that he wasn't the most shatteringly fantastic-looking man she had ever seen, because that would have been pointless. But hoping she looked in control, like a woman who had taken a long hard look at her life, edited out all the bad bits—in which he featured as the central character—and got on with her life, she dismissed the impact he made.

Reminding herself that looks counted for nothing if they hid a hard, unloving heart, she rose to her feet. Five feet five inches of severely groomed adult woman, supported by three-inch spindly heels, was a match for any man, even if he was six feet something of steel-hard muscle and twelve years her senior.

'They told me you were here,' Roman imparted in the husky, sexily accented voice that, despite everything, still had the power to send shivers careering up and down her spine. 'I'm sorry to have kept you waiting.' He removed his hat, and sent it languidly spinning across the room to land on a dour-looking table beneath one of the shuttered windows, revealing slightly overlong soft hair, as dark as the wing of a raven, and smoky charcoal-grey eyes that told her he wasn't sorry at all.

Roman had never considered her feelings when they'd lived together. There was no reason on earth why he should do so now.

'So, what brings you?' He tilted his head in enquiry, his ruthless, sensual mouth unsmiling, his dark eyes cold. 'A year away, working in a second-rate dress shop in a little town that no one has ever heard of, living in a tiny, squalid flat above the premises, has made you wake up to the fact that you're far better off with your husband? Is that it?'

His long legs were straddled, his thumbs hooked into the waistband of his jeans, his unforgettable features blanking out whatever thoughts were passing through his cold, cruel mind.

She didn't want to look at him, but couldn't avoid it without appearing to be a coward or, worse, shifty, as if she had something despicable to hide. And the burn of inner heat that pulsed so violently through her veins was anger, nothing else.

Anger at his sarcastic denigration of her work, her home, the bitter knowledge that he must have kept tabs on her over the past twelve months without her being aware of it.

Not willing to waste breath on telling him that the boutique she ran with Cindy was thriving, that the flat above the premises might be small but was light years away from being squalid, she made her features as cool and unreadable as his and told him, 'I came because Roy's in trouble and he needs me.'

'Now, I wonder why that fails to surprise me.' The words were drawled, casually sardonic, but a flicker of some dark emotion over his harshly beautiful features and the thinning of his aristocratic nostrils told her she had somehow hit a nerve.

She narrowed her tawny eyes at him, waiting for some further reaction, something she might be able to use to her advantage. And when none came, and there was nothing but the thick, uncomfortable silence, she returned to the straight-backed heavily carved chair and lowered herself into its unforgiving embrace.

Slowly, she crossed her long silk-clad legs and watched him watching the unconsciously elegant, vaguely provocative movement; she realised with a tiny shock that made her breath catch in her lungs that his brooding eyes had taken in the way her narrow skirt had ridden way above her knees and quite definitely liked what they saw.

Sex. She would not let herself think about that.

She said levelly, refusing to let him see how nervous she had suddenly become, 'I understand how angry you must be with Roy. I feel exactly the same. What he did was nothing short of disgraceful.'

'Then for once in our lives, *mi esposa*, we are in agreement.'

Smooth, cool, even very faintly amused, his riposte didn't help. Twisting her fingers together, she pulled in a breath. 'But sending him to prison wouldn't help; you must see that. It would blight the rest of his life—he is only twenty-four...and *do* remember the hallowed Fernandez name.'

A bite in her voice there. She hadn't been able to help it. Pride in their exalted ancestry, the ownership of vast tracts of land supporting vines, cattle, wheat and olives, their place in society as members of one of the old sherry families, had been the favourite, seemingly endless topic of conversation between Doña Elvira and the aunts. Indulged in, she had no doubt at all about it, to reinforce their opinion that she was nowhere near good enough to be the wife of the heir to the kingdom!

'You are suggesting that his crime goes unpunished?'

Roman was moving now, with the indolent grace that was so characteristic of him, his wide hard shoulders relaxed, his lean body tapering down to flat, narrow hips and endless legs. He opened the louvres, letting the harsh light flood the room. Probably the better to see her, she thought tiredly.

He stood with his back to the windows, his face shadowed. Enigmatic. So what else was new? She had never been able to tell what he was thinking.

But that didn't matter. He was nothing to her now. She had walked out on their empty marriage a year ago and after another year she could begin divorce proceedings. All she cared about was helping her brother out of this mess and then getting back to England.

'If you don't bring charges against him, I'll take him back home with me—that could be a condition.' She offered the solution she had been turning over in her mind ever since Roy had phoned her. 'Leaving Spain permanently would be punishment enough. He loves this country.'

'I don't think so,' Roman replied implacably. 'What he loves about Spain is being connected by your marriage to one of the wealthiest families in Andalusia. It makes him feel important.'

Cynic! Cassie swallowed the instinctive accusation. Why waste her time and her breath on stating the obvious? He had married her for purely cynical reasons and nothing had changed.

Grimly, she refused to let memories eat away at the poise she had gathered during her year away from her unloving husband and his incurably snobbish family. She was over whatever it was that she had once felt for him and was making a life for herself where she was respected and liked, and where no one tried to make her feel inferior.

She straightened her already rigid shoulders, mentally crossed her fingers, and played her ace. 'Do you really want that sort of blot on the revered family name? Somehow, I don't think so. Imagine the gossip when it becomes known that Roman Fernandez's brother-in-law is behind bars.'

He moved into her line of vision, standing over her, his height, his breadth, the power of him suddenly and unwelcomingly intimidating.

'The sympathy would all be with my family for its association with yours. We would be seen as upholding the rule of law, no matter what the cost. Quite noble, you must agree.' He smiled, but his eyes were still cold and hard. 'You will have to do better than that.'

Cassie muffled a sigh and reined back the urge to slap that beautiful, arrogant face. There was no point in appealing to his better nature. Still less point in trying to get through to him. She had never been able to do that, not even when they were first married.

'I'll repay every peseta he stole from you,' she offered without a great deal of hope. She had no idea how much that was—Roy, to put it mildly, had been incoherent on that subject. It could take her the rest of her life, but it would be worth it. She lifted eyes to him that were now sparkling with defiance—she refused to admit that the emotion raging inside her was hurt—and said, 'You'll get your money back, get me and Roy out of your sight. In a year we can divorce and you can forget your precious family was ever associated with mine! And then—' she drew in a breath, surprised by the pain that gripped her heart in a cruel vice '—you can marry that highly suitable Delfina who was always hanging around. Make your mother and the aunts happy—Delfina, too. The way she flirted with you, and the way you played up to her, used to make me sick!'

Too late, she deeply regretted the unguarded words that had revealed some of those earlier painful insecurities. She was over them now; she didn't care who he eventually married. But his ego was too large to let him believe that simple fact, as was clearly demonstrated by the upward drift of one dark brow, the knowing tilt of his head.

He thought she was jealous, that she still felt something for him. It was intolerable!

Cassie shot to her feet, smoothing the non-existent wrinkles out of her skirt with unsteady hands. She was beginning to get a headache and her stomach was tying itself in tense knots because, so far, her visit hadn't achieved a thing except to remind herself of two of the most unhappy years of her life.

Still, she had to try. She tilted her chin. 'Do we have a deal?'

She couldn't plead with him, not even for her twin's sake. She had pleaded with Roman too often in the past—to no effect whatsoever—to want to go through that humiliating experience again, to put her pride on the line for him to trample on.

'No,' he said implacably. 'At least, not the one you outline. You surprise me, Cassandra,' he added, as if he questioned her sanity. 'When we married I found work for your brother in the Jerez accounts office because, according to him, he didn't want to cut the apron strings and go back to England without you and he didn't want to follow in your father's footsteps and study medicine. In fact he almost shed tears when I reminded him that that was what his father had wanted.'

'He was barely twenty-one and he didn't know what he wanted to do with his life. He'd not long lost his father, had had to face the fact that the family home had to be sold to pay Dad's debts—and, unlike you, he hadn't come into this world cushioned by money and holding the entrenched belief that he was superior to everyone else on the planet!'

He ignored her protective outburst as if the heated words had never been said, just as he had ignored every opinion, every need of hers, in the past. 'I gave Roy a job with a living wage, then paid the rent on an apartment because after a while he complained that he wanted to be independent of the family household in Jerez. He repaid me by going in to the office late and leaving early—when he bothered to go at all—and finally betrayed me and my family by embezzling a not insubstantial amount of money.' He lifted his shoulders in a dismissive shrug, as if the conversation was beginning to bore him. 'Having you rescue him from the consequences of his crime and repay the money he stole would not build his character, I think.'

Cassie winced. She hated to admit it, but in a way he was right. But she knew her brother far better than Roman did, and a spell in prison wouldn't help Roy achieve responsible adulthood.

She put her fingers to her temples. The pain was getting worse. She'd made this journey, come face to face with Roman again, had the humiliation of seeing her offer brushed aside as if it had been made by a fool, and accomplished precisely nothing. She felt as if she'd been chewed up and spat out, and it wasn't a pleasant sensation. She pushed herself to her feet.

'If that's your final word, I'll leave, but I'd like to see Roy before I go,' she said thickly. 'I'll wait here until he finishes work.' Surely he couldn't be heartless enough to deny her that? She had to see her twin, let him know she'd done her best. Advise him to take his punishment like a man and tell him to come back to England, to her, when he was free, and she'd do everything she could to help him to make a fresh start.

'And here was I, beginning to think you'd developed a backbone,' he said lightly. 'I think you give up too easily.'

Perspiration was slicking her skin and she folded her arms jerkily across her chest as she tried to contain the feeling that she was about to have hysterics. 'And I think you don't know what you're talking about,' she said, hanging on to what little poise she had left. 'You won't listen to what I have to say so what am I supposed to do? Sit in my chair like a good little girl until I grow roots?'

'I listened,' Roman remarked with an indolence that made her hackles rise.

She felt her face go red. 'Maybe. But you still refused to consider what I said!'

'I wasn't aware that it was mandatory.' One broad shoulder lifted in a very slight shrug.

He was impossible! Swallowing fury, she hitched the strap of her bag over her shoulder. She was leaving! But easier said than done, because a graceful long-legged stride, one hand on her arm, stopped her.

She didn't want him touching her. The heat of his hand through the fine fabric of her sleeve brought back memories she had no desire to acknowledge. Her tongue, though, was welded to the roof of her mouth and, before she could unstick it, he said at a smooth tangent, 'You've gained weight. For most of our two years together you reminded me of a stick. Sometimes I used to worry about you.'

What a lie! Concern for her happiness and well-being had been so low on his list of priorities it had fallen off the bottom of the paper!

'Liar!' she accused scornfully. 'The only people who worried about my weight loss were your mother and aunts. And that, according to the precious Delfina, was because they thought I was anorexic and possibly infertile. She even told me that having your child was the only way they would ever accept me.' Seized by a wild, uncontrollable anger, she surged on, 'I should have told them that I lost weight because I was desperately unhappy. That I couldn't conceive because you never came near me!'

The words blistered her mouth but she didn't regret them. It was time Roman faced the truth.

'I thought you didn't want me to?' The sensual line of his mouth tightened. 'You rejected me, or don't you remember?'

It was framed as a question but he'd wait until hell froze over before he got an answer. She'd die before she admitted how much she'd regretted pushing him away, turning from him, lacking the courage to tell him how she felt; how later she'd ached for his touch; how his indifference, his long absences had hurt her.

She thinned her mouth as, probably in retaliation for her stubborn silence, glittering charcoal eyes veiled by thick black lashes made a lazy inventory of the curves she privately thought had grown a little too lush just lately. Her body burned hotly where his eyes touched and she tried to squirm away, aware that her breath was thick in her throat. His unanswered question and the explicitly intimate way he was looking at her was beginning to fill her with embarrassment and confusion.

What did he know about how she had felt? The sense of inadequacy, the beginnings of the shame that had grown right throughout their marriage because he had obviously decided she was frigid, not worth the trouble of going to her room at night.

His fingers tightened on her arm, his other hand resting lightly on her waist, just above the feminine roundness of her hips; his voice was sultry and wicked as he asked, 'I wonder if a year apart has made any difference? Perhaps we should try to find out. Would you still reject me if I came to you in the night?'

'Don't!' It was wrenched from her. She went rigid. She had taught herself not to cry; she wasn't going to forget those harsh lessons and disgrace herself now.

Once—it seemed like a lifetime ago now—she had thought she loved him, had worshipped him, believed him to be the most perfect being ever to draw breath.

Now she knew better. He couldn't get to her on any level if she didn't let him. She threw back her head and challenged him, 'If you think I'm going to oblige you, lie down on the floorboards while you satisfy your sexual curiosity, then you can think again!'

She slapped his hands away, one after the other, and headed for the door, her lips clamped together to stop herself screaming with all the remembered pain, and he drawled behind her, 'I had something rather more civilised in mind, *mi esposa*. Share my bed for the next three months and satisfy my…sexual curiosity, and I won't bring charges against your brother.'

CHAPTER TWO

'YOU need time to think about it?' Roman asked as the brittle silence stretched until it was painful. The soft, almost scornful strand of amusement in his voice finally snapped her out of her state of numbing shock.

'You can't be serious!' The thin, wavery bleat of her own voice secretly appalled her. She hadn't meant to sound so utterly withering. Cassie swallowed convulsively and tried again, tried to do better. 'You must be desperate if you have to resort to blackmail to get a woman to share your bed!'

This time the contempt she felt must have echoed in her tone because she saw his eyes narrow, his jawline harden. He was a passionate man; she knew that—passionate about his work, the land he loved, the family name, his women. Never about *her*, though, and they both knew it. Her taunt would have damaged his inbred, fierce Spanish pride.

'Not blackmail—a condition,' he corrected harshly. 'Non-negotiable. You are free to take my offer, or leave it.'

'My body's not a commodity to be bartered,' she stated, suddenly feeling shivery, as if her flesh had been plunged into a deep freeze. What he was suggesting was completely out of the question.

But he obviously wasn't seeing it that way because his voice roughened. 'It was before, if I remember correctly. Your body in my bed in exchange for my ring on your finger, a life of luxury, payment of your father's debts—and let's not forget that nice soft option for your brother, which we now know he abused. And again, with you, I got the rough end of the bargain and found myself sharing a bed with a block of ice. My bride made me feel like an animal with depraved and intolerable appetites—it was not an experience I wished to repeat.'

So he had left her completely alone. And he hadn't had the sense to understand that she'd been terrified.

Not of him, because she had loved him then, but scared half to death of failing the shatteringly sexy, passionate and experienced man who had swept her off her feet with one smile from those sensually moulded lips, one glance from those sultry, smoky eyes. The man who hadn't seen that his family's displeasure at his choice of wife had already made her feel inferior and totally inadequate.

And she hadn't had the courage to explain all of that to him, to at least try to tell him how she felt. Cassie shook that unwanted thought out of her head and closed her eyes as she dragged in a deep lungful of air; when she opened them he was holding the door open, his powerful body graceful, relaxed.

Showing her out? Bored? Impatient to get rid of

her now he knew she would have nothing to do with his outrageous suggestion?

So why did she feel giddy with relief when he told her, 'I'm not suggesting something immoral. You are my wife.'

'We're separated,' she reminded him, defensively putting her light-headedness down to the trauma of the last few days, the expenditure of courage that had been needed to bring her to face him again.

'Not by my wish,' he stated dismissively. He swung on his heels.

Catching her breath, she followed him along the stone-flagged passageway that connected the old farmhouse to the newer, more comfortable addition that had been built in his father's lifetime. Surely there was room for negotiation? Surely she could make him see that his cruel suggestion simply wasn't practical, then ask him to reconsider her original offer?

'Roman!' If there was a desperate edge to her voice, she couldn't help it. Her brother's future depended on her ability to make her estranged husband change his mind. 'Even if I wanted to come back to you—' which she most definitely did not '—I couldn't. I have a living to earn, a job to go back to. I told Cindy I'd only be away for a couple of days. It's one of our busiest times.'

He stopped, turned, his impressive figure framed in the archway that led into the main hall. He lifted wide shoulders dismissively. 'No problem. I'll phone my cousin and explain. She'll understand.'

Of course she would! Cindy idolised Roman, she hadn't been able to believe her ears when Cassie had returned to England with the news that her marriage was over.

The relationship wasn't as close as Roman had stated. Cindy's grandmother had been Doña Elvira's eldest sister. She'd married a Scot and they'd lived in England, producing Cindy's mother. Although the Fernandez family hadn't approved of the alliance with a mere foreigner, Doña Elvira and her surviving sisters had remained in contact.

Cassie and Cindy had been best friends since they'd met at school as five-year-olds, and it had been to her and her warm and loving family that Cassie had turned when her and Roy's father had died from a heart attack.

They couldn't have been more supportive. When the shock news had come that the house Cassie and Roy shared with their widowed father would have to be sold to cover his debts, Cindy's mother had suggested, 'We've been planning a holiday in Spain, visiting relatives on my mother's side. Why don't you and Roy come with us? I know they'll make you welcome when I explain the circumstances. And it would give you and Roy a chance to get your heads round what's happened.'

That was how she'd met Roman; that was when the short and, with hindsight, strangely distant courtship had begun. And the rest, she thought tiredly, was history. A history she wished had never been written.

'Any other objections?' he enquired flatly. 'Or is

the resumption of our marriage for three short months too high a price to pay?'

Much, much too high! Roy had done wrong and the only way Roman would allow him to avoid punishment was to punish her in her brother's stead. Their wedding night had been a total fiasco. Although they had consummated the marriage, her fear of disappointing him had made her about as responsive as a lump of rock, thereby ensuring that the experience was one she didn't want to repeat. The fear of further failure had made her push him away when he'd tried to take her in his arms on the following nights after that. So why would he want to force her to share his bed now—unless it was to dole out punishment?

Oh, her objections were legion! Moistening her dry lips with the tip of her tongue, she framed the words of the only one that wasn't personally insulting to him—which meant it was the tritest. 'I came prepared for an overnight stay in Jerez before getting a flight back to England. How can I stay when I haven't got much more than the clothes I'm wearing now?'

His smile was thin and it didn't reach his eyes. 'I think we might be able to find a store that stocks female clothing somewhere in Spain, don't you? And, Cassandra—' his eyes narrowed to slits of smoke-hazed jet '—I'm not prepared to discuss this further. You take my offer, or you leave it. Sleep on it and give me your decision in the morning.' He turned again, lobbing over his shoulder, 'I'll get someone to show you to a room you can use for tonight. We eat at nine, as you may remember, and afterwards you and Roy can have some time together to discuss your futures.'

Dispiritedly, she watched as he strode across the polished terracotta tiles of the airy, square hallway. She had honestly believed she was mature enough now to stand her ground against that overweening authoritarianism of his—that she would never again allow him to tell her what to do, where to go.

Yet she had to admit, after one of the maids—new since her own departure, just over a year ago—had shown her to a bedroom overlooking the courtyard at the back of the house, that her interview with Roman had sapped her of the energy she would have needed to arrange for a taxi to pick her up here and drive her back to Jerez, where she would have had to find overnight accommodation.

Also, this way she was guaranteed some time with her twin. She could sit through dinner with Doña Elvira and the dreadful aunts for the sake of the opportunity to speak to Roy alone afterwards. If she insisted on leaving now, Roman would make sure she didn't get so much as a glimpse of her brother.

She needed to apologise in person for having failed him. Break the news that Roman would be bringing charges against him. It made her sick just to think of it. She'd been looking out for him ever since their mother had died a few days before their eighth birthday, but the price Roman was demanding was way too high. She had worked hard to turn her life around. How could anyone expect her to put herself back in the prison she'd escaped from a year ago?

Her pale face set, she gave the room she'd been shown to a cursory glance. It was very similar to the one she'd used when she'd spent the greater part of her two years of marriage here. Roman had simply dumped her, leaving her with his mother and the aunts while he'd been away doing his own thing. Business in Jerez and Cadiz, with plenty of fringe benefits in the form of fancy restaurants, fancy females, climbing in the Himalayas, skiing at Klosters—whatever turned him on.

Shrugging, consigning her memories back into the past, she unpacked her overnight bag. Cotton nightdress, a change of underwear, make-up and toiletries. Her heart hovering somewhere beneath the floorboards, she went to the adjoining bathroom for a much-needed shower and wished she and her twin had never heard of Roman Fernandez.

Candles—dozens of them—set in shallow crystal bowls imparted a warm, flickering glow to the old silver of the elaborate place settings. Dinner at Las Colinas Verdes was always a formal affair and tonight all the stops had been pulled out because there were two guests.

Herself the unwanted one. And Delfina The Desirable, who had been flavour of the month amongst Roman's female relatives for as long as Cassie had known them.

Roman was seated at the head of the long table with the Spanish woman on his left. Delfina was as exquisite as Cassie recalled, her dark hair cut in a fashionable jaw-length bob, her slender figure clothed in ruby satin, leaving the delicate sweep of her shoulders and arms bare.

'You are looking well, Cassandra. Better than I have seen you. You are obviously happier in your own country.' Doña Elvira, remote and dignified in black silk, was seated at the foot of the table, to Cassie's right. Her remark was made in her perfect English and carried the customary barb.

'Thank you.' Cassie inclined her head coolly. She could have answered that she would have been ecstatically happy in Spain if her husband had loved her, if his family had accepted her. But what was the point raking over a past that was dead and buried as far as she was concerned? She would not let this ordeal undermine her hard-won poise. She wouldn't let any one of them intimidate her now.

Tía Agueda and Tía Carmela, Roman's aunts, were seated opposite, their small dark eyes constantly flicking between Cassie and Delfina. Delfina was speaking in animated Spanish to Roman who, naturally, took pride of place at the head of the gleaming mahogany table. Her hand was continually moving to touch the back of his, or to linger on the white fabric of his sleeve, as if to emphasis a point she was making, her dark eyes flicking and flirting beneath the lustrous sweep of her lashes.

During her time in Spain Cassie had picked up

enough of the language to get by, but the other woman's voice was pitched too low, too soft and intimate to allow her to hear what was being said.

She fingered the stem of her wine glass and, as if noting the unconsciously nervous gesture, Doña Elvira said, 'It is an uncomfortable time for all of us.'

And wasn't that the truth? Cassie speared a sliver of tender pork fillet. Her twin was conspicuous by his absence. House arrest, he'd told her. He probably had to eat in the kitchen with the servants. She laid down her fork, the food unwanted.

'I'll be returning to England tomorrow,' she stated, squashing the wicked impulse to tell her mother-in-law of her son's attempt to blackmail her into resuming their marriage. Only for three short months—but, even so, Doña Elvira and the aunts would hate that. They were probably already counting down to when Roman could be free of his unsuitable, hopeless wife and they could begin pressing him to marry someone of his own nationality, someone with breeding and lots of lovely old money!

Something clicked inside her brain. Of course! She could see it all now. Roy's fall from grace had given Roman the leverage he needed. It wasn't just sexual curiosity about her, as he'd so insultingly claimed—his family must be nagging him again to produce an heir, and this time he could put them off if it appeared that he was having another stab at making his marriage work!

Sharply, her mind skidded back to the afternoon

Roman had proposed to her. The older family members had been taking a siesta; Roy and Guy—Cindy's older brother—had taken a couple of horses out onto the *campos* while Cindy and her mother were upstairs packing. About to follow suit—the month-long holiday was over and they were leaving for home the next day—she'd been halfway up the handsomely carved staircase when Roman's softly voiced request had stopped her in her tracks.

'Cassie, got a few minutes to spare?'

Her hand had shot out and tightened on the polished banister until her knuckles stood out like white sea-shells as a wave of raw heat flooded her body. She had been sure she was in love with him, helplessly and hopelessly in love, and it had turned her into a gibbering idiot when he was around.

Cindy had said, *'Mucho macho!'*, pretending to swoon. 'He doesn't even notice me but he follows you with his eyes, you lucky pig!'

Trying not to think of the gross stupidity of that remark—why should a man as gorgeous, as self-assured and wildly wealthy as Roman spare a very ordinary woman with no social skills and about as much sex appeal as a carrot a second glance?—she had waited until the gauche heat ebbed from her face before slowly turning.

He had been watching her from the foot of the stairs. Watching. Waiting. Her throat muscles had gone into spasm.

'I want to talk to you.'

'Yes?' Had her expression been intelligent, or just

plain dumb? The latter, she suspected, because the slight shake of his dark, handsome head, the very slight abrasiveness of his voice had suggested impatience.

'Not here. In the courtyard, for privacy. Come down.'

She'd gone; of course she had. If he'd asked her to walk to the North Pole with him she'd have gone without a murmur. And the sun-soaked courtyard had been deserted except for just the two of them, the scent of the rosemary and lavender planted in the centre perfuming the hot air. And his proposal had been the very last thing she'd expected.

'As my mother and aunts never tire of telling me, it's time I married and sired an heir. They've been dangling suitable females under my nose for the past five years and now that I've reached the venerable age of thirty-three they've stepped up their campaign.

'I tell them to hold their meddling tongues, to put the succession of simpering creatures back into the boxes they dug them out of; I tell them that I will marry the woman of my choosing, not theirs. It makes no difference and, quite frankly, Cass, I am tired of it.'

At that point he had taken her hand and her whole body had melted, turning her into an amorphous mass of sensation, blanking out every last one of her brain cells. What else could explain the unseemly haste, the total lack of logical thought that had accompanied her acceptance when he'd increased the pressure of his fingers on hers and murmured, 'I think we could make a successful marriage. You're young for your years. Don't take that as a criticism—you lack the guile and artifice that bores me in other women, and I find that very appealing. I do need an heir, and for that I need to marry. I want a woman I can live with, a woman whose primary concerns aren't the perfection of her appearance, attending parties that take her days to prepare for, or empty-headed gossip.'

His mouth had indented wryly. 'The bargain wouldn't be one-sided. Since the death of your father you're a ship without a rudder; I gather that he had you convent-educated then used emotional blackmail to keep you at home acting as an unpaid housekeeper. Cass, marriage and motherhood would give you the direction you want. And no need to worry about the debts waiting for you at home—naturally, as your husband, I would discharge them. And for me—' his eyes had softened as he'd smiled into hers '—I would be free of the endless carping from my female relatives. In time, there would be our children to take their meddling minds away from me, and I could get on with my life in peace. And, more importantly, I would have a wife I'd chosen for myself. Will you think about it, dear Cassie?'

She hadn't, she thought now, defiantly draining her wine glass. She'd simply accepted him and thought about it later, when it was too late to do anything other than acknowledge the fact that he had married her because she was biddable, undemanding, a creature of no consequence, and someone he could hide in a corner and forget about. Someone to provide him with the heirs the vast Fernandez estates needed.

Only it hadn't worked out like that, had it?

'I see Delfina still visits you,' she remarked coolly to her mother-in-law. Her voice dripped with sarcasm as she added, 'So kind, don't you think, when sophisticated social events, glitzy restaurants and expensive shops are her natural milieu? Or so she always led me to believe.'

Before, she would never have dreamed of saying such a thing. She had almost literally withered away whenever her mother-in-law or the aunts had spoken to her, almost always with some criticism or other—the way she dressed, her apparent inability to conceive or keep her husband at her side, her weight loss.

'She has always been fond of my son.' Doña Elvira dabbed her mouth with her napkin. 'As I said, it has been an uncomfortable time for all of us.'

Was that sympathy in the older woman's eyes? Cassie thought so. She pulled her lower lip between her teeth. Formerly, had she only listened to the words, failing to see the concern for her well-being and happiness that lay behind the apparent criticisms?

She laid down her napkin, made her excuses, and left the room without even glancing at Roman. Sympathy from a most unexpected quarter wasn't worth thinking about. Not now. It was over.

* * *

'Sis!'

As Cassie closed the door to the formal dining room behind her Roy emerged from beneath the stone arch that led to the kitchen quarters. It took her two seconds to reach him. She wanted to shake him but he looked so wretched she hugged him instead.

'I couldn't sit through dinner, not knowing whether you'd persuaded Roman to give me another chance.'

She had meant to tell him that she'd tried and failed, that he was on his own now and had to take the consequences of his dishonesty, but she could feel his wiry body shaking. Her heart lurched. Her eyes filled with tears.

In the past she'd fought all his battles for him. Maybe he would have been a stronger character if she hadn't. Maybe she was to blame for the way he'd messed up his life.

But how could she fail him now, when he needed her most?

'It will be all right,' she told him unsteadily. 'You'll be given another chance. Make the most of it, though, because it will be your last.'

CHAPTER THREE

THE kitchen was in the older, original part of the house; the stone walls were painted white and the huge black range added to the warmth of the early morning. Asunción, who ran the household and catered for the unmarried estate workers with unruffled efficiency, was kneading dough; two of the maids sat at the other end of the central table, chattering over their toasted rolls and coffee.

'Have you seen Señor Fernandez?' Cassie asked as her appearance made the housekeeper stop pummelling and the maids fall silent.

Unless they'd changed their habits during the past twelve months, Doña Elvira and the aunts wouldn't surface until after they'd breakfasted in their rooms at ten. But when he was here Roman was always out on the estate soon after sunrise; she didn't want to miss him and hang around until lunchtime, getting more nervous and downhearted with every passing second. She wanted to get this over with.

'No, not this morning, *señora*.' Asunción planted her floury hands on her wide hips, her small dark eyes sparking with curiosity. 'Señorita Delfina waits for him also.' One of the maids smothered a giggle, earning a quick dark look from the housekeeper. 'If you join her in the courtyard, someone will bring coffee out for you.'

'Thank you, Asunción.' Cassie retreated smartly, her cheeks burning. Las Colinas Verdes was like a small village; everyone knew everyone else's business and the affairs of the family were the subject of eternal gossip and conjecture.

They would all be wondering why the runaway, unsuitable English wife had returned and why *el patrón* had taken his young brother-in-law out of his comfortable office in Jerez and put him to work like a labourer in the fields. Uncomfortably, she wondered what answers they'd come up with.

She had no wish to join Delfina but she really did need that coffee. Her night had been restless, tormented by the knowledge of what she'd let herself in for. She couldn't go back on her promise to Roy, but if Roman wanted her to pretend that they were making a fresh start, and get his relatives off his back, then she had a condition of her own to make, she thought firmly.

Delfina was sitting in the shade of the sprawling fig tree which grew against one of the high stone walls of the courtyard. She was wearing form-fitting stretch jodhpurs and a cream-coloured, heavy silk shirt; the long sleeves were casually rolled up to just beneath her elbows, displaying lightly tanned forearms and a matching pair of thin gold chain bracelets.

She looked every inch the aristocrat, as if she belonged here. Cassandra couldn't understand why Roman was going to such lengths to pretend he wanted another shot at making his marriage to an average-looking nobody like her work, when surely he could see that this beautiful, sophisticated daughter of a wealthy sherry family would make him a perfect wife. Or had he really meant it when he'd said that Delfina's type bored him?

'If you're looking for Roman, you're out of luck,' Delfina snapped. 'We had a date to go riding but he must have left without me.' The lovely, perfectly made-up face was petulant, the scarlet mouth drooping sulkily. 'He always did head for the hills rather than spend time around you, so I guess that's what's happened now.'

'Is that so?' Cassie slid on to the bench seat on the opposite side of the table, in the full glare of the already hot sun, noting that the other woman had barely touched her coffee or her juice. Roman might enjoy the flirtatious attentions of Delfina, and the way she hung around him would boost his already considerable ego. But he certainly wouldn't want to marry her, and not only because her shallowness would bore him.

Delfina had been born to elegance and style, and was accustomed to the high life. She certainly wouldn't allow herself to be isolated here, seeing her husband only when he felt like dropping by for a week or two, producing babies and closely chaperoned by his mother and aunts while he swanned off, free as a bird. She would make a demanding wife, while he had wanted a dutiful, self-effacing one, one who didn't ask questions or demand a single thing of him.

Roman Fernandez was far too selfish to completely tie himself down to a woman; he enjoyed the pleasures of a bachelor-style life far too much. But at least, Cassie knew, he wouldn't seduce the other woman. She came from an important family and he wouldn't compromise her; his Spanish code of honour wouldn't let him. Though why she should see that as a consolation, Cassie couldn't imagine. She no longer cared what he did.

'I can't think why you came back after all this time,' Delfina said pettishly. 'You're wasting your time if you expect Roman to take you back—because he won't, you know. How long are you staying, anyway?' she wanted to know. 'It can't be too long if the only thing you've got with you is the same old suit you wore to dinner last night,' Delfina added disparagingly. 'And you really shouldn't sit in the sun, not with your ginger colouring. You'll get covered in ghastly freckles, just like your brother. And what's he doing working here? I thought Roman had given him an easy life back in the office in Jerez.'

'He's learning estate management from the bottom up,' Roman's dark, velvety voice supplied. He was standing in the shadow of the pillared arcade that surrounded the courtyard on three sides. 'And you never know, if he's not otherwise engaged when Miguel retires in six years' time, Roy might make manager.'

Cassie got the message. Roy could make something of himself here on the estate, or go to prison. She shivered, despite the warmth of the sun. At least Roman hadn't confided the true situation to Delfina. She offered up a silent word of thanks for his tact.

'We had a date,' the Spanish woman cooed as Roman stepped out of the shadows. The petulance gone, she was all smiling welcome. She stood up, smoothing her hands over her prettily curved hips. 'I've waited for ages, but at least you're here now—so just this once I've decided to forgive you!'

He wasn't dressed for riding. Wearing narrow fawn-coloured cotton trousers topped by a black shirt in the finest lawn, he looked fantastic, all raw male sexuality—and then some. Cassie knew exactly why Delfina couldn't keep away from him; she could imagine how the Spanish woman's hopes would have soared when she'd learned that his failure of a wife had left him.

Cassie almost felt sorry for her!

'You're going to have to ride alone this morning,' Roman stated abruptly, as if his patience was running out. 'I have urgent business with my wife. But,' he added as a palliative, 'I had Demetrio saddle up for you. The mare's ready and waiting in the stable yard.'

His cool smile seemed to soften what was obviously a blow and pushed what petulant words Delfina might have been about to say back down her throat. Asunción, bearing down on them with a huge tray, did the rest.

As the housekeeper, with a murmured, *'Señor,*

Señora,' set out breakfast for two and cleared away the offerings Delfina had barely touched, the Spanish girl swept her eyes dismissively over Cassie, gave Roman a commiserating smile and drawled, 'I'll leave you to your boring business then, *caro*. You can make amends for letting me down when you've finished with it.' Another pointed glance in Cassie's direction and then she was walking away, leaving the sultry perfume that was her trademark behind in the hot summer air.

As Asunción left, Roman took the seat Delfina had vacated and Cassie eyed the crispy rolls, honey, fresh fruit and coffee and felt her throat close up. Alone with him, she felt wound up enough to explode, and he made it a thousand times worse when he reached out a hand and ran the back of his fingers lightly down the side of her face.

'Unlike your unidentical twin, your skin doesn't freckle.' His voice was slow, sexy and smooth, the smoky eyes following the movement of his fingers as they rested briefly on the corner of her mouth. 'And I wouldn't describe your hair as ginger—far more like burnished chestnuts, Cassie.'

After those first few disastrous days of their honeymoon he'd never touched her, except perhaps by accident. He'd certainly never touched her skin deliberately, lingeringly, seductively. So why touch her now? Why was he trying to contradict Delfina's earlier insults? Her huge eyes were bewildered.

She tried to move, to jerk her head away from the gentle stroke of his fingers, the warmth that was setting fire to her skin—but she was mesmerised, trapped beneath the intimacy of his eyes, for all the world as if she were twenty-one years old again. Vulnerable, gullible, innocent and still traumatised by recent happenings.

'Awwwk—' The sound that emerged from her painfully tight throat was more like a croak than the opening for a sensible statement. As if he knew he could sweet-talk her into a state of feeble submission where his threats had failed, one dark brow quirked upwards; a slight smile curved his sensual mouth as he dropped his hand and lifted the coffee pot.

But it wasn't that; it really wasn't. She was beyond all that self serving charm. It was just that she dreaded having to commit herself, but knew she had to if she were to save her twin.

And now—apart from that condition she was determined to make—the time had come to tell him she agreed to accept his monstrous offer.

She could hardly believe this was happening to her. It had taken courage to walk out on him, and a whole lot of determination to put him and what he had meant to her right out of her mind.

Her throat jerking, she swallowed around the constriction in her throat, stared into the rich, steaming coffee he had placed in front of her and stated as evenly as she could manage, 'If you must use me to divert your family from pestering you to provide an heir then I'll stay with you for the three months you stipulated. But—'

'A diversion? Interesting…' Roman looked almost amused.

'What other reason could you have?' Suddenly, Cassie was wary.

'None.' A glint of wickedness in the dark eyes belied the blunt disclaimer, but she was reassured by his, 'You catch on quickly; well done! You are my wife, you're here, and you suit my purposes—but don't forget, the deal includes you sleeping with me, as a good wife should…'

Cassie swallowed hard and forced an edge into her voice, 'Point taken. You don't have to paint a picture. I'll keep my part of the bargain, but not here.'

'Is that an ultimatum, *mi esposa*?'

'Take it or leave it.' She echoed his former words, trying to blank out the knowledge that he was not a man to be coerced, trying to look as if she wouldn't back down while all the time knowing that she would have to if he didn't agree.

'I wonder what it is about Las Colinas Verdes that you dislike so much?' he queried idly. Cassie shot him a suspicious glance from beneath her lashes. Buttering a roll, spreading it with honey, he gave every appearance of being totally relaxed about the whole surreal situation. 'I seem to recall a previous time when you asked if we might make a home somewhere else.'

She hadn't simply asked, she'd begged—practically pleaded with him on her knees! She hadn't been able to bear being left here, watched over and criticised by his mother and his aunts, enduring Delfina's visits—visits which had always miraculously coincided with Roman's own.

But he had barely listened. But then why should he have when her misery—the feeling of being abandoned, a prisoner—hadn't been important to him? After their disastrous wedding night, it had suited him to have her out of sight and out of mind.

'It isn't the place,' she corrected sharply. 'It's the people.' And if that was insulting to his family, tough! She had grown out of pussy-footing around him, trying to please him, vainly hoping he would start to feel something for her beyond indifference. 'If we were here, they'd be watching like hawks to see if I got pregnant. I've been there, done that. And I don't want a repetition.'

'You could have told them they were wasting their time,' he said coldly. 'That the likelihood of your conceiving my child was non-existent because you couldn't bear me to touch you.'

Cassie swallowed the instinctive, vehement response that the blame for that was just as much his as hers. After all, she'd broached this subject yesterday; the snap of his eyes and the tightening of his jaw line had showed her that her criticism of his family had made him angry.

She took a deliberate sip of coffee, then took a deep breath and made her tone entirely reasonable as she told him, 'I don't want to get into a fight, Roman. Our marriage was a mistake. It didn't work for all sorts of reasons. The past is best forgotten; it's no longer important. What matters right now is deciding how we're going to handle the next three months, and where we'll spend them.'

Another few sips while she weathered the startling frisson that racketed through her body at the mere thought of the coming three months. And, if anything, her prosaic words—meant to pour oil on waters that were beginning to look ominously turbulent—seemed to have worsened the situation, because his black brows were drawn together, his haughty Spanish disdain sharp enough to cut.

'We'll spend them together. That was the bargain.' He got to his feet, the dappled shade reinforcing the mystery of the man. He was a complex character, many-faceted; she had never been able to understand him. 'I will break the news of our reconciliation to my family. Be ready to leave in an hour.'

His mouth pulled back against his teeth, he stared down at her, as if daring her to say another word, then swung round and walked away. He left her wondering at his change of mood.

Set to charm the socks off her to start with—most probably in an attempt to persuade her to fall in with his wishes. Then showing flashes of simmering black temper after she'd agreed to what he wanted: the pretence of a reconciliation!

No, she never had been able to understand him. But it really didn't matter now, did it?

CHAPTER FOUR

BEYOND a few lines of self-consciously banal chit-chat, they had barely spoken. The prickly silence inside the air-conditioned car was beginning to get to Cassie, but it didn't seem to bother Roman and that annoyed her.

Everything had happened so quickly her throbbing head was still going round in ever accelerating circles.

Yesterday they'd driven away from the *finca*, the vast Las Colinas Verdes estate, leaving behind Doña Elvira and the aunts, who had looked as if they didn't know what had hit them, Delfina, who knew very well what had hit her and hated it very much indeed, and a suitably chastened and contrite Roy.

Roy had hurriedly assured her in a last-minute undertone that he would work his socks off on the estate to make up for what he had done, adding gruffly, 'Don't worry about me. I've got my head straightened out. Just concentrate on making a go of your marriage this time, sis. Roman's crazy about you; he's been unbearable to be around since you went away.'

Which only went to show that working under the

hot Spanish sun had sent her twin brother completely loopy.

They'd arrived in Seville in the sweltering afternoon heat and booked into a hotel where, to her knee-sagging relief, she'd been given a room of her own, complete with a four-poster bed and wonderful views of the Giralda. Then, before she'd had time to unpack her meagre belongings, Roman had knocked on the door, insisting on taking her to a surprisingly elegant boutique off the pedestrianised Calle Sierpes.

The sheer, rather stark grace of the dark-haired woman who had approached them had made Cassie sit up and take notice. The discreet decor, the clever lighting, the single garment on display—a simple cream silk suit with a designer label to die for—shrieked serious money.

'I need something practical,' Cassie had muttered at Roman, mentally digging her heels in. One or two cotton skirts, trousers and tops plus comfy sandals—stuff that could be bought cheaply at the market, not wickedly expensive designer gear. She hated the thought of being beholden to him to that extent.

A lazy look into her hot and mutinous face, the slight raising of one sable brow, and Roman had smoothly taken over. But when the pile of garments which had been brought out for his inspection and approval had reached mountainous proportions, Cassie had snapped, 'Enough!'

So here she was, with enough beautiful, expensive clothes to last her a lifetime packed into the boot of the Mercedes, driving away from Seville in the hazy warmth of the following morning, her head throbbing sullenly after another sleepless night, her body tense with the misgivings that were accumulating with remorseless rapidity and her mind buzzing with unanswered questions.

One of which was answered as they headed out of Jerez, making for the coast, through the gently undulating vineyards, miles upon miles of them beneath the vast blue sky.

'You're taking me to Sanlucar?' She could hardly believe it. Was he too insensitive to realise that the beautiful stone house, almost a mini-palace, in the old quarter of the historic port, was the last place she wanted to have to see again?

He spared her a mild sideways glance. 'You didn't want to stay on the estate, the house in Jerez is being redecorated, and I remembered how delighted you were with this area, the house. So, yes, we shall make our home in Sanlucar.'

He was talking as though it would be a permanent arrangement. 'For three months,' she reminded him stiffly, the memories she'd thought she'd successfully buried rising up to the surface of her mind to torment her.

He'd brought her to the house in Sanlucar for their honeymoon. She'd fallen in love with the place on sight and had told him as much. The tall rooms, the time-touched, lovingly tended antiques, the perfumed courtyard where water played in the ancient stone fountain and white doves called from the top of the walls where pale lemon roses arched in graceful profusion.

And it had all gone wrong, every single thing; instead of staying for several weeks, they'd left after three days. She'd been weeping silent tears of shame and hopeless inadequacy as they'd driven away and his gorgeous, beloved face had been stiff with Spanish pride. From that moment on he had virtually ignored her existence.

Had he brought her here to humiliate her? Was that another part of her punishment? Probably. A year ago he would have been incredulous, furious, when he'd received that note telling him she was leaving him. No one—not even a despised, unwanted wife—could turn their back on him and hope to get away with it.

And now she was being punished for it.

The large stone house overlooking the mouth of the Guadalquivir was deserted, the elegant, high-ceilinged rooms silent. Roman said, with no particular inflexion whatsoever, 'The caretaker and his wife are on leave. I thought it best to give them extra time off under the circumstances. So we fend for ourselves for a week or two. In view of your recent independence, I'm sure you won't find that a problem.'

'None at all,' she answered blandly. 'Housekeeping will help pass the time.' Not for the world would she let him see that their isolation worried her, that the thought of sharing his bed—as he had stipulated—horrified her, made her feel almost as if she were prostituting herself.

Her amber eyes were expressionless as they locked with his. He had married a naïve, vulnerable dreamer. Three years on she had her feet firmly on the ground, an adult woman toughened by harsh experience. It was something he was going to have to learn.

She said stiffly, 'I'll leave you to dispose of the luggage.' Heaps of it littered the shady hall. 'Is there a phone still in the small salon? I need to call Cindy.'

'That's already been taken care of.' He was watching her narrowly. 'She was delighted to hear we would be living as man and wife again,' he told her, a thread of cruelty hardening his voice. 'You have nothing to say to her that has not already been said.'

'I think,' she said calmly, ignoring the flutter of nerves that notched her heartbeats up a gear, 'that I'm the best judge of that.' She turned her back on him and began to walk away. Never again would he tell her what to do and expect her to submit in the old mindless fashion. She had moved on. She had changed.

But she was actually shaking as she dialled her friend's number, fine tremors that ruffled the surface of her skin and sent mini-icebergs bobbing through her veins. Standing up to Roman instead of taking the much easier option and acting like a doormat was strangely exhilarating. She felt as if she were stepping blindfold into unknown, scary territory.

'Dolls and Dames, how may I help you?' The

sound of Cindy's bright voice curved Cassie's mouth in a wistful smile. She could hear the chatter of customers in the background, the hypnotic beat of the latest chart-topper, and she wished ferociously that she was back there, in the thick of things, getting on with her own life.

'It's me,' she said. 'I'm sorry about what's happened—Roman said he'd already spoken to you. Look, Cin, about my job and the flat—' Would they still be waiting for her at the end of three months? 'I'll be back, I promise, I—'

'Stop fussing,' Cindy inserted blithely, her voice raised against the background noise. 'And for heaven's sake don't apologise. It's the best news I've heard in a long while. The only person who isn't celebrating because you and Roman have got back together is Guy. He looks like he's won the lottery and lost the ticket! My poor brother hoped to move in on you after you and Roman divorced, so now he's stuck in the mother and father of sulks. But don't you worry yourself about that, or anything, you hear me? Enjoy your second honeymoon—Sanlucar, Roman told me—and come back to clear your personal stuff from the flat when you feel like it. And don't worry about dropping me in the you-know-what because I hired a school-leaver yesterday—seventeen and sassy. She stepped right into your shoes as if they'd been hand-made for her.'

Glumly, Cassie gave up. Obviously, to save face, her estranged husband had intimated that the supposed reconciliation would be of a permanent duration. He had lost her a job she enjoyed and her home. However loudly she might protest that she wouldn't stay in Spain a minute longer than three months, her friend wouldn't believe her.

'I had no idea Guy felt that way,' she said disbelievingly when she was able to get a word in. 'You have to be wrong. We've been friends for ever. Just friends,' she insisted.

'Nope. My big brother started fancying his chances with you on the holiday we all had in Spain—but Roman made his move, and the next we knew you'd promised to marry him. Poor old Guy—back home he started to sow wild oats with a vengeance, but as soon as you came back, saying your marriage was over, he stopped dating and started waiting for your divorce to come through. He didn't think it right to tell you how he felt until you were free.'

'Oh, Lord!' Cassie pressed the knuckles of her free hand against her forehead. 'I promise you, I didn't realise.' Just one more thing to worry about. Guy was almost like another brother; she hated to think she had caused him misery, albeit unknowingly.

When she came off the phone she tried to put the unsettling conversation out of her mind. She had more pressing matters to deal with. Roman had disappeared, and so had the luggage.

Suddenly, all those beautiful new clothes seemed utterly desirable. Refusing to make use of them because he had bought them seemed childish. Cutting her nose off to spite her face. The suit she'd travelled to Spain in felt as if it had been on her back for a year!

She mounted the magnificent staircase, the banister supports intricately carved with clusters of grapes and exotic birds, trying to ignore the fluttery sensations in the pit of her stomach. 'Bedroom' and 'Roman' were not words she was happy to couple together.

With diminishing hope, she poked her head into one bedroom after another. No sign of her things. As she approached the master suite, the scene of their honeymoon disasters, her heart fluttered wildly. Taking a deep breath to steady it, she opened the elaborately carved door.

Nothing about the beautiful room had been changed. Tall windows overlooked the gardens and the rolling hills beyond the coastal plain. Sumptuous brocade in soft shades of rose and silver covered the walls and the graceful chairs which flanked a low antique table that was perfect for intimate breakfasts for two.

She refused to look at the splendour of the four-poster bed.

The classy carrier bags and her overnight case were piled in the centre of the floor and Roman was hanging his gear in the cavernous wardrobe. He had no intention of letting her wriggle out of her side of the bargain or even to give her a night or two of breathing space!

Well, the room hadn't changed, and he surely hadn't. But she had. She was no longer an inarticulate mouse, unable to express her feelings. She said to the back of his head, 'I see you don't intend to offer me the privacy of my own room. In at the deep end, is it? Hardly a subtle approach.'

The wide shoulders stiffened beneath the crisp white cotton. He turned slowly, his darkly glittering eyes meeting hers and holding.

'Subtlety didn't get me anywhere on our honeymoon here. Or perhaps you've forgotten how you gritted your teeth and endured my lovemaking? Do you know how that made me feel?' he demanded, a dull flush of angry colour staining his craggy cheekbones. 'Little better than an animal, taking my own pleasure and giving none! Cassie—' his tone altered, softening just a little '—I told myself to make allowances for your sheltered upbringing, your total lack of experience. After all, that was part of the attraction I felt for you. But after that first time you wouldn't let me near you. So I left you alone—as you wanted. There's a limit to how many blows to his pride a man can take.'

Her eyes dropped guiltily. She had never looked at it quite like that before. Instinctively, she'd known that what she'd secretly feared had become fact. She'd been a huge disappointment to him on their wedding night, fear of failing him making her freeze, unable to relax or respond.

And that same fear had made her instinctively reject him whenever he tried to touch her again.

If only he'd said one word of love, things might

have been so very different… But then, for all his faults, Roman wasn't a liar…

'I suggest we drop the subject,' he said flatly. 'Why don't you unpack while I find something for lunch?'

He walked out, closing the door behind him and, for no reason that she could think of, she felt totally bereft.

An hour later she descended the stairs. A shower in the luxurious green marble *en suite* had worked wonders, as had the liberal application of fragrant body oil.

And the choice of what to wear from the huge selection of shockingly expensive clothing Roman had insisted she have had been difficult. Everything was so lovely.

In the end she'd settled for white lace briefs, soft, silky wide-legged trousers in a gorgeous tawny colour and a matching halter-neck top that left her arms and most of her back bare and negated the need to wear a bra.

She'd left her hair loose and it was beginning to dry in soft curling tendrils. After adding the barest touch of lipstick and mascara, she felt ready to go downstairs. She wasn't going to think about the coming night and get herself all tense and apprehensive because she might, just might, be able to wriggle out of it.

She paused for a moment on the cool tiles of the hall, then followed the sound of cutlery. Roman was drawing the cork from a bottle of white Rioja and the kitchen table held a huge tray crammed with plates, cutlery, glasses and salads.

The arrogant Roman Fernandez, master of the vast Colinas Verdes estates, working in a kitchen? Unheard of!

'You have been busy,' she drawled from the doorway, amusement in her voice. For some reason, seeing him in an unprecedented domestic role made her feel warm inside.

He glanced up, smoky eyes veiled by twin fans of thick dark lashes. 'I have impressed myself,' he confessed in his lightly accented, sexy voice, his sudden white grin disarming her.

He straightened, placing the opened bottle that was already sporting a haze of condensation on the overburdened tray, the straight black bar of one eyebrow rising in silent appraisal.

Resting one narrow-boned hip on the side of the table, he let his eyes travel with slow deliberation from the toes of her sandalled feet to eventually lock with hers.

'I was right to insist on that outfit.' His voice was low, sultry. 'You would have thrown it back in that poor woman's face, along with everything else I chose for you. It becomes you. You have beautiful breasts. You were right not to constrict them in a bra.'

His openly sexual appraisal had made her breath catch in her throat. She felt her nipples peak as a slow ache of desire flared deep inside her. Heavens, the man was dynamite! A look, a word, could bring any woman to her knees! No wonder she had felt inadequate, way out of his league.

His narrowed charcoal eyes still held hers as a rapid pulse of embarrassed colour covered her face. 'A mere observation,' he said lightly. His mouth wasn't smiling but his eyes were dancing. 'Shall we eat? Outside?'

He lifted the heavy tray and strode out through the open door. Cassie dragged in a shuddery breath and followed.

In the past she'd only had to look at him to go dizzy with wanting him. Wanting him so badly yet unable to deliver.

If he had his way, the whole humiliating farce was due to begin all over again—unless she could convince him that it wasn't necessary.

By the time she caught up with him he was unloading the contents of the tray on to a teak table in the courtyard. Shaded by a massive almond tree, flanked by ancient stone urns filled with perfumed lilies and carnations, it was the ideal site for a relaxed meal, the prelude to a second honeymoon.

Suddenly, her legs felt hollow. She sat down quickly. It was so hot, even in the green shade that made his skin seem darker, his eyes enigmatic. The combination of the still, heavily perfumed air and nervous tension was making her dizzy.

'You have to be hungry,' he allowed, piling a plate with thin slices of the ham that was a speciality of the region, plump olives and crisp salad. 'Since you refused to eat breakfast back at the hotel. Tell me—' his eyes skimmed her wilting body as he poured the wine '—do I ruin your appetite, Cassie *mia*? Whenever I was at the *finca* I saw you pick at your food, yet you've gained weight during this last year. A very becoming amount of weight.'

Cassie reached for a crusty roll, broke it and drizzled olive oil over the two halves. She took a deliberate bite and speared a succulent morsel of ham with her fork.

'You intimidated me,' she told him honestly. If nothing else, a year away from him had given her back the ability to give an opinion, vocalise her thoughts. 'I was dumped in that isolated farmhouse with nothing to do but endure the disapproval of your female relatives. When you did put in an appearance, you barely seemed to see me—'

'Oh, I saw you,' he slid in, his mouth compressing. 'Whenever I was foolish enough to try to get near you I saw a pair of frightened eyes, I saw panic. *Por Dios!* Is it any wonder I stopped trying?'

'That was just sex,' she shot back. 'You wanted an heir. That was the only use you had for me!' Her fingers tightened convulsively on the misty surface of her wine glass. 'When it was obvious that it wasn't going to happen, you washed your hands of me—you couldn't even be bothered to ask why!' she told him stormily. 'What *I* wanted was never important, was it? When I asked—*begged* you to let us make a home away from the *finca*—'

'You were hysterical,' he reminded coldly. 'In those days I needed to be away often—'

'You could have taken me with you,' Cassie snapped back, wishing the subject didn't still have the power to make her so angry. The past was dead, so why couldn't she bury it? She drained her glass in one long swallow, hoping the chilled wine would cool her temper.

And when he dismissed, 'My mother was worried about you; the aunts, too, decided you needed guidance, looking after,' she could have hurled the empty glass straight at his head.

As if he read the intention in her eyes he calmly refilled the prospective missile, then put his forearms on the table, leaning towards her.

The shock of soft dark hair that fell over his forehead and his sudden, disarming smile made him look younger than his thirty-six years. And his voice was husky as he told her, '*Querida*, we are not here to quarrel. You have your wish. We are away from the *finca* and my relatives. Now we can see if your attitude in the bedroom has changed as radically as your figure and your ability to answer me back.'

He reached out and touched her hand and the whole of her body caught fire as he said, 'I am looking forward to finding out, *mi esposa*.'

CHAPTER FIVE

THE fluid music of the fountain as the water splashed into the shallow stone basin seemed unnaturally loud in the silence that lay over the courtyard. The way he was still looking at her, the things he had said, released a flood of shattering sensation inside her, making her flesh quiver, her blood pound hotly through her veins. It took her breath away

Responding to the way he looked, the sound of his voice, his vital masculinity, had never been a problem. Nothing had changed in that respect. But she couldn't deliver, couldn't hope to please and enthrall a man of his sophistication and experience.

Could she?

Feeling as if her bones were about to disintegrate, she gripped the stem of her wine glass and said thickly, 'It needn't happen—the bed thing,' and felt her face go red beneath those steady, watchful eyes.

'I see.' Long fingers lazily plucked a grape from the terracotta platter. She heard the wine-dark fruit crunch between his strong white teeth. 'And how do you work that out?'

At least he wasn't forcefully reminding her of the bargain they'd made, she thought, as she thankfully released the breath she'd been holding. He wasn't getting all macho and Spanish and breathing fire and brimstone from those aristocratically sculpted nostrils! In fact, he looked completely relaxed, one arm hooked across the back of his chair, the other reaching towards the grapes.

Roman in a reasonable, listening mood was pretty bewildering—it made her feel as if she were on another planet, but she wasn't going to knock it!

Hoping it was going to last, she said levelly, 'Tell me if I'm wrong, but this supposed reconciliation of ours is being staged to get your family and Delfina off your case, isn't it?'

No response. He crunched another grape and refilled the wine glass she hadn't noticed emptying.

Despite her best intentions, her voice rose a level. 'When you marry again it won't be to that type of spoiled, demanding socialite. Unless you've altered your mind radically, it will be to a quiet breeding machine, content to stay home while you go out to play.'

Cassie huffed in an infuriated breath. He could at least show some interest in what she'd been saying and agree with her, because she knew she was right. 'Why don't you say something? Anything! Or are we having a one-sided conversation here?'

His slow smile was indulgent, his eyes lazy. 'You have an opinion, Cassandra; I am merely doing you the courtesy of listening to it. So far you've not said anything that invited comment.' His brows lifted just slightly. 'I'm patiently waiting to hear what you have to say about the—what did you call it?—the Bed Thing.'

Patronising horror! But losing her temper wouldn't help. 'Exactly,' she said grittily. 'Just putting the picture straight. So sorry to bore you. If you can't be up-front about it and tell Delfina and your family to get lost instead of insisting on this subterfuge to get you out of a corner—'

Now she was being sarcastic. She really couldn't afford to ruffle his feathers, so she deliberately relaxed her shoulders and sugared her tone a little. 'What I'm trying to say is, I've agreed to live with you for three months. To the interested parties back at the *finca*, it will appear that we're making our marriage work. That's enough. They won't have posted spies here, or put hidden cameras in all the rooms. There's absolutely no need for us to actually sleep together.'

There, she'd said it. Holding her breath, feeling the prickle of perspiration gather on her forehead, she waited for his reaction. Surely he would recognise that her being here with him was enough to get Darling Delfina and his matchmaking relatives off his back? Surely he could have no wish to repeat the frustrating and humiliating experiences of three years ago?

Smoky eyes regarded her narrowly. He stretched his endless legs further under the table and clasped his hands behind his head. In the green shade of the almond tree his expression was shadowed, unreadable.

'Are you on the pill, Cass?'

She widened her eyes at him. With a handful of words he'd pushed her thoughts right out of gear. What had her being on the pill got to do with anything?

'Are you?'

'Yes,' she grudged, and felt her face go hot.

'Ah. I see.' His tone might be smooth, but something dark and dangerous flashed in his eyes as he shifted his position, leaning slightly forwards. 'Who's the lucky man? My cousin Guy? He ogled you when he thought no one was looking, when you visited that first time. You certainly headed in his direction when you left me.'

'Don't be ridiculous!' She moved uncomfortably in her seat. Poor Guy. She'd had no idea he'd thought of her in that way. On that fatal visit she'd had eyes for no one but Roman.

'Who, then?'

He looked unpredictable, dangerous. His pose might be studiedly relaxed but she knew better. He was like a coiled spring. Touch him and he'd snap every which way.

Despite being separated for a year, they were still man and wife. If he thought she'd been making love with someone else after rejecting him, the knife-thrust to his monumental Spanish pride would produce an explosion of awesome proportions.

'No one. My GP recommended I go on the pill to regulate my monthly cycle. It had gone haywire. No other reason. Unlike you, I don't look on sex as being the be-all and end-all of everything,' she said stiltedly.

'Of that, *mi esposa*, I am fully aware.' His mouth curled wryly as he swung down his arms and pushed back his chair. 'So I choose to believe you. I had to ask, you understand. One of us has to use protection.'

So he wasn't prepared to listen to reason!

Her heart leapt and fluttered like a frightened bird. But he wasn't to know that. She wouldn't give him the satisfaction of seeing her in a panic.

'Protection? Here was I, thinking that the only reason you married me was to get an heir!' Her voice was commendably cool, she'd even managed a slight underlying note of amusement. And knew she'd hit a nerve when his face tightened.

'I do want an heir. But not one given grudgingly.'

Grudgingly? What did he know about it? What did he know about the lonely heart that had wished things could have been different, wished he could have understood her fears, the way she'd hated and despised herself for her failings?

She would have loved to have had his child, to have made a real and loving home with him, away from his critical relatives.

She stood up quickly; the way he was looming over her was making her jittery. If he weren't so bone-shakingly gorgeous she could handle him better. Forget that once she had loved him.

And now they were too close.

Cassie took a quick step back, trying not to think that when he made her keep her side of their fiendish bargain they would be a whole lot closer. No point in getting in a state before she had to!

'So—' One large, finely made hand gestured vaguely at the table. 'We clear away? Wash the dishes? Then, maybe, siesta?'

His abrupt change of mood, that slow sexy smile, took her breath away all over again. But she recovered it, recovered herself, turned away and told him, '*You* dismissed the staff. *You* do the dishes. And sex in the afternoon wasn't part of the bargain, as I remember.'

She walked away.

As she stepped beneath the rose-covered arch in the stone wall that separated the courtyard from the extensive gardens her skin prickled, the fine hairs standing on end. It felt as if an army of ants wearing red-hot spiky boots were marching all over her body. Knowing him, he would command her to come right back—and if she refused he'd make her.

But he didn't. Only the sleepy sound of the doves, the faint rustle of a breeze in the gently swaying tops of the eucalyptus trees disturbed the peace of the slow Spanish afternoon. She expelled a shaky breath.

Reprieve.

But not for long. Only until tonight.

And did she mind? Really mind?

The sudden, unwelcome question had her rooted to the spot, her feet seemingly glued to the narrow, paved path. Something sharp and fierce twisted deep inside her, making her squeeze her eyelids together. Her lungs expanded as she dragged air into them, inhaling the scents of the billowing borders, heady lilies, hot spicy geraniums, sweet oleander…

She forced her eyes open. What kind of stupid question was that? Of course she minded! She hated the thought of being used to satisfy his warped curiosity, of being punished for what her twin had done!

What sane woman would want to be forced to share Roman's bed? Loads, she answered herself honestly. And it wouldn't be a question of forcing.

Deeply uncomfortable with the way her thoughts were shaping, she marched on, covering all the winding paths that curved around the massive flowerbeds and passing the airless summer house covered with deep red roses. She finally came to a halt at the barrier of wooden poles that overhung the deep and shady ravine.

Steep sides and tall trees offered shade, and far below she could hear the stream from the hills fall over rocks and chatter its way between moss-covered boulders. It was tempting. Up here, at this time of day and at this time of year, the Andalusian sun was merciless.

She felt as if she were melting, her clothes sticking to her overheated body, an ache building up at the back of her eyes. But the only way down was a steep staircase of stone and her legs felt so wobbly she didn't think she'd be able to make it.

Roman, she thought crossly, was probably lolling in the salon, an electric fan cooling the air, a glass of something long and cold to hand. While she—

'You punish yourself.' His voice was slow and soft, the hands he placed on her shoulders gut-wrenchingly gentle.

She hadn't heard him walk up to her, but the sound of his voice in the sleepy silence of the garden, the touch of his hands, hadn't startled her. Almost as if she had known he would come and she'd been waiting.

The tips of his fingers moved over her burning skin and she thought: No, *you* punish me. You make me face the things about myself I don't like—the fear, and the cowardice that stopped me doing anything about that fear. I should have told you I was afraid, and made you listen. I wasn't brave enough.

'Too much sun, your skin burns.' He lifted the heavy swathe of hair away from the back of her neck and her breath snagged as his lips touched her nape. 'You taste of salt.' His voice purred. 'And woman.'

Her head was beginning to swim, and it wasn't just the effects of the hot afternoon sun. She wanted to move away, to reinforce the distance that had been growing between them ever since their wedding night, but couldn't make her legs function.

Instead she said shakily, 'I was thinking of climbing down there, into the shade,' and sagged weakly back against him as his hands slid down her naked arms, cupping her elbows.

A year ago, if he'd come to her, touched her like this, she would have leapt away like a startled rabbit, terrified to let things go further and allow him to rediscover just how frigid she was.

Now, she was incapable of any movement at all; her body wanted to stay exactly where it was, close to him, and her brain had gone AWOL.

'I've got a better idea.' His hands slid around her body, resting on her midriff. The light pressure of his fingertips sent a shock of feverish tension zinging through her. She could feel the hard jut of his pelvis against the lower part of her back and felt faint at the contact, desperately willing his hands to move higher to cup her breasts, to discover for himself the evidence of erect nipples that strained against the insubstantial barrier of silk.

She wanted to cry out, to beg him to touch her, and almost did, but was achingly glad she hadn't when he said lightly, 'We go back to the house and you can shower and rest. Alone. I won't bother you—if that's why you're staying out here and inviting sunstroke. Later, we'll go out for supper. I can't face doing any more dishes!'

He moved away, walking back towards the house, his stride loose and graceful, and Cassie followed, her face flaming.

He hadn't noticed how her body had become so supple and willing, so eager for his touch, how her breath had shortened. But then, why should he? In his limited experience of her, she had never responded. He wouldn't expect anything to have changed.

Which begged the question of why he had stipulated that they share a bed at all.

To punish her.

Which meant he was cruel, had an unfeeling heart and thought of her as nothing more than an experiment. With the side-effect of getting Delfina and his family off his back.

Well, for Roy's sake she could get through the next three months. Roman expected a wooden woman in his bed and that was what he'd get. The aching desire she'd felt just a few moments ago was nothing to worry about.

She'd wanted Roman to make love to her on their wedding night, but when it had come right down to it she'd turned into a block of ice. The same thing would happen again. He'd soon tire of the silly game and remove himself to another room.

And that would be the end of it.

CHAPTER SIX

'YOU are safe to walk home?' Roman's voice was threaded with dry amusement and Cassie's amber eyes answered his relaxed mood, gleaming up at him.

Moonlight suited him; he looked really spectacular. But then, when did he not?

'I may have had one glass of Rioja too many—'

'Don't forget the Manzanilla—'

'I'm not.' She wrinkled her nose at him. 'Besides, I ate like a horse—those *langostinos* were to die for, and that sauce!' She kissed her fingers in the air and swallowed a husky giggle. 'Besides, what option do I have? Unless you're offering to carry me?'

For answer he gave her a long assessing look, sweeping from head to toe. Cassie felt the sexual awareness that had been hovering between them all evening crank up another notch or two. Or two hundred. The breeze was moulding the fine cotton of the understatedly elegant shift dress she was wearing tightly to her body and his eyes lingered like a lover's touch on each and every lush curve.

She shivered deliciously, the punch of desire inside her making her legs go weak, and he told her, 'It wouldn't be a problem, but I think the walk would sober you up.'

'I'm not drunk!'

'Tipsy, then?' His gorgeous mouth was straight now, unsmiling, making her want to reach up and touch his lips with hers, to feel them soften, remind him of the promise this night held. For both of them.

'Only a little.' She did her best to sound haughty and dismally failed. And didn't really mind. She was beyond being annoyed with him, having to be forever on the defensive. The evening spent in the little restaurant in the Barrio Alto, the oldest part of the port, had been wonderful from start to finish, and if she'd had too much wine it had only been because she'd decided to dull her senses so that the prospect of the coming night might take on less alarming proportions.

Instead, she realised as she took his proffered arm, the alcohol had crept insidiously through her veins, whetting her sexual appetite, making her near delirious in her need to act the wanton, fling herself on him, beg him to make love to her, and hope to hell she didn't freeze up on him again.

Not that she felt like freezing, not one little bit, she recognised dizzily as they threaded slowly through the narrow, ancient streets. The playful breeze was warm and she could smell the sea, and the river, and the orange trees that seemed to be planted everywhere.

She belonged here; she really did. It made her feel so happy. This place, and being here with him, intoxicated her far more than the wine had done.

'I'd forgotten how relaxing this corner of Spain

could be,' she said on a breathy little sigh, and dropped her glossy chestnut head against his powerful shoulder.

'Andalusia? Or the best part of a bottle of wine?' he queried dryly, slipping an arm around her waist for greater support. 'Not long now; almost home.'

Home. Oh, it sounded so good! Far too good to be true. A tear formed in the corner of each eye. If only they could have spent their married life here, away from...

'Whoops!' She stumbled over an uneven cobblestone and the momentary plunge into misery was forgotten as Roman, with a darkly muttered imprecation, swept her up into his arms and carried her the rest of the short distance and then beneath the stone portal of the house.

'You didn't carry me over the threshold on our honeymoon,' she murmured, knowing her words were all slurring together in a way that made her want to giggle irrepressibly.

And it wasn't really the effects of alcohol, either. It was being held in his arms, pressed against that gorgeous, macho male body, her arms clinging around his neck, her face so very close to his. Definitely close enough to kiss...

'We had an audience, remember?' he answered lightly, as if he were trying to humour a difficult child. 'You were such a timid little thing, I didn't want to embarrass you. The slightest thing made your face turn into a beetroot and sent you scurrying for cover.'

He had a point, she conceded. Three years ago she'd been a pathetic wimp. She responded airily, 'I remember. All the staff gathered to give the master's new bride the once-over. Staring, picking me to pieces!'

She felt his whole body tense, the arms that held her turning to steel bars. She wound her arms more tightly around his neck. Hey ho! What did the past matter? They were alone now; that was the important thing. No old family retainers to exclaim over the total unsuitability of *el patrón*'s new wife, as she'd had no doubt they had done in the privacy of their own quarters.

Not that that sort of thing would bother her now, of course. Suddenly, she felt liberated, her own woman, capable of facing anyone and anything. Best of all, she wasn't afraid of disappointing Roman in bed. What she didn't know he could teach her. She would be a willing pupil!

'You get some strange ideas.' His long stride carried him across the cool, dimly lit hall. 'But then I never had the privilege of knowing what was going on inside your head.'

Because he hadn't asked? Or because she hadn't told him? Were they equally to blame for the complete lack of communication between them?

Cassie was in no fit state to come up with an answer to that; she was simply a mass of sensation, minus a brain. Her blood was singing through her veins, red-hot, burning her up. She'd expected him to put her down but he didn't. He carried her up the stairs as if she weighed no more than a kitten.

Tonight wasn't going to be a problem. Tonight she was more ready for him than she could ever have dreamed possible.

The fiendish bargain he'd struck had seemed like a violation of the worst possible kind. Until tonight. Tonight, making love with her husband—wholeheartedly responding to his incredible, overpowering, fantastic masculinity—was nothing short of natural, totally and overwhelmingly right.

She gave a long sigh of blissful anticipation as he paced his way to the side of the sumptuous bed by the light of the moon that slanted through the louvres, and slid her down to her feet, flicking on the bedside lamp at the same time.

Her arms still looped around his neck, Cassie stared up into the strong planes of his heartstoppingly arresting features and electrifying, bone-melting excitement made her sway on her feet, her breath coming rapidly, shallowly.

She tried to say his name but her mouth couldn't form the word; her lips parted uselessly. Ever since they'd arrived here this morning she'd been more and more sexually aware of him, trying to deny it because she hadn't wanted a repeat performance of their wedding night.

She knew now that wouldn't happen. During the last year she had finally grown up.

'Por Dios!' Roman muttered beneath his breath. Swiftly, he lifted his hands to remove hers from

around his neck where her fingers had begun playing with the soft dark hairs at his nape.

Then, without any effort at all, he swung her round, found the zip at the back of her dress and pulled it down. The tiny rasping sound seemed unnaturally loud. Cassie held her breath, her heartbeats thudding wildly as deft fingers slid the fabric from her shoulders, down her arms, loosing the garment to let it pool at her feet.

Her need for him was so hot and heavy now, she could barely stand.

When he unclipped the back fastening of her bra and released her throbbing breasts Cassie felt she might expire on the spot from the wild clamour of sexual excitement, and a husky moan was dredged from deep inside her when he slid her brief black lace panties down the length of her trembling legs.

She made to turn, her mouth running dry, wanting to undress him, to touch her nakedness to his, but he propelled her forward with one firm hand, the other pulling down the thin, silky bed-sheet.

'Sleep it off, Cass,' he advised grimly. 'You obviously decided to get drunk—' he laid cruel emphasis on the word '—to help you through the night. Well, I've got news for you, *mi esposa*. I find that a definite turn-off.'

He marched back to the door, then paused, his tone dry, 'I'll join you later, if only to make sure you don't raid the wine cellar for more Dutch courage. But, never fear, I won't touch you. So sleep well.'

CHAPTER SEVEN

CASSIE stirred fretfully and came awake. And wished she hadn't. Asleep, she didn't have to relive the scene of her humiliation, the way her red-hot anticipation of the night ahead had been so effectively doused by the ice of his parting words.

Drunk.

It was still only the middle of the night and the room was in total darkness. She'd been too busy crying herself to sleep to think about anything practical, like turning off the bedside lamp.

Roman must have done it.

For the first time amid the internal racket of her clamouring waking thoughts she heard the sound of his breathing. And held her own breath, her naked body going tense beneath the fine silky sheet.

He had joined her. He had said he would.

But the bed was huge and he was lying as far away from her as he could get without falling off the edge.

He had said he wouldn't touch her.

Because he believed she'd deliberately got drunk so that when it came to keeping her side of his Machiavellian bargain she would be too fuddled to take any notice of what was going on! Well, it had sort of started off that way, she admitted honestly, but somewhere along the line it had changed.

Quite when she had realised that she still loved her husband, always had and always would, she couldn't really recall.

It hadn't hit her like a bolt of lightning, but had been gradually unfurling inside her, like the newly opening petals of a rose, becoming more certain with every breath she took.

She loved him so.

Her heart leapt, twisted, and ended up somewhere in her throat.

Her life with Roman, before she'd gathered enough courage to leave him, had been liberally spattered with mistakes. Far too many mistakes, the greatest of which had been her inability to communicate with him and explain her feelings.

Never again!

Whatever the future held—and as far as she knew he wasn't looking beyond three months—she owed it to both of them to be open and honest. Starting with telling him that if she'd given the impression that she was about to sink into an alcoholic heap, it had only been because the thought of spending the night with him had intoxicated her!

She hoisted herself up on one elbow, gingerly narrowing the distance between them. Her eyes were growing more accustomed to the darkness now and she could see the outline of his dark, beautifully shaped head against the white pillow. The sheet was tangled around his hips, and the shadowy sweep of his tautly muscled back was a temptation too far.

Her heart lurching, her mouth running dry, she reached out a hand and touched him. Just gently. From the warm nape of his neck her fingers slipped between his shoulder blades, loving the warmth of his skin, the slick texture, and down, down the ridge of vertebrae, sliding across to the hard prominence of his hipbone, exploring him as she had never dared to do before.

The arm he wasn't lying on was flung upwards, covering his face, giving her tenderly roving fingers access to the lower part of his chest. And lower, trailing down the washboard flatness of his stomach, her fingers stilling as they tangled in crisp, thick body hair.

Her heart was beating wildly, clamouring beneath her breast, her breathing difficult to regulate. She could touch him if she wanted to, and she did want to, but it would be an invasion of his personal privacy, wouldn't it? While he was asleep?

Forcing her hand to stay quietly and exactly where it was, she pulled in a ragged breath and bent forward to put her lips against the oiled satin skin of his shoulder, her throbbing, almost painfully aroused breasts meeting the hard plane of his back.

She wriggled against him, pressing closer; she couldn't help it. Her mind had gone on holiday and she was acting on instinctive, primitive need. Being so breathtakingly close to him, skin to burning skin, felt so right, so natural. She couldn't begin to imagine why she'd ever been unable to respond to him.

A small mew of pleasure escaped her throat, her whole body so sensitised now she knew she was about to wrap herself round him, make him wake, force him to bring her the release that only he could give.

But if he didn't want to give it?

The thought cooled her like a dash of icy water. If he rejected her, as she had formerly rejected him, pushing him away whenever he came near her after the awkwardness of their wedding night, she would be utterly devastated, humiliated…

She sucked in a savagely painful hiss of breath, realising for the very first time exactly how he must have felt and why, after a time, he had stayed away from her so often.

Sudden tears burned behind her eyes. How could she have done that to him when she'd been so much in love with him? How could she have been so self-centred, never giving a thought to how he must have felt, absorbed in her own immature hang-ups?

A tear of bitter regret fell on his shoulder blade. Unthinkingly, she bent her head and lapped it away with the tip of her tongue. And heard him moan softly, deep in his throat.

Awake? For how long? When had the rhythm of his breathing altered, become shallower, more rapid? Cassie's body went still. Waiting. Tense with the dread of having the tables turned on her. And he said, his voice husky with need, 'Touch me, Cass.'

Relief drenched through her. He wasn't going to take his revenge by telling her to keep her hands to herself. Relief and something stronger, wilder, had her pressing her naked body to his, fitting her thighs beneath his, her hand dipping lower.

Fully aroused, he was sensational. She shuddered with deep, spiralling ecstasy, her head spinning wildly as he groaned raggedly and swept round towards her, crushing her in his arms, parting her legs with a strong hair-roughened thigh.

'Wait—' She freed her trapped hand and raised it to gently touch his face, the heel of her palm resting along his tough, stubbly jawline, her fingers against one jutting cheekbone. 'I want to tell you—I promise you it wasn't just that I'd had a bit too much to drink. It was the thought of tonight that intoxicated me…'

If he believed her, he didn't say so. But perhaps the way his mouth took hers was answer enough. The hungry mastery of his kiss made her feel as if she were drowning; the hands that caressed and tormented every inch of her body sent her into a state of delirium and there were no words spoken when he finally plunged into her willing, receptive body.

But who needed words when two desperately needy bodies, two loving souls were communing in the darkness of the warm, sweetly scented Spanish night?

'If I didn't know better, I'd say you were not the woman I married.' Roman's slightly accented voice was soft and sultry and Cassie smiled dreamily into his smoky eyes.

The tone of his voice told her that he liked the woman she had become in his bed far better than the woman he had married. She wasn't going to spoil the magic they'd created together by reminding him of why he'd chosen an immature, biddable little thing to be his wife.

Around dawn they'd fallen asleep in each other's arms and, moments ago, his light kisses on her eyelids had woken her. Last night had been spectacular; they hadn't been able to get enough of each other, like starving people suddenly coming across a banquet.

Untutored as she was, her responses to him had surprised her. She'd been quite shameless, very much more than merely willing, wanting to give to him as much as he had given to her.

'Same beautiful hair,' he murmured, running his fingers through the long silky strands that were splayed out over the pillow, burnished to copper by the sunlight that filtered through the partly opened louvres. 'Same eyes—like the finest topaz—but with a light behind them that was never there before.'

The tips of his fingers slid across her cheek, found her parted lips and she reached up, looping her hands behind his head, pulling him down to her, and the kiss was like a drug, sending her spinning out of control and when he broke it she gave a tiny sob of denial.

'Shh—' he murmured, his eyes wicked, his sultry

mouth curving. 'Patience, *mi esposa*. I have not yet finished my inventory. Indulge me.'

She placed a shaky hand on his broad, bronzed chest, her body trembling with sharp awareness, her voice thick as she protested, 'Do you like tormenting me?'

'I love it.' His sensual mouth framed the words softly, liquid grey eyes gleaming beneath the thick black lashes. 'Almost as much as I love touching you, looking at you. Cassie, *mia*, you have matured beautifully.'

A languid hand slid the silk sheet away from her body. 'Lie back for me; let me look at you,' he commanded lazily as his hands swept over her engorged breasts, over her slender waist, following the feminine flare of her hips, then trailing inwards, to the apex of her thighs. Cassie reached for him, writhing with the burning fever of desire, parting her legs in wanton invitation, glorying in the release of knowing her feeble hang-ups were a thing of the past, that she could at last show him how much she loved him.

Then briefly, like a shadow, she saw a frown gather between his eyes, his jawline tightening as he pulled in his breath.

Something was wrong. Hadn't she pleased him as much as she'd thought she had? Despite what he'd just said, did he suddenly find her eagerness distasteful? Anxiety clouded Cassie's eyes as she lifted a tentative hand and laid it against the side of his face.

'Roman?'

At her touch, the sound of her voice, the frown

disappeared and the stillness that had held his body rigid melted away. She saw dark colour streak his hard, jutting cheekbones as he gave a rough growl low in his throat and demonstrated the full power of his possession.

She hadn't known it could be like this, Cassie mused one hour later as they exited the shower, wrapped around each other. The physical expression of love was so addictive.

She felt so sated she could barely move, and closed her eyes as he reached for a fluffy bath sheet and gently patted her dry before mopping the moisture from his own superb body. Thankfully, whatever had briefly troubled him had been forgotten. Or perhaps she had simply imagined it...

'The day is half gone,' he told her as he rubbed the towel over his hair, leaving it sticking up in endearing spikes. 'What would you like to do with the rest of it? Take a picnic to the beach? Or perhaps you'd prefer a restaurant?'

'I'd rather stay here,' she admitted huskily, her golden eyes drenched with soft emotion.

Roman grinned at her, his teeth very white against the bronze tones of his skin, his eyes glinting wickedly. 'I hoped you'd say that. Far more interesting things can happen in the privacy of our own home.' He dropped the towel, closed the small gap between them and put a brief kiss across her mouth. 'I'll make coffee and find something to eat. Come down when you're ready. And Cass—' he was already at the door to their adjoining bedroom '—wear something easy to get out of!'

Waves of love rolled over her, making her giddy. She wanted to stay here with him for ever, just the two of them.

Just the two? She suddenly remembered that she'd forgotten to take her pill last night. They might already be a threesome! She couldn't recall how many times they'd made love.

But it didn't matter, did it? Surely now that the lovemaking side of their marriage had been put so magnificently right he would want her to stay, want to make their marriage work? He had never pretended to be in love with her, but after last night he would put their troubled past behind him and build on what they now had.

Of course he would!

And even if he didn't love her now, love could grow, couldn't it?

Rough-drying her hair with the towel he'd discarded, she wandered through to the bedroom, the prickle of excitement deep inside her beginning all over again as she wondered which of her many new garments would be the most flattering and the simplest to remove!

CHAPTER EIGHT

'YOU are certainly a different person now,' Roman commented smoothly. He looked at ease, one arm draped along the back of the bench seat, his fingers touching the tousled copper strands of her hair as it tumbled over her shoulders. But his relaxed smile didn't reach eyes that seemed, in the half-light of a misty dawn, strangely wary. 'Is it the year away from me, from Spain, that has made you so? Being back in England has made you happier?'

Cassie glanced quickly away, swung her legs up on the upholstered bench seat that hugged the far side of the rose-smothered summer house and leant back against him.

She really didn't want to think about that year of separation, or the two years that had gone before. What had started out as a cold-blooded, wicked bargain had turned into a truly wonderful second honeymoon. She didn't want anything to spoil it.

Five weeks of wedded bliss, of lazy sun-drenched days, velvet, perfumed nights, wild bursts of passion in the most unexpected places, at the most unexpected times—lovers getting to know every intimate detail of each other's bodies in their own secluded paradise. Being shut away from the outside world had left her feeling she inhabited a haven of magical unreality.

But unfortunately reality was about to poke its nose in, she conceded reluctantly. Of course he would want to know why she'd walked out on their marriage. Only by raking over the past could they hope to put the future right. And if she looked reality squarely and bravely in the face she would have to admit that she still didn't know whether he wanted her to stay with him beyond the three-month limit he'd set.

And she was almost certain she was pregnant.

She dragged a sigh up from the bottom of her lungs. The cold breath of reality was definitely uncomfortable.

Roman said, his voice controlled, 'It is a subject that interests me, even if you would prefer not to think about our misguided marriage.'

'Misguided?' she echoed tremulously. After these last rapturous weeks, did he still think their marriage had been a mistake? How could that be, when they had become so close? Physically, at least, though there had been times when she'd been sure something was troubling him.

He snatched in an impatient breath. 'Look at me when I'm talking to you!' he commanded gruffly, placing strong hands on her hips and swinging her round so that her feet hit the tiled floor and she was slewed across the cushions, facing him.

Cassie could feel his anger and it made her want to weep. Something was wrong, very wrong, and she had to face it, not keep brushing it under the carpet, pretending it was all in her imagination. She asked, as calmly as she could, 'Roman, what's on your mind? Something is.' She met his brooding eyes, trying not to show her anxiety, her very real fear. 'We've been happy together, you know we have, yet there have been times when you've seemed to distance yourself…times when you've looked at me with something like disgust. I want to know why.'

He gave her a lancing look, his mouth tight round the words that suddenly poured from him. 'When we first married I thought I could make you content—happy, even. But after our wedding night together it became painfully obvious that I couldn't. You couldn't bear it when I touched you. Now it seems you can't get enough of sex,' he uttered darkly. 'So who taught you? You certainly didn't allow me that privilege.'

'Oh!' She felt her face burn with sudden outraged colour. How could he think such a thing, let alone say it? The morning sun was beginning to break through the mist, the air shimmering with opaline colours; outside the summer house, a stand of eucalyptus trees swayed gracefully in the slight breeze, their misty white branches and silver leaves ghostly in the growing light. But inside it was darker, Roman's face shadowed and suddenly somehow forbidding.

A shudder rocked her body.

'You are cold? Or have I touched a nerve?' Roman asked drily.

'Not cold, angry,' she framed vehemently. 'How could you think that of me, after the way we've been together? I don't sleep around! You're the only man I've ever made love with!'

Even though she was only wearing a pair of brief turquoise cotton shorts and a matching bra-style top, the morning was warm. Too warm, really. She felt a band of perspiration form above her short upper lip and saw by the tightening of his mobile, utterly sensuous mouth that her instinctive and truthful reply hadn't impressed him.

He believed his assumption was the correct one, that since leaving him she'd been indulging in multiple affairs. And was he jealous? Roman, jealous! She squashed the surge of hope very decisively. Letting herself believe that her husband really did love her could be dangerous, could lead to a disappointment that would be almost impossible to bear.

'Why are you asking all this? Why now?' she asked dully, hopelessness dousing all that vehement anger as she at last understood the insulting reality of what had been troubling him.

Was everything about to end? It certainly looked that way, especially since he obviously didn't believe her assertion that she hadn't been with any other man.

For the first time since they'd been back together they hadn't instinctively turned to each other, making love until the sun burned holes in the sea mist, taking it in turns to fetch breakfast in bed. This morning the kiss that had woken her had been perfunctory, but his suggestion that they take their coffee down to the summer house hadn't bothered her. Not until now. Was he already tiring of her, as had once been stringently prophesised? Was his stubborn belief that she'd been unfaithful the excuse he was looking for?

Cassie hugged her arms around her midriff, shaking inside now. Everything seemed spoiled, about to fall apart. 'Leaving aside your insulting remarks about my supposed promiscuity, I thought we'd—' she lifted her slender shoulders in a hopeless gesture '—we'd settled our differences.'

'With sex? I think not.' The white shirt he was wearing gleamed in a sudden shaft of sunlight. Impressive shoulders lifted in a dismissive shrug. 'I admit that at first I found your unexpected response to me astonishing, and, being a normal male, I delighted in your sexual generosity. But that was the froth, was it not? It is what's beneath the surface that interests me.'

Male lust—was this Roman's way of warning her that mere lust was what the last five weeks had been about? Cassie pondered miserably. She was a hundred per cent thankful that she hadn't let herself hope that he was learning to love her. Well, she hadn't, not really.

She didn't know what he wanted to hear her say, but at least he was giving her a little breathing space as he bent over the coffee tray on the low table, pouring from the silver pot, sugaring hers.

Lost in disquieting thoughts, unprepared for his

next question, she gave a shocked gasp as he asked levelly, 'Tell me, did you marry me for money?'

'What put that in your head?' she demanded when she could get her mouth to frame the words. 'So I'm a gold-digger now, as well as a slut!'

'It was suggested. Before our marriage.'

'Who by?' she spluttered hotly. 'One of your aunts, at a guess neither of them liked me!'

'I refused to believe it at the time,' he stated, as if she hadn't spoken. 'You were sweet, unspoiled; you didn't demand designer dresses or fancy jewels—the exact opposite of the society creatures I was used to having pushed under my nose. I had a hard enough time persuading you to let me buy your wedding dress and a suitable trousseau. Do you remember?'

Of course she remembered! He'd already discharged those of her father's debts that the sale of the house hadn't covered, and she hadn't wanted to be a further drain on him, even if he could well afford it.

She and Roy hadn't had much, but they could have pooled their resources. She could have kitted herself out with something his exalted family wouldn't have been too ashamed to see her wearing. But, no, even that amount of independence had been denied her!

'So what changed your mind?' she demanded furiously. If he wanted a fight, he could have one, even if the thought of being at odds with him tore her apart. 'Just when have I ever asked you for money?'

'Our wedding night, and the years that followed,'

he answered flatly. 'That changed my mind. You weren't interested in me as a husband, the father of your children. You were free of those debts you felt morally bound to discharge, and as soon as enough time had passed for you to be sure your brother was settled, drawing a healthy salary, you ran away, informing me that you'd be suing for divorce. I did wonder then if laying your hands on a hefty chunk of alimony had been your intention all along.'

He spread his hands expressively. 'What else was I to think? It was the only explanation that made any kind of sense. And of course,' he added with a dryness that sent a shaft of pain through her heart, 'the only reason you are here with me now, allowing me to use your body, comes down to money—stolen money.'

That he should think her a mercenary little gold-digger incensed her, but she clamped her soft lips together and forced back the blistering words she wanted to throw at him. He did have a point.

And now, if nothing else came of their time together, he had to hear her side of the story.

'I was *never* interested in your money,' she told him shortly. 'I was grateful when you offered to pay the outstanding debts—especially when you insisted that the sum involved represented no more to you than the loose change in your pocket. It meant that the remaining creditors didn't have to suffer—that Roy and I wouldn't have to live on the breadline, taking what jobs we could get to pay off the rest of the debts. So I guess, where that was concerned, I took the easy way out.

'But,' she emphasised firmly, 'if I hadn't been madly in love with you I would never have married you. Roy and I would have gone back to England and found some kind of work.' She gave him a fierce glare. If he was worried she might demand half his wretched estate, then she could put him out of his misery.

These last few weeks together had meant nothing to him, apart from fantastic sex—which was probably already beginning to bore him.

Been there, done that!

Otherwise why would he be trying to pick a fight, as good as accusing her of marrying him for his money?

'I have no intention of asking for a single peseta on our divorce!'

Why was she talking of divorce when for the past few weeks she'd been hoping that their marriage was mended? she groaned silently. The knot of misery behind her breastbone tightened, spread down into her stomach. She felt distinctly queasy. And she knew the answer to her own question. Of course she did. He wouldn't be throwing these vile accusations at her if he wanted their marriage to continue.

She stumbled to her feet. Everything was going wrong. When they'd wandered down through the gardens this morning everything had been touched with magic, and now—

A commanding hand closed around her wrist, halting her attempts at a dignified flight, edging her back onto the seat beside him.

'You said, and I quote, that you were ''madly in love'' with me when we married—I believe you are lying because I saw no evidence of it.'

It was an accusation; of course it was. But gently said. His fingers slid away from her wrist. Meaning she was free to go now he'd made his point? Meaning she could defend herself or not? That he was indifferent?

Any moment now she would burst into tears and humiliate herself. She could feel her lungs tremble, the pressure building up in her throat and behind her eyes. But she wasn't going to let it happen.

'You already know the truth, Roman. But I'll refresh your memory.' The words emerged more acidly than she'd intended. Deliberately, she pulled in a slow breath and softened her tone. 'When we married, I was an anachronism—a nineteenth-century woman living in the late twentieth. I was brought up by a domineering father, convent-educated, and had no experience of men—barring Father, Roy, and Cindy's brother, of course. Father thought females were put on this earth to be of use to males, and for no other reason.'

She took a gulp of hot coffee and replaced the cup with a clatter that threatened to break the saucer. 'When I left school at eighteen, he used the strength of his character, plus a large dollop of emotional blackmail, to convince me it was my duty to stay home and replace the part-time housekeeper he'd had to employ after Mum died. So when I met you, fell in love, my self-confidence was already about floor level. I'd fallen for you in a big way, but I knew you were way out of my league—wealthy, sophisticated, oozing with self-confidence. Everything I wasn't.'

But she'd married him anyway, because she'd been so in love with him it had hurt. She'd known he hadn't loved her, but she'd had his affection, and that had seemed very much better than having any other man's doting adoration.

'So I was the object of a rather belated juvenile infatuation.' He dismissed the love that had swamped her life with a tired smile. 'What went wrong? I did everything possible to see that you were comfortable, free from anxieties. Did I not try to ease you into your new role, your new lifestyle?'

'Ease?' she scorned. 'Leaving me with your mother and the aunts while you flew to England—?'

'It was for the best,' Roman said bluntly. 'I had to sort out the financial mess your father had left behind. Seeing the family home sold up, dealing with lawyers and creditors would have upset you unnecessarily. It was far more important that you got to know my family—your new family—better, acclimatised yourself, began arrangements for our wedding. So please don't try to accuse me of doing the wrong thing.'

'No? You acted exactly as my father would have done. Arrogantly,' she derided. 'And don't look so affronted! I may have been unable to voice any opinion three years ago, but I can now! *You* decided what was *best* for me without asking me what *I* wanted. I was so well conditioned that I never even thought of objecting. I did as I was told to do. And suffered for it. By the time we were married I had been thoroughly brainwashed. I was nowhere good enough for you.' She ticked off on her fingers, her voice tight with the memory of how humiliated she'd been made to feel. 'I was a foreigner, had no breeding, no money, no looks to speak of. You, naturally, were the cat's flaming whiskers! But you were being typically difficult, only marrying me to spite your family. You were highly sexed and experienced; I would very soon bore you. As soon as I'd given you the heir the estate needed, I'd be pensioned off, hidden away.'

His stillness following her heated, heartfelt outburst emanated tension. His eyes looked black and chillingly cold and his voice was low and dangerous as he asked, 'Who said these things?'

'Does it matter now?' She suddenly felt empty, drained, as if a light had gone out inside her. Recalling those earlier, desperate insecurities, and how they'd been fostered—no doubt with the intention of making her call the wedding off—had reminded her that they were indeed worlds apart, in culture, social standing, everything; the past few weeks had been nothing but a fantasy, a foolish dream.

'It matters. *Tell* me.'

As forceful as ever, she thought defeatedly. Well, what the heck? The women of his family hadn't earned her loyalty. He probably wouldn't believe her, anyway. He'd already accused her of marrying him for his money and of sleeping around during their separation. Calling her a liar as well wouldn't make a whole lot of difference.

'Your aunts,' she said shortly. 'To give her her due, your mother didn't take part in those intimate family discussions—she made her point by being rather chillingly polite.'

'Por Dios!' He shot to his feet, his wide shoulders rigid, the now bright sunlight accentuating the hard lines of his face. 'You were *my* choice—how dared they?' he growled.

Cassie shivered. Roman in a temper was a sight to behold, brooding eyes glowering, his hands bunched into savage-looking fists, tucked hard against the sides of his long lean legs.

But at least he hadn't called her a liar or accused her of impugning his exalted family. That thought took root, warmed her a little and then blossomed sweetly as he held out a hand to her, his voice soft when he said, 'Come here.'

She went. Well, wouldn't she always? His arms enfolded her and she leant her head against the angle of his shoulder, her heart lurching with the love she could no more banish than fly as he murmured, 'I begin to understand a little. By the time we got to our wedding night, what little confidence you'd had in yourself had been well and truly shattered. Faced with an experienced bridegroom who was supposedly prepared to hide you away and pension you off when you'd done your duty and provided the estate with an heir, you froze.

'Naturally, you didn't want to make love with me because it could lead to a pregnancy, and you didn't want to spend the rest of your life hidden away, closely chaperoned by the females who had already made you feel unwanted.'

He sounded almost smug, Cassie thought with a weak smile, and he was patting her back as if she were a lap dog in need of quieting. Never mind all those earlier unpleasant accusations, being held in his arms was having the usual effect. She couldn't fight the way her body now needed his so desperately.

'You should have told me all this at the time,' he chided gently. 'I could then have put your fears at rest.' A final comforting pat and his hands slid up to her shoulders, holding her away from him. 'But you always did seem tongue-tied around me, though you could chatter nineteen to the dozen with Cindy and her brother. It is a pity that you were so in awe of me. A few words of explanation would have made all the difference.'

Spoken like a true feudal overlord—a Spanish one at that. Lofty, patronising. He was back to treating her like a silly child without an atom of sense in her head or an opinion worth listening to.

At one time she would have meekly agreed with anything he said. She'd been brought up to believe that men were superior beings, that they always knew best.

Now she tipped back her head. 'Pregnant or not,

I was pretty effectively hidden away, wasn't I? Besides…' She gave him a radiant smile to soften the criticism. Being held by him was giving her the confidence she needed to delve into the past, display all her earlier failings. And maybe, in doing so, she could convince him she wasn't the promiscuous madam he'd accused her of being. 'I would never have married you if I'd thought I'd get put in a cupboard and locked away as soon as I gave birth to your heir. I knew you weren't cruel. It was…' She splayed her hands out against his chest, feeling his body heat, the heavy thud of his heartbeats beneath the soft white silk.

She wanted to move closer, very much closer, but that must wait. Already the closeness of him was making her tremble, making her heart race. 'I'd been told you were highly sexed, experienced,' she went on shakily, her breath coming raggedly. 'Your aunts were at pains to mention your affairs—models, dancers, all beautiful. Not for marrying, of course, but necessary for a young man, provided discretion was observed.'

She moved closer, fitting her body to his. She was so hungry for him; surely he knew that now? Surely he would understand?

She felt the tug of his breath just before he abruptly moved away, and anxiety peaked her brows as she said to his rigidly held back, 'Roman—I was a virgin, and, worse than that, I'd never had a proper boyfriend. I was afraid of disappointing you. The fear stuck in my head and I couldn't get it out. Do you understand? I kept thinking you'd compare me with those others—the beautiful, experienced ones who knew how to please a man.'

Why wouldn't he turn and look at her? Why?

'That first night fear of disappointing you made me freeze. I knew—knew—' She was beginning to stumble over her words; the ungiving rigidity of his spine and the way he was holding his head was turning her back into the tongue-tied wretch she had been before.

She gathered herself and said more firmly, 'I knew you didn't love me—you'd picked me because I'd make no demands on you that you wouldn't be happy to meet. But you did have affection for me, and I thought that would be enough. It wasn't, though,' she confirmed bleakly. 'If you'd loved me I'd have been able to tell you how I felt. If you'd loved me you wouldn't have been comparing me to those others; you would have taught me how to respond, taken away the fear. But I knew you weren't in love with me and I was too ashamed of myself to explain. I just pushed you away whenever you came near. I couldn't face more humiliation.'

Silence. Just the soft call of a dove, the lazy rustle of light wind in the trees. Her throat went tight. Was he turning her words over in his mind, testing them for validity?

'Say something,' she begged thickly. He did turn then, and what she saw in his eyes pushed her breath back into her lungs.

Regret? Sadness? How could she be sure?

'Then I must accept the larger part of the blame,' he said stiffly. She had never heard him sound quite so Spanish. He withdrew his hands from the side pockets of the tailored grey chinos he was wearing and glanced at his watch. His eyes were blank as he imparted coolly, 'When you left me my first instinct was to get over to England and drag you back.'

He was speaking slowly, that sexy accent more marked than usual, as if he were carefully picking his words. Cassie couldn't believe he hadn't been only too happy to see the back of his unsatisfactory wife.

'Why would you have wanted to do that?'

He acknowledged the incredulity of her tone with a slight dip of his dark, breathtakingly handsome head. 'Why? Because you were mine.'

And Roman Fernandez didn't relinquish his possessions easily—not even when they were worthless, she acknowledged mutely. 'So why didn't you follow me?'

Would she have returned to Spain with him? Perhaps. During those first few weeks back in England she'd been a mess. She had destroyed her marriage before it had started. She had loathed herself. If he had come for her, demanding her return, she would have gone, hoping that by some miracle things would improve.

But he hadn't come—had made no attempt to contact her—and she'd known she was on her own, had to make a life for herself.

'I changed my mind.' Another restless glance at

his watch. He seemed to be avoiding her eyes, as if he again wished to distance himself from her. 'You were, to put it mildly, very immature. Not in a giggly, schoolgirl way—that would never have attracted me to you—but lacking in a sense of who you were. Introverted and insecure. I believed that having to stand on your own two feet for a while—be entirely responsible for your own well-being, without a father or a husband to tell you what to do—would allow you to grow up.'

If his eyes were suddenly hard, his voice was even more so, 'And I was right. You grew up with a vengeance, *mi esposa*. Certainly, you have no more fear of sex. I have ample evidence of that. The only thing I do not know—or wish to know—is who tutored you so thoroughly.'

CHAPTER NINE

'ROMAN!'

But he was already walking rapidly away, striding along the winding path that led back towards the house, his feet brushing the bordering lavender plants, releasing the sweetly astringent perfume into the sparkling air. If he'd heard her anguished cry he gave no sign of it.

Casting an agitated glance at the coffee tray, Cassie decided to come back for it later. It seemed pretty hopeless, but she had to make another attempt to convince him that no way had she been sleeping around during their year apart. He was the only man she had made love with, or wanted to be with.

She caught up with him as he entered the courtyard through the arched doorway in the stone wall. Her heart was pounding and she knew her face had turned a fiery, anxious red.

'Roman—wait!'

In complete contrast he was cool, composed. She had never seen him look so solemn. One dark brow lifted slightly in silent enquiry as he glanced down into her troubled features.

'I want to talk—and I want you to listen.' Her tongue felt too big for her mouth. Would she ever be able to make him believe she hadn't been tutored in the art of pleasing a man in bed by a string of experts? The subject had obviously been troubling him for the last five weeks and now he couldn't get it out of his head.

'The talking has been done, *querida*,' he intoned with a bleak finality that cut deep into her soul, his beautiful smoky eyes devoid of all expression. 'It was cathartic but necessary, you understand. The last few weeks have been—' wide shoulders drifted eloquently upwards '—what can I say? A dream. But always one must wake and face reality. We had to discover why our marriage had been such…' He paused, as if searching for a word that wouldn't be too hurtful. 'So uncomfortable. Now—' again that infuriating, frustrating glance at his watch '—I'm expected in Seville for a business meeting later this morning. I shall be away for two days. We will talk again on my return. Not of the past, but of the future.'

Take me with you! she wanted to plead. But didn't. She felt as if she'd been hit with a brick. He had spoken as if he had every intention of giving her the divorce she'd asked for a year ago and the old pattern was repeating itself. Business trips taking him away for longer and longer periods. Always leaving her behind.

Yet it *had* been different this time, she told herself wildly. This time their coming together had been gloriously successful; they'd been like two halves of a whole, blissfully inseparable. Did that, in the end, count for nothing?

As the cool silence of the house swallowed him, she sank onto a stone bench in the courtyard and listened to the cool music of the fountain, breathing the scent of the sweetly perfumed oleanders into labouring lungs, doing her very best to calm down. A divorce was the very last thing she wanted. She loved him so much.

He'd asked questions and she'd answered them as honestly as she knew how. His curiosity had been satisfied and he now knew why she had been forced to leave him, why their marriage had been such a failure to begin with.

That his conclusions were the wrong ones simply wouldn't occur to him. The past lived. The mistakes hadn't been erased, and a new and equally devastating misconception—that she'd been sleeping with other men—had been born. His whole attitude told her that he was set on continuing what she had started—the ending of their marriage.

The mental pain was so overwhelming she didn't know how she was ever going to be able to cope with it. And when, minutes later, he stood over her, she looked at him blankly, the sparkle blanketed from her eyes beneath the weight of her misery.

He looked cool and fresh, and she could smell the tangy cologne he always wore, a scent that would live in her memory for ever. His car keys were in one hand, a slim overnight case in the other.

He said levelly, 'I've recalled Manuel and Teresa;

they should be here within the hour. After our less than wholehearted attention, the house and the garden need some supervision,' he explained, dauntingly practical and chillingly cool.

Cassie shivered. So the second honeymoon was well and truly over. Her heart was hurting and her mind felt as if someone had ripped it apart and flung the ragged pieces to the four winds. Useless to ask him to listen to what she wanted to say while she was in this state. He wouldn't welcome near-hysterical protestations of innocence or tearful pleas to take her back on a permanent basis.

Besides, she didn't want to come over as a gibbering wreck. She needed time to wind down, gather some control and come to terms with what had happened this morning. His absence would at least give her that.

'Fine.' She returned his glance as coolly as she could manage and turned away before he could see the tears that were brimming in her eyes. 'See you in two days. Take care.'

Ten minutes later Cassie was dressed in a cool cotton shift dress in clear lemon-yellow, comfy flat sandals with a floppy-brimmed straw sun hat covering her coiled-back hair. No way was she going to be here when the housekeeper and her gardener husband returned to take up their duties.

She needed to be on her own, away from the house where everything was a bittersweet reminder of Roman. She needed to think, to get herself together, face what looked like being the final breakdown of her marriage. She also had to discover whether there was any truth in what she was beginning to believe...

Out in the shade of the narrow street that wound down into the heart of the old town she gave a small sigh of relief, feeling marginally more in control of her emotions. Teresa, as she remembered the short but heftily built woman, was a bit of a martinet, ruling the seeming army of staff with a rod of iron, making sure *el patrón*'s slightest wish was anticipated, treating the unsuitable new bride with decidedly sniffy disdain.

That, Cassie decided, she could do without right now!

Her first port of call was the chemist in the main square, and as she tucked the package into the bottom of the straw bag that teamed with her hat and stepped out into the sizzling sunlight she gave a slight shiver.

Soon she would know, one way or the other.

Had she conceived Roman's child? Or had her periods gone back to being all over the place because she'd forgotten to take the pill on that first fateful, never-to-be-forgotten night?

But she wouldn't think about that right now, not when there was so much other stuff going on inside her head. She had taken the day to get her mind straightened out, not add to the muddle. She would think about the consequences of having conceived Roman's child when and if she knew for sure she had.

Nevertheless, she felt distinctly shaky inside as she

headed for one of the pavement cafés and sank down at a table beneath the shade of a huge striped umbrella. She ordered freshly squeezed orange juice with lots of ice and tried to make her mind a blank, watching the life of the ancient Spanish town pass by.

But it didn't work. Her mind was filled with one thought alone: Roman's child—how she would love it!

It was almost dusk when she returned to the great stone house that dominated the narrow street. Her hair had come adrift from the neat coil and tumbled riotously around her shoulders and the wind from the sea had whipped away her straw hat as she'd walked on the long sandy beach. She felt hot and sticky and her feet hurt.

But it had been worth it. Her mind had gradually cleared and she felt a million times more hopeful than when she had set out. Hopeful enough to greet Teresa with a confident smile as she entered the huge, marble paved hall and found the housekeeper waiting.

'Good evening, Teresa. I hope you and your husband have settled back in.' A skeleton staff now, where once there had been an army. Had Roman refused to make use of this lovely place since their disastrous first honeymoon?

'*Señora.*' If anything, the housekeeper's impressive girth had much increased since Cassie had last seen her, and her features were, as ever, stony with disapproval. 'You wish for supper?'

Cassie permitted herself a tiny wry smile at the martyred tone. Three years ago she would have shaken her head and scuttled away, not wanting to be a nuisance. Now she said pleasantly, 'Please. Something light in the small *sala* in one hour. I need to shower and change.'

And do that test. Find out for sure if what she hoped with all her heart was true or just wishful thinking.

'*Sí, señora*. In one hour.' Was there a look of grudging approval in the older woman's small black eyes? Cassie couldn't be sure until the housekeeper said, a bit stiffly but nevertheless said, 'Welcome home. It has been too long,' and waddled away.

Sucking in a breath of pleased surprise Cassie flew up the great, curving staircase. Everything was going to be all right—it had to be! Teresa's acceptance of her had to be an omen. Didn't it?

But that was a minor thing. What really counted was the way she'd been able to go over the talk she and Roman had had this morning, rationally and calmly, picking up clues.

He had mentioned that he'd been attracted to her, that he hadn't wanted her to leave him, but had let her go for her own sake, allowing her time to become an adult woman who could stand on her own feet. And there had been no mistaking his anger when she'd confessed that his aunts had robbed her of what little self-confidence she'd had.

On his return they'd talk again. He had promised her that. Talk of the future. Their future together? The past had been dealt with, a necessary exercise but leaving him with that misconception over who else she'd been sleeping with.

She would try again to put that right. On that she was utterly determined.

Once that was out of the way—she permitted herself a dreamy, pleasurable sigh—there'd be no more pussy-footing around the subject. She'd come right out with it and ask him if he was willing to give their marriage a second chance.

She wanted to stay married to him. She needed him; it felt as if her whole life depended on it.

An hour later she floated down the stairs. She felt as if her feet were treading on air. She was carrying Roman's child within her body. She had never felt more blessed.

Today. If he kept to his word, Roman would be back today. Some time today.

Cassie paced the bedroom floor restlessly, too wound up with a mixture of excitement and apprehension to even try to relax. And it was only midday. It could be hours before he returned.

Oh, how she longed to see him again, to kiss him and touch him. To hold him close, will him to love her, just a little. A little would do for starters.

Hours of suspense, hours of waiting to discover whether she could finally make him believe that her supposed promiscuity was only in his mind, whether he'd be willing to take their marriage forward into the future.

And it was so hot. Airless. They were in for a storm, Manuel had said as she'd been helping him in the garden this morning—well, pottering, really, anything to pass the time until Roman's return. But she'd felt dizzy with the heat, the lack of sleep and lack of food. Her appetite had disappeared under the welter of growing emotions.

She'd already taken two cool showers. She was only wearing a half-cup white lace bra and the briefest of matching panties and she was still burning up with the oppressive heat.

Soon she'd have to dress. He might make it back by lunchtime. She wanted to be ready and waiting, looking her best. But what to wear?

She padded barefoot to the huge hanging cupboards and finally reached out a gossamer-fine floaty number patterned in soft swirls of cool blues and green. Her hands were shaking.

'Cass.'

The sound of his voice in the hot, sultry silence of the room startled her witless. She turned to face him, the light-as-air dress drifting from her fingers, pooling at her feet. She couldn't speak, not if her life had depended on it. Her heart was pounding roughly against her breastbone and her throat muscles had gone into spasm.

He was here, and now it was time to do what she'd promised herself. She'd get everything out into the open, tell him the truth—tell him she loved him and wanted to spend the rest of her life with him.

She wouldn't tell him about the baby, though. Not yet. He might look on it as emotional blackmail. He had to freely agree to keep their marriage going because he wanted it that way, not because he felt it was an inescapable duty.

Tentatively, she moistened her dry-as-dust lips and tried to swallow. Her throat still wouldn't work.

As soon as she could speak coherently, she would know whether he wanted her or not. Permanently. Her head began to spin dizzily as she watched him avidly. Scrub 'permanently', for the moment—she could tell he wanted her right now, if only for a brief hour of unreasoning rapture.

He'd closed the door behind him and had walked a couple of paces into the room. He looked tired. The lines of strain made his features harsher, but the dark smudges around his eyes didn't detract from the slow, simmering, brooding gaze that lingered over every lush curve of her scantily clad body.

Flesh burning, her stomach quivering, she instinctively raised her hands to him in mute supplication. He'd removed his jacket, dragged off his tie, dropping them on the floor, his eyes still riveted to her, a dull flush stealing over his hard cheekbones.

Slowly, his eyes lifted to hers, locking. She felt dizzy with longing, with needing him. Desperate. Her heart lurched. He wanted her, too—now. She knew he did. The truthful little speech she'd run over and over in her head evaporated in the sizzling heat of mutual desire.

With a tiny moan she ran towards him, her arms outstretched. Words were superfluous. What was needed was a whole lot of the sensuous lovemaking that they'd become so demonstrably good at. Together.

CHAPTER TEN

HIS eyes had turned to deepest smouldering silver, Cassie noted with a delirious kick of her heart as she impulsively wound her arms around his neck and wriggled her nearly naked body as close to his as she could possibly get.

She knew there were things she had to say to him, things she should tell him—plus the million-dollar question that had to be asked. But not now, not just yet… She needed this… Needed to feel close to him…

Her fingers tangled in the hair at his nape. It was damp with perspiration, the rest of it soft and ruffled, falling over his forehead in dark wayward strands, touching the clenched black bar of his brows.

His eyes were closed now, his mouth compressed. Cassie slid her hands down the strong column of his neck, splaying her fingers out over the intimidating width of his shoulders. He made no move to hold her but she knew he wanted to, that at any moment the power of her love for him would break through his resistance.

Her tingling breasts were pressed against the broad span of his chest and she could feel the heavy, rapid beat of his heart and the firm leap of his arousal against the yielding softness of her bare tummy, and that told her all she needed to know.

'I missed you,' she said, her voice thick with longing. She knew he wanted her, so why didn't he hold her? Why was he holding back, denying himself the reaffirmation of her love?

Her heart missing a beat, she slipped his shirt buttons from their moorings and slid her hands beneath the soft fabric, her palms moving frantically over the hot satin of his skin.

'So it would seem.' His voice was gritty, his eyes opening at last to spear her with silver intensity. 'As I've already said, the change in your attitude to sex is mind-blowing.'

'Don't!' She dropped her bright head, burrowing her face into his tautly muscled chest. 'This isn't just about sex,' she promised, the frenzied need to have him believe her making her slur her words. 'I know what you think of me, but don't! You mustn't—it simply isn't true!'

Any hope of coherency left her then; the warmth of his skin was burning her, the tangy, clean male scent of him drugging her senses. The power he had over her knocked her senseless, made her dizzy with a need that would never go away.

With a tiny smothered groan she pressed her mouth to his flat male nipple, tasting him recklessly, and dragged her hands over the hard arch of his rib-cage and down over the tight muscles of his stomach and heard him pull air between his teeth just before he muttered, 'So be it!' and enfolded her, one hand pressing against the small of her back, pulling her closer into the thrusting power of him, the other tangling in the wild fall of her hair, dragging her head back.

'Por Dios!' The harsh words cut through the thick sultry silence as his mouth took hers with a raw passion that was almost savage. Cassie gave a cry of willing, exultant capitulation as his sensual mouth moulded hers, his tongue clashing with hers as he sought her inner sweetness.

Wild fingers tangled in the soft rich darkness of his hair, anchoring his head, holding him to her as if she would never let him go. And she wouldn't, not if she could help it. That was her last clear thought as his thighs thrust between the quivering shakiness of hers and he edged her back towards the bed.

Together they fell onto the soft silk that covered the deep mattress and he rolled over and pinned her beneath his weight, finding the front fastening of her bra with impatient fingers, releasing the lush fullness of her breasts to the urgency of his hungry hands.

Only then did he break the demand of his kiss, dipping his dark head to suckle her, and Cassie gasped out loud, flinging her arms above her head in wild and wanton abandon, his for the taking, now and always.

And then the phone rang.

It was the internal house phone. It sat on a small table beneath one of the tall windows. Roman's lithe body stiffened and Cassie wrapped her arms around his neck and held him. 'Ignore it,' she breathed raggedly.

But Roman reached for her clasped hands and released himself, swung his long legs over the side of the bed, dragged in a long shuddering breath then stalked across to the strident instrument.

Would he come back to her? Cassie wondered unhappily. His face in profile looked remote. Guarded. All passion gone. She knew—who better?—that he'd returned as full of reservations as he'd been when he'd left two days ago—but she'd broken through his defences, hadn't she? And in the sweet, lazy aftermath of loving she would have told him what he needed to know, pleaded with him if necessary to give her another chance to make their marriage work.

She watched him, her eyes willing him to come back to her. After listening in silence he gave a brief response in Spanish and replaced the receiver. Turning, he hitched his shirt from the waistband of his trousers, his dark features as rigid as stone, his eyes slightly hooded, impaling her as he let the shirt drop to the floor.

Her heart leapt.

Whatever the call had been about, it hadn't spoiled things. He was coming back to her. He was! Smiling softly, her heart in her eyes, she held out loving arms to him as he reached for the buckle of his belt.

'Teresa tells me my mother has just arrived. She is to lunch with us. Go down to her while I shower and change,' he instructed flatly. 'Tell her I will be ten minutes, no more.'

Her heart sank.

Doña Elvira couldn't have arrived at a worse moment, Cassie thought wretchedly as she watched him turn and walk to the bathroom. Naked now, the lines of his body long and fluid. Perfect. There was a lump in her throat. No word of regret, no soft apology. Nothing. Just a flatly delivered instruction, a long level look that withered her soul.

Was that his way of showing her that he was a mere man after all, pushed by his hormones into accepting what had been so flagrantly offered—despite his reservations?

No. She wouldn't let herself believe that.

There was more than mere lust between them; she knew there was. Briskly, hanging on to that thought, she refastened the lacy bra and swung off the rumpled bed. Their five-week-long idyll told her there was more, much more. Hadn't she got to know the more relaxed side of the man she'd married—the side that was funny, deeply charming, sexy yet tender, sometimes impossibly arrogant but always endlessly endearing?

He was suffering from the effects of plain, old-fashioned sexual frustration. Just as she was. It was perfectly simple, she told herself firmly.

The filmy, flirty, ultra-feminine dress wasn't something she would have normally chosen to wear for lunch with her starchy, ultra-conservative mother-in-law, she thought light-headedly as she slipped it over her head and pulled up the fine side zipper. But these days she dressed to please Roman—she didn't stick to things she hoped her in-laws would deem suitable.

And because she knew her husband's eyes would openly admire the way the narrow seam at the top of the bodice left her lightly tanned arms and most of her shoulders bare, the neckline dipping into a tantalising V, the soft gauzy fabric moulding her breasts and nipping in at her waist to fall with a floaty fullness to just below her knees, the dress pleased her, too.

As usual, Doña Elvira was dressed in black, relieved slightly by just a touch of white silk at her throat. Cassie found her in the small *sala*, where Teresa had set the circular table with the very best china, glass and heavy antique silver.

Meeting the steady, cool assessment of a pair of dark eyes, Cassie gave a small smile and said, 'How nice to see you,' and knew she didn't mean it at all. She hoped this was to be a flying visit only, but she couldn't ask and appear impossibly rude.

'Roman apologises,' Cassie added lightly. 'He's only just back from some business or other in Seville. He'll be a few more minutes and then Teresa will give us lunch.'

'Sanlucar suits you,' the older woman announced from the seat in the window that overlooked the sun-baked terrace, the great Guadalquivir river and the vast Coto Doñana nature reserve. 'I find you—' a pale, long-fingered hand moved questingly '—much improved.'

Coming from one of her severest critics, Cassie

had to take that as a compliment. She spread her hands, 'I find the town, this house, quite beautiful. Who could not be happy here?'

'You were not. Before.'

The words dropped like heavy stones into a deep, dark pool and Cassie knew why the older woman had come here. Curiosity. Uneasy suspicions. She wanted to judge for herself whether the supposed reconciliation was real or just a blind to stop her and her sisters pressing Roman to go ahead with the divorce and marry someone they found acceptable—with Delfina being the obvious and prime candidate.

What would be the other woman's reaction if Cassie told her she was already expecting her son's child?

Suddenly, a wave of compassionate understanding engulfed her. Already she felt fiercely protective of the tiny new life she was carrying inside her. Of course Doña Elvira wanted the best for her son. What mother wouldn't? And three years ago Cassie hadn't been the best.

But she had changed, become more self-confident, able to physically express her love for her husband. This time, if Roman wanted it, the marriage would work.

So she said, gently reassuring, 'No, back then there were problems, mainly of my own making.'

'And they've been resolved?' The tone, as always, was carefully polite, but the cool dark eyes had narrowed watchfully. 'I want only happiness for my son, you understand?'

'I believe so. I believe I could make him happy,' Cassie said, with a sudden and unwelcome hollow feeling inside her.

Some problems had been swept away but others had crowded in to take their place. But it was up to her to resolve that, wasn't it?

She forced herself into a more optimistic frame of mind but couldn't stop her nerves from jangling when Roman said from behind her, 'So what brings you here, *Madre*? So far as I know, you haven't set foot inside this house for fifteen years. Has Cassandra given you something to drink? No? Then let me repair the omission.'

Cool, urbane, totally controlled—who would have thought that ten minutes ago he had succumbed to the wild call of the flesh, against all his obvious mental reservations, had been on the point of making wild, passionate love to her? Cassie thought as she sank on to the padded seat in the deep window embrasure.

Watching him as he poured pale Manzanilla into three tulip glasses, her heart twisted over with regret. Wearing white—beautifully tailored narrow trousers and a silk shirt that fell in long graceful folds from his impressive shoulders—he looked as gorgeous and as remote as a man could get.

Why hadn't she said those things she'd been mentally rehearsing over the last two days the moment he'd walked into the bedroom they shared—instead of flinging herself at him like the sex-mad creature he believed her to have become?

Because she loved him so much, had missed him so badly, she answered herself as he handed her a glass, looking carefully at some point over her left shoulder yet somehow avoiding any contact of their fingers. Her instincts had taken over and her instincts had been wrong. Far better that their short time alone had been occupied in putting him straight.

But she hadn't known that her mother-in-law was about to descend on them, and that lady was saying, her cool features warm now as she spoke to her son, 'True, I haven't been here since your father died. I prefer to keep my memories intact. Remember the summers we spent here—you, your father and I? The horse races on the river beach you both took part in? With me shouting your names and urging you on as loudly as any farmhand? The picnics, the long treks through the Coto Doñana? How happy we were in those days! After he died it could never be the same.'

Her smile faded. She took a sip of her Manzanilla and set the glass down on the small table at her side. 'Perhaps when you give me grandchildren I will be able to spend more happy summers here.'

Here we go again, Cassie thought as she surreptitiously emptied her own drink into the nearest pot plant. Emotional blackmail. She wasn't the only one who'd been subjected to it. Roman obviously had, ever since he'd reached marriageable age.

Thankfully, Teresa arrived, moving deftly around despite her bulk, laying dishes on the table. Doña Elvira said less mournfully, 'I am visiting the house in Jerez now that the decorators have finished. I want to make sure all is exactly as it should be. Tomás is driving me; Teresa is looking after him. I thought I would make this diversion to bring you the news before Tomás and I retrace ourselves to Jerez.'

She stood up, leading the way to the table, and Roman, an indulgent smile on his face for the difficulties his mother sometimes had with the English language, asked, 'And that is?'

Cassie followed, hoping her mother-in-law's news didn't involve Roy and some further misdeed; she felt more miserable by the minute, because Roman had barely looked at her since he'd entered the room—and when he had his expression had been cold.

'I hope it won't come as too much of a shock,' Doña Elvira said as she helped herself generously to swordfish with a luscious prawn and clam sauce, adding a portion of Teresa's roast red pepper and tomato salad. 'I know how close the two of you are—were—and I didn't want you to hear of it through the newspapers. Delfina is engaged to be married.'

'Now why should that shock me?' He spoke softly, as if he were humouring a child. But Cassie had seen the flicker of relief cross his face.

His ploy had paid off. Darling Delfina was off his back. But what had started off as a tactical manoeuvre, with her playing the part of a returning loving wife in exchange for Roy's freedom from prosecution, had turned into something wonderful. A marriage that could truly work. Surely to God it had?

Her hands were knotted together in her lap, her knuckles white. She barely heard Doña Elvira's, 'Delfina's such a lovely girl. Your aunts and I, we always hoped—'

'I know what you hoped,' Roman cut in sardonically, helping himself to a chunk of crusty bread to mop up the delicious sauce. 'And I think you know I won't tolerate any more meddling. Don't even think about dredging up some other suitable, shallow creature to dangle in front of my nose now Delfina's out of the frame. I forbid it.'

Cassie's stomach twisted alarmingly. Her throat went tight. Why didn't he remind his mother that he already had a wife? Sitting right here! Why were they both ignoring her? Doña Elvira quite naturally, probably because she believed Cassie wasn't worth noticing, and Roman studiedly, as if he didn't want to be reminded that she existed.

Well, she *did* exist—she *would* be noticed! She unstuck her tongue from the roof of her mouth and asked firmly, 'So, who is the lucky man?'

A heartbeat of silence, then Doña Elvira said lightly, 'You wouldn't know him.' She turned to her son. 'Rodrigo Talavera. They are to be married in Brazil, where most of his family is. They leave in a few days; her mother goes with her, naturally.'

'He's old enough to be her father.'

Roman looked faintly amused, the smile that played around the corner of his mouth deepening as his mother defended, 'But wealthy. He will dote on her and spoil her thoroughly. She will be happy. And you, Cassandra, you are not eating?'

Suddenly, the attention was on Cassie. She felt her face go hot.

'I'm not really hungry,' she said truthfully. How could she eat a thing when her stomach was tied in squirming knots? She wanted the meal over and done with, her mother-in-law out of the way so that she could talk to Roman, really talk to him, tell him what was in her heart and discover what was in his.

'Is it Spain that robs you of your appetite? It is obvious that you ate well when you were in your own country.' Dark eyes pointedly raked the fullness of the breasts emphasised by the clinging bodice, the smoothly rounded arms. 'You were happier back in your own country, I think?'

The implication being she should go right back there, Cassie thought on a flash of temper. She fingered the stem of her water glass, looking at Roman from beneath her lashes, and said with a trace of defiance, 'I've been wonderfully happy here and, yes, if the record needs straightening, I was happy back in England, too.'

She wasn't going to pull any punches. Roman, in particular, needed to know what had happened to her. He hadn't really asked, and she'd been too bound up in the enchantment of getting to know him physically, in the strong rebirth of her love for him, to tell him.

Aware of his brooding attention, she said, 'At the risk of sounding fanciful, I discovered who I was during my year away. I'd never had to be responsible for myself; all decisions had been made for me—by my father, my husband, my in-laws.'

She heard Doña Elvira's intake of breath and ignored it. 'For the first time in my life I was responsible for myself. It was scary at first, but exhilarating. I headed for my home town because I knew it, had friends there.' She met Roman's thoughtful eyes head-on. 'I found a cheap bed-sit, walked into a waitressing job, enrolled in a couple of evening classes—upholstery and furniture restoration—and made a few new friends. I was in charge of my own life, my own well-being and making a reasonable fist of it.

'Then, six weeks or so later, Cindy offered me a job helping her run the boutique. One of the perks was the rent-free flat above it. I took it—of course I did. It was a far better proposition than what I was doing, where I was living.' She took a breath.

'But most important of all, it was *my* decision. Nobody was telling me what to do and how to do it. Nobody was making me feel inferior and pretty damn useless. And at last I had a home I could call my own. Could decorate it and furnish it just as I wanted to—mainly cheap second-hand stuff—and that's where the evening classes came in useful.'

No need to say that Guy had helped her trawl the auction rooms, had wielded a paintbrush pretty niftily. No need to put suspicions in Roman's mind that had no right to be there.

No need to mention how very much she'd missed

her arrogant Spanish husband, or how hard she'd tried not to, how hard she'd tried to put the past behind her. Not now, not while she could feel Doña Elvira's eyes on her, absorbing every word she said. Later, when they were alone, she would tell him that missing him had been the hardest part of all.

'So.' She tugged in a breath. 'In a nutshell, I finally grew up. Learned to stand on my own two feet, got some self-respect. Now—' she glanced around the table. '—we appear to have finished. Shall I ask Teresa for coffee?' She looked at her mother-in-law and caught the slightly astonished gleam of admiration in the older woman's eyes as she proffered, 'Or shall I ask her to tell Tomás to bring the car round? You must be eager to settle into the newly decorated house. If you're staying there for more than a day or two, maybe Roman and I will descend on you for a tour of inspection.'

Half an hour later, after seeing Doña Elvira off—very upright and dignified in the back of the ancient Daimler that was kept for ferrying his elderly relatives around—Roman said, 'Among other things, you've learned how to handle her.'

It was the 'other things' that had to be sorted out, Cassie thought, following him back inside into the relatively cool, echoing dimness of the massive hall.

Would he believe her when she insisted she hadn't spent that year away sleeping around, learning by experience? He hadn't so far, but that didn't mean she wasn't going to try again.

Would he truly understand that, apart from his monumental Spanish pride being damaged by having a runaway wife, that year had been necessary? He'd said she'd needed to grow up, but more than that, she had needed to find out who she was, what she was capable of—had needed to find the self-respect that had been missing for most of her life.

Roman looked so sombre. She had her misgivings, and they deepened when he turned to face her, his features shadowed and stark in the cool dim light.

'I want you to know that I made a bad mistake when I blackmailed you into staying with me, sleeping with me. I've thought hard about this over the past few days. What I did was unworthy, dishonourable. Unforgivable.' He pushed his hands into his trouser pockets, his mouth a straight hard line, his eyes dark and unreadable.

A current of fear arced through her. What was going on here? Was this some kind of coded message? Would she ever be able to breach those vast, remote defences of his? Could her words alone touch him? He had retreated to a place where she couldn't reach him, just as he had done when he'd decided she was frigid and had ceased to bother with her.

At least she could try! 'You don't have to apologise for anything,' she said quickly.

'I'm not. Haven't I already said that what I did was unforgivable? So,' he went on in a flat monotone, 'you are free to go now. I release you from our bargain. And before you start worrying about that brother of yours—who should be old enough to look after himself—if he keeps his nose clean, works hard, he can enjoy a good position on the *finca*.'

Dismissed. Just like that! These few weeks had meant nothing to him. A woman to sleep with, that was all she'd been to him, and now she'd served her purpose she could go.

Anger sparked in her eyes. 'Let me get this straight—Delfina's safely engaged and due to leave the country in a day or two, and,' she added for good measure, 'you've satisfied your curiosity about my present attitude to sex, so I can leave!'

She hadn't known she could feel this betrayed, so surplus to requirements. Or so blisteringly angry! At least anger was keeping the hurt away—for the moment.

He seemed to be having a problem with her anger, judging by the frowning bar of his brows. And then he tilted his head just slightly. 'If that's how you want to see it. I am merely explaining you are free to go.'

Or stay? But he hadn't mentioned anything about her staying. And she could tell by the closed-in look on his face that her presence was suddenly distasteful to him. But she'd give him one last chance; she owed that to herself and to their unborn child.

'What about the divorce?' she asked, and wished she hadn't sounded quite so humble. She prayed he'd say he didn't want that to happen, prayed so hard her heart hurt.

'If that's what you want,' Roman conceded slowly. His minimal shrug looked decidedly dismissive. 'But in the meantime I'll make you a generous allowance. I know, because you've told me—' his mouth curved bitterly, '—that you're quite capable of looking after yourself, but the job and the flat you had have gone. For that I take full responsibility—and I don't like the idea of you having to wait on tables, or serve behind some seedy bar because you're unqualified for anything better, living on a low wage in some squalid room.'

It was like a slap in the face. A hard slap. Holding herself together was going to be tough. She lifted her chin and said staunchly, 'Then I'll pack. I'll stay overnight in Seville and catch the first available flight back to England.'

She headed for the stairs, but his harsh voice halted her. 'Tell me when you're ready and I'll drive you.'

She didn't turn. She couldn't. Why let him see the tears that were now flowing unstoppably? She swallowed hard. 'Thanks but I'd much prefer Manuel's company. Perhaps you could tell him I'll be ready to leave in twenty minutes.'

CHAPTER ELEVEN

ROMAN dismounted and handed the reins of his sweat-lathered horse to the groom who came hurrying from the stable block to meet him. Beneath the straight brim of his black, dust-covered Cordoban hat his features were scored with harsh lines.

The sun was setting, casting long shadows over the sweeping upland valley; a pair of eagles planed overhead in a cloudless sky that was deepening to amethyst.

His boots rang on the cobbles of the yard as he strode towards the main house, slapping the dust from the sleeves of his heavy-duty canvas jacket.

Nothing had worked during the month since Cassie had left. Not a damn thing. Not the long hours of unremitting physical hard work here on the estate, the endless cold showers, stern and lengthy lectures to himself on the advisability of cutting his losses, getting on with his life, etc, etc.

Something had died inside him when she'd walked out of their marriage for the second time. Only his ingrained pride had stopped him from going after her, up the sweeping staircase he never wanted to have to see again in the whole of his life, begging her to forgive him, pleading with her to stay.

The first time she'd left him had been hard. This time it was a whole lot tougher.

He'd given her the opportunity to leave, and against all his hopes she'd taken it. But what else, with honour, could he have done? To have put pressure on her to stay with him would have been unthinkable, given what he'd already done to her.

Initially, the idea of forcing her to stay with him had seemed logical. It would have given them the chance to get to know each other all over again, allow him to prove that he could be good husband material. Not the remote figure he'd turned into during the first two years of their marriage, too insensitive, or too damn proud to ask why she flinched and looked at him with frightened eyes whenever he came near her.

But later the idea of blackmail had left a sour taste in his mouth. He'd come to despise himself for using her natural concern for her brother against her. And, yes, if he was honest with himself, jealousy had come into it. Where and how had she learned to be so sexually responsive? And who with?

Now that side of it didn't seem to matter. Provided it was in the past.

As usual, Asunción had left a cold supper on a tray in his study. Food had been the last thing on his mind these past weeks.

And, thankfully, the aunts had joined his mother in Jerez for the Sherry Harvest that had been celebrated earlier this month. He could do without the presence of chattering females and he guessed the icy tongue-lashing he'd doled out on the subject of their less than helpful treatment of Cass in the past had sent them scuttling for cover, staying at the house in Jerez for much longer than usual, hoping that time would improve his temper.

Time wouldn't alter a thing; he knew that. Only his wife's love could make him feel whole again.

Roy, too, had moved out to one of the self-contained *cabañas* on the estate, so that meant he was alone here and no one but himself had to suffer from his perpetual black mood.

If it weren't for his pride he might not have been alone. He might have had Cass. His wife. His adored wife. But he hadn't told her how beloved she was. He ground his teeth together, raging against himself. He'd been on the brink of it, willing himself to swallow his pride, tell her how he felt and put his future happiness in her hands—when two things had happened.

A sudden brain-boiling hatred for the man—or men—who had taught Cassie to enjoy sex, and an equally explosive reaction to the way he'd blackmailed her into agreeing to live with him.

Ignoring his supper, as he did more often than not, he tossed his hat onto a chair and reached for the phone.

Stiff-necked, arrogant pride.

It didn't warm his bed or fill his heart with joy. One thing was for sure: he had to see her one more time, swallow that wretched pride of his—go down on his knees if necessary and humbly ask if she would forget the idea of a divorce and spend the rest of her life with him. And if she would, he'd make sure she never regretted a single moment of their time together.

And if she didn't—well, he didn't want to think about that. But he'd be no worse off than he was now. What did loss of pride matter?

His face grimly determined, he punched in the numbers for Air Iberia.

Cassie stepped out of the bath and smothered her glowing body in the swamping towelling robe Guy had loaned her and felt marginally better.

The weather on this first day of October had turned wet and decidedly chilly, an unpleasant and unseasonal foretaste of winter. She'd got soaked to the skin as she'd walked back to the ground-floor flat from the antiquarian bookshop where she'd found part-time, temporary work.

Four days a week, from ten in the morning until four in the afternoon, Robert Greaves—the owner—had told her. The job would end in November, when his partner returned from visiting relatives in New Zealand.

It wasn't much but it was better than nothing and at least the pay packet meant she didn't have to dip into her savings account. Soon she would have to start looking for something else.

A sudden mental image of the cheque Roman had sent through Cindy flashed into her consciousness.

She blinked it rapidly away as she dragged a comb through her tangled wet hair.

As an allowance it had been more than generous. She wouldn't have had to find work to keep her and the baby growing inside her. But she hadn't even been tempted. She wanted nothing from him. He'd virtually accused her of marrying him in the first place for what she could get out of him, deliberately causing the breakdown of their relationship so that on their divorce she could take him to the cleaners.

Well, he could stuff his wretched money! She could manage without it!

'Send it straight back to him,' she'd instructed Cindy tersely, tearing the cheque to tiny pieces.

'Are you mad?' Cindy's blue eyes had gone wide. 'I don't know what went wrong this time—I've lost patience with the pair of you—but why scratch around for a living when Roman can afford to keep you in comfort?'

'Because I don't want his hand-outs.' She wanted his love, and because she knew she couldn't have it she was damned if she'd settle for anything less. Besides, regular contact, even if it was only through a monthly allowance cheque, would remind her of him, hamper her resolve to forget he'd ever existed.

'Then *you* return it,' Cindy had ordered, refusing to take the confetti-like scraps of paper. 'You do know his address! Besides, this not speaking to each other is childish. You could at least talk things over like rational human beings. Heaven knows, he can afford to keep you until you get back on your feet. Absolutely childish!' she'd repeated vehemently.

Perhaps. But the pain of what he had done to Cassie, using her body until he got bored then giving her her marching orders, was entirely adult and ferocious.

'You haven't told him where I am?' Cassie had asked, her eyes narrowing suspiciously.

'Nope. He didn't ask. When he phoned he just said he'd be sending a cheque once a month and would I see you got it.'

Yet another savage stab of pain. He wasn't interested in her whereabouts, what she was doing. For all he knew or cared, she could have emigrated to Australia!

Though why that should hurt when she'd already decided that she had no interest in him either, she couldn't fathom. She'd drawn a decisive line beneath her ill-fated marriage to Roman Fernandez—hadn't she?

Cassie slammed the door firmly on memories that had anything at all to do with Roman—something, she reflected uneasily, she was having to do several times a day. She put the hairbrush down on the dressing table and walked out of the tiny spare bedroom, tightening the belt of her robe around her waist.

It was almost five o'clock and Guy would be home in an hour, from the high street travel agency he managed, and since making use of his spare room she'd insisted on cooking supper. It was the least she could do.

She would put the remains of yesterday's casserole in the oven and then throw on a pair of jeans and a warm sweater. Then, while the casserole was heating through, she'd prepare a salad to go with it and cut up the crusty loaf she'd bought on her way home.

She was straightening up after sliding the heavy cast-iron pot into the oven when she caught the sound of a key in the door.

'You're back early,' she said, her breath snagging at the rapt expression in Guy's warm hazel eyes as he looked at her from the open kitchen doorway. She knew her face had to be flushed from the blast of heat she'd received from the oven, all mixed up with a tide of uneasy embarrassment. She'd meant to be dressed before he got back.

The robe was smothering enough in all conscience, but the implication was that she was naked beneath it, and the way Guy was looking at her told her he was fully aware of that fact.

The situation here was growing more awkward by the day.

Thankfully, it would soon be over.

'Yes. I decided to shut up shop early. There's no business around. Time of year, I guess. Plus, people appear to be organising their own holidays on the internet.'

Guy closed the door behind him, walking further into the room. The kitchen was doll's-house size and Cassie was beginning to feel claustrophobic. Cindy had told her how her brother felt about her, and Roman had suspected it. She should never have allowed herself to be pressured into staying here. He was a dear friend and hurting him was the last thing she wanted to do.

'I thought we might eat out this evening,' Guy said, removing his tie, his eyes never leaving her face. 'There's something I want to say to you.'

'Then say it here,' she responded lightly.

But her throat tightened miserably. She hoped it wasn't what she thought it was. Ever since he'd found out about her pregnancy—she hadn't been able to keep it from him; her regular bouts of morning sickness would have alerted a fool—he had been different. More serious, more watchful—possessive, even.

'Bastard!' he'd said when she'd reluctantly admitted his suspicions were right, pressing him to promise to keep the knowledge to himself, at least until she'd sorted herself out. Because, much as she loved her friend, she couldn't absolutely trust Cindy not to pass the news on to Roman. 'If I could get my hands on him I'd throttle him for what he's done to you!'

She reached a head of lettuce from the fridge. 'Supper's already on the way. I've been soaked through once, and so, by the looks of it, have you. I don't fancy a repeat performance. Why don't you change while I finish off? And, by the way—' she reached for a knife and began to shred the lettuce into a colander '—I'll be moving out at the end of the week. I found a bed-sit in Church Street today.'

She turned on the tap—anything to break the sudden stinging silence. Then he said, 'There's no need for that. You know there isn't.'

'There's every need,' she responded seriously. 'I want to be independent. It was good of you to take me in—'

'Good!' His mouth twisted on the interruption. 'Don't go all mealy-mouthed on me! Cin and I had to practically twist your arm before you'd take up my offer. Mum and Dad were in the process of selling up and retiring to the Lakes and Cin had just moved in with her boyfriend. Staying here was the last and least-favoured option, so don't try to pretend it wasn't,' he challenged bitterly.

The only other option being a bed and breakfast place, as they'd both been at pains to point out. For the first few days back in the small Shropshire market town where she'd lived for most of her life she'd stayed in a run-down boarding house on the outskirts and had seen what a drain it could make on her modest savings.

Finding a job had been her first priority, and she'd only reluctantly agreed to accept Guy's offer of a roof over her head until she could find a place of her own.

What could she say? In the past she'd been thankful for his friendship, his help, looking on him as a brother—one more reliable than the one she had! It was only since learning how he really felt about her that she'd wanted as little to do with him as possible.

She had first-hand knowledge of how it felt to love

and not be loved in return. She didn't want to make him hurt any more than he already was.

She gave him what she hoped was a pacifying smile and turned back to the sink. 'I have been grateful, truly. But it's time to move on. It never was a permanent arrangement; you know that. Besides—think about it—you don't want a divorcee plus child cluttering up your space. It would seriously cramp your style. From what I've heard—' she injected a note of wry humour to let him know she wasn't being judgemental or the least bit envious, was merely stating a fact '—you've accumulated a fair few notches on your bedpost in the past.'

She heard Guy approach. Felt his hand on her shoulder, tightening just briefly, heard the complacency in his voice as he said, 'If that's all that's bothering you, we don't have a problem. We'll sort this out over supper.'

He walked out of the room and she knew she'd blown it. He had misread her—believed she'd been fishing for reassurance about her place in his life, his intentions.

Roman paid off the taxi as the clock on the church tower struck five and turned up the collar of his leather jacket against the cold driving rain. The brightly lit windows of the boutique reflected splashes of orange and gold on the wet pavements.

The sign on the glass door said 'closed', but he could see Cindy's blonde head bent over some paperwork on the desk at the back of the bright little shop.

His stride was as confident as ever, his knuckle-rap on the glass of the door imperious. But inside his heart he was terrified.

He had little doubt that he could persuade his distant cousin to tell him how to find his runaway wife. But would Cassie agree to come back to him? Could she ever learn to love him again? Once, she had loved him—she'd told him as much. But had the precious magic gone for ever?

Cindy's pretty face was wreathed in smiles as she unlocked the door and held it open. 'You've come for Cass,' she stated. 'About time, too.'

He followed her in, the warm, cheerful atmosphere barely impinging, and Cindy said, 'Come through to the back before you drip all over those silk blouses.'

Carefully negotiating the racks of colourful garments, he sank into a chair opposite the one she'd been using, stuffing his hands into the pockets of his black denims, his long legs outstretched and his booted feet crossed at the ankles.

'I take it she hasn't sworn you to secrecy on the subject of her whereabouts?' he divined from her opening remarks.

'Of course she has!' Cindy answered blithely, turning to the small counter behind her to switch on an electric kettle. 'But, like the first time she did a runner, I'm prepared to break my word for the good of all concerned. One thing I do promise, though, I'll never tell her that I reported regularly to you, that you persuaded me to give her a job here when Kelly left to have her baby, or that you paid the rent on the flat that was supposed to be one of the perks.'

She spooned coffee granules into two heavy earthenware mugs. 'Cass grew wonderfully in self-confidence during that year. It would knock her back if she knew you'd been keeping a watching brief. She's such an innocent in a lot of ways. She never questioned why her job with me was so well paid—thanks to your top-up cheques. I don't think she'd be all that happy to know you've been there behind the scenes, helping her. I thought I should warn you against letting that cat out of the bag!'

'Thanks.' He managed a smile but his face felt stiff with tension. Cindy had a point. It had been a joy to see Cassie's new aura of self-assurance, to see her reach her full potential as a woman.

When she'd left him that first time he'd been frantic, stunned by the realisation of how much she meant to him. Despite the seeming failure of their marriage, the bitter knowledge that he hadn't done enough to try and make it work had made him hate himself.

His first instinct had been to follow her, do something positive about the situation. Sober reflection had stopped him. Only then had he been able to see clearly. All her life she'd been dominated, one way or another. She'd never had the chance to find out who she really was or what she was capable of. Time on her own, without a father, a husband or a clutch of in-laws to tell her what to do and how to do it, would only help her.

With him keeping an eye on her through Cindy, giving an unseen helping hand. And one day, when the time was right, when he judged she would believe herself to be his equal, he would ask her to come back to him.

But fate, in the shape of her brother's criminal activities, had intervened. And he'd made an unholy mess of it.

One day, though, when their marriage was firm, her love for him as strong and enduring as his was for her, then he would tell her how carefully he'd watched over her well-being. There were to be no secrets between them.

'Drink that. You look as if you need it.' Cindy put a mug of steaming coffee in front of him, breaking into his teeming thoughts. 'You look as if you haven't eaten or slept for weeks.'

It was too near the truth to bother arguing with. He took a gulp of the scalding brew, watching intently as she found a piece of paper, her pen flying as she scrawled an address.

'I don't know what went wrong; she didn't tell me. I was really sure the two of you would make a go of it this time, but when she arrived back here she looked as if her world had fallen apart.'

'My fault,' he admitted tightly, his heart beating with sudden hope. If he'd been no more than a stud to her, a way of satisfying her new-found sexuality while she'd been blackmailed into staying with him;

if she'd been happy to see the back of him—as her headlong flight had suggested—then she wouldn't have appeared to be so shattered, would she?

Cindy pushed the scrap of paper over the desk, her eyes narrowing as she debated the wisdom of telling him or not that his wife was temporarily staying with her brother.

Not, she decided. Roman's pride was legendary. He might turn round and go straight back to Spain if he knew Cassie was sharing a roof with another man.

On the other hand, Roman knew that the three of them had been close friends for practically the whole of their lives. He didn't know Guy was in love with Cass. And Cass wasn't interested; she was still in love with her husband.

Cindy sighed. They would have to sort it out for themselves. By telling him where to find Cass she'd done more than her fair share of meddling. 'It's a ten-minute walk, if that,' she told him. 'But I could call a cab; it's still pouring down outside.'

'I'll walk, if you'll give me directions.' He stood up, impatient to be gone. It would probably take a cab more than ten minutes to turn up here and a drop of rain wouldn't hurt him.

At the door, after giving him the simple directions, Cindy said, almost diffidently, 'I don't know what your plans are, and I know you're great at granting favours but lousy at taking them, but you can stay with us tonight. Fraser and I only have the one bed at the moment, but you could kip on the sofa. Cass has our number—call. One of us can pick you up.'

'So you see this as something of a wild-goose chase?' The forced lightness of his tone hid the sudden swamping ache that tightened his heart. 'What's to say I won't be spending the night, the rest of my life, with Cass?'

The hope was so great it tore at him savagely. But if it didn't turn out that way—his body went cold, his heart contracting beneath a layer of ice—then company would be the last thing he wanted. He would rather walk the streets, or find an all-night cab company and get himself straight back to the airport.

He gave Cindy a bleak smile and strode out into the rain.

Her hands unsteady, Cassie hastily chopped red peppers, sweet onions and celery and dumped them into the bowl of lettuce. She'd make the dressing later.

She had to get dressed before Guy had finished getting showered and changed. Suitably armoured against the hungry look she'd seen in his eyes, she'd be more able to explain that he'd made the wrong assumptions, that she would never see him as anything other than a friend.

Explain, perhaps, that she still loved Roman and probably always would, despite what had happened. Not that Guy had any idea, of course. He only knew what she'd told him and Cindy—that the reconciliation hadn't worked out. That didn't stop him being anti-Roman. Guy blamed him for everything bad that had happened in her life.

And maybe he was right.

But there were good things, too, memories she would always treasure. Memories of a time when she'd believed that their lives would run together, always. Those lazy, languid weeks in Sanlucar. The sun and the teasing wind from the Atlantic. Wandering through the old town together, hand in hand, sipping *café solos* at their favourite café, where the taped voices of *cante jondo* singers came from the dim interior and a fragrant orange tree cast a welcome shade over their chosen table. And the nights, the long, sultry nights of loving…

The knife she'd been holding slipped from her nerveless fingers, skittering over the tiled floor. Blinking, biting her lip as she came back to stark reality, she muttered under her breath and went down on her knees to fish it out from under the fridge.

And heard the kitchen door open.

Damn!

She'd been day-dreaming, masochistically indulging in memories that only served to heighten her pain, when she should have been starching herself up, dressing in sexless old jeans and a baggy sweater, scraping back her hair.

Now she would really have to scuttle if Guy weren't to get the wrong ideas about her state of undress.

Giving up on the knife that seemed to have got well and truly wedged, she peered through the nearly-dry mane of her hair, her startled eyes fastening on a pair of boots, travelling slowly up long, lithely muscled legs encased in narrow black denim, a black leather jacket spangled with raindrops.

Roman!

His black hair was plastered to his skull and there were lines of strain etched deeply at the sides of his mouth, but his eyes glowed with something that made her breath catch in her throat, her heartbeats race, sending her giddy.

'The door was on the latch. I walked straight in.' His voice was like velvet, the voice of the lover who had haunted her dreams. 'You should be more security-conscious, Cass. I worry about you.' A slow, almost tentative smile curved his mouth. 'At least something smells good. You are not neglecting yourself, as I feared.'

The casserole! she thought manically, trying to hold on to the mundane and normal to counteract the shock of his sudden appearance, the crazy hopes that against all common sense were clamouring for recognition in her painfully agitated brain.

It was an effort to scramble to her feet, an effort to make her voice work. 'Why are you here?' It was scarcely more than a whisper. She couldn't tear her eyes from his face. So dear to her, so loved. Yet strangely older, with deeper hollows beneath his slashing cheekbones. Compassion stirred strongly, making her ache. Had he, too, suffered, just as she had?

His slightly hooded eyes swept her, a line of quick

colour touching his skin, and Cassie, shell-shocked, knew why when she glanced down and saw how during her undignified knife-hunt the edges of her borrowed robe had come apart, revealing the heavy globes of her breasts, or most of them, the line of her still-flat tummy and the tangle of springy hair at the apex of her thighs.

Swallowing convulsively, she snatched at the edges, wrapping them tightly around her, and he said thickly, moving closer, 'Don't hide your body from me. You are so beautiful you make my heart ache, *querida*. I have come for you, if you will have me. Will you, my Cassie?'

With tears in her eyes, dazed wonder numbing her mind, her body suddenly shaking, Cassie could only struggle to get control of her vocal cords, tell him yes, and yes again, to be with him was what she had always wanted.

A sound emerged, but thickly, making no sense. Her hands flew to her face as shattering emotions racked her body. She made her feet move somehow towards him, to reply to his question with physical contact, since she seemed incapable of doing it verbally—her body against his, her arms around him, her mouth finding his, giving him his answer.

'Stop hounding her, dammit!' Guy's voice was thin and high, ragged with temper. 'Haven't you done enough damage?'

In the doorway his face was red. He was wearing a thin silky robe that did little to disguise the fact that he wore nothing under it.

The silence following his outburst was still and sharp. Cassie didn't know whether to giggle hysterically or to burst into tears.

Roman turned cold eyes on his distant cousin, his patrician nostrils pinched with arctic displeasure.

'And don't look at me like that,' Guy blustered. 'This is my home, and I'm telling you we don't want you in it. If you need to contact Cassie, do it through your solicitor.'

Cassie's eyes went wide. Guy's face was purple now. She was afraid he'd have a stroke! 'Guy,' she commanded, as firmly as she could under these surreal circumstances, 'don't I have a say here?'

'No!' His voice rose a full octave. 'I'm handling this. And I'll tell you something for nothing, Fernandez. I'm looking after Cass, I'm marrying her and taking care of the baby—'

A single fiery Spanish expletive cut him off in full flow. Tormented charcoal eyes flicked briefly in Cassie's direction. And then, with Guy stepping smartly aside, Roman strode through the doorway, disappearing into the dark wet night.

CHAPTER TWELVE

'THIS is a total dump!' Cindy censured, parking herself on the only armchair the dingy room boasted. The best that could be said of it was that it had broken springs and stained upholstery. 'Guy was in a right state when he phoned this morning and told me you'd moved out, and where you'd gone. I came as soon as I shut up shop. Where's Roman?' she demanded. 'And what the hell do you think you're doing in this grot-hole? Honestly, sometimes I think you should be locked up for your own safety!'

Glumly, Cassie had to agree with her friend's scathing assessment of the bed-sit she'd just moved into. But it was cheap and, more importantly, she was no longer sharing with Guy.

Last night he'd gone to bed in a chastened mood after she'd told him he'd ruined everything for her, reminding him that if he'd thought by saying he was planning on marrying her and looking after the baby had been an act of chivalry, he was utterly and hopelessly wrong.

What he'd said, giving Roman the wrong impression of their relationship, had been totally destructive and completely out of order.

She'd spent the night in anguish, stuffing her few

possessions in carrier bags, then pacing the floor as she waited for dawn when she could remove herself; sleep had been out of the question.

Roman had wanted her back, wanted to make their marriage work. Now he believed she'd shacked up with Guy, leapt straight into bed with him and had conceived his child. What other interpretation could he have put on what Guy had said? No wonder he'd walked straight out. He would think she was a slut and would have washed his hands of her!

'So,' Cindy prompted sharply, 'what happened? Roman had come for you; I know that because I gave him Guy's address. Don't tell me you sent him packing?'

Still in shock over what had happened the previous evening, and cursing the weak tears that flooded her eyes, Cassie muttered dully, 'It's a long story.' She really didn't want to talk about it. It was too close, too painful. But she knew she would have to. Cindy wouldn't leave until she did.

Buying herself a few extra moments, she offered tiredly, 'Why don't I make us some coffee?'

There was a sink and a gas ring in one corner, divided from the rest of the room by a shabby brown curtain. She'd shopped for a few basics on her way back from the bookshop but hadn't been motivated enough to unpack them.

Now she hunted through the carrier for the jar of granules, and when the brew was made and she couldn't delay any longer she perched on the edge of the single bed and haltingly told her friend everything.

'Hell's teeth!' Cindy exploded, putting her empty mug down on the floor. 'How could my stupid brother have done that? I honestly thought it would be all right—he kept his feelings to himself, was the perfect gentleman, in fact, when you came back that first time.'

She moved her hands expressively, her frown ferocious. 'The only time he ever really came clean about what he felt for you, he definitely told me he wouldn't say a word to you, or give you a hint, while you were still legally married to Roman. I really thought it would be the same this time, otherwise—' She shook her head helplessly. 'I'm so sorry, Cass!'

'You're not your brother's keeper,' Cassie said dully. 'It's done now.'

'But not dusted,' Cindy replied decisively. 'When did you find out you were pregnant?'

'Some time towards the end of August, I suppose. Just before everything went wrong.'

'So why didn't you tell Roman then? Surely he'd have been delighted—why keep it a secret?'

'Because.'

Cassie sucked in a long breath. Her whole body was shaking with inner tension. She didn't think she could take much more.

'Because what?'

Another dredging sigh, then Cassie spilled out edgily, 'Because even though we were getting along fine and the sex was great, he hadn't said a word about loving me or wanting me with him permanently. So far as I knew, he still expected me to leave at the end of the three months—he never said a single thing to make me believe anything else. As it happened,' she tacked on stiffly, 'he as good as gave me my marching orders well before then—as soon as he heard Delfina was no longer a problem.'

'All that tells me is that both of you are hopeless when it comes to communication. It doesn't tell me why he doesn't know he's about to be a father,' the other woman pointed out drily.

'If I'd told him about the baby he would have insisted I stay. I do know that much!' Cassie bit down on her trembling lower lip. 'Can't you understand? I needed him to want me for my own sake, not because I was carrying his baby. He wants an heir. And you know him—if I'd refused to stay on permanently because I couldn't bear to stay married to a man who couldn't love me, he would have done everything he could to get custody. I *want* this baby!'

His child.

'It's *his* baby, too,' Cindy pointed out. 'You have to tell him.'

'He thinks it's Guy's.'

'Then you'll have to tell him it isn't, won't you?' Cindy stood up, pointing out firmly, 'You're understandably upset, and in no mood to think straight. But believe me, Roman does love you. Why else would he have asked you to go back to him? But my stupid brother went and put his foot in it. No big deal—just a minor spanner in the works. It's up to you to get everything running smoothly again.'

Cindy had offered to come to Las Colinas Verdes with her for moral support. Now, drawing the hired car up in front of the large stone-built farmhouse at the heart of the sprawling estate, Cassie wished she'd accepted her offer.

It was almost dark. The wind blowing from the distant mountains carried an autumnal chill. She shivered, but the palms of her hands were clammy with sweat.

After Cindy had left her, a couple of evenings ago, she had eventually emerged from her traumatised state and everything had seemed so simple.

Follow Roman back to Spain and tell him the truth.

The baby was his, not Guy's.

Despite the way things had looked, he would believe her—surely he would? After all, he must have missed her, missed the closeness they'd shared, thought things over and regretted having told her to go. He must have done; there could be no other reason for his coming to England, asking her to come back to him.

Simple. The outcome a foregone happy conclusion. She'd felt so sure of herself, and of him, that she'd told her boss at the bookshop that she wouldn't be returning; given up the bed-sit; burned all her bridges.

Now, within moments of coming face to face with

Roman, it didn't seem simple at all. Scary was nearer the mark. What did she know of him? Really know? That he could be tender, caring, a considerate lover, a wildly passionate lover, a wonderful companion—and could change in the blink of an eye into a remote and quelling stranger, keeping his thoughts to himself, his motives an enigma, shutting her out.

She shuddered and forced herself to leave the car, wiping her damp palms down the sides of the cream-coloured linen trousers she wore. It was no use hanging around outside, regretting the impulsive decision that had brought her here. Get it over with. Stop dithering; find some of that self-confidence you were so proud of having achieved, she instructed herself.

Surely it hadn't all gone. Surely she wasn't back right where she'd started at the beginning of their marriage—a timid, tongue-tied little doormat?

However, deciding not to tempt fate, she left her overnight case right where it was on the passenger seat, tucked a few wayward strands of copper-coloured curls behind her ears, resolutely straightened her spine and walked briskly towards the main door.

As always, the heavy, carved door was unlocked. Trying to ignore the shudders of apprehension that were starting up again, playing havoc with her insides, she pushed it open.

What if he threw her straight back out again, refused to even listen to her?

Or what if he did listen, did believe the baby was his, and wanted the baby but not her? He'd already voiced suspicions that she'd been taught by some other man—or men—to be sexually responsive.

Seeing her and Guy together in a virtual state of undress—sharing the same flat only weeks after leaving his bed—would have confirmed everything bad he'd thought about her. Would he fight her through the courts for custody of his child? Would he win?

Either scenario was intolerable, would inflict a wound that would never heal. Trouble was, as Roy had once said, Roman had a mind like a maze. No one ever knew what he was thinking.

Swallowing convulsively, she bit her lip and listened. The main part of the house was silent. The atmosphere empty. No one here. Dragging in a breath, she made for the kitchen regions.

She opened the door to be met by a waft of heat, the aroma of cooking. The sound of rapid Spanish male voices ceased abruptly and Asunción turned from the range, an iron skillet in one hand. Her broad face beamed.

'*Señora*—you have come. It is good!'

She advanced, edging round the end of the long table where the unmarried estate workers were eating. 'We did not expect, did not know—*el patrón* he did not say. But I will have Maria make a fire for you. I will make you *huevos flamencos*—very quick, not much waiting for you.'

'Thanks, Asunción.' Cassie managed a weak smile. 'But I'm not hungry, truly. And please don't go to the trouble of lighting a fire.'

The family was away; it was obvious. And where

was Roman? She'd been so certain he would have come back to his estate in Andalusia when he'd turned on his heel, his head high, his back rigid with that ingrained Spanish pride as he'd stalked out on her.

She'd already glimpsed Roy's bright head among the dark ones around the long table; now he pushed his half eaten meal away and stood up. There was relief on his face as he walked towards her.

Conversation gradually picked up around the table. Cutlery scraped against plates and someone laughed, the atmosphere going back to normal. Reaching her side, Roy more or less echoed the housekeeper's greeting.

'Sis—thank God you've finally come back!' He gripped her arm, just above her elbow, his fingers urgent through the sleeve of her light linen jacket, marching her back out of the kitchen door, closing it behind them. 'We need to talk.'

Cassie dug her heels in. Much as she loved her brother, she was in no state to listen to his problems, whatever they were. 'Where's Roman?' she asked sharply. 'Do you know?'

'Sanlucar. Look, I'll tell you what I know when we get to my place. We won't be disturbed and there won't be anyone listening at doors. There's enough gossip going the rounds as it is.'

'He is all right, isn't he?' She cast him a worried look. It all sounded ominous.

'Apart from a thunderous black temper, yes. So far as I know.'

Knowing she wouldn't get any more out of him, she gave in and followed as he strode through the stable yard and into a walled quadrangle. Lights glowed from the windows of a dozen stone built *cabañas*, some large, for the married workers and their families, and others smaller, for the bachelors.

'You're not still living with the family?' Cassie observed as her brother pushed open a door and flicked on a light, her voice drained of life, her energy levels on the floor.

Psyching herself up to the point when she could have argued her case with her husband, only to discover he was miles away, had been an anticlimax of near-stupefying proportions.

'No, thank the Lord!' He ushered her through to a sitting room, comfortably furnished with a couple of armchairs, colourful rugs on the polished boards of the floor.

'I guess I deserved every last bit of it, but the way the three old ladies kept watching me, as if they expected me to sneak out with the family silver, was doing my head in. I think Roman knew that. Anyway, he offered me the use of this place.'

Roy crossed to a plain wooden cupboard and produced a bottle of wine, two glasses. Cassie, uncomfortably conscious of forgetting her twin's problems while she wallowed in her own, asked, 'You're settling in?'

'Sure.' He drew the cork. 'Don't hover; park yourself. It's basic but it's comfortable. It's good to have my own space.'

'I meant—' Cassie sank into an armchair, trying not to worry about him '—the work here on the estate, Roman's attitude.'

'He hasn't got one, not like the old ladies. In fact, he's quite a guy when you stop to think about it. I offered to pay back the money I'd borrowed—' He reddened as he saw her eyebrows practically hit the ceiling. 'Right—the money I *took*. Said he could dock some out of my wages each week. But he said no. Provided I toed the line here, the whole thing was forgotten.'

'And are you? Toeing the line?'

For the sake of the tiny new life inside her she refused the glass of wine he offered her, suddenly too weary to ask for a glass of water to ease her dry mouth and throat.

The drive to Sanlucar tonight was out of the question. Apparently Roman could forgive her twin for stealing from him, abusing his trust. Would he forgive her own supposed misdemeanours, believe her when she told him she hadn't committed any?

'Don't worry, sis. I've learnt my lesson,' Roy said quietly, sitting on the low, chunky table in front of her. 'At first I thought I'd hate it here, thought I'd miss the night life, the pretty *señoritas* and fast cars, the fancy restaurants. But you know what? I didn't. I enjoy the work, learning how the estate's managed and that sort of stuff. I'm not going to mess up again or do anything to spoil my opportunities here. Roman as good as promised that if I shape up I can take over when the present manager retires in a few years' time.

'Trouble is—' he spread his hands '—Roman's talking of selling up—everything except the house in Jerez—and taking off. It was a real bombshell, believe me. That's why we were so relieved to see you. You can talk some sense into him.'

Cassie felt the colour drain from her face. 'I don't understand,' she whispered. This vast estate had been in his family for countless generations; he was fiercely proud of his heritage. How could he even think of selling up, denying his future heir his enviable inheritance?

'Nor do the rest of us. I thought you, as his wife, might be able to throw some light on the situation,' he answered soberly. 'There was the reconciliation, the second honeymoon. Then—' He made a slashing movement with one hand. 'He was back here. Alone. Nobody knew what had happened to you. Twenty-four hours later, the aunts scuttled off. Talk about a black mood; nobody dared go near him!

'Then, a few weeks later, he took off. To England, by all accounts. Late the next day he was back here—breathing more thunder, according to Asunción. He told the estate manager he was selling up, then, so gossip has it, got blind drunk, and that's a first as far as anyone here knows.

'This morning he went to Sanlucar. The property there will be the first to go. Perhaps you can fill in some details—like what broke the two of you up this time. Something must have done; everyone thinks so. You must have really rattled his cage!'

She could give him details in plenty, but she wasn't going to. This was between her and her husband. And she would do anything she could to make things right between them.

'I'll do what I can,' she promised, her voice firm now, her resolve strong and her energy flooding back. If he was hurting as badly as his astounding decision to sell up would suggest, then she needed to be with him.

She stood up. Forget resting up, tackling the journey to the coast in the morning. She'd go right now. 'If you'll point me at the bathroom, then fix me a flask of coffee, I'll be on my way.'

'But Cass—it's over a hundred miles. Leave it until the morning.' He looked startled. 'There's no point—'

'If I leave now I'll be there before midnight.' She glanced at her watch, cutting through his common sense objections. She would drive until dawn if she had to.

Nothing was going to keep her away from Roman. Not now, and not in the future.

CHAPTER THIRTEEN

CASSIE made the midnight deadline she'd set herself with half an hour to spare. She parked the hired car in one of the small Moorish squares, grabbed her overnight bag from the passenger seat and straightened up, stretching the kinks out of her spine and shoulders, blinking her eyes as she tried to rid them of the uncomfortably hot and gritty feeling.

The pavement tables outside the café that she and Roman had favoured were still fully occupied. Couples, mostly, enjoying a late supper; people in the south kept late hours. She could hear the sound of guitar music, melancholy and haunting, the counterpoint of soft laughter.

A sudden draining sense of loss and hopelessness swamped her. Would she and Roman ever wander hand in hand down to their favourite café, sit in the shade of the orange tree and watch the world go by, cocooned in a warm and loving relationship?

Or would tonight bring the end of everything?

The square was sheltered from the Atlantic winds and Cassie dragged in a deep, steadying gulp of the soft, dark night air, then headed upwards through the warren of narrow streets, lit by lamps high up on the walls of the jumbled buildings.

She wasn't nervous, she told herself, trying to quiet the manic pitter-patter of her heart. Just keyed-up. Tonight would be a turning point. Could she and Roman at last begin to communicate? They had to if they were to make any sense of the emotional mess they were in!

And she was as much to blame as he was, unable to tell him of her needs, the way she felt, how very deeply she loved him.

The house she had always instinctively been drawn to was in darkness, the many windows overlooking the narrow cobbled street tightly shuttered. It seemed withdrawn, closed in on itself, the usual feeling of welcome absent.

She hated to think of this lovely place, where she and Roman had been so briefly happy, passing into the hands of strangers.

But that wasn't going to happen, she told herself staunchly. She wouldn't be here at all if she didn't think that somehow, if they both opened up, they could work things out.

Thankfully, Manuel hadn't yet locked up for the night, and the huge, ornately carved door swung open at her touch. The hall was in darkness. Feeling for the domed brass switch, she depressed it and the overhead chandelier sprang to glittering life.

The feeling of alienation became stronger, something to dread. Several cardboard boxes filled with books stood at the foot of the stairs.

She swallowed round the hard, painful lump in her throat. Roman was already packing his personal belongings, those books he treasured from the extensive library here, which had been built up over the generations by the Fernandez family.

Somehow she had to stop him.

She called his name but her voice echoed, unanswered, in the silence of the ancient house. She had half expected the housekeeper, or her husband, at least, to emerge from their private quarters at the rear of the building, but no one came.

Biting her lip, she searched the ground-floor rooms. Nothing. Only the few gaps on the library shelves, the open wall safe and the briefcase on the table told her that he was somewhere on the premises.

She was panting slightly when she reached the top of the stairs, her hair coming adrift from the pins that had secured it in a neat pleat at the back of her head. She pushed it away from her face with an impatient hand.

A thin sliver of muted light showed beneath the door of the master bedroom, the room they had shared with such passion, giving of their bodies unreservedly yet keeping the things that really mattered hidden. Openness, trusting each other enough to discuss their feelings, hopes and fears.

Not allowing herself to even think that the coming encounter might have an unhappy outcome for both her and her precious unborn child, she opened the door and walked into the bedroom.

Only the bedside lamp was lit, casting shadows into the corners of the room. Roman was dragging his clothes from the hanging cupboard by the dim light, tossing them haphazardly into an open suitcase.

Hers, the clothes he had insisted on buying her all those weeks ago, were in a pile on the bed. A huge lump formed in her throat.

Without missing a beat, without turning, he said, 'If you've come for your things, you needn't have bothered. Teresa returns tomorrow; I was going to ask her to pack them up and send them on.'

He did turn then, slowly. The light from the lamp picked out his features, emphasising a new and disquieting harshness. He was wearing a white shirt tucked into slate-grey trousers; it made his skin look dark by contrast, his eyes black and unforgiving.

She swallowed convulsively and blurted, trying to lighten the tense atmosphere, 'How did you know it was me? It could have been anyone—a burglar!'

'I knew,' he said, almost uninterestedly. 'And "burglar" fits. You stole something from me, and I don't for a moment think you've come to give it back.'

A mind like a maze didn't come near describing his tortuous thought processes. She'd left here taking only the things she'd brought with her! But now wasn't the time to ask why he was adding theft to the long list of things he'd stacked up against her.

He gave her a last, penetrating look from beneath his brows, his mouth a hard, straight line, then closed the open suitcase with his foot, bent to fasten it and straightened up again.

He was leaving, she thought, panicking, as he

hefted the heavy case and strode towards the door where she was standing. As far as he was concerned she didn't even merit the title of unfinished business.

Her heart gave a violent twist of anguish. It couldn't end liked this—she wouldn't let it!

'We need to talk.' Her voice sounded ragged. Cassie stood her ground, though. If he wanted to go through that door he would have to lift her bodily off her feet. And she was getting the distinct impression that touching her in any way at all was the last thing he wanted to have to do.

'Why?' The question was flat. But he did stop, keeping distance between them, his eyes coldly dismissive.

First things first. Conscious for the first time of her travel-stained clothes, her hair all over the place, her possibly manic appearance, she levelled her voice and told him, 'I was at Las Colinas earlier this evening. Roy said it was common knowledge by now that you intend to sell up. Everything.'

One black brow tilted upwards fractionally. 'And you followed me all the way down here? *Por dios!* you must be eager. For the clothes you left behind? Or were you intending to wheedle your way back into my life via the bedroom? Decided you prefer living in luxury in Spain to sharing a flat with your lover?'

Cassie closed her eyes briefly, her head going back as if to force the threatening tears back right where they came from. She'd expected initial difficulties, but they were turning out to be more painful than she could ever have imagined.

'And not quite everything,' he corrected, loosing his grip on the case, letting it drop to the floor. 'The house in Jerez will stay in the family, for the benefit of the older generation.' He lifted his shoulders in an uncaring shrug. 'After the place has served its purpose, who knows? It will probably go the same way as the estate and this house.'

'You can't do it!' Her throat tightened up again, the words emerging thickly. He would spend the rest of his life regretting it; his heritage was the most important thing in his life.

He crossed his arms across his chest, his long legs straddled, his aristocratic nostrils narrowed. 'No one tells me what I can and cannot do.'

His arrogance pricked her on the raw, despite her compassion. Knowing what his proud heritage meant to him, she knew that something deeply traumatic had forced him to this decision. 'A law unto yourself?' she snapped sardonically. 'What was it you used to say? That you were merely the custodian of your inheritance, honour-bound to hand it on to the next generation in a better state than when it came to you. Or have you conveniently forgotten that?'

She saw a muscle jerk at the side of his mouth, another clench along his hard jawline. 'As there is to be no future generation, I see no point in tying myself to places that hold nothing but bad memories of a woman I don't know any more. I thought I did know you. For a few perfect weeks you had me fooled.'

Her heart lifted. The feeling was so strong it was almost a pain. He had followed her to England to ask her to go back to him, of course he had, and she hadn't lost sight of that. Was it possible that he was feeling as bereft as she was? How could she prove that she loved him, that there had never been anyone else for her?

'Roman—' She wanted to go to him, to hold him, to take the pain away. But even though the hope in her heart was a great and desperate thing, she knew it was too soon. She had to convince him that what he'd seen and heard back at Guy's flat wasn't what it must have seemed.

'Roman.' She repeated his name softly. 'There is a point. You do have an heir.' Unconsciously, her hand rested against her still-flat tummy, then dropped shakily back to her side as she registered the immediate and contemptuous curl of his mouth.

'You try to pass your lover's child off as mine? You insult me, *señora*!'

'The baby is *not* Guy's!'

'Nor mine. You were protected by the contraceptive pill when we were—were together. Or have you, too, very conveniently forgotten you told me that? Do you take me for a fool?' His fists were clenched at his sides, a white line of temper around his mouth. 'I saw you together with my own eyes. Barely dressed. I heard what he said. You were living with him. Well, *señora*, you may go right back to him, with my blessing!'

Shakily, she passed a hand over her burning forehead. This was her worst nightmare. But, unlike a nightmare, she knew she wouldn't wake and leave the horrors behind.

They would stay with her until the end of her days.

Weariness swamped her. It had been a long, long day. The flight out to Jerez, the seemingly endless drive, hither and thither. And nothing accomplished. Zilch. Zero. He would never believe she loved him; more than anything in the world she loved him...

Even if she told him?

She filled her lungs with much needed oxygen. She had to make him believe her. She had to! 'Roman—I always loved you. I've never made love with any other man, despite what you thought. I was able to express my love for you physically because I'd finally grown up, begun to rate myself as a human being—a woman. And I believe—' she dragged in a shaky breath '—that you had finally learned to love me, too.'

She couldn't look at him, couldn't bear to see the cynical disbelief in his eyes which would mean she'd failed. She began to pace the floor, nervous energy overcoming her tiredness, making her restless.

'I'd hoped you'd tell me you wanted me to stay beyond the three months you'd stipulated. Hoped you wanted to make our marriage work as much as I did. But you said I was free to go. I took it that I was no longer any use to you because you'd just heard that Delfina had got herself engaged. What else was I to think?

'Thanks to you, my old flat above Cindy's shop was no longer available. I had nowhere to stay. Guy offered to put me up until I got back on my feet. Against my better judgement, I accepted. I don't know why he said the things he did. Only that—'

'He's in love with you,' Roman injected blankly.

'Unfortunately.'

Silence. She had her back to him; he wasn't responding to her declarations of love. She had opened her heart and he could say nothing in return. Because he thought she was lying?

There was nothing left for her to say except, 'Later, a paternity test can be arranged. It will prove beyond any doubt that you are the father of my child.'

Tears clogged her throat. That it should come down to this. A clinical procedure when, in a perfect world, all it needed was love. And trust.

But this wasn't a perfect world. And very few people in it were free of imperfections.

And still the silence was deafening. He had decided that what he had felt for her wasn't worth the hassle. He could do without her.

But could he do without his child?

The thought of the tiny, precious life within her tore her apart. She pressed her fingertips to her throbbing temples and reached the hardest, most painful decision of her life.

'When you're satisfied that the baby is yours, then

I will hand him or her over to you. To your safe-keeping. Hang on to your heritage for the sake of your heir. I'll—' her voice faltered, the words choking her. But she knew it had to be this way, there wasn't any other.

It would kill her to give up her baby—all the joy in the world would end for her on that dreadful day—but she loved Roman far too much to allow him to be deprived of the child he had always wanted to carry on his name.

'I'll ask only one thing. To be kept...informed...of progress. I'll keep out of the way, never interfere. The occasional photograph...would be welcome.'

CHAPTER FOURTEEN

'CASS.' His voice was harsh. 'Do you know what you're saying?'

He was standing behind her now. Not near enough to touch. But she could feel his warmth, the strength and sheer male vitality of him.

She shuddered convulsively, wanting him to take her in his arms and tell her everything would be all right. Knowing he wouldn't.

'Yes.' It was as much as she could do to get the word out. Her whole body felt as if it were wired to a detonator. Any moment now she could disintegrate, fragment into a million ragged pieces.

'Why?' A heartbeat of silence. Then, 'You do not want our child? You want to be rid of it?' he asked, ice in his voice.

At last he believed the baby was his. Because she'd offered the solution of a paternity test? She folded her arms tightly around her body, trying to hold herself together.

'Of course I want my child! Damn you!' The emotional protestation was torn from her, her voice high and hard, splintering the soft warm air. How could he think that of her? *Why* was he so cruelly intent on thinking the very worst of her?

'Then why would you give your baby away? To me? Cass, I need to know,' he persisted, his voice low, deeper than she had ever heard it.

Her shoulders were held high, rigid with tension, with the effort of keeping herself together. He touched her then, lightly massaging the knots along her collarbone, and the touch of the hands that had brought so much magic into her life for such a brief time was almost her undoing. 'Tell me,' he insisted quietly.

'You—you could give our child a far better quality of life than I ever could,' she said raggedly, wanting to get this over before she broke down completely. 'But that's—that's not the most important consideration.'

Her voice roughened, every word she said seeming to distance her from the new life she carried. 'The dynasty your family founded, the sense of history and pride that you seem intent on throwing away is your child's birthright. Having an heir would stop you from making the greatest mistake of your life—turning your back on your heritage because of the bad memories I made for you. I can't let you do that! Don't you see?'

Reined-in sobs were building up pressure in her chest; it was getting more and more difficult to control the misery that was overwhelming her. 'I know—know you would love our child. Believe me, I wouldn't be doing this if I had any doubts about that.'

Her slight shoulders shook, her hands flying to

cover her face as the pent-up sobs finally escaped. She had made her decision and it had been the hardest thing she'd ever had to do. She'd said what had to be said. The only pity was she hadn't been able to walk away from this traumatic scene with some kind of dignity.

Why couldn't he love her as much as she knew he would love their child? Why had whatever it was he had felt for her turned into bitterness? Why, when he surely must have accepted the truth of what she'd told him—that she had always loved him, that there had never been any other man for her?

He said nothing. By now his very silence told her that the quite obviously tenuous feelings he'd once had for her were now well and truly dead. But he did turn her gently round, enfolding her loosely within the circle of his arms, allowing her head to droop forward against the broad expanse of his chest.

Just as anyone with an ounce of compassion in their make-up would offer brief comfort to another distraught human being. She wouldn't let herself read any more into it than that.

'Cass,' he said moments later, one of his hands straying to her hair, the other still clasped loosely around her waist. 'Enough. Getting rid of tension's all very well. Too much weeping will harm you and our baby.'

That effectively stopped the feeble outpourings, stiffened her spine. Of course. The baby she was carrying would be his prime consideration.

She lifted her head from his thoroughly wettened

shirt, 'I have no intention of harming my baby! So don't worry—getting an heir was the only reason you married me in the first place, other than getting your family off your back. You've won on both counts. Just don't—don't rub it in!'

She wasn't going to cry again. She was not! What was done was done, by her own decree. Now she had to learn to live with it. Somehow.

'Shh. Stop torturing yourself. You will make yourself ill.' He lifted her bodily and carried her to the huge double bed, stacking the pillows carefully behind her, one hand holding her down as she tried to scramble to her feet again.

'Be still,' he commanded gently, and the fight went out of her, utter tiredness seeping into her bones. 'You are quite right,' he told her as she slumped back against the pillows.

Keeping his eyes on her troubled, tear-stained face, he bent over her to remove her shoes, then sat on the edge of the mattress and eased his fingers through her long tousled hair, gently removing the few remaining pins. 'I have won. You stole something from me and now you have brought it back.'

'What?' she demanded truculently. She disliked this new mood of consideration and caring as much as she disliked his earlier stiff silences.

He was only concerned about the baby she'd promised to give over to him. If she hadn't been pregnant he would have probably told her to go jump in the wide waters of the Guadalquiver. 'I've never taken a thing from you—don't mix me up with my twin!'

She didn't want to be here; she wanted to be somewhere else. Somewhere dark and private where she could lick her wounds and try to come to terms with the promise she'd made him.

And she didn't want him to see her in this state; overemotional, her face red and puffy from crying, her hair a mess, the linen jacket and trousers crumpled, spotted with the coffee stains that had resulted from her tussle with the recalcitrant top of the flask Roy had filled for her.

'You stole my happiness,' he told her softly. 'My pride in my heritage—just about everything that made life worthwhile.' He took her hands in his, lifting them to his lips, his kisses as light as butterfly wings on her knuckles. 'And now you have brought it back.' He raised his head, his features solemn. 'And you are right again. I needed an heir. But that was not the reason I married you. I felt this great affection for you, my Cass. I had this huge urge to protect you and care for you. This I had never felt for any other woman. I knew—well, I hoped—that you had a fondness for me, too.

'But sexually, you didn't want to know. It used to tear me apart because at that time I didn't understand it. So I used to absent myself for long periods of time. It was only when you went away that first time that I realised how much I loved you—despite the way our marriage had turned out.'

'My fault!' she blurted miserably, hating her

younger self. She'd been such a timid fool back then. But was she just as big an idiot now, going out of her mind, hearing things she so desperately wanted to hear? Or did he really, truly mean he had once loved her?

'No!' he countered vehemently. 'Mine entirely. But we're not going to argue about it. All that's over, it is—what do you say in your country?—water under the bridge. What matters now is what we make of our future.'

Cassie bit down on her wobbly lower lip, then asked bluntly, because she just had to know. 'You do want me, as well as the baby? You do believe I have never made love with any other man?'

'Cass—' He drew in a long breath. 'I believe you implicitly.' His eyes softened. They suddenly looked suspiciously moist. 'You were willing to make the biggest sacrifice a woman can make, for my sake,' he said emotionally. 'That told me how much you love me; it made my unworthy suspicions ridiculous. The depth of your love humbles me, *querida*.'

He stood up, his mood changing abruptly. 'You are exhausted, my Cass. I am going to take very great care of you. That is my first duty. Tomorrow, I will make an immediate appointment for you to see an obstetrician—one of the best. I will, of course, accompany you. I will be with you every step of the way through this pregnancy. But now I will run a bath, and while you relax in warm water I will make you hot milk. And you will eat?'

His dark brows furrowed. 'In your mad dash

around the countryside I don't suppose you thought of food,' he accused, planting his feet apart. 'You must take better care of yourself, and if you won't do it, then I must,' he stated firmly. 'Teresa and Manuel don't return until tomorrow—a family birthday celebration. She left me things that are probably too spicy for your condition. You will like a good plain omelette—'

'Stop!' Cassie wriggled round onto her knees, her eyes wet with emotional tears, her mouth curving in a tender smile. Roman had never looked or sounded so utterly Spanish as he did at this moment. And so determined to get things right.

'Pamper me if you must—I'm not complaining! But eating's low on my list of priorities at the moment.' She held out her hands to him. 'Forget your duty, just for a minute, and come and talk to me. Tell me, did you mean it—about realising you really did love me when—?'

'When you left me. I was utterly shattered. I couldn't believe how empty I felt.' He sucked in his lower lip, and it was the first time she had seen him appear indecisive. 'You are sure you are up to more talk?'

He capitulated gladly at her bright-eyed nod and moved back towards her, his own eyes soft as he took her outstretched hands in his. 'My instinct was to drag you back, so that we could sit down together, somewhere away from my family, and try to find out what had turned our marriage into a disaster zone.'

Sitting on the side of the bed, he held her hands

against his chest. 'But the sensible side of me said that would be wrong. From what I knew of your past, and my misguided handling of you during our marriage, all your life you'd been told what to do, pushed into being what other people wanted you to be. You needed time to get to know yourself.'

He smiled gently into her bright, tear-spangled eyes. 'I kept a watching brief—and one day I'll tell you how I did this—and told myself to be patient for one year. Then I would come for you, and bring you flowers and perfume and jewels. And my love. And woo my bride back to me.'

'But I came to you first,' she murmured thoughtfully.

If Roy hadn't stolen that money, she wouldn't have gone to Roman; he would have come to her. To woo her back to him. She wouldn't have been able to resist him, she knew she wouldn't, because he had always been all she had ever wanted. So much misery would have been avoided.

'That was when the sensible part of me went on holiday.' He leant over and kissed the end of her nose. 'I'd expected to see a change in you, but the extent of it took me by surprise. You'd regained all that lost weight, lost the haunted look that used to worry me so much—you had poise, confidence. You did not look like a woman who would be easily wooed—not unless you wanted to be, and I was sure at that stage that you did not. So I got this crazy idea of using blackmail and later deeply regretted it. It was so unworthy.'

Cassie wriggled forward, snuggling into his side. She was home; she and her baby were loved and wanted. 'Which was why,' she said, smothering a yawn, 'you were so stiff and proper when you told me I was free to go. I thought—'

'I know what you thought,' he said gravely. 'But you couldn't have been further from the truth. I had to give you the choice—no pressure. I wanted, with all my heart, to hear you say you wanted to stay with me. And now I know you will.'

'Always,' she responded sleepily, her bright head drooping into the hollow of his shoulder. 'Tell me you love me.'

'I love you.' She heard the smile in his voice. 'So much so, I knew I had to go far away from memories if I wanted to stay sane,' he murmured against her hair. 'Now all that is over—and for you,' he went on briskly, 'bath, bed and food.'

He lifted her effortlessly and she looped her arms around his neck. 'No food. It's very late and I'm too sleepy to eat.' The truth was, she didn't want to let him out of her sight. If she did, she would begin to think this was all a dream.

She gave an enormous yawn to prove her point and he shot her a frowning look of concern as he flicked on the light in the *en suite* and slid her down the length of his body, steadying her with one hand, turning on the taps to fill the bath with the other.

The water gushing, steam misting the marble walls, he slid her crumpled jacket from her shoulders, revealing the pretty lace bra that barely constrained her full, creamy breasts. She heard the rough, urgent tug of his breath and smiled softly as she suggested huskily, 'Why don't you join me?'

'Believe me—' he ran a finger slowly down the inviting indentation of her cleavage '—there is nothing in the world I would enjoy more.' There were pinpoints of searing light in the smoky depths of his eyes and a wry smile tugged at the corners of his long, sensual mouth as he added dryly, 'But it would be a very bad idea. You need to rest. One thing would lead to another and neither of us would get any sleep at all, you understand me?'

Only too well, she thought, already swaying on her feet as he turned off the taps and tested the water. But it would have been heavenly…

Cassie stirred lazily beneath the soft covers. It was dawn. A new day. A new beginning. A contented smile curved her soft lips.

She could only dimly remember climbing out of the scented bath water, Roman stepping forward to smother her in a huge towel, gently patting her dry.

Her overnight bag was still in the hall. It had seemed too much effort to ask him to bring it to her. Besides, he had gathered her into his arms and slid her, boneless and naked, between the silky sheets…

And now he slept beside her, his tough features relaxed and almost vulnerable, his soft dark hair rumpled, his jaw darkly stubbled. Her heart lurched with tenderness as she stretched out a hand to touch him.

He, too, was naked. Her smile was wicked now,

her amber eyes glinting as she wriggled closer and wrapped her arms around him, glorying in the sensation of loving and being loved in return.

She felt his lithe body stir, as if her touch had brought him immediately awake. And then he turned, pulling her close before lifting himself on one elbow, his face only inches from hers, his eyes soft, liquid silver, as he asked, 'You are feeling good now?'

'Mmm,' she murmured, wriggling closer, her breath snagging as she felt his hard response against the softness of her tummy. 'But I could feel better.'

'How?' His brows peaked, emphasising the line between them, and she put her hand against the side of his face, the rough dark texture sparking tremors of electric sensation deep inside her.

'This—' She rubbed the ball of her thumb across the carved sensuality of his mouth, then claimed it with her own, and his answering kiss was deeper, more tender than she had ever known it, touching her soul, claiming it, making it his own.

'Cassie,' he said raggedly when lack of breath parted them, 'I adore you.' He pushed his fingers through her hair, dark colour suffusing the skin along his taut cheekbones. 'I want you so badly. But is that all right for you, and for the baby? If I am slow? And careful?'

'Well…' she said consideringly, smoothing her hands over his shoulders and then down his chest to the tautness of his stomach. 'Slow and careful? I don't believe we've done that before.' Her eyes glinted wickedly into his as her hands slid between his thighs. 'Let's see how it works out, shall we?'

'Delicious,' she husked an hour later. 'Divine, pure ecstasy.' Her arms lay above her head, their legs tangled together, supine and sated.

Roman shifted on to one shoulder and bent his head to her breasts, burying it between their lushness. 'For me, it was heaven. You are heaven.' A hand strayed to her tummy, fingers rubbing through the tangle of springy curls just below. 'Cassie, *amada*, when did you know we were having a child?' he queried softly, his head lifting, his eyes intent on what his fingers were doing, the way her creamy thighs immediately parted for him.

She told him, her breath coming faster. How could this be happening again, so soon after the last mind-blowing hour?

'And you kept it secret. Why, Cassie *mia*?'

'I wanted to be sure—' Oh, dear heaven, what was he doing? It was almost too much pleasure! 'Be sure you wanted me for me, not because I was to be the mother of your child.'

'Then I think,' he said with a decided glint in his eyes, 'that it is my pleasant duty to reassure you.'

And he proceeded to do exactly that.

Nine months later.

Three-month-old Sebastian Roman Fernandez looked adorable in his white lace christening robes.

He'd inherited his golden eyes from his mother, but the rest of him was pure Roman.

The family party was going with a swing. Teresa, now Cassie's staunch admirer, had coped magnificently with the preparations, and the guests were spilling out into the courtyard.

The aunts had pronounced Sebastian the most beautiful baby in the whole of Spain, and Doña Elvira had admitted, 'You have made my son happy. I didn't believe you could but you have proved me wrong. My dear, you are a most welcome addition to the family.'

Cassie, her figure restored to normal—apart from a greater fullness in the bosom area which Roman vowed he adored—was dressed in a sleek cream silk shift, the pearls her husband had presented her with on the birth of their son around her elegant neck, her chestnut hair upswept to show them off.

The photographs had been taken and she'd socialised with all of the guests. Now she had gravitated back to the crib, watching her baby son sleep, with love-drenched eyes.

'To the three of us.' Roman joined her, looking incredibly handsome in his lightweight handcrafted suit. He handed her a champagne flute and touched his glass to hers. 'To my beautiful wife, my handsome son, and the happiest, proudest husband and father alive.'

Her smile was radiant as she reached up to put a kiss on the side of his gorgeous mouth. 'I missed you. Where have you been?'

'Talking to Roy. I managed to prise him away from Consuela for long enough to discuss a few projects with him, get his opinions.' His grin was disarming.

'Do you think it's serious—I mean between him and Consuela?'

Her brother and the dark-haired pretty youngest daughter of the estate manager had been inseparable. Cassie could see the attraction between them.

Roy had matured out of all recognition. Deeply tanned, his features tougher and more serious, her brother had turned into one hunky man, the hard work around the estate broadening his shoulders and narrowing a waistline that had formerly tended to bulge.

'Could be,' Roman confirmed. 'In fact, I think it definitely is. And the way Roy's shaping up, he'll step into the job of manager when Miguel retires. And, Cass—' he slipped an arm around her shoulders. '—how would you feel about visiting Las Colinas for a few weeks, introducing young Seb around the place? I know how you love Sanlucar, and this house will always be our permanent home, but—'

'But you yearn for the wide open spaces? You want to poke your long nose in?' Her eyes sparkled for him. 'That's fine by me.'

Where Roman was she would always want to be. He successfully ran his many other businesses from Sanlucar, visiting Seville occasionally for a few hours, but Las Colinas was in his blood.

'You're sure?' He held her eyes. These days they kept nothing from each other; they were almost like one person—with infinitely exciting differences, he had to concede. 'The aunts and my mother could be tactfully moved to Jerez for the length of our stay,' he suggested.

But Cassie shook her head. 'I'm perfectly happy to share space with them. They won't criticise the mother of your heir!'

His smile was wicked. 'No, I don't think they'd dare! Well, if you're happy with that?'

'Happy, full-stop.' She slipped a hand into his and raised her glass. 'To the three of us.' She tilted her head, her smile enigmatic. 'How about four? The heir needs at least one brother or sister to stop him being disgracefully spoiled.'

'Your wish is my command,' he said, his fingers tightening around hers, his smile sleepy and utterly fascinating. 'Mind you,' he added, the incandescence of her answering smile making his heart leap crazily, 'as commands go, I can't think of anything I'd rather put more effort into.'

THE SOCIETY BRIDE

FIONA HOOD-STEWART

CHAPTER ONE

HE'D been summoned, Ramon Villalba realised. He frowned as he sat astride his fine Passo Fino and stared across the wide, green open spaces where several thousand heads of cattle—all belonging to him—grazed, oblivious of the fact that their owner was once again about to board his company jet in Buenos Aires and head for London.

It was rare these days that his father summoned him. After all, Ramon was thirty-two, and had cut his eye-teeth a long while ago. So the matter must be extremely important and the summons immediately met.

He experienced a moment's concern. Could it be the health of one of his parents' that was the issue here? Surely not. His mother, with whom he had an exceptionally close relationship, would have confided in him. Still, he wasted no time in galloping back to the gracious *hacienda*, its ancient terracotta walls bathed in late-afternoon sunlight, and having Juanito, his manservant, pack his bags in readiness for the journey.

Twenty-four hours later he was sitting in the book-lined study of his family's home in Eaton Square, trying to absorb the impact of what his father had just said.

'But that's utterly preposterous!' Ramon exclaimed, dragging his fingers through his thick black hair and shaking his head. 'As I recollect, Nena Carvajal is not twenty yet—a mere girl. How can you and old Don Rodrigo even contemplate marriage for her?'

'Really, Ramon. Stop being prissy. You sound as if you've never heard of a marriage of convenience.'

'Well, certainly not one like this,' Ramon countered with feeling, letting his long legs stretch before him and crossing his ankles. His bronzed brow creased. 'I don't know what's got into your heads. If Nena thinks of me as anything at all it's probably in the light of an—'

'Rubbish.' His father, a well-dressed man in his late seventies, cut him short briskly. 'I doubt if she remembers you at all—which may be for the best.'

'Wonderful.'

'There is a very strong reason for this arrangement.'

'Oh? And what might that be?' Ramon raised a haughty brow.

'Simply put, Don Rodrigo, her grandfather, is dying.'

Ramon frowned and sat up straighter. 'What's wrong with him?'

'The big C, I'm afraid. He has six months at the most. Now, can you imagine what might happen to that girl if she's let loose on the world with the kind of money she will inherit? Not to mention the running of Rodrigo's empire,' he added, with a quick, sharp look at his son.

'So that's what this is all about,' Ramon said slowly. 'Rodrigo thinks I might be a suitable candidate to take over, does he?'

'I would say that is a great compliment, considering the vastness and complexity of his empire.'

'I suppose that's one way of looking at it,' Ramon conceded irritably. 'There's only one problem.'

'Oh?' Don Pedro raised an eyebrow and waited.

'I have no desire to be married.'

A moment's silence followed before the older man answered. 'Ramon, this marriage to Nena—'

'Who could practically be my daughter,' Ramon dismissed disparagingly.

'Hardly. Unless you plan to enter the *Guinness Book of Records* as a very young father,' his parent murmured with a touch of wry humour. 'Now, this marriage—as I was saying before you so rudely interrupted me—will hardly curtail your er—lifestyle. I'm sure that Nena has been brought up to expect a marriage of this kind. I haven't, I admit, seen her for several years. She has been at boarding school—the Convent of the Sacré Coeur,' he continued with a small satisfied smile. 'That in itself is a good omen.'

'Father, this whole notion is totally absurd!' Ramon exploded. He jumped up from the chair, his lean, athletic figure clad in an exquisitely cut Italian navy silk suit, and began pacing the study. 'You'd think it was the Middle Ages. I cannot agree to such a plan.'

'At least give it some thought—think about it,' Don

Pedro said reasonably. 'It would, of course, be an incredible opportunity for you. Businesswise, I mean.'

Ramon's eyes flashed and he drew himself up taller. 'If you think, Father, that I would get myself tangled up in a marriage of convenience out of a desire to improve my already not so shabby business ventures, then let me relieve you of the notion immediately,' he replied witheringly.

'I didn't mean it like that,' Don Pedro responded carefully, measuring his son's reaction. 'Think of your mother and I. We barely knew one another before our marriage. And look how wonderfully it has turned out. The truth is I have never looked at another woman since, and I can assure you I was quite a lad in my day.' He let out a long, low laugh. 'And as for age—why, your mother's twenty years my junior. You are barely thirteen years older than Nena. I cannot take that as a consideration. And besides, at thirty-two it is time you thought of setting up your nursery.'

'Whatever, Father,' Ramon growled, suddenly needing to be alone, to think, to straighten this mess out.

'May I tell my old friend Don Rodrigo that you will at least think about the proposal? To turn it down out of hand would be nothing short of an insult.'

This last was true. The honour of being selected by one of the richest men in the world to be his future grandson-in-law, heir to all his responsibilities, was no light matter. Handled wrongly, this could affect a lifelong friendship.

Reluctantly Ramon nodded. 'Very well, Father. But

on one condition,' he declared, his chin jutting firmly, 'that I get to see Nena. I presume she has been made aware of the circumstances?'

'Uh, not that I'm aware of,' Don Pedro murmured, carefully shuffling a pile of papers on his desk. 'All in good time.'

'Great,' Ramon replied cynically, rolling his eyes. Then, for some inexplicable reason, he avoided delivering the rest of the sentence about to escape his lips.

'The Villalbas?' Nena's well-shaped brows creased and she tilted her lovely, lightly tanned face to one side, her flashing green eyes fixed on her grandfather. 'I don't seem to remember them. Did we know them back in Argentina?'

'Of course, my love. But it has been quite a while since they last visited. Certainly not since you went off to school. Pedro Villalba is an old and trusted friend of mine, and his wife Augusta is in some way related to your late grandmother's family.'

'Ah.' Nena nodded and smiled. Everyone was always somehow related to the family.

'They are coming to tea tomorrow with their son, Ramon, whom you may remember. He came over once or twice when he was at Eton and then Oxford.'

'Sorry, I haven't a clue who he is.' She shook her tawny gold-flecked hair, highlighted by two weeks of playing tennis every day in the South of France, and jumped up. 'I'm off to the tournament now. Do you need anything before I go? Water for your pills?' she asked, suddenly concerned.

Her grandfather seemed to have aged much during

the past weeks, and she worried about him. Not for nothing had she inherited her deceased French mother's perception and innate capability for running Thurston Manor, their lovely country house near Windsor, and for making sure that her beloved grandfather was cosseted.

'No, no, my child. Off you run. Just make sure to be back on time for tea tomorrow.'

'I'll try. But we have the semi-finals, and if I get through today I may be playing.'

Don Rodrigo smiled at her benignly. He loved her so dearly, and wished—oh, how he wished—that he could live to see her bloom into the flower he perceived emerging, watch as she travelled towards womanhood. But that was not to be, he reminded himself with an inner sigh, accepting the soft kiss on his withered old cheek. And he must make sure she was safely provided for. Not just financially—there she was only too well provided for. If anything that was half the worry. In fact what truly concerned him were the fortune-hunters that he knew would hover like anxious vultures from here to Tierra del Fuego the minute he was dead and buried.

It was four by the time the Bentley drew up on the gravel drive before the splendid country house. Ramon experienced another wave of distaste. The whole thing was utterly absurd, and left him feeling as though he were participating in a very bad B movie. Still, he'd listened to his mother's urgings and his father's request to at least honour the visit. And he would, he supposed, alighting from the vehicle. At least after this he might be able to bring his father and Don Rodrigo to reason.

Several minutes later they were being conducted by the dignified white-haired butler onto the lawn, where Don Rodrigo heaved himself with some difficulty out of a wicker chair.

'*Amigos,*' he said, embracing Pedro and kissing Augusta. 'What a pleasure it is to receive you in my home.' Then he turned towards Ramon and eyed him closely. 'How do you do, Ramon? It is several years since we last met, but I've followed your may I say rather brilliant progress?' He quirked a brow and smiled. 'Knowing your father, I am not surprised. But impressed. Very impressed.'

'Coming from you, that is a compliment indeed,' Ramon murmured, shaking the other man's hand. He sensed the slight shaking and frailty in the fingers and realised that the sharp grey eyes belied failing health. He also realised that Don Pedro would not easily be fobbed off. As he sat down next to his mother at the table, already laid for afternoon tea, he wondered just how hard it was going to be to get out of this marriage. There was no sign of Nena, he observed a sudden spark of hope flashing. Perhaps she'd been told and had refused to agree to the arrangement. She was, after all, nearly twenty.

If so, all the better.

He was quite willing to help her out, advise her financially—even be a trustee, if Don Rodrigo so wished.

The thought began to take shape. Perhaps that was the way to work the situation, he mused, his quick brain already solving the matter. If Nena didn't agree to the marriage then he could bow out gracefully and not be blamed, and it would all work out for the best. It was, he reflected, allowing wishful thinking to take the upper hand, a mere question of initiating the correct strategy.

'Have they arrived?' Nena asked breathlessly as she jumped out of her new Audi TT. After throwing her tennis racket onto one of the hall chairs, she glanced at herself in the gilt mirror. 'I look a mess. But I suppose I'd better dash out and say hello, or Grandfather will kill me,' she exclaimed to Worthing, the butler, who was eyeing her severely as he closed the door.

'Don Rodrigo and the guests are on the lawn, Miss Nena.' He still called her by her childhood name.

'Good. Well, do see that tea is served, won't you? Oh, and Worthing? Please ask Cook to serve both China and Ceylon. I don't know which the guests would prefer.'

'Of course, Miss Nena,' he replied, pursing his lips and shaking his head fondly as she flew across the hall, through the drawing room, and down the steps to the lawn, where the group was seated under the chestnut tree facing the lake.

Smoothing her hair back, she hurried across the grass. How nice for her grandfather to have some people to entertain. He saw so few nowadays. She was sure it wasn't good for him to lead such a solitary existence, she reflected as she drew up on them from behind, but perhaps a lot of social activity might tire him.

'Hello, I'm so sorry I'm late.'

Ramon turned.

'Aunt Augusta, Uncle Rodrigo, it's been ages,' she said, kissing Ramon's parents while he looked in frank admiration at the gorgeous, lithe young woman—at her never-ending long bronzed legs that eradicated for ever the fuzzy image he'd formed of a rather dowdy, plump adolescent. Her smile, he reflected, was dazzling, her teeth white and perfect, and her lightly tanned skin set off the beauty of her huge almond-shaped green eyes in a manner fit to leave even a seasoned womaniser like himself dazed.

And her hair…

It fell in feathery wisps from a ponytail, giving her the air of having tumbled straight out of bed, and leaving him in dire danger of an embarrassing physical reaction.

Pulling himself together, Ramon rose and shook hands, hoping none of these untoward emotions showed, and reminded himself of the true nature of their visit here.

'Will you excuse me if I pop upstairs and change?' she was saying to his mother in a charmingly assured manner that belied her youth. 'I look a dreadful fright.'

He watched as she retreated swiftly across the lawn, trying to suppress the delightful image of that long, curved, slim body uncoiling amongst bedsheets, finding himself distressingly prey to a sensual twisting tug. He must not, he realised, removing his eyes from her, lose track of reality here. He caught his father's approving eye and quickly concentrated once more on the conversation.

But if his father thought that Nena's astonishing beauty and charm might make the marriage any more acceptable he was wrong. Instead it somehow made it worse. It was one thing to do a poor dowdy creature a favour, another to place under his protection a paragon whom, when she found her feet, would be the toast of society in every city they visited. The thought was strangely disturbing and he banished it.

'Ramon, I hope you have thought about your father's and my proposition,' Don Rodrigo said, easing himself with obvious difficulty in the wicker chair, reminding Ramon of just how much was at stake here. 'After one look at my lovely granddaughter I'm sure you are aware how impossible it would be for me to allow her to go out alone and unchaperoned into the world.'

'Well, I don't altogether agree, no,' Ramon countered. 'After all, sir, we are in the twenty-first century. A well-selected board of trustees could easily take care of her affairs. She seems a confident young woman, quite able to look after herself,' he added.

'Ha!' Don Rodrigo let out a harsh exclamation. 'Much you know about it. Oh, she's got confidence and charm and excellent manners, of course. But she would be swept off her feet by the first fortune-hunter that walked into her life. And, believe me, they're already lining up,' he said darkly.

'That I can believe,' Pedro Villalba replied, sending

his son a meaningful look from under his thick silver brows.

'And it's not only my little Nena I'm concerned about,' Don Pedro continued, meeting Ramon's eyes with a look as steady as his own. 'It's the future of all I've built up over a lifetime. I have no intention for that to go to rack and ruin, frittered away by some spendthrift. Trustees, as you mentioned earlier, are all fine and dandy, but they will not direct her sentimental life, look after her as a woman needs looking after.'

'Excuse me for being so bold,' Ramon said, leaning forward, 'but does Nena have any idea of what's going on here?'

'Up until now I deemed it preferable to stay silent. After all, I do not want her to be unduly upset. And when she learns of my illness,' he said stifling a sigh, 'she *will* be most upset.'

'Of course.' Ramon looked down. 'Don Rodrigo, although I would be more than willing to accept a role in an advisory capacity, I don't feel that—'

'One moment, young man. I am aware that all this has been thrust upon you in a most impromptu manner. But will you not at least take the opportunity, now that you have come all this way, of getting to know my granddaughter a little better? I am not suggesting that the two of you fall in love, or anything of that nature, merely that together you establish a well-balanced relationship. Nena has been brought up in the strictest possible manner. She would make you a good wife.

'Many marriages work out very well under these

conditions,' he added with a thin, tired smile. 'I know that in this day and age you young people all believe in Hollywood-style relationships—marriage one day, divorce the next. But real life, my boy, is very different. Look rather at your parents, and at myself. Our marriages were planned, and they worked out brilliantly.'

'That's all very well,' Ramon countered, but then, seeing the butler carrying a large silver tray piled with scones and sandwiches, he closed his mouth.

Nena rushed into the large marble bathroom of her suite of rooms and took a rapid shower, her mind filled with the incredibly good-looking son of her grandfather's friends. She had been quite taken aback, but hoped that her surprise had not been in any way evident.

He was older, of course, and rather forbidding and arrogant-looking, with his thick black hair, straight Roman nose, high slashed cheekbones and chestnut golden-flecked eyes. A bit like an actor, she reflected, rubbing herself with a thick terry towel before stepping into the dressing room and choosing a short pink linen Gucci dress.

Minutes later she tripped down the stairs and joined the others. She sat in the only available chair, next to Ramon, determined not to let his intense masculine aura distract her as she proceeded to serve the tea. The next few minutes were occupied with handing round sandwiches, and it was only when she sat back down that she realised Ramon was looking at her rather fiercely.

She shifted uncomfortably and suppressed a desire to pull her skirt lower. A delicious shiver coursed through her. She'd heard of men looking at you and leaving you feeling undressed. Now she knew what it meant. For a moment she wondered if she was dreaming. Perhaps she'd spilled something on her dress and that was why he was looking her over in that confident manner.

She glanced down, but there was nothing, and she felt cross with herself for allowing this man to leave her feeling both self-conscious and—something else that she couldn't quite define. Shifting closer to his mother, she half turned her back on him and chit-chatted about this and that for a while, trying not to be aware of his eyes upon her.

'You must come and see the garden properly,' she said to Augusta. 'I've had some new flowerbeds laid out near the lake, and the little wood over there is charming to walk in.'

'Thank you, my love,' Augusta replied with a gracious smile. 'But I'm afraid I find walking a bit of a strain these days, particularly in the heat. But Ramon, I'm sure, would be delighted to see the garden.'

'Oh, no. I don't think you'd like it at all,' Nena said hastily, turning towards him, embarrassed and biting her lip while hoping she hadn't sounded too rude. She could hardly refuse to take him, but the last place she wanted to go was for a walk in his austere, rather autocratic company.

'Yes, Nena, that's a good idea,' her grandfather insisted. 'You take Ramon for a walk while we old folks chat.' Don Rodrigo smiled approvingly.

Unwilling to distress her grandfather by refusing, Nena turned and glanced at Ramon. 'If you like we can go,' she said, her tone unenthusiastic, hoping he'd refuse.

'Fine. Let's go.'

Reluctantly she rose and began walking down towards the lake with Ramon close by her side. He was tall, she observed, at least six foot two or more, and his shoulders were broad. There was something powerful and engulfing in his presence, she realised, an authority about him that reminded her in a way of her grandfather. Now, as they walked, he slipped off his jacket and threw it casually over his shoulder while Nena wondered what on earth to say to him.

Soon they'd reached the lakeside, and Ramon still hadn't made any effort at conversation—although Nena could feel his eyes boring into her. It was really most uncomfortable, especially since he was so close to her. She was catching whiffs of his musky aftershave—and something else indefinable, something she'd never experienced next to any man before.

'Those are peonies and delphiniums,' she blabbered, pointing out the flowers, 'and over there are a number of dahlias. But I'm sure you're not really interested in flowers,' she added quickly, pressing her hands together and wondering why she felt so wound up and nervous when usually she was perfectly at ease with visitors.

'You're right,' he replied, his face breaking into a sudden charming smile that lit up his face as he looked down at her. 'I'm no expert on flowers. But my parents and your grandfather seemed pretty determined that we should come for a walk together, don't you think?' he asked, testing the terrain.

'Yes.' She frowned, looking up at him, puzzled. 'They did, didn't they? Do you have any idea why?'

Ramon wished he'd kept his mouth shut. For now he felt like a cad, as though he was deceiving this young woman by not telling her the truth. Yet how could he come clean when she had not the slightest idea that her grandfather was dying?

'I suppose they thought that we are nearer in age and might find more to talk about on our own,' he said with a non-committal shrug. He found it hard to resist her enquiring gaze, that lovely frank innocence in her eyes and in her charming smile, and the underlying trace of sensuality that he'd be willing to bet she still hadn't recognised in herself. The thought left him in dire danger of another embarrassing physical reaction and he turned quickly towards the lake. 'Look, why don't we keep them happy and you show me this famous wood?' he said, pointing to his left with forced interest.

'Okay,' she agreed, glad that the atmosphere had lightened up. Perhaps he was just someone you needed to get to know better.

'Tell me about yourself,' he said, taking her arm lightly as they reached a small bridge that crossed the lake to a path that led to the wood.

Another curious new sensation coursed through Nena at his touch on her flesh, and she was hard put to it not to shudder.

'There's not much to tell,' she said, allowing him to guide her across, although she knew the bridge by heart. 'I finished school last year. I wanted to go to university—was accepted by a couple, in fact,' she added hastily. For some reason she didn't want him to assume she was stupid. 'But then Grandfather seemed increasingly unwell and I didn't feel I could abandon him.' She stopped and shrugged, then smiled up at him through long thick lashes. 'He doesn't seem any better lately, and I don't want to make him unhappy.'

'But of course you must go to university,' Ramon replied. Part of him was shocked that her future might be compromised. The other part, the part that didn't want to recognise just how attractive he found her, thought how appealing it was that in this day and age, when most women he came across thought only of their own wellbeing and personal ambition, she should place her grandfather first. Which, in turn, reminded him of all the pain she was going to experience when she learned of his terminal illness.

'Maybe one day I'll be able to go to college,' she replied with a shrug. 'I'd really like to. But please,' she said, her brows creasing suddenly, 'promise you won't tell Grandfather? I would hate for him to be upset or worried.'

'Of course I won't say anything. Anyway, it's none of my business. Still, it seems odd that he won't—' Suddenly Ramon remembered. Of course Don Rodrigo didn't want her out there, in the midst of people over whom he had no control. 'Where were you accepted?' he asked.

'Oxford and the Sorbonne.'

He looked at her, brows raised. 'That's pretty good.'

'You seem surprised,' she countered, challenging him. 'I suppose it's because I'm a woman?'

'Guilty,' he said, a new and delicious twinkle brightening his eyes. 'I'm afraid I'm not used to coming across women who are as lovely as you and yet who are obviously also highly gifted and intelligent.'

Nena's cheeks flushed and she looked quickly away. 'Oh, I'm not really that bright. I just like studying, that's all. There's the wood,' she mumbled hastily.

'What about your boyfriend?' he probed. 'Does he want you to go to university?'

'Boyfriend?' Nena frowned again, then laughed, a natural spontaneous gurgle that left Ramon swallowing. 'Oh, I see. No, I don't have a boyfriend. Well, I have friends, of course, like Jimmy Chandler and David Onslow at the tennis club, but that's different.'

'And have none of them ever tried to kiss you?' he asked in an amused, bantering tone, unable to resist the temptation of finding out more about this alluring creature to whom he was becoming increasingly drawn, despite the strange situation they were in.

'Oh, Lord, no—they're just pals.' Nena gave an embarrassed shrug and their eyes met as they reached the edge of the wood. 'This is the wood. Do you want to see it?'

'Honestly?' His eyes flashed wickedly.

'Honestly,' she responded, lips twitching.

'Honestly, I have no interest whatsoever in seeing

your wood—though if it is half as charming as its owner I suppose I should.'

'Oh, shut up.' She giggled, feeling now as though she'd known him a while. 'That's totally silly.'

'Why don't we sit over there by the lake for a few minutes and relax?'

'All right.'

They walked back across the bridge and down to the water's edge. 'Here, let me lay this on the grass; it may be damp,' he said, spreading out his jacket for her, trying to sort out the conflict raging in his mind.

'Thanks.' She sat on part of the jacket, leaving room for him, and he lowered himself next to her.

'Tell me, what's it like living with your grandfather?' he asked suddenly, throwing a pebble spinning into the still waters of the lake.

'I love him dearly. I mean, of course at times it's a bit restrictive, but I need to look after him. That's why I didn't tell him I'd been accepted at Oxford, or he might have changed his mind and felt obliged to let me go. Then there would have been no one to look after him.'

'But surely the staff would take care of him?'

'Yes, but that's not the same at all,' she dismissed, raising her lovely determined chin. 'Lately he seems to be so frail. I can't quite explain it, but…' She hesitated and pressed her fingers together, a sudden frown creasing her brow. 'I'm just being silly, I suppose, but it worries me.' She looked up and their eyes met. 'Your parents seem so nice,' she said, changing the subject. 'Do you live with them or on your own?'

'Oh, on my own. I have several houses—my

hacienda, a loft in Puert Madero in Buenos Aires. In London I stay at my parents' place in Eaton Square, though. Quite a change,' he added, aware that he could hardly tell her that he shared his life with Luisa, his official mistress, and on occasion a smattering of models, who drifted in and out. Luisa was not officially in-house, of course, but it was an ongoing relationship. And although she knew he had no intention of marrying her—she was twice divorced—they had a very pleasant time together.

Which brought him back to the matter at hand. What would happen to Luisa if, by some twist of fate, he decided to accept Don Rodrigo's proposition?

Ramon glanced down at Nena once more. She was lovely, and unaware of it. Just as she was unaware of what awaited her just around the corner. Her grandfather's death would shake her for ever from the safe cocoon she'd lived in all her life. It would be harsh and painful, he realised sadly. For as an only grandchild she was probably even more protected from the world than if her parents had been alive. Also she'd have no one—except some friends and her financial advisors—to turn to. Perhaps, he reflected sombrely, Don Rodrigo was not so wrong to want to protect her from all that might be waiting for her out there. All at once Ramon shared the old man's fears for her.

'Maybe we should be getting back,' he said abruptly, glancing at the thin gold watch on his tanned wrist. 'My parents will be wanting to leave soon.'

'All right.' She jumped up and he picked up the jacket, throwing it over his shoulder again as they made their way back to the group on the lawn.

It was odd, he reflected, that a plan which only an hour ago had struck him as absolutely preposterous now seemed considerably less so. Plus, as both Don Rodrigo and his father had pointed out, it was a marriage, not an affair. He was thirty-two, and would have to think of marriage and a family shortly anyway. Wouldn't it be infinitely preferable to be married to a lovely creature like Nena, whom he could mould to his liking, teach the art of love, yet continue enjoying the Luisas of this world on the side? he reflected somewhat ruthlessly. All in all, having a beautiful, well-mannered society wife, whom he could take pleasure with in bed from time to time without changing his routine, might not be such a bad thing after all.

'My love, I have something I need to speak to you about,' Don Rodrigo said to his granddaughter the next evening over dinner.

'Yes, Grandfather?' Nena looked at him closely. He seemed very tired. In the past few days he had barely left his room, except to sit on the lawn yesterday afternoon with the Villalbas. 'Is something wrong?' she enquired anxiously.

'After dinner we shall retire to the study and have a chat,' he said, knowing the moment had finally arrived when he must tell her the truth.

Since the acceptance that morning of the proposition of marriage by Ramon Villalba he had known it was essential she learn about his illness and what the future held, however painful.

Don Rodrigo sampled a tiny spoonful of chocolate

mousse. It turned bitter on his tongue. He had faced many hard moments in his life, but telling this child whom he loved so dearly that the end was near would rank among the cruellest blows life had dealt him. His only solace was that Ramon Villalba had, for whatever reason, accepted his proposition.

Half an hour later, seated as always on the tapestried footstool at his feet, Nena listened in anguished horror to her grandfather's words.

'But that's impossible,' she cried, grabbing his hands and squeezing them tight. 'It can't be true, Grandfather, there must be a mistake. You must have other tests—other opinions. It simply can't be right,' she ended, sobbing.

'I'm afraid I've already done all that,' he responded sadly, stroking the mane of tawny hair fanned out on his lap and soothing her tears. 'That is why I have had to make provision for you.'

'Pro-provision?' she gulped, raising her head, still trying to absorb the horrible news he'd imparted.

'Yes, my love. You must be taken care of, provided for.'

'Please, Grandfather, don't talk about it,' she sobbed.

'I'm afraid I must. Time is short and measures must be taken.'

'Wh-what measures?' she gulped sadly, trying to regain some control as the truth sank in.

Don Rodrigo hesitated, then, with a sigh, forged ahead. 'Yesterday you met Ramon Villalba.'

'Yes,' she whispered, taking his handkerchief and blowing her nose hard.

'And you found him—pleasant?'

'Yes, I suppose so. He was polite. Look, Grandfather, what has that got to do with you being ill?' she burst out, leaning back on her heels, eyes pleading.

'Ramon Villalba has proposed marriage.'

'Marriage?' Nena let out a horrified gasp and stood up, clutching the damp handkerchief between her nervous fingers. 'But that is absurd, Grandfather. How can I get married to a man I don't know, whom I don't love? I don't want to get married. I—'

'Shush, child, do not get so agitated. Come here.' He held out his hand and she sank once more to the footstool. 'I have talked to the Villalbas. We all agree that this marriage is a good thing.'

'How—how can you say that, Grandfather? It's archaic. Nobody is forced to marry any longer; it's unheard of. Oh, please, Grandfather, this can't be real. There must be a mistake. I'm sure if you went to another doctor—'

'Now, now. I want you to listen, Nena. Carefully. I am absolutely decided on this marriage. And I want the wedding to take place as soon as possible.'

'You mean he came here to inspect me, as he might a horse or a piece of cattle?' she cried. 'Why would he propose an arrangement like this?'

'I can think of several reasons—all of them perfectly valid,' Don Rodrigo answered firmly. 'He needs a wife from a good family and of excellent upbringing who is unsoiled. Also he is adequately prepared to take care of our business ventures.'

'So that's it,' she whispered bitterly. 'A business

arrangement. Oh, Grandfather, how can you auction me off like this? It's all too horrible.' She turned, and her shoulders shook as she sobbed. Her pain at learning of her grandfather's terminal illness was somehow increased by the knowledge that a man whom she'd ended the afternoon finding most agreeable was in fact nothing but a dirtbag. 'You talked with him without knowing if I wanted this?' she whispered at last, turning back to him, her eyes glistening with tears.

'Yes, Nena, I did. Villalba is a practical man. I have informed myself, followed his career over a period of several years. He will take care of you, look out for you and the fortune you are going to inherit.'

'I don't care about any of that!' she exclaimed.

'Maybe not, but I do. Please do this for me,' he added, a softer, pleading note entering his voice. 'I can die in peace knowing that you are in his hands.'

'Oh, please don't talk like that,' she begged once more, kneeling next to him.

'Then agree to my request,' Don Rodrigo said, exercising a considerable amount of emotional pressure. He sighed inwardly. It was the only way to bring the matter to a fast and satisfactory conclusion. 'Answer me, Nena. Tell me you'll do as I ask.'

Nena stared through her tears at the carpet, her emotions in turmoil. The last thing she wanted was to be married to a man she barely knew. A wave of frustration overtook her. This was, after all, the most important step in her life—yet she had no control over it. Despite her feelings, she already knew what the answer must be.

'I'll do it, Grandfather,' she whispered.

At that moment she hated Ramon Villalba.

CHAPTER TWO

THE wedding—a small, intimate affair, with only the two families present—took place at the fashionable church of St James, Spanish Place, in London, two weeks later. Afterwards they returned to Don Rodrigo's house in Chester Square to quietly celebrate the nuptials.

Nena wafted through the ceremony in a daze, her emotions blunted, the pain of seeing her grandfather withering daily barely allowing her to think clearly about what the future next to a man she despised would hold.

'Are you okay?' Ramon asked quietly, touching her arm as they moved into the hall. She deposited the bouquet of flowers on the hall table and allowed the butler to take her wrap.

'I'm perfectly all right,' she answered coldly.

'Are you sure?' He looked down at her, noting the dark rings around her beautiful green eyes and the sadness they held. 'A bride should be happy on her wedding day.'

'Happy?' she jeered, sending him a glare. 'How could any bride be happy, married in these circumstances?'

'I know these are not the happiest of times,' he

agreed levelly, glancing at Don Rodrigo, mounting the stairs with extreme difficulty. 'Still, I want you to know, Nena, that as your husband I shall do my best to make you happy.'

'How very gracious of you,' she responded bitterly, barely attempting to conceal the anger in her voice. How dared he pretend he cared? Wasn't it bad enough that she was losing her grandfather, whom she adored, without having Ramon's odious presence thrust upon her?

She sent him an angry look, then spun on the heel of her designer shoe and marched towards the stairs.

Ramon followed her at a distance. To his consternation Nena had not unbent, as he'd hoped she would. She had refused to receive him again before the wedding and had barely addressed a word to him since leaving the church. He sighed. This did not bode well for the future. But it was done now. The knot had been tied and the vows exchanged. All that remained was for them both to make the best of it.

'I thought you would prefer to come here to the island rather than be with a crowd,' Ramon said above the purr of the engine as the helicopter hovered over the Aegean.

Nena could distinguish an island below, and a small port, with a yacht and a number of colourful fishing boats bobbing in the harbour. Then she saw a rambling white villa, surrounded by smaller dwellings with little blue shutters and, in the distance, a windmill. At any other time she would have been enchanted. But right now being in Greece on her bridegroom's private island or being in Battersea would have meant about the same to her. All she wanted was to be alone, to think, to assimilate the shock that having her world tipped topsy-turvy from one moment to the other had left her in.

As they alighted Ramon took her hand firmly, and they walked up a small winding path from the beach where the chopper had landed. A soft evening breeze blew in from the sea, gulls twirled overhead, and villagers sat on the wall waving at them with bright smiles. As they approached the villa a little girl ran forward and, curtseying, handed her a bouquet of wild flowers. Despite her numb state and her sadness, Nena smiled down at the child and thanked her.

She gazed at the flowers, reminded that this was her wedding day.

The saddest day of her life.

For a moment tears welled, but she suppressed them as fast as they came. She had no right to be unhappy. At least her grandfather would have a happy end to his life. And that mattered more than anything.

Then all at once she became deeply conscious of Ramon standing next to her, his powerful body so close he almost touched her. And she shivered. What came next in this awful sequence of events? she wondered as slowly they moved on up towards the steps of the house. What would he expect from her as his wife?

For the first time, as they entered the huge hall, then stepped into the tiled drawing room and out onto the low-walled terrace overlooking the cerulean sea beyond, Nena faced her dilemma. Suddenly she glanced at

Ramon, who was speaking to one of the servants. He looked like a man not used to being thwarted. Everyone jumped at his quiet, polite commands. What, she wondered, would he want from her?

'I've ordered some champagne,' he said, looking down at her. 'Afterwards you might like to tour the first of your new homes,' he added, with that same touch of sardonic humour she'd observed the first day by the lake. *Remember,* she told herself, *he doesn't care about you. You're nothing more than a lucrative asset.*

'I feel rather tired,' she said, seating herself on the colourful woven cushions that were spread over the white-washed stone sofa surrounding the wall that formed a cozy niche. 'I think I'll go and rest in a minute, if you don't mind. Perhaps one of the maids could show me to my room.'

'To *our* room, you mean,' he returned firmly.

Her eyes flew up to meet his and she shivered. 'I—I think we need to talk about that.' She clasped her hands together and felt her cheeks go bright pink.

'What is there to talk about?' Ramon asked, leaning lazily back against the wall in his immaculate grey suit. He managed to look at ease in it, despite being on a relaxed Greek island.

'A lot, I think.'

'Oh?' He raised an enquiring brow.

'Yes. We—this is a marriage of convenience. You, for whatever reason, decided that it suited you to propose,' she replied hotly, sending him an angry glare. 'I accepted because I love my grandfather and don't want him to end his days worrying and miserable. I don't think that either of those reasons constitutes grounds for—for intimacy.' She ended hurriedly, wishing this conversation wasn't taking place.

'I see.' Ramon gazed at her speculatively. He hadn't reckoned with this—had thought that once he had her to himself things would somehow smooth themselves out. Perhaps, he reflected reluctantly, he would have to give her some time to get used to the idea that she was his.

The thought sent a slash of heat racing through his body and he stood straighter. 'We'll talk about this later on,' he said, seeing a servant appear with the champagne. 'For now, let's relax and have a drink.'

Seconds later he was handing her a glass filled with sparkling champagne. 'Welcome to Agapos,' he said, raising his glass. 'May you be happy and contented here, *señora mia*.'

Nena made a minute gesture of acknowledgement with her glass, and instead of the sip she'd intended took a large, long gulp. She certainly needed something to get her through the next few hours…days—nights.

Ramon watched her. He would have to restrain the desire that had been consuming him for the past two weeks and control the powerful urge he had to take her to his bed. There was time for that, he told himself. No need to rush things. He was willing to pander to her present needs—for a while. Still, there was a limit to his patience.

But she was experiencing a period of deep trauma, caused by her grandfather's illness, and their marriage must have come as something of a surprise, he realised soberly. Then there was the fact that she was very young, and apparently had very little or no sexual experience. She was perhaps afraid. It would be up to him to make sure that it all happened smoothly, that her initiation to the bedroom and its pleasures was an enjoyable experience. He took a deep breath and forced his mind onto something else before his body betrayed him.

Three nights later Ramon was feeling considerably less amenable. Nena had barely spoken to him, and when she did she was grudgingly polite. They'd spent several stonily silent hours on the beach, on the yacht, driving around the island. If he proposed a plan she agreed neither happily nor unhappily.

Indifferent.

That was what she was. And it was driving him crazy. He could have handled raw anger, tears, a show of passion. But this blatant unresponsiveness and determination to remain as distant from him as possible was intolerable.

He sent her a scorching glance across the table which had been tastefully laid on the terrace. The moon was rising and the night was dotted with stars. The perfect night to be with a woman, he thought. They could have spent wonderful hours together, yet she refused to budge from this tenacious position she'd assumed. What was going on inside that lovely head? he wondered. What thoughts rankled? What was it that was eating her?

'Nena, I think that if there is something disturbing you, you should tell me about it. I've tried to be as accommodating as possible,' he added, thinking of the separate bedrooms he'd instructed the staff to arrange, 'but I think you owe me an explanation.'

'An explanation?' She lowered her fork to her plate and sent an icy stare across the crisp white cloth. 'I don't think I owe you anything, Ramon. Neither of us owes the other. We cut a deal. We each, apparently—though I don't quite see it that way—are supposed to benefit from this arrangement. I can see the advantages for you. I have yet to find out what mine are.'

'Is that how you see this? Purely as a business arrangement?' he said, shocked that someone so young could be so level-headed, so…

'That's exactly how I think of it. And the sooner you do so as well, the better it will be for both of us. Why don't we end this farce of a honeymoon at once and get back home?'

'We are home,' he replied coldly. 'Home, from now on, is where I reside. My homes have now become your homes.'

'I have to go back to my grandfather,' she said doggedly staring at her plate.

'I have no objection to remaining in England for the present. But in our home.'

'But—'

'There are no buts,' he returned autocratically. 'We shall stay with my parents. I have instructed my estate agents to look for a place for us.'

'I don't want to go to Eaton Square,' Nena muttered through gritted teeth, her fingers clenched as she tried not to cry. 'I want to go home—to Thurston.

Why don't you just go back to Buenos Aires and—?'

She stopped herself in time from saying *back to your mistress.* He had no idea that she'd seen the pictures of him and Luisa Somebody-or-other in *Hola!* magazine. The pictures had been taken in Gstaad, where they'd been winter sporting. In fact Ramon had no notion that she knew about his lifestyle. She had found out quite by chance about the woman in his life, as she'd flipped through an old copy of the magazine that Doña Augusta had brought for her grandfather.

And, surprisingly, it had hurt.

It didn't matter that she despised the man for agreeing to marry her, despised his motives and everything he stood for. The sight of him—arm possessively around the shoulders of a lush, luscious, stunning brunette, obviously a highly worldly and sophisticated woman, near to his own age—had left her inordinately troubled. Not that it was anything to do with her, she'd reasoned then as she did now. What did she care how many women he slept with? She had no intention of being one of them, did she?

Ramon leaned forward and touched her hand. 'Nena, I have no objection to your visiting your grandfather, spending time with him, and of course there will come a time—' He cut off, unwilling to say the words he knew would hurt her so much, while deeply aware that it was his duty to prepare her for what he suspected would take place in a very short time. 'But I do require that your official and permanent residence be under my roof,' he finished firmly as she drew her trembling fingers from his grasp. 'I will not allow my wife to live anywhere but with me.'

He'd never thought he would feel so strongly possessive the day he married. Had never thought about it much at all. But now that it had happened he felt a need to control, to be in the driving seat. He had never bothered being jealous in the past. If a woman lost interest—why, he usually had long before, and was sticking around out of courtesy.

But Nena was different. He sensed it deep down in a part of himself he hadn't known existed, some deep, primeval instinct that he'd tapped into on his wedding day and wouldn't leave him be; the same instinct that was leaving him ever more antsy as he passed her closed door each night on his way to bed.

Patience, he repeated to himself once again. She's young. Give her time. But it was becoming increasingly difficult.

That night Nena was unable to sleep. She had slipped on one of the beautiful, flimsy, spaghetti-strapped lawn nightdresses that were part of her hastily put together trousseau, chosen by her personal shopper. She looked down at it and sighed. She'd taken no interest in her trousseau, had merely agreed with anything Maureen had shown her. Now, half-afraid, she looked at herself in the mirror. She could see the shadow of her body peeping through the thin fabric and closed her eyes. How hard it was to admit to herself that despite her wish to alienate him, she was constantly thinking of her husband, that when he came close to her every nerve vibrated, that a new, torrid heat she'd never known charged through her being with an alien vibrance that left her damp in places she was embarrassed to think of. Desperately she searched for answers, unable to pinpoint this new, unquenchable thirst that had invaded her being and couldn't be satiated.

Angry with herself, and desperate to be in the open, she moved out onto the vast balcony that contoured the upper story of the villa. Leaning her hands on the balustrade, her long hair flowing about her shoulders, Nena gazed out over the Aegean at the starlit night and listened to the sea softly lapping the shore. This was her honeymoon, and should have been the most wonderful moment of her life, yet here she was, miserable in more ways than one. She let out a long sigh.

'Aren't you sleepy?' The deep husky voice just behind her made her spin round and gasp, another thrust of emotion rushing through her.

Ramon stood before her, more handsome than ever in silk pyjama pants, the top open revealing an expanse of bronzed chest. In the pool of lantern light she could see a gleam flashing in his golden-flecked chestnut eyes as they flicked over her, taking in each detail of her body in a cool, possessive manner, as an owner might look over a thoroughbred. The thin nightdress, she knew, left little to the imagination.

Ashamed, Nena moved her hands behind her against the balustrade, unaware that by doing so her small, delicious breasts were thrust towards him invitingly as her hair fell back from her shoulders and her perfect throat glistened in the moonlight.

God, she was lovely, Ramon acknowledged, a shaft

of untamed desire taking hold once more as he moved towards her, unable to resist. And she was his wife. He had every right to possess her.

'Nena,' he whispered, his voice low and sultry, 'let me love you. Let me be your husband.'

'I—I can't—' she responded hoarsely, only too conscious of his scent, of the maleness of him, of everything about him that drew her even while she tried desperately to remind herself of all the reasons why she couldn't let it happen.

'I promise not to hurt you,' he said reasonably, leaning his hands on each side of the balustrade, his tanned face and sensual lips only inches from hers.

It was then Nena realised, with a tingling shudder that left her weak, that he was about to kiss her.

And she could do nothing to stop him. Knew that however much she tried to justify it to herself she wouldn't stop him. She must resist, must not show him that she cared, that in spite of the fact that she despised him she also longed for his touch, to discover in his arms what it would be like to become a woman.

Then, before she could think further, his lips came down on hers, and Nena gave way to her first real kiss. She felt his lips prying hers open. For a moment she tried to draw back and protest, but the firm yet gentle insistence of his tongue working its way cunningly into her mouth, left her clutching his hard shoulders instead, trying to hold on to something as the earth swayed beneath her feet.

Ramon drew her into his arms, and, pressing his hand into the small of her back, felt the delicious curve of her bottom, her small taut breasts pressed against his chest. What would she do when she felt his hardness against her? he wondered. He was careful not to rush her as his tongue probed further, thrusting carefully, leading her gently to a response, containing his rampant desire to possess her until she was ready for more, aware that this was her first everything.

So he took it slowly, sensing her waning resistance, the fight between her brain and her body, her instinct and her soul. Then, just as smoothly and firmly, he drew her closer—until she could feel the length of him, until her tongue began tentatively seeking his, guiding her all the way, hands caressing her back, the soft curve of her perfect thighs.

Then all at once he felt her arms tighten about him, heard her tiny gasp as he left her mouth and began kissing her throat, and knew he was well on his way.

Nena threw her head back and moaned, giving herself up to his caresses. She let out another tiny gasp of delight and surprise when his lips reached her breast, encircling her taut nipple, taunting it through the soft texture of her nightdress, making her want to scream with joy and pain, to reach for more, to feel free of the fabric that stood between them. But still Ramon lingered.

Slipping a hand from behind her, he gently fondled her other breast until Nena thought she couldn't bear the searing rush of heat that stabbed her somewhere down in a place she'd never been entirely conscious of until this moment, but that now begged for some new kind of fulfilment and release.

Then a primal, tight, knotted spiral that she'd never before experienced rose within her, mounting until she thought she'd scream. And just as she could bear it no longer, as her fingers raked his thick black hair and she wanted to beg for mercy, for him to stop, a miracle happened and the hot, intense, coiled build-up crashed, simply let loose, wafted into an ecstatic joyride that lingered on and on for several seconds, leaving her limp and weak, her knees giving way beneath her as Ramon held her up and she fell extenuated against him.

'Mi linda,' he whispered, lifting her in his arms then carrying her through the French windows into his bedroom with the male satisfaction and pride of knowing he'd just introduced her to her first sexual experience.

'What happened?' she whispered as he laid her down in the middle of the huge bamboo four-poster bed, with its voile curtains and soft, cool linen sheets.

'You just experienced your first orgasm,' he said, slipping next to her onto the bed, his smile as arrogant as it was possessive.

'Oh.' Slowly Nena recouped her breath. Then suddenly she became aware that Ramon was about to remove his pyjama pants. Exercising every ounce of will-power, she sat up and brushed her hair aside, little aware of how tantalising she looked in the glow of the soft bedside lamps.

'Ramon, what are you doing?'

'Nena, you may be young and a virgin,' he said with a touch of humour in his flashing brown eyes, 'but I think you know very well what I'm doing. It's time I made you truly my wife.'

'No. I don't want to.' She moved back against the pillows and drew her legs up under her nightdress.

'Nena, after what just happened out there that is a ridiculous statement,' he said with a low, husky laugh that left her once again prey to the rush of heat that had assailed her previously. 'You want me just as much as I want you,' he said softly, trailing his long dark fingers from her throat to her breast, where he stopped just above her nipple and looked deep into her eyes. 'Tell me you don't want me to start all over again,' he said with quiet, yet arrogant assurance, 'and I'll leave you alone.'

Nena tried to think straight, to resist the tantalising caress that was fuzzing her brain. 'I don't—I can't—'

'Yes, you can, *mi linda,* of course you can. Remember, I'm your husband. You can do anything with me, Nena, anything at all. I'll show you, take you places you've never dreamed of.'

Her better judgement now fading into complete oblivion, Nena let her head sink back against the pillow with a long sigh.

'No,' Ramon said in an authoritative tone, 'don't run away from me. I want you here with me. I want you to know who is loving you and when. Nena, take off your nightgown.'

Again she tried to shy away. 'No. Please, Ramon, I—'

'Nena, might I remind you that a few days ago you vowed to obey me? I would hate to see you not keep your word.' His eyes pinned her now, allowing no room for flight. 'I am your husband, the man who has the right to see you, to possess you.'

It was a command, she realised, wishing she had the will-power to refuse him. Part of her hated him for what he was doing; the other submitted with intense female surrender. After all, he was right. The vow to obey had been part of their marriage ceremony; she had pronounced the words. But she hadn't thought of their meaning. Now, seeing him rise and stand over her next to the bed, his face unsmiling as his gaze held hers, she knew that the words were for real.

Slowly, very slowly, Nena slipped to the edge of the bed.

'Stand up,' he ordered softly.

Nena did as he bade her—standing, cheeks flushed, clenching her hands, as gently but firmly he pulled up the nightdress and slipped it over her head, leaving her before him with nothing but the long strands of her silky tawny mane for protection.

Then Ramon took a step back and feasted his eyes on her. 'You're beautiful—lovely,' he whispered hoarsely, letting his fingers trail over her, past her breast on down to her belly.

Despite her embarrassment Nena experienced another mind-wrenching tingle rush through her when his fingers reached further. All at once she realised she felt damp and hot, filled with a desire so great she could barely control the moan that escaped her when his fingers fondled her soft mound of golden curls, then slipped between her legs, probing further as he drew her close with his other arm.

And all at once she wanted to experience his skin

on hers, to know what he felt like, and it was she who began tugging at the tie of his pyjamas.

'Not so fast, *cariña,*' he murmured, close to her ear. 'There's time for that.'

'No,' she muttered, gasping as he touched a place deep inside her, provoking thrusts of pain and joy, leaving her increasingly ragged and wanting. 'You saw me. Now I want to see you.'

Ramon let out a low, satisfied laugh. 'Very well, my darling.' With that he continued caressing her with one hand while with the other he helped her remove the offending garments.

Soon they were standing naked, facing one another. Then Ramon gently removed his fingers and looked into her eyes. 'I am your husband, Nena, don't be ashamed.'

And the amazing thing, Nena realised, baffled, was that she wasn't. In fact she felt a strange new power take hold as he looked at her, and—tentatively at first—she allowed herself to look at his body, feast on his strong, bronzed and muscled limbs, his broad yet lean torso, then on down.

Firmly Ramon slipped his hand over hers and drew it towards him. 'I want you to feel me as I've felt you,' he said, drawing her back into his arms and gently placing her hand upon him, strangely enchanted to know that this was the first time she'd been with a man, that he was the first to teach her. Another sudden rush of possessiveness and then something far stronger hit him with utter surprise: for all at once he hoped he would be the last.

It was a strange, overwhelming feeling that left him

more emotionally touched than he could have believed possible. Now, as his arms slipped around her once more and he drew her back onto the bed, he tried to reason with himself, keep up the control. But he couldn't—could think only of reaching further, knowing her thoroughly, and he kissed her, not gently, as before, but with a new, surging passion that eradicated all trace of hesitation. The latter was replaced by a passionate, gnawing hunger that he'd rarely known but that needed to be assuaged.

Nena held her breath and let her feelings take over, her heart beating so loudly she was sure he would hear it, delighting in the hard wall of muscled male body cleaving against her. And something more, something much more troubling yet stirring, a primal need, grew inside her that she knew she had to pursue, as Ramon began a thorough and delicious investigation of her body, starting with feathery kisses at her throat that descended, further and further, taunting her aching swollen nipples, then moved on down until he reached her core.

Nena let out a gasp as his tongue flicked over the little nub of sensitive flesh she'd been unaware existed until this very moment. Seconds later she was moaning, writhing, unable to restrain the need to rake her fingers through his hair.

'Ramon!' she cried, and shattered again into a myriad of indescribable sensations, only to end up curled in his arms as he whispered sweet nothings in her ear and soothed her gently as every pulse in her body beat wildly.

And there was more to come.

Just as Nena was beginning to steady herself Ramon slipped his fingers between her thighs once more and probed, slowly, feeling the soft liquid honey, making sure she was ready for what was to happen next.

'Nena, *mi amor,*' he whispered huskily. 'I'm going to make you mine, all mine.' His almost imperceptible Spanish lilt thickened with passion as firmly he slid on top of her and parted her thighs.

Nena felt her body tense.

'Don't be afraid, *querida*. I'll do my best not to hurt you.'

'I—I've never—'

'I know, *corazon*, just leave it to me.' He dropped a long kiss on her mouth and at the same time eased himself gently into her.

Nena experienced a moment's shock as she felt him reach within her, just a little at first, as though letting her get used to the novelty. Then all at once he penetrated further. Nena gave a gasp of pain when he thrust deep, and dug her nails into his shoulders.

'It's all right, *mi amor,*' he murmured softly, his kisses almost reverent in their gentleness, his eyes dark and bright and filled with a gleam she didn't recognise. And the pain was quickly replaced by another of those lingering, rising coils of desire. At each new thrust Nena felt herself arching involuntarily towards him, her hips moving in a new and wonderful cadence. Then all became hazy, fuzzy, as she felt him join her, knew that he was somehow experiencing the same incredible sensation she was. And together they soared, swept away on a powerful, forceful wave of passion so strong that when it came to their climax they cried together, then fell exhausted onto the rumpled sheets, too spent to do more than listen to the beat of each other's hearts.

CHAPTER THREE

'DON RAMON?'

After several knocks Ramon awoke and realised that Juanito, his manservant, who'd accompanied he and Nena on the honeymoon, was outside the door, urgently calling his name.

Rising quickly from the rumpled bed, Ramon pulled on his discarded pyjama pants and dragged his fingers through his hair. He glanced down at Nena, still fast asleep, curled up like a kitten under the sheet, her hair fanned over the pillow, and smiled before he turned and went to the door. Opening it carefully, so as not to wake her, he slipped into the corridor.

'What is it, Juanito?' he asked, smothering a yawn. '*Que pasa?*'

'It is Don Rodrigo, *señor*. *Doña* Augusta called to advise you that he has taken a turn for the worse. She and Don Pedro feel you should return to London immediately.'

'My God.' Ramon was fully awake now, his mind working nineteen to the dozen. He glanced at the door. How would she react? he wondered, heart sinking, knowing he would have to go back into the room, wake Nena from her slumber and tell her the devastating news.

'Muy bien,' he said with a firm nod. 'See that the chopper is here within the hour, and tell the pilot to have the plane ready for take-off. We should be at Athens International Airport shortly.'

With that he turned on his heel and faced the daunting task of telling the woman to whom he had made love last night, for the first time, that the honeymoon he'd begun to have such hopes for was about to end. He entered, watched her, still curled up on the bed, then moved towards it. He sat down on the edge, next to her, face softening as his fingers gently smoothed the amazing mane of hair that was neither dark nor light, but a unique shade, highlighted with a myriad of golden streaks.

Bracing himself, he dropped a light kiss on her eyelids, then her mouth.

'Nena,' he whispered, gently shaking her shoulder, 'You must wake up, *cariña.*'

Slowly, very slowly, Nena emerged from a delicious dream. At first she kept her eyes closed, still basking in the aftermath of a wonderful night's sleep. Then all at once she stretched, became conscious of her body, of a slight pain when she moved, and little by little she recalled and pieced together the events of the night before.

Opening her eyes with a start, she looked up into Ramon's face.

'Good morning, *señora mia,*' he said softly. 'How did you sleep?' There was a gleam in his eyes as he spoke, and Nena felt her cheeks warm as in a sudden instant the lovemaking of the previous evening flashed before her.

'Fi-fine,' she muttered, looking away as Ramon leaned down and slipped an arm under her, drawing her close.

'Don't be embarrassed by what occurred between us, *mi linda,*' he said cajolingly, 'it is how it should be.'

He did not add that he'd been struck by the intensity of feeling that had hit him when at last he'd penetrated her fully and made her his. He had never experienced anything quite so powerful. And there had been women in his life, many women—younger ones, older ones—all of them exciting experiences who had taught him to perfect the art of lovemaking, of becoming a skilled and thoughtful lover as well as satisfying his own needs. But never before had he experienced such sheer, unadulterated passion as he had with his virgin wife.

But now was not the moment to be thinking of those things, he reminded himself, regretting that he couldn't prolong the aftermath and start all over again. Duty, after all, came first.

Pulling her gently to a sitting position, careful to help her wrap the sheet decorously about her, he placed his hands on her shoulders. 'Nena, I'm afraid I have some bad news.'

'Oh? What is it?' She frowned, fully awake now, her eyes wide with sudden fear.

'I'm afraid it's your grandfather. He's taken a turn for the worse.'

'Oh, no!' She pulled back from him and gazed up in horror. 'I must go at once,' she whispered, suddenly aware that here she was, making love with this man who'd been thrust upon her and whom she'd allowed to take possession of her body, when her grandfather was lying ill and probably needing her. 'I must leave!' she cried, struggling to get up.

Ramon rose quickly, leaving her room to move. 'I have arranged for the chopper to be here shortly.'

'Thank you,' she replied stiffly, rising, the sheet wrapped around her like a toga. 'I shall be ready.'

'Right, then we'll leave as soon as it lands.'

'We?'

'Of course,' he responded haughtily.

'But I can go alone,' Nena said, suddenly anguished at the thought of having him along, wanting to be by herself, to try and forget the shame she was experiencing.

How could she have allowed last night to happen? How could she have forgotten her grandfather and let herself be sucked into Ramon's bed and—? Oh! It was all too awful, and too frustrating. This man, after all, wanted nothing from her but to own her—make her part of his already vast array of possessions. And now he'd branded her, asserted his ownership, and he probably imagined he could take her whenever he wanted, use her to satisfy his needs, like the rest of his belongings.

Gathering together some last shreds of dignity, Nena nodded curtly, head high, and moved towards the huge marble bathroom she perceived through the half-open door. But even the hot jet of water blasting her from the shower didn't erase the tormented and uneasy feelings of guilt and shame that assailed her.

Ramon sighed as she closed the door behind her.

He could read her like a book—the doubts, the anger, the shock, the self-recrimination written in her eyes—and wished only that there was time to help assuage some of the inevitable emotions she was experiencing. But he shrugged and made his way to the other bathroom of the suite. Priorities came first. He must get her back to Don Rodrigo as soon as possible.

And he hoped desperately that it wouldn't be too late.

Nena barely spoke a word during the flight back to London. When they arrived at Heathrow customs officers came quickly on board and formalities were rapidly dealt with. Then they climbed into Ramon's Bentley, waiting on the tarmac to pick them up, and roared off immediately towards Windsor.

Several calls on Ramon's mobile phone had kept them abreast of Don Rodrigo's progress, which was not good. He would very probably be moved to hospital if he didn't improve by the afternoon.

Nena sat in the corner of the leather seat, as far from Ramon as possible, and clasped her hands in her lap, hating herself. How would she ever forgive herself for not being here when her grandfather had most needed her? She should never have consented to the wretched honeymoon in the first place—should have been more attentive to all the arrangements. In fact she simply should have refused. They could easily have stayed somewhere nearby. There had been no need to go all the way to Greece.

Over and over she chastised herself, so that by the time they arrived at Thurston Manor she was jumping out of the car before the chauffeur could so much as open the door.

As Ramon alighted he watched her burst into the house and run up the stairs towards her grandfather's apartments, heedless of the nurse and Doña Augusta standing in the corridor.

It was only when she finally reached the door of his room that she slowed down, took a deep breath, straightened her hair, then opened it quietly and tiptoed in, so as not to disturb the patient.

The room was dark, the curtains closed to keep out the glaring sunlight. Don Rodrigo lay very still in the middle of the large oak bed. He seemed so much smaller, frailer than when she had last seen him. And as she approached the bed Nena stifled a sob before slipping soundlessly into the chair next to it. Gently she laid her hand on his wax-like one, lying motionless on the coverlet.

'I'm here, Grandfather,' she whispered softly, a sob catching in her throat. 'Please forgive me for having been away when you needed me.'

'Nena?' Slowly the old eyes opened and his head moved stiffly on the pillow. 'Ah, my child, you are here.' He closed them again and squeezed her hand weakly. 'So silly of me to get worse just at the moment,' he added in a faint voice.

'Oh, Grandfather, I'm sure that now you'll get better!' Nena exclaimed, passing her hand over his brow, determined that somehow she would make him recover, despite the doctor's dire prognosis.

Don Rodrigo managed a dim smile. 'Ah, my Nena.

You were always such a sweet, determined little thing,' he whispered.

Just then the door opened, and she looked up to see Doña Augusta and Ramon enter, followed by the middle-aged uniformed nurse.

'I'm afraid he mustn't get too tired,' the nurse said gently, coming forward with a tray. 'If you would excuse us, Mrs Villalba? I need to give Don Rodrigo his medication.'

Nena experienced a jolt at being called Mrs Villalba. Since their marriage they'd been on the island, and the servants had addressed her as Doña Nena or Kiria Nena, in Greek. It was similar to the way she'd been addressed during her many stays in Argentina. Now the truth of her situation and all its implications sank in as never before.

'Very well,' she said, rising and dropping a kiss on her grandfather's withered brow. 'I'll be back later, darling,' she whispered.

He nodded faintly, but she could see that already he looked paler, that even the few minutes spent with her had exhausted him.

Biting her lip, she turned without so much as a glance at her husband and left the room.

Doña Augusta took her arm. 'I'm so sorry, Nena,' she said, slipping her hand over the young girl's, pained to see her suffering so intensely. 'Now, come downstairs and have a cup of tea or a drink. You need it. Your grandfather is getting the best possible care.'

Nena merely nodded. Her mind was full of so many troubled thoughts that she could barely concentrate on what her mother-in-law was saying. Once they were in the drawing room she remained vaguely aware of Ramon, standing near the fireplace, his mouth set in a hard line and a frown creasing his thick dark brows. Maybe he was upset that the honeymoon had been interrupted. Well, that was just tough luck. She shouldn't have been away in the first place, let alone doing what she had been doing.

But despite her sadness and worry Nena couldn't entirely banish the immediate undercurrent that flowed the instant she recalled last night. She glanced fleetingly at her husband, then turned away. It was wrong to feel like this when so much was at stake, with the end of her grandfather's life in the offing. Entirely wrong.

Ramon stood, impeccable as always in a well-tailored dark grey silk suit, leaning his arm on the corner of the mantelpiece. He carried on a stilted conversation with his mother, and watched as the butler brought in some tea and accepted a cup from him. He was aware that Nena just sat, looking numb, as though her world were crumbling about her. One look at Don Rodrigo and a quickly exchanged glance with his mother had been enough to tell him that the end was close at hand. Perhaps that was why they hadn't already taken him to hospital, he reflected sadly. Perhaps the old gentleman preferred to die at home in his own bed. And if that was the case then his wish should be respected.

He glanced over at Nena, seeing the determined line of her mouth. He must make her realise the truth. He could not allow her to drag her grandfather off, subject him to treatment that would do no good anyway just because of her need to keep him alive. At that moment Ramon understood that there was a lot more to marriage than just sleeping with his wife. The role of husband was also to help her take the right course of action. Nena and he might very well be up against their first hurdle, he realised with a flash of enlightenment.

For a minute he looked over at his mother, sitting gracefully near Nena, her silver hair perfectly coiffed, her Chanel suit worn with such elegance, and wondered what it could have been like for a young girl of eighteen to marry a man twenty years her elder, a man whom she'd barely known before the wedding, and asked himself if she'd ever regretted it. His parents certainly didn't ever give the impression of being unhappy. Quite the opposite, now he came to think of it. Perhaps there was something to be said for an arrangement of this sort after all.

The thought brought him up with a jolt.

God, he realised, horrified. In the flurry of the past few weeks he had completely forgotten to tell Luisa about the wedding and the changes in his life!

The sudden realisation left him raking his fingers savagely through his hair and wondering how on earth he was going to find a free moment to call her. How could he have been so thoughtless and remiss? He glanced over at Nena, realising, much to his surprise, that she had occupied his mind fully from the moment he'd first set eyes on her, and that since that day he'd barely thought about Luisa. But it would be discourteous and callous of him to allow the woman with whom he'd spent the better part of his leisure time over the past couple of years to learn of his nuptials in the press.

Strangely, his initial idea of maintaining Luisa on the side as his mistress seemed out of the question after last night. He shifted sideways and crossed one leg over the other. Merely recalling the previous evening's activities was causing an embarrassing change in his physical state.

Stop it, he ordered himself. *Stop acting like a teenager with a hormonal overdose.* He tried desperately to think of things that would dampen his ardour. But nothing sufficed to completely do the trick.

That night they stayed at Thurston Manor. Nena made it plain that they would be sleeping in separate bedrooms. Ramon was about to protest, then with a flash of insight realised that maybe she needed to be alone at this difficult time, and so he shut up.

Don Pedro had driven down from London to join them, and together they sat through a desultory dinner. No one was very hungry. Nena could barely eat a bite, her thoughts concentrated on her grandfather's room upstairs, where she'd spent the better part of the afternoon, sitting quietly in the chair next to the bed, stroking Don Rodrigo's frail white hand and praying that a miracle would occur to save him.

Despite her initial desire to sweep him off to hospital she had listened to her mother-in-law's words when Doña Augusta had gently suggested that perhaps her grandfather was happier where he was.

Later Ramon spoke to her in similar terms, and in spite of a profound desire to flout him—since she felt he was in a way responsible for her absence—and to whisk her grandfather onto a helicopter and off to hospital, she listened to the painful truth.

'Nena, I know how difficult this is for you to accept, but I think you must face the fact that the end may be close at hand,' Ramon said to her when they were alone in the hall. He made no attempt to take her hand or approach her, and stood several feet away.

'But he can't be that ill. There must be a solution,' she repeated for the hundredth time. 'Surely something can be done.'

'You heard the doctor, *querida,*' he said, gently but firmly. 'There is not much that can be done except keep him as comfortable as possible.'

At that Nena turned, her eyes full of tears, and ran up the stairs while he watched her, his bronzed hand fixed on the newel post, sensing that it was better to leave her be.

Again Ramon wanted to query the separate bedrooms issue. Not because he planned to have sex with her but because, he realised, he wanted to hold her—take her in his arms and give her the comfort he knew she so desperately needed. But, seeing how distant she'd become, he kept quiet. There would be time enough to console her once Don Rodrigo had passed on to a better world and when Nena realised the full truth of it. How wise the old gentleman had been to foresee the situation so clearly, he reflected. Soon it would be up to him to give his wife the kind of support she would need.

Still, the night alone would give him an opportunity to make the much needed phone call to Luisa, and once he was in his room Ramon braced himself, punched the quick-dial on his cellphone and waited while it rang over in Buenos Aires.

'Dígame.'

He heard Luisa's musical, throaty voice on the line and, surprisingly, did not experience the usual reaction.

'Lu, it's me,' he said automatically.

'Really, *querido?* And where might you be?'

'In England.'

'I see. If rumour has it right, you have been quite a busy boy of late.' Her voice was as icy as the waters of Antarctica.

'Look, Lu, I should have called you earlier, told you what was going on. But somehow I just didn't get around to it.' He closed his eyes and grimaced, imagining Luisa's livid face.

'So it's true,' she said, after a small hesitation.

'Yes, I'm afraid it is.'

'And you didn't even have the decency to call me and tell me personally?'

'I'm afraid I forgot.'

'You forgot. Well, Ramon, that is just wonderful. We spend two years having a white-hot affair, which has been splattered all over the press, and you simply "forget" to tell me that you're getting married. My congratulations,' she added frigidly.

'Lu, it's all my fault, I know, and I should have told you—of course I should. I could kick myself for not ringing you, but—'

'But what? Your child bride was taking up too much of your attention?' she asked sweetly.

'Don't be ridiculous. And she's not a child, she's—'

'Oh, shut up, Ramon. I don't even know why I'm talking to you. You deserve to be hung, drawn and quartered—and, believe me, if you were anywhere close by I'd do something a hell of a lot worse.'

Ramon shuddered, then smiled. 'Lu,' he said, his tone cajoling, 'you know that even though it's over between us I'll always adore you.'

'Hmm. Don't try and cajole me with your golden tongue, Ramon Villalba.' But she relented a little and laughed all the same. They were, after all, two of a kind—sophisticated jet-setters who knew the rules of the game and could remain friends.

The rest of the conversation was inconsequential and when it was over Ramon rang off, relieved. After reading a while he turned off the light to go to sleep.

He might have been considerably less at ease had he known that Nena, upon leaving her grandfather's room, had passed Ramon's closed door and overheard a single phrase that had left her running, anguished and furious with him and herself, to her own apartment.

I'll always adore you.

The words throbbed like cymbals in her ears. How could he? How could he make love to her, call her those endearing names one night, and the next be telling another woman that he would always adore her?

Nena threw off her dressing gown and climbed miserably into bed. This was the saddest, most awful time of her life. Her grandfather was no better and she was slowly coming to terms with the inevitable outcome. And now just as she'd been telling herself that perhaps there was something to be said for his insistence that she marry and not be left out in the world all on her own, she had overheard those dreadful words.

Well, she consoled herself, huddling under the covers and blowing her nose determinedly, it was probably better to know the truth and not make a complete fool of herself again, as she had the previous night.

But that was it.

From now on she would insist they sleep separately. Ramon was obviously a very talented actor. But now she had been well and thoroughly alerted. And, she reflected, throwing a pillow furiously out of the bed, she would do well to heed the warning that inadvertently she'd been privileged to overhear.

CHAPTER FOUR

THREE days later, at three thirty-eight a.m., Don Rodrigo passed away. Nena, who had barely left his side for the past seventy-two hours, finally collapsed from emotional exhaustion and, laying her head on her grandfather's still chest, cried her heart out. It wasn't just losing him, but also all that had changed, all that would change for ever in her life. In the space of three weeks she'd been thrown into a tailspin, and now her one point of gravity, her grandfather, was gone.

It was thus that Ramon found her when he came quietly into the room two hours later.

'Nena—oh, my God,' he muttered, hurrying to her side and laying his hand on her head to stroke her hair. 'I'm so sorry, *amor mio,* so dreadfully sorry.'

After several minutes he forced her to sit up, to move her stiff limbs, to take her eyes off the wax-like figure lying motionless in the bed.

The nurse, who had tactfully remained out of sight until the moment was over and Nena had said her final goodbye to her grandfather, came forward. Ramon, his arm firmly gripping her shoulders, shepherded her from the room.

'You must rest,' he insisted, guiding her in the direction of her bedroom. Then, seeing that she could barely walk from exhaustion, he scooped her into his arms and carried her, as he would a child, then deposited her gently onto the bed.

'Now let me cover you,' he murmured, pulling back the covers and sliding her legs under them before tucking her in and sitting on the edge of the bed. Her eyes seemed vacant, her limbs numb. But he knew that for now all he could do was try and soothe her to sleep.

Nena's eyes closed, and after several minutes she glided into an exhausted sleep. Somewhere through the haze of her mind and soul the gentle movement of Ramon's fingers massaging her neck and stroking her hair reached her. But it barely registered. Only when she woke several hours later and found him still seated next to her, dressed, his hand on her shoulder, having fallen asleep against the pillows, did she become fully aware of his presence.

Nena sat up, careful not to wake him. Despite her antipathy, and her anger at the words she'd heard him say the other night, she could not help but be touched by this unselfish display of solidarity. A rush of sudden affection swept over her and gently she tried to accommodate him better.

Ramon shifted towards the centre of the bed and instinctively pulled his legs up onto it. Then, as naturally as though they'd been sleeping together for years, he flung an arm across her and drew her close, murmuring something indistinguishable in his sleep.

For a moment Nena held her breath and lay stiffly, a prisoner in his grip, unwilling to wake him. Then, hearing the regular breathing and certain he really was asleep, she slowly relaxed, closed her eyes once more, and willed reality to stay away for as long as possible.

She felt strangely warm and protected in her husband's arms. Maybe he had told another woman he adored her, and maybe this was all fake, she conceded, but right now—just at this crucial moment—she needed the human companionship and warmth that he was offering, albeit in sleep.

At ten o'clock Doña Augusta decided to check on Nena. Peeping round the door she was surprised to see her lying in her son's embrace. Both were fast asleep. Her face broke into a soft smile, lessening some of the tension of the past few hours. Then gently she closed the door behind her and descended the stairs to find her husband.

There was so much to be attended to—funeral arrangements, the gathering afterwards. Nena was incapable of handling such responsibilities in her present state, and with the natural grace of habit Doña Augusta took over. The relieved servants turned to her for their instructions, instinctively bowing to her well-bred automatic sense of command, glad to delegate responsibility.

And so it was that when Nena and Ramon finally woke and blinked into each other's eyes, downstairs nothing had been left to chance.

As soon as she became conscious of her situation Nena wriggled and tried to escape.

'Don't go,' Ramon said, pulling a hand through his

tousled hair. 'You're too tired to get up. You need to rest, Nena.'

'I have to get up. There is so much to do—so much to take care of. Grandfather would have expected me to be on board, whatever my feelings,' she answered, feeling her limbs stiff with tension and trying to stretch.

'Here, let me give you a massage.' Not waiting for an answer, Ramon turned her peremptorily on her tummy and began kneading her shoulders.

'I—'

'Shut up and relax,' he commanded in an authoritative tone. 'You'll be no good to anyone if you're all wound up. And, as you said, there is much to be dealt with.'

Too tired to argue, Nena gave way, experiencing a thrill as her muscles began to relax. She closed her eyes and let him work on her back, down and down, unable to do more than let out the odd sigh from time to time, exhale and allow the tension to dissipate as his hands pressed exactly the right pressure points, the ones that were aching. Then all at once the massaging turned to caressing, and still she didn't move. When his hands slipped from her lower back to her bottom she lay totally still, allowing him to follow the rounded curves without protest.

Slowly Ramon slipped his hand under her nightdress, stroking her thighs lightly, relaxing them, unable to resist the temptation or the powerful tug that drew him to this woman, to her body, her mind and soul. He needed to enter her, feel her, to let her know that she was not alone, that he was here for her, to cherish and protect her, to help expedite the pain. Wasn't that, after all, what he had promised to do?

His hand reached further, until he parted her thighs and let his thumb roam, and a thrill of delight coursed through him when he felt the delicious wetness that told him more than words could just how much she needed him. Leaning over, he kissed the back of her neck and stroked her intimately, hearing the tiny moan, feeling her buttocks arch up to meet him.

Nena let out a long sigh. Part of her protested inwardly while another craved more. And she could do no more than submit to his caresses. Then, when she let out an involuntary cry of pleasure and relived once more that same wonderful release she'd experienced several days earlier, Ramon turned her around.

She saw the raw passion written in his eyes and gasped, felt him all but tear her nightgown from her, then arched back as he thrust deep within her, joining him in a tempestuous encounter, perfectly rhymed, an intuitive dance of which both seemed to know the steps. He was gripping her small waist, pulling down on her hips, delving into her core, as though determined to drive away sorrow, death and the anguish of the previous hours, to let life take hold. Then once again they crashed together in that rollicking surf before falling, embracing among the sheets and into another much needed bout of sleep.

'I think we should return to Buenos Aires,' Ramon said several days later.

'But I don't think that's a good idea at all,' Nena protested, thinking suddenly of the woman whom he'd told he adored. Surely she must be there in Buenos Aires, waiting for him? Maybe, she reflected bitterly, that was why he was in such a hurry to go.

It was a lowering thought that made her remember all too clearly the lovemaking of the past days. Ramon had not left her bed again, had insisted they sleep together, and because she was too overwhelmed by the events going on about her, and because—although she hated to admit it—the feel of his arms about her was so wonderfully comforting, and his body next to and inside hers was so incredibly reassuring, she'd conceded.

Now the truth came ramming home and she sat bolt upright in her chair and looked at the floor.

'Why don't you go to Buenos Aires, Ramon? I have nothing to do there. Plus, I need to wrap up so many things here—see people, take care of some of Grandfather's affairs. I wasn't able to talk to many of his friends at the funeral, and I need to write thank-you notes and—'

'Nena, that's ridiculous and you know it. We met with all your grandfather's legal advisors yesterday. And I will be dealing with the Carvajal interests from now on, you know that. As for thank-you notes—well, we have perfectly good writing paper in BA.'

'I don't see why we have to go,' she said stubbornly, the thought of going back to Argentina clouded by all she knew awaited him there—principally Luisa, too much to handle.

'I would have thought it was obvious,' he answered firmly. 'I have my companies to deal with, my *hacienda*. My businesses to run as well as yours,' he added with a touch of humour. 'Why are you so reluctant to go?'

For a brief moment she nearly told him about the magazine and the article she'd read. Then dignity and pride got the better of her, and, tossing her tawny head, she looked straight at him.

'I don't think it's the right time.'

'Quite the contrary. You know it has to happen some time. Much better to go now, let all this settle. You need a break—to get away and relax after all the strain.'

'I hardly think BA will be relaxing,' she murmured witheringly.

'I don't see why not. It's a very pleasant part of the world. You'll make friends, have a life there as well as in London and Paris and all the other places we live. But it is, after all, going to be our main home. I want to buy a new house or an apartment.'

'Oh? What's wrong with the one you've got?' she enquired, eyes challenging.

'Nothing. But it's more of a bachelor's pad than anything else. Far too small for a family.'

'We're only two people,' she said, raising a brow. 'And who knows? I might just like it.'

'No,' he said firmly, and she saw a flicker of determination in his eyes. 'We'll stay in a suite at the Alvear until we find something that suits us.'

Nena did not argue. She had realised by now that when Ramon made up his mind about something there was little use fighting it. He didn't shout or bark or lose his temper, he merely used a quiet, very commanding tone of voice that allowed the listener no doubt as to the outcome of the matter.

Well, so be it, she reflected, with a sigh. In a way maybe it *was* better to get going. One day she would have to face the truth, and perhaps the sooner she did—came out of this fantasy world she'd been living in for the past few weeks—the better it would be. She must face life alone, she realised sadly, watching his turned back with a pang of sadness and something more. It was hard to know that he could be so passionate in bed with her and be just as powerful and giving with another woman.

The thought hurt, and Nena turned, gazing fiercely towards the window, determined that he shouldn't see her anguish. She'd deal with it—get it under control, rid herself of this stupid jealousy she was experiencing as the picture in the magazine flashed before her once more.

And in the end she'd win.

Ever since she was a child it had always struck Nena as strange to leave London in midsummer and arrive in Buenos Aires with a heavy coat on her arm.

Now they had arrived at the Alvear Palace, the *grande dame* of hotels in Buenos Aires, and some of her initial qualms were appeased. Ramon was attentive and thoughtful, making sure she was not relegated to second place, as had been her fear, but very much in the limelight.

Still grieving for her grandfather, Nena didn't feel like any social activities. But Ramon insisted he take her out on their first evening, to an amusing restaurant on the Ricoletta. They would eat wonderful *assados,* composed of fabulous Argentinian meat, and maybe watch the tango danced at the Viejo Almazen.

And then he came up with a complete surprise that, despite her efforts to regard him in an uncompromising light, touched her heart just the same.

They were at dinner, and reaching the pudding stage, when suddenly Ramon leaned across the table.

'Nena, *mi linda,*' he said, his voice low, his eyes penetrating, 'I owe you.'

'Owe me?' She frowned, not understanding. 'You don't owe me anything that I can think of.' Actually, if she were truthful, she probably owed him. Ramon had taken charge of her grandfather's affairs in a forceful and efficient manner that had left the advisors and trustees in no doubt as to who was in charge.

'Oh, but I do,' he insisted. At the same time he removed two small leather boxes from his jacket pocket. 'This is the first thing I owe you.' He slid a red Cartier box across the table.

Nena hesitated, her pulse beating suddenly faster. Then tentatively she opened the box. A beautiful diamond ring sparkled up at her. Ramon reached across and removed it from its velvet bed. Smiling at Nena, he lifted her left hand and slipped the ring onto her finger, next to her wedding band. 'That,' he said, eyes gazing straight into hers, 'is your engagement ring. If you don't like it we can have it changed.'

'Oh, no, I love it. It's perfectly lovely,' she assured him, gazing down at the perfect jewel, touched that he'd taken the trouble to remember such a detail.

'And this,' he said, opening a long thin jewel box,

'is your wedding present.' He removed a glistening, delicately woven diamond and sapphire bracelet.

Nena held up her wrist, enchanted. 'It's perfectly gorgeous, Ramon. It's vintage, isn't it?' she exclaimed, eyeing the bracelet and biting her lip, unable to express just how much the gesture meant.

'Yes. I saw it in a catalogue for a Sotheby's sale and had my man in Paris bid for it. I know you probably inherited masses of vintage jewellery from your mother and grandmother, but this struck me as a rather special piece.'

'Oh, it is!' she exclaimed, fighting back the tears that welled in her eyes. She felt suddenly bad. For here she was, trying to reject this man, when he was making every effort to make a success of their marriage. Perhaps she was being very silly and immature.

She looked up at him and smiled tenderly across the table. 'Thank you, Ramon, I'm very touched. It was lovely to think of this.'

'It's the least I owe you,' he said gruffly. Then, taking her hand, he turned it around and kissed the inside of her wrist, sending delicious shudders up her arm and reminding her that the evening was not entirely over. She had been reticent near him since their arrival in BA, afraid that Luisa might be just around the corner.

But now he'd dispelled most of her fears. Here, in the quiet, well-attended restaurant, with its sophisticated décor and discreet waiters, she felt suddenly very, very happy—glad that she was here with him and not back in England, mourning her beloved grandfather all on her own.

They decided to walk down the wide avenues back to the hotel. Nena had vague memories of taking tea there with her grandparents and her mother and father when she must have been a very little girl.

'I can still just recall coming here with my mother,' she told Ramon as they stepped into the lobby. 'Do they still have English afternoon tea with scones?' she asked, with a touch of nostalgia for her mother, the woman who had flitted so briefly through her life.

'Of course. The Alvear never loses its touch or its old traditions. I can see that it must have been very hard for you, growing up with no parents,' he added, glancing at her and securing her arm more firmly in his.

'In a way, but then I had my grandparents. They were wonderful to me.'

'When did your grandmother die?'

'Four years ago. Grandfather never got over her death. He was never quite the same after that. They loved one another so much.'

'Yet they had an arranged marriage?' he said thoughtfully.

'Yes. And so, apparently, did your parents. They seem very happy too. They've been so kind to me.'

'So they should—they've just acquired a daughter.'

'Is that really how they feel?' she asked, turning and looking up at him. 'Or are you just saying that to make me feel better about all this?'

'No. I really mean it. My mother adores you and my father's half in love with you himself.'

She giggled as they tripped up the steps and

through the blue-carpeted lobby to the elevator, then on up to their suite.

'Tomorrow we're meeting with the estate agents,' Ramon said as they reached their door. 'They have a number of houses and apartments to show us. Which do you think you'd prefer?' he asked casually as they entered the drawing room of the suite, taking off his jacket and slinging it over the back of a chair while Nena hung up her coat in the cupboard.

'What? You mean a house or an apartment?' she asked, tilting her head. 'I really don't know. I—you see, I never thought of getting a house of my—our—own so soon. It's all rather a novelty.'

'Good. We'll have fun choosing then,' he said, sitting down on the sofa. 'I don't suppose you want to watch TV, do you?'

'Why not? Let's see what's on.' She sent him a dazzling smile and curled next to him on the sofa as if they'd been doing this for aeons. It felt good. It felt natural. And Nena sensed a chill of fear at just how used she was getting to sharing her life with this man whom she barely knew.

Ramon flipped the remote control. 'Oh, Lord. Look—it's the Britcoms. *Fawlty Towers* and Manuel!'

'Oh, please, leave it on!' she exclaimed, touching his arm. 'It's so funny.'

'I doubt there's anything much else on, except CNN and the news,' he answered, leaning back and slipping his arm around her while laughing at one of John Cleese's inimitable gestures.

An hour later they were both doubled over with laughter, relaxed and enjoying every minute of the evening. Nena had kicked off her shoes and Ramon had his feet up on the ottoman, ankles crossed.

It had been a perfect evening, she reflected, glancing down at her wrist and her finger. All the fears she'd had about coming here were suddenly obliterated by his gesture and the manner in which he'd managed to set her at ease. She felt excited now about choosing their new home, and imagined what it might be like, thought of how she would decorate it. Doña Augusta would have to help her get to know the various shops and decorators when she returned from London.

'Okay, sleepyhead,' he said, ruffling her hair and dropping a kiss on her brow, 'Time for bed, I think. We have quite a day tomorrow.'

Nena smiled, smothered a yawn, stretched and let him pull her up from the sofa. Then all at once there was an imperceptible change in the atmosphere. Their eyes locked and in one swift movement Ramon pressed her hard against him.

'I want you,' he growled, slipping his hands on her bottom and pressing her against him, letting her feel his hardness.

'And I want you,' she whispered back, gazing up at him, feeling herself go completely liquid inside.

'Then what are we waiting for?'

In one quick gesture Ramon unzipped her dress. It fell in a circle about her feet. Then he flicked open her bra hook and flipped it aside. 'My beautiful, gorgeous *señora,*' he muttered, cupping her breasts and grazing her nipples with his thumb, causing her to draw in her breath as she worked desperately on the buttons of his shirt and the buckle of his belt.

Minutes later they were lying naked in the huge Empire bed, Ramon's tongue working magic on her. But this time Nena wanted to adventure herself, and when he lifted his head she pushed him back on the bed.

Ramon quirked a surprised eyebrow, then, seeing her determined expression, gave way as she tentatively began kissing his throat, his chest, and down, down, until her lips closed falteringly around him.

She heard him draw in his breath.

'Mi amor,' he muttered, huskily surprised.

That was all the encouragement she needed. Soon they were writhing together, kissing, biting. Ramon thrust deep within her, possessing every inch of her, and she possessed him.

And Nena knew a new and powerful satisfaction: that of having truly pleased her man.

At ten o'clock the estate agent picked them up in a smart four-wheel drive to visit several addresses on his list. The first two were not suitable, and were immediately discarded, the third was a lovely house, but had a garden that needed a complete overhaul, but the fourth, a thousand-square-metre penthouse in an attractive building in the upmarket district of Palermo, enchanted them.

'What a magnificient view!' Nena exclaimed, gazing out over the city. 'It looks so like Paris, doesn't it?'

'Yes, it does. Do you like this place, Nena?'

'Yes. I think it's wonderful.'

'Nice ample bedroom,' Ramon muttered, out of earshot of the agent.

'Hmm,' she murmured, trying not to giggle and digging her elbow into his ribs to keep him quiet.

'And room for a nursery,' he added, slipping his arm about her as they walked out onto the wide wrap-around balcony.

'I don't plan on having kids for a long time,' Nena pronounced briskly.

'No, of course not.' He nodded blandly. 'Still, it's good not to have to move too often, don't you think?'

'Absolutely,' she agreed. 'Much more practical.'

'Shall we take it, then?'

'Yes,' she said, her face lighting up with a radiant smile that left him wanting to return immediately to the hotel.

It was quite amazing, he reflected as he went back inside the living room to discuss the terms with the agent, just how Nena had captured his whole being. And, if he was really truthful, he realised ruefully, his heart. He had never experienced such tenderness for a woman, such a feeling of warmth, such an intense need to be with her, return to her when they were separated even for a few hours.

Was this what marriage was all about?

Two days later Ramon called Nena on her cellphone.

'*Mi amor,* I have to go to the *hacienda* for a few days. A problem has cropped up that I must deal with personally.'

'Oh. Shall I come with you?'

'No. I don't think it's worth it. I'll have to be on

the go the whole time. I want to be able to spend time with you the first time you go there.'

'All right. I can get going with the apartment, then. I have a few addresses. Your cousin Pablo's wife, Elisa, kindly said she'd take me to several decorating establishments.'

'Good. She's a great girl. I'm glad you've made a friend.'

'When will you be flying out?' Nena asked, the thought of him being away leaving her lonely.

'Early tomorrow morning. Don't worry, *cariña,* we still have tonight,' he murmured, leaving her blushing at the feelings his words evoked.

The next day Nena met Elisa to go shopping, and then continued with her on for lunch at Santi's, a trendy lunch spot in the Ricoletta. They were seated at a corner table which offered them a full view of the busy restaurant.

It was obviously the 'in' place for ladies' lunches, Nena realised, watching a positive catwalk of the latest fashions, worn by rake-thin, angular, good-looking Argentine women who walked by with a self-assured, slightly arrogant air, as though they owned the world.

Nena ordered a salad, and Elisa a thin entrecôte.

'I'm dieting—low carbs,' she said, grinning.

'But you're so thin already.'

'Must keep it up, darling. You're young, but I'm hitting thirty. Positively ancient. Have to preserve my figure.'

Nena laughed and shook her head. Everyone here seemed so conscious of the way they looked and dressed and projected themselves. It made her feel rather young and unsophisticated, despite her exposure to London and Paris. It was just a different way of life where the physical was more interwoven into the general consciousness.

'Ah, there's Ana and Mariella over there,' Elisa said, waving to two friends. 'I must introduce them to you. You'll like them. They're great fun.'

It was just as the waiter was laying their espressos on the table that Nena looked up and, to her amazement, recognised the woman standing at a nearby table, chatting. She shuddered, certain it was the woman she'd seen pictured in *Hola!* magazine. And not ten feet away. She caught her breath and swallowed a gasp. Of course this would have happened some day, she supposed. She just wished it hadn't been when her husband was away.

'Do you know her?' Elisa asked curiously, seeing Nena's gaze fixed on Luisa.

'Oh, no. But she's very good-looking, isn't she?'

'Yes,' Elisa responded warily, 'she is. Very.'

Nena took a sidelong glance at Elisa and caught the troubled expression in her eyes.

'Don't worry,' she said, trying to sound nonchalant and very grown-up, 'I know all about her and Ramon.'

'You do?' Elisa looked surprised.

'Yes. It doesn't bother me,' she lied with a shrug.

'That's very sensible of you,' Elisa responded approvingly. 'Much better to be realistic about these things.'

Nena didn't add that she felt confident that now

that she and Ramon were spending every day together and every night passionately making love his affair with Luisa must be over.

The woman turned and sent a long glance in her direction, then leaned forward and murmured something to the woman she was sitting down next to, who in turn murmured to her neighbour. Suddenly they were all looking at her critically, and Nena felt herself blushing despite her determination to carry on as if nothing untoward had taken place.

'Pay no attention to them,' Elisa said, waving blithely at Luisa and her table. 'They don't mean any harm; they're just curious about you. After all, Ramon is a very big catch. Luisa and he had been going together for a couple of years, and frankly the whole thing must have come as a great shock to her.'

'Naturally. It must have,' Nena agreed, suddenly seeing the flipside of the coin. It must have been very difficult for Luisa to be ousted from one day to the next. For a moment she felt sorry for the older woman. Other people's feelings had no place in their arranged marriage, and she wondered suddenly if Ramon had really broken off with Luisa after all.

A niggling doubt assailed her as she recalled the night at Thurston Manor when she'd passed Ramon's door and heard him say *I'll always adore you.* Had it been Luisa he'd been talking to?

She glanced furtively in the other woman's direction, not wanting to be obvious. Luisa looked proud and beautifully groomed. Her long, glistening dark hair hung straight on the shoulders of her white cashmere jersey, she wore suede pants and high-heeled boots and looked sure of every inch of herself, Nena reflected. Would a woman who'd just been abandoned by a man like Ramon, with whom she'd had such a public affair, be flaunting herself like this in a restaurant? Laughing, elbows lightly poised on the table, her perfectly manicured fingers with their sparkling diamonds elegantly clasped, chattering as though she hadn't a worry in the world?

Perhaps it was just an act, and inside she was suffering, but the woman's exuberance and self-confidence left Nena feeling a little—not dowdy, exactly—but not quite up to par.

'Let's go clothes-shopping this afternoon,' she said suddenly to her companion. 'I'd like to buy some of the wonderful suede things they have here—some pants, skirts and things.'

'Why, of course,' Elisa said, smiling, brushing her pretty brown hair back from her attractive tanned face. 'I'll take you to my favourite boutique right now.'

Nena felt relieved when they exited the restaurant and she was finally free of the prying eyes she'd felt following her.

As the afternoon flew by and they visited various shops and boutiques the uncomfortable, uneasy feeling that had gripped her gradually wore off, and by the time she reached the Alvear, loaded with huge shopping bags, she felt back to her old self again.

Ramon exited the company plane in Cordoba, where his manager was waiting to drive him to the *hacienda*. But first he had a meeting scheduled with the governor of the province, and a few banking details to be dealt with.

However, by four p.m. he was saddled up and galloping over the pampas, inspecting his cattle, his mind busy with the details that needed to be attended to.

Then finally, as he turned his horse around and began cantering back towards the *hacienda,* he had time to reflect upon all that had taken place over the past few weeks—how his life had made a three-hundred-and-sixty-degree turn and how strangely happy he felt in this new existence. The only thing that bothered him was his unforgivable behaviour towards Luisa. After all, she must have learned that he was back in town by now, somebody would have made sure to tell her, and she must be wondering why he hadn't been in touch.

In fact, he rather wondered himself.

Okay, he'd been taken up with showing Nena around, finding the apartment and one thing and another, but still it did not explain his reluctance to face Luisa and have the final conversation he knew he owed her, which would have to take place at some time or another in the near future.

He sighed and slowed to a trot. Perhaps the best thing would be to stop off and see her on his way back to town. That way he wouldn't be obliged to lie to his wife—wouldn't have to mix apples and pears. Somehow it was important that the fragile confidence he'd established with Nena endured. The last thing he needed was to have his mistress—ex-mistress, he reminded himself quickly—thrust upon her at any given moment.

Seeing Luisa for the last time and getting the whole thing straightened out, he decided, returning to the stables, was definitely the right way to manage this whole affair.

Satisfied that he'd found the correct solution, Ramon dismounted and walked slowly back to the lovely colonial farmhouse that had been in his family for several generations, since the King of Spain had given his ancestor these tracts of land. He looked forward to bringing Nena here, showing her the place and letting her get her hands wet redecorating. The place certainly needed it. His mother very rarely came to Santa Clara any more, finding the climate too rude, but he had the feeling Nena would enjoy riding in the pampas and sharing this place with him—something he had never done with any other woman before, he mused. This had always been his private enclave. Now, to his utter surprise, he had no qualms about sharing it.

CHAPTER FIVE

'I KNOW I should have told you,' Ramon repeated, looking over at Luisa sitting opposite him on an ultra-modern sofa in her exquisitely decorated apartment that he knew so well. 'I am entirely to blame in this whole affair, Luisa.'

'So you keep saying,' Luisa replied, eyeing him askance and wondering, now that they were face to face, if there might not be a way of hanging on to him despite his marriage to the girl she'd seen the other day at Santi's. Okay, his new wife was young and lovely. But wouldn't that youth and lack of experience bore him after a little? And, when the novelty wore off, wouldn't he prefer to take a break in her arms once in a while?

Luisa thought it over warily. She must be careful not to push him. She knew Ramon well enough to recognise that stubborn twitch around his lips, knew that when he was committed to something he went for it full throttle. Still, handled with kid gloves, there was no saying what might happen. She might just be able to revert this situation in her favour. Of course, it would never be quite the same again—but what in life was?

She sighed inwardly. She had strong feelings for

Ramon, and was not disposed, she realised suddenly, to just let him disappear out of her life without so much as a by-your-leave. At first she'd been furiously angry, insulted and hurt. Now the hurt remained, but common sense prevailed.

'I'm famished!' she exclaimed, stretching and reaching over to touch his arm. 'Why don't we go and have a bite in one of our special haunts, for old times' sake?' She smiled at him winningly.

Ramon had little desire to be seen publicly in Luisa's company, but to refuse the invitation after she'd been such a good sport—had taken the rejection in such a well-spirited manner—would be churlish.

'Okay,' he agreed, disguising his reluctance as he rose. 'I'm afraid I can't stay too late, though.'

'Of course not,' she said in a cajoling tone, while slipping her smooth bronzed arm through his and letting him get a whiff of her perfume. 'You're a married man now, and you have obligations after all.'

'Uh, yes.' He laughed uncomfortably while Luisa made sure that her thigh rubbed gently against his as they moved towards the hall to slip on their jackets.

'Let's go to Santi's. It should be pretty quiet on a Thursday at lunchtime,' she proposed, tossing her large leather handbag over her shoulder.

'Fine. Great idea,' he replied, all in favour of a place that would not be jampacked with half their friends and acquaintances.

But Luisa's prognostication proved to be wrong. Santi's was, in fact, filled with just the kind of people Ramon had hoped to avoid, and it took them a full ten minutes to get from the door to their table, there were so many friends to greet.

'Hi, Ramon, good to see you back in town. Let's get together.'

The greetings were endless, and the curious looks and interested murmurs that followed them in no way suppressed.

Luisa smothered a grin of satisfaction. Her plan had worked after all. She pretended to pay no attention to the disturbance they were causing, to the chattering couples all speculating as to what was going on in Ramon's life. Well, let them. The more the merrier, Luisa decided as she studied her menu.

Ramon sat silently furious, but could do nothing without causing a scene. He could see now what Luisa's game was, and was thoroughly annoyed with himself for having fallen for it. Well, let the games begin, he decided, calmly ordering his favourite dish. 'Oh, and don't forget the *chimi churri* sauce, will you?' he said to the waiter, with a grin that belied his inner anger.

He thought of Nena. He'd told her he would be back today but didn't know what time. Was she back at the hotel waiting for him? he wondered impatiently. God, Luisa could be a bitch when she set her mind to it. And somehow now all her faults glared straight at him. How come, he wondered, carrying on a light-hearted and amusing conversation with her, hadn't he recognised them clearly before?

'Oh, he won't be back until late,' Elisa assured Nena as they left the boutique where Nena had had to pick up several articles of suede clothing she'd ordered. 'Let's have a bite of lunch, and afterwards I can drop you off at the Alvear on my way home.'

'Okay, sounds good,' Nena responded with a smile.

She felt good in a new pair of trousers, a smart polo-neck cashmere top, a suede vest bordered with fur, and a very smart pair of Chanel sunglasses that set off her glistening well-trimmed hair, swinging around her shoulders. She had been to Carlos, Elisa's top-of-the-line hairdresser, and felt more a part of the elegant lifestyle of the women in this sophisticated city. She found it fun and amusing. And, although her grandfather was never far from her mind, her propulsion into this entirely different new existence had done wonders to help overcome her initial sadness.

But she missed Ramon.

It was extraordinary to think that only a month or so ago she hadn't even known the man who had made such a mark upon her being, and without whom she now found it difficult to imagine life.

'Santi's, as usual?' Elisa asked with a grin.

She liked Nena very much, was thrilled that Ramon had finally—through no merit of his own—fallen on someone so perfect for him, and had enthusiastically taken Nena under her wing, introducing her to friends and showing her the ropes. But she knew that of all the places she'd taken the girl, the fashionable and trendy Santi's was her favourite.

'If you don't mind going there again, I'd love to,' Nena replied, laughing. 'It's always such fun. And I love their *empanados.*'

'I just hope that Franco will be able to give us a

decent table. If worse comes to worst we can have a glass of champagne or something at the bar while we wait.'

But when they entered the packed restaurant Franco had no hesitation in finding them a small table for two tucked in a corner that had just been vacated, and the girls wound their way among the busy tables. Nena even had a few people to say hello to herself now, and everyone seemed pleased to see her.

It was Elisa who first caught the furtive glances directed upwards, towards the elevated gallery. That and the overly bright smiles. She frowned, her radar immediately picking up the silent messages being sent her way. But it was too late. Nena looked up too soon.

Words could not describe the chill, the utter horror she experienced when she saw them—the woman, Luisa, from the magazine, leaning towards Ramon touching his cheek in a manner denoting complete intimacy and familiarity.

At first Nena could hardly move as indescribable pain seared through her. Then, as though by some miracle of will, she reacted, pulled herself together in the space of a few seconds and went on talking as though nothing untoward had happened. But it seemed hours until they reached the table, where she sat on the edge of the bench, barely able to breathe.

'What's the matter, Nena? You look pale,' Elisa said with a worried frown.

'I'm fine.' She sent the other woman a bright, brittle smile and tossed her hair back elegantly, damned if she was going to make a complete idiot of herself.

She'd been a fool to think Ramon would give up

his old lifestyle so easily, that just because he spent so much time in her bed he'd forsake his mistress. Stupid and naïve were the correct terms. Why, oh, why hadn't she followed her initial instinct and kept the marriage as it had been initially conceived? An arrangement. A satisfactory solution to a problem. But, no. She'd allowed herself to be swept off her feet, to fall victim to his immense charm, to his delightful manners, falling prey to his demonstrations of kindness and, let's face it, to the passion and intimacy he'd taught her and that now formed an integral part of her existence.

Foolish and unprepared. That was what she was. Perhaps it had amused Ramon to teach her a few things, men liked to be the first man in a woman's life, to show her the ropes, she reflected cynically, determined not to peek up towards the gallery but to maintain her dignity. She'd thought he too was enjoying their being together. Ha! What a stupid illusion. In point of fact where he really enjoyed himself was with the sophisticated Luisa, a woman of the world, one with whom he shared similar interests, friends and a life. All she was, Nena realised suddenly, swallowing back the tears welling inside and determined not to give way, was a fish out of water.

Not now.

She would not, she vowed, *could* not make a spectacle of herself in public. Whatever it cost, she would hold it together, eat the food that was put before her and carry on a normal, civilised conversation with Elisa as if nothing had happened. She would not, she assured herself, give that woman up there the pleasure of seeing her defeated.

Uneasily, Elisa glanced towards the gallery. She wondered if Nena had seen the couple and hesitated, caught between her desire to warn the girl and her doubt as to whether she'd noticed them. Better not mention it, she decided, in case she hadn't. But the girl looked so pale, so drawn. And despite her efforts to make conversation and appear at ease Elisa could tell something was wrong.

She must have seen them, Elisa figured, her heart going out to Ramon's young wife, admiring her dignity and her pride, and the fact that she hadn't made a scene or rushed from the restaurant in tears. It took guts to face up to something like this, and she was pleased to see that Nena was no lightweight. In fact, she reflected, taking a quick peek at Ramon, apparently engrossed in conversation with Luisa, she sincerely hoped that Nena would give him a run for his money. It would do him no harm at all.

Okay, many men had double lives. The story of the *casa grande* and the *casa pequeña* was all too common—it was almost a status thing for a man to keep a beautiful mistress. But somehow Elisa felt this situation was different. There was a streak of determination in Nena that was not to be messed with. And she would not be the least surprised, Elisa reflected, if in the end Nena didn't win the day.

Ramon rose from the table and moved aside for Luisa to pass ahead of him. Again she made sure her thigh grazed his, then turned back and spoke to him in an intimate manner as they descended the few steps from the gallery to the main part of the restaurant, touching his arm possessively.

It was at that precise moment that he saw Nena, seated at a table straight in their passage.

'Madre de Dios,' he muttered under his breath.

Luisa walked ahead, smiling at their friends, stopping from time to time, making sure the whole place saw them together. He could throttle her! How had he allowed himself to be sucked into this? Should he talk to Nena or pretend he hadn't seen her? From all he could see she appeared to be having an animated conversation with his cousin's wife Elisa.

But there was no way he could avoid direct contact with their table. Allowing Luisa to walk on ahead, heart sinking, he approached the two women, aware that every eye in the restaurant was fixed upon him. He knew the crowd only too well—knew all the restaurant was waiting in titillating suspense to see what he'd do. For a moment he hesitated. Then he made up his mind.

Damn Luisa and her below-the-belt tricks! His wife was more important, he realised suddenly, aching for her, admiring the way she was pretending to be oblivious of the scene when she must have seen him.

'Hola,' he said, dropping a hand on Elisa's shoulder and a kiss on the top of her head. His eyes met Nena's glittering ones across the table. 'Nena. I—'

'Hello, Ramon.' She sent him a brittle smile that cost her a fortune in will-power. She wished she could get up right there and send a ringing slap onto that bronzed cheek of his. Instead she posed her hands elegantly on the table. 'What a coincidence that we should find ourselves in the same restaurant. I thought you were returning later in the day.'

'I was,' he muttered. 'When will you be back at the hotel?' he asked curtly.

'I have no idea,' she responded coldly. 'Oh, look, you'd better run along. Your friend is waiting at the door.'

'Very well,' he agreed stiffly. 'I'll see you at the Alvear later.'

Nena gave him a nod and a smile for the benefit of the crowd, pretending not to stare. She had never been so humiliated in the entire course of her short existence, and once, she vowed, rage stirring in her as never before, was enough.

'Bravo, Nena,' Elisa whispered fervently across the table once Ramon had disappeared. 'You were simply terrific. I can't admire you enough for the way you behaved. Luisa must have brought him here to try and prove to people that they are still together.'

'Well, she was just proving the truth by the looks of it, wasn't she?' Nena responded, the neutral tone of her voice belying her boiling inner turmoil. She could kill the man, quite literally strangle him for the pain she was feeling, the utter humiliation and sheer anguish of seeing him so intimately next to another woman.

And Luisa in particular.

She would tear Luisa's eyes out too, if she got half a chance, she realised, a sudden new emotion that she recognised as jealousy searing though her like a white-hot arrow.

As they silently returned to the hotel Nena's mind was on fire. She wondered when Ramon would make his appearance. If he would be there when she walked in, or if he would only come back later. But what did it really matter? She had no intention of staying anyway.

After thanking Elisa for her kindness and saying goodbye, Nena went hurriedly up to the suite and, hand trembling unlocked the door.

There was no sign of Ramon, she realised, relieved, throwing her shopping bags onto the bed and heading straight for the closet, where she dragged out her two large suitcases.

Then turning around she picked up the phone.

'Ah, concierge? Yes. I'd like you to book me a place on the British Airways flight to London tonight, please. Yes, first class. By the window. Thank you.'

She laid down the receiver and swallowed. She'd been foolish to follow him here, to do his bidding, but it was still not too late to remedy matters.

Determined not to give way to her pent-up rage, Nena folded each item of clothing carefully before inserting it in the case. She would not allow him the satisfaction of seeing her fall apart—would not let him know how deeply he'd affected her feelings, how much the past few days and weeks had come to mean to her. They obviously represented very little to him, so what was the point?

Half an hour later she was packed and ready to leave. She called for a bellboy, still mustering all her control. The tears that had been fighting their way to the fore would just have to wait until she was by herself. Well away from him and this place.

Ramon drove furiously back to the hotel. His leave-taking from Luisa had been cold and angry. She'd set him up, and for that he would never forgive her. Maybe she hadn't known Nena would actually be in the restaurant—that was simply an added bonus—but she must have calculated that it would be jam-packed with every curious Tom, Dick and Harry. And he was even more to blame; he should have known better.

Now he had to deal with explaining to his wife just what he'd been doing, lunching there with his former mistress. It didn't take a rocket scientist to imagine what was going through Nena's mind. Of course someone—probably Elisa—would have told her who Luisa was by now. He could hardly blame his cousin's wife. It had been blatantly obvious by the manner in which Luisa communicated with him that there was intimacy between them.

'Damn, damn, damn!' he exclaimed as he rode the elevator up to the suite, glancing at his watch, wishing he could have put off his meeting at the Casa Rosada with the President. But that, of course, would have been impossible. And naturally the President had been late, and the meeting had lasted longer than he'd expected.

And just as everything was going so well, he reflected furiously, when Nena was finally opening up to him like a blooming flower, this had to happen.

He opened the door carefully.

The sitting room of the suite was empty. Then he

moved towards the door of the bedroom and stood in the doorway. But that room was empty too. Hurrying towards the closet, he flung it open, only to have his suspicions confirmed as he confronted a row of empty hangers. She'd gone, he realised, glancing at his watch again and seeing that it was too late to reach the airport in time to impede her flight.

Two minutes later he'd confirmed it with the concierge. So she was off to London. Well, at least that was home territory for her and he knew where to catch up with her. Still, the rift that now loomed between them would be hard to bridge.

Several minutes later he decided the best course of action was to warn his mother and then get himself to London as soon as he could.

Upon arrival at Heathrow Nena went straight to Thurston Manor. The servants were surprised, but glad to see her, and after getting through their greetings and the inevitable congratulations Nena sank onto her old bed, content just to lie there, eyes closed and let go a little of the tension that had travelled with her from Buenos Aires.

She was exhausted, she realised. Not just by the trip, but from the rollercoaster of emotions she'd been through in the past few hours. She hadn't slept during the journey, her mind too taken up with the events of the afternoon to allow her to relax sufficiently to close her eyes. But now, at least, she was home. Really home. Not on *his* territory but on hers, where she called the shots and no one, least of all Ramon, could force her to do anything.

She'd made up her mind what to do on the plane. Tomorrow, once she was more rested, she would phone the lawyers and find out how to go ahead with a divorce. She would not stay married to this man a moment more than necessary. He'd played with her feelings, her heart and her pride and she'd had enough.

For a moment her grandfather flashed before her. But she braced herself. It was too late to worry about her word, which she'd given him. Anyway, she doubted he would have expected Ramon to behave in such a callous, ungentlemanly manner. She could not be expected to just back down, lower her eyes and accept his infidelities like a doormat, could she?

Nena shifted on the bed, too agitated to sleep, too tired to get up and do anything. If only they'd had more time to get to know one another none of this would have happened. Or perhaps she should have paid real attention to that magazine article, shown it to her grandfather. Certainly, she should have asked a few questions before entering naïvely into this wretched arranged marriage.

Finally, after much tossing and turning, Nena managed to fall into a troubled sleep. But her dreams were filled with visions of a tall, dark and handsome man, whose hands created magic when they touched her and for whom, despite all her anger and ire, she still felt desire.

Doña Augusta was a practical woman, and it was frankly no surprise to her when she heard of Nena's sudden return to England. What did surprise her—

actually encouraged her to harbour new hopes for her son—was Ramon's obvious discomfort at the fact. Truth was she had never, in the course of his thirty-two-years, heard him so discomfited.

Well, Augusta thought, as she laid down the telephone receiver, it would do him no harm at all to stew in his own juice for a few days. She was secretly thrilled to know that his relationship with Luisa was terminated. She had never approved of it from the beginning, and had feared that Ramon might, like so many of his peers, get married and continue to live the same life as he had before, paying small heed to his lovely young wife.

But apparently that was not the case.

Gleefully Doña Augusta set about advising her husband of the facts. Not all of them, of course. Just the essentials. There was no earthly use interfering, she pointed out firmly to Don Pedro; it was just important to let Nena know that she had Doña Augusta's friendly ear, should Nena need it. Don Pedro agreed. The couple must, they decided, work it out for themselves.

After having said this, the first thing Doña Augusta did was to invite her daughter-in-law to lunch at Mark's Club *à deux*, where she determined to discover exactly what was going on between the pair. Ramon had been irritatingly vague and Nena excruciatingly polite on the phone. But Doña Augusta sensed that things were in a worse state than she'd let her husband believe. It was time for a little probing, she decided. Not that she meant to interfere, of course, but a little well-placed adjusting could do no harm.

* * *

She could hardly refuse the invitation, Nena decided with a sigh. Not that she had the least desire to go to London. As far as she was concerned she could wallow here at Thurston Manor for ever and never show her face again. She felt stupid, ugly and unkempt, and had refused to take any of Ramon's numerous calls. She hadn't washed her hair in days, and her nails needed a serious manicure.

She looked at herself in the mirror, disgusted. Look at what you've become, she threw at herself. With a weary sigh she realised that she couldn't go to lunch looking like this and would simply have to go and have a makeover before meeting her mother-in-law. Reluctantly she picked up the phone and made the necessary appointments.

'So,' Doña Augusta said, settling on the moss green velvet bench of Mark's select dining room, near the window, with Nena seated beside her, 'I hear that you and Ramon have found an apartment in Buenos Aires?'

'Uh, well, we did look at something,' Nena said hesitantly, not wanting to tell Doña Augusta about her decision to get a divorce without first speaking to Ramon. She still hadn't contacted her lawyers, but that, she'd persuaded herself, was because she hadn't had time. After all there had been all those thank-you letters to write for all those wretched wedding presents that she would have gladly packed up and returned.

'Oh, but I thought it was definite?' Augusta raised a perfectly plucked brow.

'Yes—no. Well, it's all rather complicated, to tell you the truth,' Nena conceded. Somehow it was very difficult to look Doña Augusta—the woman who had been so wonderful to her during her grandfather's illness—straight in the eye and tell a blatant lie.

Touching her beautifully coiffed silver hair with a bejewelled hand, Doña Augusta patted Nena's with the other. 'I have the feeling,' she said, taking a sip of crisp champagne, 'that perhaps all is not perfectly harmonious between you and Ramon.'

'Yes, well, no—I mean, it's not really—'

'Nena, I would like you to consider me as a friend rather than your mother-in-law—such a daunting term, isn't it?' she added with a low conspiratorial laugh. 'After all, you have neither your mother nor your grandmother to guide you, *querida*. Let me add, before we go any further, that I have a very realistic view of my son. I am not one of those doting parents who believe their child can do no wrong,' she added firmly. 'I am very well aware of Ramon's—er—faults.'

Nena took a long gulp of champagne. She'd been turning the problem over and over, back and forth in her own mind now for several days. But to open up to Ramon's mother? Would it be right? Would it be wise? Yet as she looked into the other woman's clear grey eyes she suddenly knew she must confide in someone before she went crazy.

'I don't know how to tell you,' she began, staring down at her napkin. 'I thought everything was all right. I was beginning to believe that perhaps the whole idea of our marriage was not such a bad one, and then—' Just the thought of Ramon in Buenos

Aires, looking down into Luisa's face as she'd been walking down those steps, left Nena seething, another rush of hot tears ready to be shed.

As though sensing her torment, Doña Augusta laid a hand gently on hers.

'Nena, dear, why don't you just tell me what happened? Keeping it to yourself is far worse. We are women; we need to talk when things bother us. I assure you that what you confide in me will go no further.'

'Well—' Nena took a deep breath '—he has a mistress.'

'Ah! Luisa, I suppose.' Doña Augusta gave a knowing nod. 'Most unsuitable and a thorough nuisance. I had the impression she was on her way out.'

'Not from where I was sitting,' Nena said with a sniff.

'Sitting? You mean you've seen her?'

'Oh, yes,' Nena answered bitterly. 'Rather, I saw *them.*'

'I see.' Doña Augusta's expression turned to consternation. 'Where was that, Nena?'

'At Santi's. Ramon was supposed to be in Cordoba,' she blurted out. 'I went to lunch with Elisa, who'd kindly taken me shopping. I like Santi's, so we went there. It was at the end of the meal, as we were having coffee. I looked up and there he was staring down, smiling at this woman. I knew who she was—I saw them together in that magazine you brought over for Grandfather—I just thought…just imagined that now he was married…' Her voice trailed off and she took another long sip of champagne to ease the pain, though talking about it had made her feel slightly better.

'I'm very sorry you were subjected to that,' Doña Augusta replied, her expression concerned. 'I know from experience that these things are sometimes difficult to deal with. Pedro was quite a Don Juan when we were married, and I had a few run-ins myself. I suppose that is why you came back to London in such a hurry?'

'What else could I do,' Nena replied defensively.

'I'm not criticising,' the older woman responded with a gentle smile. 'In fact I think you did exactly the right thing. It will do Ramon no harm to realise how silly he's been.'

'Doña Augusta, I think it is only fair to warn you—though I wanted to tell him first—that I plan to get a divorce.' Nena held her head up and Doña Augusta noted the determined line of her mouth.

'That is quite a radical decision to take,' the older woman replied carefully.

'I see no future for us under the present circumstances.'

'Of course. But tell me, Nena, what exactly are the present circumstances?'

Nena hesitated. What could she say? That she thought she loved a man who obviously saw her just as a convenience? That to know he was leaving her to see another woman would quite simply kill her?

'Nena, I am much older than you, and so perhaps am able to have a better inkling of what is going on,' Doña Augusta said in a smooth, soothing voice. 'Please correct me if I'm wrong, *querida,* but would

I be right in assuming that you have feelings for my son?'

Swallowing once more, Nena nodded. 'Which is why it would be impossible to bear,' she murmured, clasping her hands tight. 'Totally impossible. I know some women do it, but I couldn't stand seeing him leave every day, never knowing if—if he was going to see her.'

'And neither should you have to go through any such thing,' the older woman replied briskly.

'The best thing is to put an immediate end to the whole thing,' Nena said with a sigh. 'We never should have been forced into this situation. It's not natural. I suppose there was a lot of pressure on Ramon as well.'

'Rubbish. You are both in it now, and I think you at least owe each other a chance. A divorce at the first sign of adversity is for the faint-hearted, Nena, and I have the impression that you are anything but that,' she finished shrewdly.

'I don't want to run away, if that's what you mean,' she replied, squaring her shoulders and sitting up straighter. She hadn't actually thought of the problem in this light before.

Doña Augusta contemplated telling Nena what her son had said on the phone, that the affair with Luisa was most definitely over. But after a short moment's reflection she decided not to. It was up to them to work things out. Still, she considered it time for Ramon to put in an appearance and start fighting for what she was certain he truly wanted. She could hardly wait to see his face when Nena told him she wanted a divorce. It would do him a world of good not to have everything going exactly his way.

It would, indeed.

CHAPTER SIX

'DON RAMON is in the library,' Worthing announced two days later as Nena thankfully finished the last wedding thank-you note.

'Show him in, Worthing,' she said, swallowing, aware that the meeting had to take place and that the sooner she told him of her decision the better.

A minute later Ramon marched into the room. In spite of her resolve, Nena felt her heart lurch when his tall, dark, handsome figure, clad in an immaculate grey suit, entered.

She stood by the window and waited while Worthing closed the door.

'Good morning,' she said, as formally as she could, head held high, her body rigid.

Ramon could read all the tension in her body language. Nena was a little trooper, he realised. She had carried the whole restaurant thing off with such grace and dignity, like the true lady she was. Now, as he watched her across the drawing room, he experienced a surge of admiration—and something else so strong it made him stop and hesitate. It took his breath away and for a moment he remained silent, watching her, thinking what an extraordinary woman she was turning out to be, despite her youth. Then he cleared his throat.

Nena looked him over coldly, hiding her racing pulse, eyes ablaze.

'Why did you run away?' he asked, breaking the silence, with a flash of anger at her sudden disappearance without either his knowledge or permission.

'I should have thought that would have been blatantly obvious,' she replied icily.

'I don't see why you should have gone anywhere.'

'Don't you?' she asked sweetly. 'Well, I'm afraid I disagree. There was obviously not room for me *and* your mistress in Buenos Aires. Apparently we frequent the same establishments,' she threw. 'How very unfortunate.'

'That was bad luck.'

'Really? Well, I'm afraid I don't know the rules of this game, Ramon, and I can't say that I want to learn them. Now that you're here we can discuss the terms of the divorce, once I've seen my lawyers.'

'Divorce?' Ramon took a shocked step forward.

'Yes, divorce. You can't truly expect me to stay married to you after what happened. Surely even *you* can't imagine that I would tolerate that kind of behaviour?'

'Nena, we need to talk about this.'

'No, we don't. The least said the better.'

'Don't be ridiculous.'

'I'm not being ridiculous. I'm being realistic—something that I apparently haven't been over the past few weeks,' she added bitterly, turning away and staring out of the window, through the summer rain and across the lawn.

'Nena, *mi amor,* please—give me a chance to explain.'

'Explain what?' she exclaimed, spinning on her heel. 'That you keep a mistress, a woman who you've been having an affair with for the past couple of years?'

'It's all over.'

'Really? Well, you could have fooled me. I may look young and stupid, Ramon, but I have a minimal amount of brain cells. I find it impossible to believe that you would abandon a woman that you've even been photographed with in *Hola!* magazine, and whom you still see fit to lunch with in the most fashionable restaurant in town, despite the very unimportant fact that you're married,' she replied witheringly.

'Nena, this is absurd,' he said, moving forward and grabbing her arms. 'It was not as you imagine. I had to see Luisa—explain to her. I hadn't advised her properly of our marriage. I owed it to her to take a proper farewell.'

'At Santi's.' Her eyes blazed up at him. 'How dare you treat me like a simpleton?' she threw, pulling away from him, tears burning despite her every effort to quell them. 'How dare you, Ramon?' Before she could stop herself Nena brought the force of her hand across his cheek, then backed off, horrified at her own lack of control.

Ramon stood perfectly still, then raised his hand to his cheek. His face broke into a rueful smile. 'I deserved that. But now, please, calmly, let me explain.'

'No.' She burst into tears. 'I don't want to hear another word about it. Go on—go back to her. She obviously satisfies your every need. I was a fool to think that we—that I—that—' She turned again to the window, shoulders shaking, unable to contain the flow of tears rushing down her cheeks.

'*Mi niña,*' he said, coming up behind her and slipping his arms around her shaking body. 'There is no need for all this agitation. If only you'd listen to me, let me tell you how things really are—'

'I don't want to know,' she said stubbornly, trying to get out of his arms. 'I don't believe a word of what you say. You're just trying to placate me. Well, I'm not going to be fobbed off.'

He spun her around and faced her, his face set in hard, determined lines. 'I am not a liar, Nena. What happened is unfortunate, but I will not have my wife questioning my word.'

'I didn't say that—'

'Yes, you did. You said you didn't believe me, won't even listen to my version of what happened, and you talk about divorce with the greatest of ease. Is that how you regard marriage?'

His eyes burned into hers and his hands gripped her upper arms. 'I repeat—is that how you view marriage? As something to be thrown out of the window as soon as there is a problem?'

'I—' Nena was taken aback by his sudden change in attitude, and the true and real anger she read in his eyes.

'Answer me,' he ordered, his voice cold and quiet, cutting the silence. 'I want to hear it from your lips.'

Nena swallowed. 'N-no. That is not how I think of marriage. It's just that—'

'Just that what? That you saw me with a woman and presumed I was still sleeping with her?'

Nena felt heat rush to her cheeks.

'Yes.'

'I see. And is there anything else you'd like to share?'

Nena hesitated. 'I don't trust you.'

Ramon drew back, and his face took on a rigid, hard expression. 'I see. Then there is effectively very little for us to talk about. I'll bid you good day.' With a small bow he turned on his heel and marched from the room, leaving Nena standing alone, the wind completely blown out of her sails.

She hadn't meant that—well, not exactly. Perhaps she'd worded it badly. Oh, what had she done? she wondered, remembering the forbidding expression on his face as he'd taken his leave. She hadn't meant to hurt or insult him. And now it was too late. She'd thrown the dice and played her hand and now there was no going back.

A sob caught in her throat and she threw herself on the sofa, where she indulged in a long, stormy cry that brought little relief.

'I want a full report on the Carvajal oil companies,' Ramon told Morton, the late Rodrigo Carvajal's personal secretary, who was now serving as his assistant at the offices of Carvajal Enterprises in Dover Street. 'And get me an audit on the import-export firm too, please.'

'Yes, sir. Will that be all?'

'For the moment, yes. Thanks, Morton.' Ramon looked up and smiled. 'Is Sir Wilfred in yet?'

'He should be in by ten, sir. Shall I tell him you've been asking for him?'

'Please. And Andrew Trenton as well. Do they always come in so late?'

'They usually appear by ten,' Morton replied uncomfortably, sensing disapproval in the new boss's tone.

'Ah, well. That's fine. Please advise them that I need a word, will you?'

'Of course, sir.'

With that Morton withdrew, and Ramon set about going through several thick files. He needed to become totally familiar with all the Carvajal companies and their assets, their management and how they were run. Also, it helped take his mind off Nena.

After their disastrous talk the other day he'd driven back to London and discovered his mother alone in the drawing room in Eaton Square.

'Well, darling? Have you seen Nena?' his mother had asked casually, laying down a copy of *Country Life*.

'I have.'

'And?'

'Not good, I'm afraid. She's talking divorce.' He sat down on the opposite sofa and swung an ankle over his knee. 'I don't know what's the matter with her. It wasn't that terrible after all.'

'Oh? You think that a newly wed bride being faced with her husband's mistress in a restaurant is an everyday occurrence of which she should take no heed?'

'That wasn't what I said,' Ramon replied, irritated. He knew perfectly well he appeared to be in the wrong, and didn't need salt rubbed in the wound.

'Mmm. Then what exactly did you say?'

'That there was no need to make such a to-do about it. She wouldn't even let me explain properly.'

Doña Augusta sent him a long, speculative look. 'Has it occurred to you how that young girl must have felt?'

'Of course it has.'

'Here she is, thrust into a marriage of convenience, having lost her grandfather, whom she adored, dropped into a new society of people she has never seen before, who are considerably older and more sophisticated than she, and from a different culture. And on top of that she's expected to handle a situation like this? Don't you think you're expecting rather a lot?'

'Actually, she handled it brilliantly,' he said, staring at the oriental carpet gracing the hardwood floor. 'She was so dignified and cool you'd have thought she dealt with things like this every day of the week.'

'Good for her. That doesn't mean she's prepared to put up with your lifestyle.'

'I never intended to keep Luisa in my life.'

'You've told me that already,' Doña Augusta said sharply. 'The point is that you don't seem to have made that clear to Nena.'

'She won't listen.'

'If I were you,' Doña Augusta said, rising and picking up her magazine, 'I'd give it a little time and let the dust settle. Life has a funny way of taking care of things.'

Ramon watched her leave the room. He was damned if he'd wait. Yet…his mother had an uncanny way of being right. Oh, well. He would stay here in London and get on with familiarising himself with Don Rodrigo's affairs. After all, he had a moral obligation where they were concerned. He'd given Don Rodrigo his word as a gentleman, and whatever the outcome of his marriage he would not renege on that.

Several days went by, but still Nena hadn't picked up the phone to call her lawyers. She knew that was what she should do, and chided herself for not getting on with it. But somehow every time she was about to look up the number something inexplicable stopped her and she would start thinking about Ramon, about those wonderful, unforgettable nights spent in his arms.

It was absurd and ridiculous to think of them when she knew—perfectly well—that it could never be. She wouldn't be able to live with him knowing he was doing the same things in another bed with another woman. She shuddered, the same mix of pain and anger assailing her. Why, oh, why had she let her heart get involved?

Nena sat at her desk and determinedly filled out applications for several universities. She must think of getting on with her life, of getting an education, instead of mooning over a man who had proved himself worthless and a cheat. But the prospect of college, which before had seemed so thrilling and which she'd longed for so dearly, no longer held the same allure. Plus the past few days she'd been feeling dreadfully tired and listless. Perhaps she should take some vitamins, or something, to boost her metabolism…

But next morning when she woke she felt no better. In fact quite the opposite. Just as she was getting out of bed she found herself rushing to the bathroom, feeling awful. Leaning over the sink, she retched.

The bout of nausea passed and Nena leaned back, staring at her pale face in the mirror. She looked like hell. Oh, well, what did it matter? She'd probably caught some bug in Argentina that had incubated for a while and had now decided to invade her system. As though the place hadn't bugged her enough already. She was very glad to have wiped the dust of it from her shoes. Still, the image of the luscious, sophisticated Luisa gazing up possessively at Ramon kept flashing at odd moments. No wonder she felt sick, she reflected crossly, weaving her way back across the room and collapsing thankfully onto the bed.

At that moment the telephone rang. She very nearly let it be answered downstairs, but then thought better of it.

'Hello?'

'Hello.'

At the sound of Ramon's deep, rich voice, Nena's pulse leaped. How she wished she could get her feelings under control.

'What do you want?' she said, somewhat rudely.

'I was just calling to see if by any chance we could

get together for lunch—say tomorrow? I have a number of things I need to discuss with you.'

He sounded impersonal, almost cold, and Nena felt suddenly downcast. Deep down, he was probably glad to be rid of her.

'What sort of things?' she asked warily.

'Oh, paperwork, a couple of matters concerning the Carvajal oil companies that I think you should be aware of. Particularly if you're going to take over running the companies yourself,' he added coldly.

'I—' It had never occurred to her that if she and Ramon divorced he would hand over his duties. The thought was daunting. 'Well, I suppose we could meet. Where do you want to go?'

'Would Harry's Bar suit you?'

'Fine. What time?' He sounded so dreadfully formal, so distant, as though all they'd shared was somehow in the past.

'A quarter to one?'

'Fine,' she repeated, seeking any kind of change in the tone of his voice.

'I'll see you then.'

He rang off and Nena flopped back against the pillows, wondering why she felt so teary. It was she, after all, who'd suggested the divorce, wasn't it? So what was she whining about? She'd made her bed and now she'd have to lie on it.

Letting out a long sigh, and fighting another bout of nausea, Nena turned on the pillow and buried her head in it. Right now all she wished was for the earth to swallow her up. She'd had enough of facing one wretched thing after another.

But her will got the better of her and soon she was in the shower, determined to remain calm and face whatever was coming with dignity and courage.

Harry's Bar was busy. The waitresses in their pretty uniforms hurried hither and thither, and the sound of social chit-chat reigned as Nena made her way towards a corner table where Ramon was rising to meet her.

She wished he wasn't so handsome, so utterly sexy in his light suit. It was not surprising that most of the women in the place were taking a peek at him out of the corners of their eyes. Some were even quite blatant about it.

'Hello, Nena.' Ramon looked her over, immediately noting how pale and thin she looked.

'Hello, Ramon.'

They didn't kiss, just sort of nodded formally.

'How have you been?' he asked, as though talking politely to a distant acquaintance.

'I'm doing well, thank you. And you?'

'Oh, fine,' he responded.

'And your parents?'

'Fine as well. In fact my mother was wondering whether she could persuade you to come for dinner tonight at Eaton Square.'

'Oh, I don't think I—' Nena said hurriedly, then, remembering how kind Doña Augusta had been, felt bad.

'It would give them great pleasure,' Ramon said, pushing every button he knew might pressure her into staying. 'I can always pick you up, if it's too long for you to remain in town all that time.'

'All right, I'll come.'

'Then we could meet somewhere and I'll drive you over there.'

'That's perfectly all right, thank you,' she said, dismissing his offer. 'I have a number of things to get done this afternoon. You can pick me up at Chester Square.'

'Fine. At seven.'

The next few minutes were spent studying the menu. Nena wondered what she should eat. The nausea had passed, but she feared that should she make the wrong choice it might return, and the last thing she wanted was to make a scene. In the end she declined a starter and opted for some grilled chicken and vegetables.

Ramon quirked a brow. 'No shrimp cocktail? I seem to recall you liked that.'

'No—no, thanks,' Nena replied hurriedly, the mere thought of the stuff making her queasy. 'I'm not very hungry today.'

'I see. Well, you must take care of your health. You look a little off colour.'

'Oh, it's nothing. Just a bug I think I must have picked up somewhere. It'll pass.'

He sent her a long, piercing look but made no comment.

'What are the things you need to talk to me about?' she asked, tentatively sipping her champagne, hoping it wouldn't have dire effects upon her queasy system.

He frowned. 'Talk about? Oh, yes. Well, there are

a couple of matters that you should be aware of. In fact, if you are considering taking a participating interest in the Carvajal companies I think you should spend some time in the office becoming familiar with them. I was going to bring a couple of files with me, but then I thought better of it. Easier for you to come to Dover Street and look them over at a desk.'

'I see.' And she did, in more ways than one.

A tiny flutter circled her heart and she peered at him from under her thick lashes. He looked so cold, so formal, his mouth set in a determined line and that arrogant head held high. But she couldn't help wondering if perhaps, despite the forbidding countenance, he hadn't arranged this lunch as an excuse to see her. The thought sent a thrill coursing through her and she took another quick sip of champagne, surprised to see that her glass was almost empty.

Before she could protest Ramon had ordered another one. Oh, well. She might need it at this rate.

She was lovely. Though so pale and waif-like. Nena was a proud woman and he'd hurt her—not only her feelings, but her self esteem, Ramon realised. He of all people knew how much that could rankle. The good news was that she apparently hadn't gone ahead with any phone calls to lawyers regarding the divorce she'd talked of. Perhaps she was thinking better of it. Living without her, spending his days cloistered in the office and nights alone in his bed in Eaton Square, recalling how they'd made love together, were not proving easy to handle.

He eyed her cool, calm and collected front. She

was quite an adversary, he realised ruefully, but one he was determined to vanquish in the end.

But these thoughts he kept to himself.

By the end of lunch Nena was amazed that they'd ended up chit-chatting about this and that in a surprisingly relaxed manner. She pulled herself up with a bang. This man was dangerous, far too smooth an operator. She must be careful and try and know her own mind, she reflected crossly as she walked into the Harvey Nichols department store later that afternoon. After all, hadn't she decided what she wanted?

With a sigh—because she obviously hadn't—Nena headed to the designer floor, and without much interest began looking at clothes.

Dining at Eaton Square was a potentially embarrassing situation, Nena realised uneasily as she lingered in the bath. What did Don Pedro and Doña Augusta think about all that was happening? After all, it was obvious all was not right between her and Ramon, since they were living apart. Her mother-in-law had seemed very tolerant of the whole thing. But what about Don Pedro? Would he express recrimination at her abandoning the conjugal domicile?

But Nena's fears were immediately allayed by the warm reception she received. Ramon had phoned and suggested he pick her up on foot, as it was just around the corner and the evening was lovely. And she'd agreed. She could think of nothing nicer than a walk before dinner.

Soon they'd arrived at the mansion on the corner of Eaton Square. Once again Nena was impressed by the exquisitely decorated rooms, the collection of paintings hung on the stairs and the more contemporary works in the vast living room.

'How lovely to see you, Nena.' Don Pedro welcomed her with a broad smile and drew her next to him on the sofa. 'We have missed you the past few days. But I'm certain you must be very busy, with much to do at Thurston.'

'Uh, yes,' she said, grateful to him for making it look as if the separation were a natural one, forced by circumstance rather than the rift that existed between Ramon and herself. Eyeing her mother-in-law out of the corner of her eye, she wondered just how much she'd told her husband. And appreciated Doña Augusta's obvious discretion, glad that she was proving to be the friend she'd professed.

Nena felt a rush of affection. There had been no older woman in her life since the untimely death of her grandmother four years earlier—no one to talk to or to seek advice from. Suddenly, knowing that Doña Augusta had really meant what she'd said the other day at lunch made her feel better. Perhaps she could talk to the older woman about how rotten she was feeling physically. Of course she could always go to Dr Grainger, the family physician in Harley Street, but for some reason she didn't want to. Perhaps the best thing, she decided as she chatted with Don Pedro, laughing at his jokes and feeling more at ease, was to let it cure itself.

Ramon was at his most charming. She could feel his eyes on her practically all the time, and she blushed. It was impossible not to remember, not to long for what he'd taught her, what he'd wakened within her.

By the end of an excellent dinner in such pleasant surroundings Nena felt positively sad that it was time to leave. She was very fond of Ramon's parents, and appreciated the kind way they'd embraced her into their family. She wished—oh, how she wished—that things might have been different.

But they weren't, she reminded herself as Ramon prepared to escort her back to Chester Square.

Night was just beginning to fall as they stepped outside, even though it was nearly ten o'clock. They began walking and Ramon slipped his arm in hers. Nena stiffened, then realised it would be churlish to reject what was probably nothing more than a gentlemanly gesture, and together they proceeded. Soon they were passing St Michael's Church, and nearing her front door. Ramon slowed.

'Nena, would you mind if I came inside and we had a talk?' he asked, his expression softer than it had been all day. 'I know you're very angry with me, and I deserve that, but I think you owe me the courtesy of listening to my side of the story.'

'Does it have to be tonight?' she enquired, looking away, wondering how she could avoid the inevitable confrontation. It was bad enough having him so close, breathing the scent of him—musky cologne mixed with that unforgettable male scent she'd remember for as long as she lived.

'Well?' Ramon quirked his dark brow at her, eyes piercing hers, filled with determination.

He was not going to be fobbed off, Nena realised,

giving in despite her reluctance. 'Okay,' she said with a shrug. 'You might as well come in and have a night-cap.'

'Don't sound so enthusiastic about it,' he murmured, making her smile in spite of everything.

'Sorry—I didn't mean to sound unwelcoming. I'm just rather tired tonight.'

'You look tired,' he said as they walked up the front steps and she pulled out her key, not waiting for the servants to come to the door. 'Are you sure you're okay?'

'Fine. Just that bug, I think. I'll be better in a couple of days. Nothing to worry about,' she replied as he held the door for her to pass into the hall.

'I certainly hope so. I don't want you getting ill.'

'It's really none of your business any longer,' she said, raising her determined chin and facing him.

Ramon stiffened and his eyes blazed. 'You are still my wife,' he uttered bitingly, 'and as such you are under my protection.'

'Oh, don't be so archaic,' Nena countered, surprised at his reaction.

'Archaic?' Ramon took a step forward. 'That may very well be. But I'll remind you that I'm your husband and it is therefore my right to be informed about your wellbeing.'

He was standing over her now, looking down into her face, eyes hard and gleaming, his mouth set in a harsh, determined line that left no room for argument. And Nena was unable to take her eyes away from his, unable to pull away, to flee the hypnotic gaze riveting her to the spot.

Before she could react his hand touched her cheek. It trailed to her lips. Then just as suddenly she was in his arms and his mouth came down on hers, crushing, forcing open her lips, demanding her to bend to his will.

For a moment Nena resisted—pushed her fists against his chest and tried to escape his hold. Then all at once his tongue touched a spot so sensitive, so tender and so vulnerable that all she could do was allow him to press her against him, feel the hardness of his body and his desire, and submit, allow his hands to roam down her back, knead her neck, and possessively caress the curve of her buttocks.

'I want you,' he growled when he came up for breath. 'God, how I want you, my Nena, how I've missed you. Come upstairs and let's finish what we've begun.'

'I—I thought you wanted to talk,' she gasped, trying to compose herself long enough to regain her sanity.

'We can do that afterwards—whenever,' he responded, pushing her firmly towards the stairs.

'No. No. Ramon, wait.' She pushed her hands against his chest and took a step back. 'This is all so simple for you, isn't it? Just kiss and make up and we'll all be friends and a happy little family again. Well, it isn't that simple. Not for me, at any rate,' she said hoarsely, her heart beating so hard she could almost hear it. 'I am not about to become some kind of carpet for you to walk all over. If you wanted us to be an item you should have thought your life out before we got married, not afterwards.'

'You're being childish and petty,' he replied, unwilling to give up.

'Maybe. But for now that's how I feel.'

'What about the divorce? I haven't had any calls from your lawyers as yet,' he challenged, eyes gleaming with contempt. 'Empty threats, Nena, not so easy to follow up on when it comes to the crunch, are they?'

'Is that what you think?' She drew back and glared at him, feeling foolish and belittled. 'Then, very well, you shall hear from my lawyers, if that is what you want.'

'I never said that, so stop trying to put words into my mouth.'

'Yes, you did. You said—'

Ramon stepped forward and in one swift movement pulled her hard against him. 'I married you for better or worse, not for you to walk out as soon as the going got rough,' he spat angrily. Then before Nena could move he'd crushed her mouth under his again and forced her to open to him.

It was so hard to resist, so awfully hard, and Nena found herself yielding when every instinct told her not to. Then his hand found her breast and fondled it. Not gently, but expertly, leaving her wet and wanting, her legs buckling as his hand came swiftly down and he touched that most sensitive spot of her body, which reacted even through the fabric of her dress and panties. Then, as she gasped, he drew away.

'A very good night to you, *señora mia.* I hope you enjoy your lonely bed.'

With that he turned on his heel and, letting himself

out, marched down the front steps and walked furiously in the direction of Eaton Square.

Nena sank onto the third step of the long flight of stairs and let out a tiny moan. It was all so confusing, so difficult to contend with. One minute she wanted to loathe him, the next to love him. The feel of his hands on her body had awakened every nerve, set alight every sensation. Now she stared at the closed door, asking herself what on earth was going to happen next. He'd almost dared her to call her lawyer—yet he'd touched her and kissed her in such a way that—

It was all too frustrating! And he was impossible. Entirely impossible.

Steadying herself on the banister, Nena rose, and trailed upstairs. In her room she undressed slowly, eyeing her body in the mirror as she undressed, touching the spot on her breast where his fingers had left a mark, seeing her nipples aroused, swollen with naked desire. She could feel the soft dampness between her thighs and closed her eyes, wishing, longing for one lingering, dreamy moment that she'd given in, let him stay, let him come upstairs and make love to her, let him ease this delicious ache that persisted, begging for completion.

Then common sense asserted itself and she turned her eyes away and grabbed an old pair of flannel pyjamas. At least they weren't sexy, didn't remind her of the honeymoon, of the way he'd told her to remove her nightdress and how deliciously sensual, how powerful she'd suddenly felt, standing naked before him.

Stop it, she ordered, marching into the bathroom

and squirting toothpaste onto her brush. She was acting like a brainless idiot, like those girls she'd so despised at school who had always been drooling over men. Surely she had more self-control than that?

But as she slipped between the covers, with the scent and feel of Ramon still impinged upon her brain and her being, Nena wondered if she had any sense left at all.

The best thing was to try and get a decent night's sleep, she decided, switching off the light and staring out of the window. Perhaps he was sleepless too, and not five minutes away, she reflected, tossing in the bed, eyeing the starry night.

It was all so desperately frustrating, she concluded, letting go an irritated sigh. And the worst part was she'd asked for it by not even allowing him to tell her what his version of the Luisa tale was.

Suddenly Nena sat up in bed, her hair falling wildly about her shoulders. What if it was actually true and he *had* been seeing Luisa for the last time?

'Oh, hell!' she exclaimed, punching her pillow angrily. She was sick and tired of this game, and the sooner it was over the better off they'd all be.

'Well?'

Ramon saw his mother mounting the wide flight of stairs as he entered the hall and hesitated.

'Well, nothing. I dropped Nena off, that's all,' he replied curtly.

'I gathered that,' Doña Augusta said patiently. 'How are things between the two of you?'

'If you want the truth, I have no damn idea,'

Ramon exploded. 'And please don't go on about it, Mother. I've had just about enough of this whole nonsense. Did you see how Nena looked? How unwell? It's ridiculous, the way she's behaving.'

'She did strike me as somewhat pale,' Doña Augusta agreed, coming back down the stairs and leading the way to the sitting room. 'Perhaps I'd better ring her tomorrow and see if she's all right.'

'Well, I hope you get a better reception than I did,' he muttered, heading straight for the silver drinks tray and pouring himself a stiff brandy. 'There's just so much of Nena's nonsense I'm prepared to tolerate,' he added through gritted teeth. 'I've had about enough of her antics.'

'Maybe she's had enough of yours,' Doña Augusta murmured, disguising a smile at her son's fury.

'Whatever. Either way, this ridiculous situation has to be put a stop to one way or another. I'm damned if I'm having my wife sleep under her own roof. It's disgraceful.'

'Tell me, *querido,* just out of interest, is it your heart or your pride that is suffering most right now?' his mother asked casually. 'That is perhaps a matter you should ask yourself.'

'Oh, Mother, leave me alone, please. I'm not in the mood for philosophical conversations. I'm off to bed.'

'Goodnight, my son. Sweet dreams.'

'Goodnight,' Ramon muttered, then stalked from the room, leaving Doña Augusta staring into the empty fireplace, a smile twitching the corner of her lips.

CHAPTER SEVEN

'DOÑA AUGUSTA is in the living room,' the maid said as Nena made her way downstairs. She felt washed out, and the bouts of sickness hadn't stopped as she'd believed they would. Could she have something serious? she wondered, taking a deep breath as she reached the hall. What was Doña Augusta doing here at ten-thirty in the morning? She felt rather dizzy, and disinclined to talk, but could hardly turn her mother-in-law out.

'Nena.' Doña Augusta rose from the sofa and Nena went over to kiss her. 'Sit down, child, and tell me what is wrong with you,' she said immediately. 'You look very pale and unwell. Have you seen a doctor?'

'No. I haven't. I don't know what's wrong with me. For several days now I've felt so queasy, but only when I wake up. By the end of the morning I feel so much better that I think I'm on the mend. I think I must have caught some sort of bug,' she said gloomily.

'Only in the morning, you say?' Doña Augusta asked casually.

'Yes. It's the oddest thing. I can't bear the thought of breakfast, but by lunchtime I'm quite hungry.'

'Hmm. Excuse me asking you something so personal, *querida,* but when did you last have your period?'

'Oh, I don't know—a few weeks ago.' Nena closed her eyes a moment and waited for the wave of dizziness to pass. 'I'm sorry,' she said. 'I'll be fine in a minute.'

Doña Augusta smiled. The child had no idea what was happening to her, she realised ruefully, wondering how the news would affect the situation between Ramon and her, and knowing she must tread carefully.

'Nena, have you thought that perhaps it might not be a bug?'

'Well, no. I don't really see what else it could be.' Then all at once Doña Augusta's previous question rang loud and clear in her head and she sat up straighter. 'Oh! You don't think that I might be—?' She turned towards her mother-in-law, her eyes wide.

'Expecting a baby?' she asked softly.

'But I can't be. I mean, these things don't happen just like that, do they?'

'That depends. Have you been using any form of contraception?'

'Uh, no. I didn't think about it. I—'

'Well, in that case I think there is a strong possibility that you may be pregnant. Morning sickness is one of the first symptoms. I had it dreadfully when I was expecting Ramon.'

Nena sat on the sofa in shock. Pregnant. Expecting Ramon's baby. What was she going to do?

'Doña Augusta, please don't tell Ramon. At least until I've found out for sure if I am really pregnant.

Things aren't—well, you know they're not—going too well between us now. I need to be able to make my own decisions.'

'I understand, my dear, but let me make an appointment for you with an excellent gynaecologist. He will be able to tell you if you are expecting or not, and then we'll take it from there. As for now, I want you to lie down on the sofa and put your legs up. Here.' Doña Augusta placed another cushion behind Nena's back. 'And some herb tea might help. I'll get the maid to make some immediately,' she said, taking charge.

A baby.

What would it be like? Was it a boy or a girl? And what if she and Ramon—? The thought didn't bear thinking about. How would he react if she was pregnant? This couldn't have come at a worse time, she decided, caught between the newborn emotions of imagining a tiny person growing inside her womb and the fact that she and Ramon were so torn apart.

She sighed, closed her eyes and let Doña Augusta fuss, ordering tea and covering her legs with a cashmere throw before she headed for the telephone and began making calls.

Several minutes later she returned to Nena's side. 'Good. I have got you an appointment for tomorrow morning at eleven. I can come with you, but quite understand if you would prefer to go alone.'

'Thank you.' Nena smiled gratefully. 'If you don't mind, I think I'd better go by myself.'

'I understand, *querida*. But please phone me when he tells you the result.'

'And you won't tell Ramon?'

'Didn't I promise this would remain our secret? That is on the condition that you allow me to take proper care of you. After all, you may be expecting my grandchild,' she added with a conspiratorial smile.

'Of course. You've been wonderful. Thank you so much.'

'Not at all. I'm thrilled to finally have a daughter to spoil.'

'Yes,' Nena replied hesitantly. What if she and Ramon split up? What then?

But right now she mustn't think of that, must just get through the rest of the day, then go to the doctor and find out the truth. There would be time then to find answers to the rest of her dilemmas.

There was something wrong with the numbers.

Ramon frowned. He'd been over the audits several times and something didn't fly. He picked up the pages where he'd circled several items in red and reviewed them once more. And that wasn't all, he reflected, leaning back in the leather swivel chair. He had a feeling there were other issues going on at management level in several of Don Rodrigo Carvajal's companies. But as yet he hadn't pinned them down, and he was loath to show his hand before he was certain of his facts.

And it might take him a little time to find out.

He didn't trust the urbane Sir Wilfred, with his suave, ready answers and slightly patronising attitude. In fact he wondered for just how long he'd been ripping Don Rodrigo off. Too long, probably. Certainly since the old gentleman had become ill and had been obliged to hand over the everyday running of his affairs to the man. Then there was that team of high-powered savvy lawyers, who seemed to have an excessive amount of power within the structure of the holding company.

It would take him some sleuthing, but Ramon was determined to get to the bottom of it. Still, these problems, and a number of others he was dealing with in his own affairs back home, did not stop him from wondering just how he was going to handle the biggest problem of all: his wife.

Nena was being recalcitrant and difficult. He'd thought yesterday that she would finally listen to him, allow him to explain, and that maybe they could get over the hurdle that had risen between them. He thought of her, pliant and yielding in his arms, and his body reacted immediately. She was lovely. That she should believe he could possibly want another woman when he had her was almost amusing. But that was precisely what Nena thought, that he had married her out of convenience—which he had—and that he planned to continue with his old life as well.

The other thing worrying him was the state of her health. She'd seemed better last night, but when he'd phoned half an hour ago to talk to her, in the hope that he might persuade her to meet him for lunch, the maid had said she was unwell and couldn't be disturbed.

Suddenly Ramon got up. This was ridiculous. If she was ill then he must get her to the doctor. Grabbing his suit jacket from the back of the chair, he slipped it on and made his way out of the office.

'I'll be back later, Miss Brown. Please advise Morton,' he told Don Rodrigo's dragon-like secretary, who sat behind a large desk, ramrod-straight, wearing a pair of horn-rimmed glasses that made her look like an owl.

'Very well, sir.'

'I'll phone in and you can tell me if there are any important calls. Is Sir Wilfred in yet?'

'No, sir. He has a meeting in the City this morning, with the American bankers for Carvajal Oil.'

'But I specifically said I needed to be at that meeting.' Ramon frowned, torn between his desire to go to Nena and the knowledge that he should definitely stay and be informed of what was going on. 'Damn it. Why wasn't I advised?'

'I'm afraid I only learned the news by chance myself, sir.' Miss Brown pursed her lips, and for the first time she exchanged a long glance with him.

'I see. Well, in future I think we should keep our eyes and ears well open, Miss Brown,' Ramon responded carefully, mindful of the fact that Miss Brown, like Morton, had worked for over thirty years with Don Rodrigo, who had held the highest opinion of her. If he had to trust someone, she was certainly his best bet.

Turning on his heel, he took the ancient cage elevator down to the ground floor, then grabbed a taxi. Nena would just have to wait. The issues at hand were too important to let slip. It would do no harm for the

Americans to know he was actively on board at Carvajal, and that from now on they'd be dealing with him.

In the doctor's office Nena slipped her clothes back on, returned from behind the screen and sat down on the opposite side of Dr Langtry's desk.

'Just a few minutes, Mrs Carvajal, while we verify the test. All your symptoms seem to indicate that you are expecting a baby, but we'd better be certain.' He smiled at her and she smiled back weakly, her mind in a frenzy as little by little the reality of the whole thing sank in.

At that moment the nurse entered and handed him a slip of paper.

'Thank you.' The doctor skimmed over the results.

'Well, Mrs Carvajal, see for yourself,' he said handing her the typed piece of paper. 'You are expecting a baby for next April.'

Hand trembling, Nena stared at the word 'positive'. She swallowed. Was she happy? Sad? Or just overwhelmed?

'Thank you, Doctor,' she said hoarsely.

'Come back in two weeks and we'll see how you're faring. The morning sickness should pass after the first three months, maybe sooner. Dry toast and tea is the best remedy. But then you must eat properly—plenty of vegetables and nourishing food—and lots of exercise, of course. I recommend swimming and walking.'

'What about tennis?' Nena asked weakly.

'You mentioned slight pain, so I'd say nothing too vigorous just at the moment.'

'Okay.' Nena nodded.

Five minutes later she was seated in the back of her grandfather's Bentley, wondering what to do. She must tell Doña Augusta, but what about Ramon? Would he assume that this simply obliterated the problems they had? Would he see this as a way of sorting things out exactly as he wanted?

Nena experienced a sudden pang of hunger and knew she simply must eat roast beef. Odd. She'd never been very partial to roast beef, but now the mere thought of it made her mouth water and she could barely think of anything else.

All at once her mobile phone rang.

'Hello?'

'Hi, it's me. I've been looking for you.'

'Who's me?' she asked haughtily, her lips twitching. He was so dreadfully arrogant and presumptuous she couldn't resist.

'What are you doing for lunch?'

'Eating roast beef.' The words were out before she could stop herself.

'Eating roast—? Well, all right. Why don't I join you? Where are you?'

'I'm in the car, coming up to Piccadilly Circus.'

'Then meet me at Wilton's. I'll be there in twenty minutes.'

'But—' Nena was about to say that she didn't know if she wanted to lunch with him, then gave up. Frankly, the roast beef was more important, and Wilton's certainly prepared some of the best in town.

The car drew up in Jermyn Street and she alighted and entered the restaurant.

'I believe my—my husband—' the word still

caught on her lips '—phoned to reserve a table,' she said to the *maître d'*.

'Why, of course, Mrs Villalba. This way, please.'

Nena followed him through the restaurant and was shown into one of the booths, where she sat down thankfully. She was about to order a glass of champagne, then hesitated. Alcohol wasn't good for the baby.

'Some mineral water, please. Still.'

All at once it wasn't just her desires and wishes that counted any longer. She had a being inside her whom she must protect and shield from harm. The thought sent a wave of emotion coursing through her. Instinctively she touched her belly and took a deep breath. But she still had no inkling of what she would tell Ramon.

Then he was standing there, leaning over her, and her heart did a somersault. As he sat down on the opposite banquette she looked over at him, this man whom despite everything she longed for—and the father of her child, she reminded herself unsteadily.

'Ah. Champagne, Nena?'

'No, thanks. I'll just stick to water for now.'

Ramon frowned. 'Are you still feeling unwell?' he asked, eyes filled with concern.

'No, no. I'm fine, actually. Just rather hungry.'

'I see. Well, that's a good sign. I suppose we'd better order right away. Is the roast beef still on?'

'Absolutely.' She laughed, and they smiled at each other, their eyes lingering. 'With all the trimmings.'

Ramon ordered, then watched her. She looked tense and he wondered what was troubling her. Surely not just the problems they were facing? She hadn't mentioned the divorce again, and had seemed quite amenable to having lunch. But he would not repeat pushing matters too fast too soon. It might pay off to retreat a little.

'I'll be going away for a few days,' he remarked casually, after the waiter had served him a glass of wine.

'Oh? Where are you going. Back to Buenos Aires?' He caught the edge in her voice and smothered a smile.

'No. Actually, I'm going to New York. I need to visit your grandfather's office there, and deal with some personal business of my own as well.'

'I see.' Nena waited a moment, then experienced a sudden flash of disappointment that he hadn't asked her to join him. Not that she would have gone, of course, but he could have at least asked.

'No wine?' Ramon asked.

'No, thanks.' Nena glanced at the bottle and felt her tummy flip at the mere thought of the stuff.

'Are you sure you're all right?' Ramon queried, his brows creasing once more. She'd looked rather green at the mention of the wine and he wondered why.

Nena's brain was working nineteen to the dozen now.

'When are you leaving?' she asked, torn between telling him her news now or waiting till he got back and she'd made up her mind what she wanted to do.

'I'm flying out tomorrow morning.'

'I see. And how long do you plan to stay in New York?'

'A few days. Not sure exactly how many,' he added casually. 'It depends on what's going on over there. I might take the weekend and pop over to Newport. I have friends who own a beautiful sloop. She's sailed in the Americas Cup. I thought I might fit in a little sailing.'

Nena leaned back, trying to control her emotions. Here she was, with the biggest piece of news to hit her young life, and he was going sailing. She might have known it. Well, let him go sailing, and whatever else he planned to do. What did she care? She was damned if she was going to tell him now. Let him wait.

The roast beef arrived, but for some inexplicable reason she seemed to have lost her appetite.

'I thought you were desperately hungry, *querida?* What happened?' Ramon asked innocently, noting the slight glare in her eyes.

'I'm fine. I must have just misjudged my own appetite.' She sent a bright, brittle smile across the table and began to talk of inconsequential mundane subjects.

'Are you sure you'll be all right while I'm away?' he asked, as they finally rose from the table.

'Of course,' she scoffed. 'Why shouldn't I be?'

'I don't know.' He shrugged and sent her a rueful smile. 'No reason.'

Outside the restaurant Nena's car was waiting. 'Do you want a lift to Dover Street?'

'No, thanks, I'll walk.'

'Fine. Then *bon voyage.*'

'Thanks. I'll see you when I get back.' He dropped a light kiss on her cheek and saw her into the vehicle.

'He'll see me when he gets back,' Nena muttered angrily to herself, watching his tall, broad-shouldered figure march off down the street. 'We'll see about that.'

But she had to admit that it was awfully comforting to know he was at the helm of all her grandfather's affairs, that she was not left high and dry in the hands of those suave, well-spoken lawyers whom she didn't understand half the time and whom for some reason she didn't entirely trust.

Then she remembered Doña Augusta, and sighed. She felt bad about telling anyone of her pregnancy before she told Ramon. But then she'd had her chance and hadn't taken it. Oh, well. She supposed there was nothing for it but to confide in the older woman and hope she wouldn't tell him. Somehow she felt that she could trust her mother-in-law. There was something very trustworthy about Doña Augusta. And she had the feeling that what she'd said was true—she had a surprisingly unbiased and realistic opinion of her own son.

Slowly she picked up the mobile and arranged to pop over to Eaton Square, where a few minutes later Doña Augusta was waiting for her.

'Come in, my dear. Let's have a cup of tea in the sitting room.' She gave the order to the butler, then accompanied Nena into a small, intimate room, decorated with flowered cushions and a window seat, that was obviously her own private little enclave.

'How pretty this is!' Nena exclaimed.

'Well, I have to have somewhere that is feminine in a house full of male energy,' her mother-in-law replied, laughing. 'Now sit down, *querida,* and tell me what the doctor said.'

Nena sat obediently on one of the plump sofas and took a deep breath.

'It's true,' she said in a rush. 'I'm pregnant. He says the baby will be born in April.'

'Well, many congratulations, my love. That is wonderful news. When do you plan to tell Ramon?'

'I don't know. It's—it's all so difficult. I thought of telling him at lunch, but—'

'You lunched together?'

'Yes. At Wilton's. I felt like roast beef.'

'Ah!'

'Oh, I don't know what to do.' Suddenly Nena burst into a flood of unbidden tears that she couldn't control. 'I d-don't know what's the matter with me,' she hiccupped, feeling for a non-existent hanky. 'I'm never up and down like this—all undecided. It's as if my reasoning mind has flown out the window.'

'But, Nena, *mi querida,* that is only natural.' Doña Augusta sat next to her on the sofa and took her hand. 'When we are expecting a baby all our emotions change. We cry for no reason, see things as black when in fact they're not, and have all sorts of unexpected feelings. Remember, your body and your mind are acclimatising to being a mother. It is no longer you alone, but the two of you to be taken care of.'

Nena sniffed and nodded. 'I know. I thought about that today in the restaurant.'

'So tell me,' Doña Augusta said soothingly, 'why didn't you tell him?'

'Because he said he was going to New York and then going sailing in Newport. Sailing! Can you imagine? I mean, what does he need to go sailing for? Why can't he just come—?' Realising suddenly how foolish she must sound, Nena clamped her mouth shut.

'Perhaps you have not shown him that you want him back,' her mother-in-law murmured softly. 'Men have a funny way of retiring into their shells. They can be very proud. Did you let Ramon talk to you about what happened in BA?'

Nena shook her head and stared at her hands. 'No, I didn't.'

'You won't be cross with me if I say that was perhaps a little foolish? He deserved to be punished, I agree. And I'm sure it did him a world of good to know he couldn't have everything his own way. But I honestly believe he was telling the truth when he said his affair with Luisa was over.'

'Do you?' Nena turned her big streaming eyes, filled with tears and uncertainty, towards her. 'But she's so lovely, so beautiful, so worldly and sophisticated. I can see why he'd want to be with her rather than with me. After all, I'm really just a commitment he took on.' She swallowed. 'I didn't realise that I would—'

'Fall in love?' her mother-in-law supplied gently, a tender smile curving her lips. 'Why not? I fell in love with my husband after we were married. And I have good reason to believe he did the same. Has it never occurred to you, Nena, that Ramon might be in love with you?'

'No. Of course not. I mean, why should he be? If you'd seen the way he and Luisa were looking at each other, like a couple—I'm sure he loves her.'

'Rubbish,' Doña Augusta dismissed briskly. 'Luisa and he were good companions. They frequented the same crowd, and all that, and I'm sure they had a well-attuned sex-life together while it lasted. But that's not what I'm referring to. I'm talking about passion, about true love—that feeling that comes once in a lifetime and never lets go.'

'Well, if he loves me why would he go off to New York and stay for the weekend for his wretched sailing when he doesn't have to?' she muttered, sniffing, and accepting the hanky Doña Augusta handed her.

'Because you've been holding him at arm's length, *querida.* What man wouldn't salvage his pride at some point? Particularly an arrogant, self-confident creature like Ramon. This has probably never happened to him before.'

'I suppose not,' Nena answered dully.

'Now, my recommendation is that you go home, relax, and take this week to think out very clearly what it is you want to do. Then when he gets back you can decide.'

'You're probably right,' Nena murmured dejectedly. 'And you won't tell him about the baby, will you?' she asked, suddenly worried.

'Of course not, *querida.* It will be our secret until the time you decide to reveal it. That is your privilege,' Doña Augusta added, smiling and squeezing

Nena's hand. 'And if you need me—and even if you don't,' she added ruefully, 'I shall be close by, making sure you're all right.'

After tea Nena went home, feeling a little calmer but very tired. She was meant to be having dinner with her old schoolfriends, Venetia and Tania, but she felt suddenly too tired, exhausted by the emotions of the day, and ready to make it an early night.

As the plane took off Ramon nursed a whisky and gazed down through the summer drizzle at the landscape below. There was much to be straightened out, and he had every intention of settling matters as soon as he could. Still, an uneasy feeling accompanied him as he leaned back in the wide, comfortable seat and pondered on all that had occurred over the past few weeks.

Nena had seemed so up and down yesterday—not her usual self at all. But there was little use worrying about it. He'd be much better served by studying the files he'd brought with him.

With a sigh Ramon opened his briefcase and settled in for the long flight. At least it would give him time to review all the issues that were worrying him about Carvajal's, and which he needed to get to the bottom of.

Plus, a week away from Nena might not do either of them any harm. As long as she was more amenable by the time he got back…

CHAPTER EIGHT

THREE nights later Nena woke in the middle of the night conscious of a stabbing pain in her lower abdomen. At first she turned over and tried to find a more comfortable position in the bed and go back to sleep. But when it persisted—got stronger—she became worried.

Switching the bedside lamp on, she tried to sit up, but simply doubled over. Then as she removed the bedcovers and tried to lower her feet to the ground she suddenly realised she was bleeding.

'Oh, no,' she uttered, horrified. What could be happening to her? Surely she couldn't be losing the baby?

Cold fear gripped her as she sat on the edge of the bed, perfectly still, as though by doing so she could somehow stop the upheaval occurring inside her body. Then another twinge had her gasping. Instinctively she reached as best she could for the phone, while falling back against the pillows.

After several deep breaths she rang the Villalba number and waited anxiously for someone to answer the phone.

'Hello?'

Don Pedro's voice reached her down the line and she squirmed, wishing it had been Doña Augusta who'd answered. This was so embarrassing—phoning in the middle of the night. What would her father-in-law think? Though frankly she was past caring.

'It's Nena,' she answered, her voice tremulous. 'I'm so sorry to disturb you so late,' she said breathlessly. 'Is—is Doña Augusta there?'

'Of course she's here—but, Nena,' he said, suddenly coming fully awake, 'is something the matter?'

'Yes—well, could I speak to her?'

'Of course, my dear, at once.' She heard him murmuring something to his wife as he passed the phone.

'Nena, tell me what is wrong?' Doña Augusta asked anxiously.

'I—well, I woke up with this awful pain, and it's not getting better. And then when I sat up I realised I was—well, that I was bleeding,' she said in a rush.

'Oh, my goodness. Stay right where you are and I shall be there in a few minutes. In the meantime don't move. I shall call an ambulance immediately.'

'Ambulance?' Nena said hoarsely.

'Yes. You must be taken to hospital at once, my love, or you may lose the baby.'

'Oh, no.' Nena felt tears surfacing once more. 'Oh, please God, no. I want this baby so much. I—'

'Calm down, Nena, it will be all right. We'll be there as soon as we can.'

Nena hung up and stayed motionless against the pillows, tears coursing down her cheeks. How could she have been so idiotic? Why hadn't she told Ramon about the baby? Now maybe it would be too late. Nena closed her eyes and tried to stay calm. For the baby's sake, she kept repeating to herself. For that tiny, crucial wisp of life growing inside her that she was determined to preserve whatever the cost.

Several minutes later she heard footsteps on the landing and a knock on the door.

'Come in.'

'Ah, Nena.' Doña Augusta came hurrying across the room, having been let in by Worthing, who was now waiting for the ambulance. 'My poor child. Now stay quiet. We will go with you to the hospital.'

'We?' Nena asked in a small voice.

'I had to tell Pedro, I'm afraid.'

'Oh, never mind.' Nena smiled as best she could and closed her eyes as another pain loomed. 'It doesn't matter any longer.'

'There, that's better,' Doña Augusta soothed. 'We'll be at the hospital very shortly, and all will be well, I'm certain. But in the future we must take better care of you.'

Ramon felt his cellphone vibrating and excused himself to Grant Connelly, the high-flying New York attorney he was dining with at Cipriani's restaurant on Fifth Avenue. The place was noisy and he could hardly hear. In desperation he got up and went outside.

'Father, I can hear you now. Why are you phoning me at two-thirty in the morning your time? Nothing's wrong, is it?'

'I'm afraid it is, Ramon.'

'What? What is wrong?' he asked hoarsely, fear clutching him.

'It is Nena.'

'What's happened to her?' He nearly shouted, pacing the pavement impatiently.

'She's being driven to hospital as we speak. I'm afraid she may lose the baby.'

'The baby? What baby?' he asked, mystified. Then all at once he grasped his father's meaning. 'You mean she's pregnant?' he exclaimed, a new and unprecedented emotion taking hold.

'Yes. Didn't you know?'

'No, I— Is she all right? Oh, what an idiot I've been.'

'Now, calm down, my son. I think you should try and get on the first flight out.'

'Of course. If I leave here immediately I can catch the British Airways flight out of Kennedy,' he said, glancing at his watch, his mind in a frenzy. 'Oh, God, how could this have happened?'

'In the usual way, I imagine,' his father responded dryly. 'Just make sure that in the future you take proper care of your wife. I don't understand all these goings-on between the two of you. It's perfectly ridiculous.'

'Yes, Father. I'll explain when I see you. Please, just make sure she—she and the baby are all right.'

'Very well. I'm on my way to the Chelsea and Westminster Hospital now. Your mother is in the ambulance with Nena. Thank goodness she confided in her, otherwise I dread to think what might have happened.'

Ramon stood on the pavement and gazed blindly at Central Park, at the carriage passing before him with a young couple in the rear, holding hands and hugging, at the lights of the Plaza across the street, seeing nothing but her face, replaying each expression, each moment, each tender look, each instant since that dreadful misunderstanding that had caused so much grief.

Then he took a deep breath and walked back inside the restaurant to explain to his dinner companion what was happening. Without a moment's hesitation Connelly offered to drive him to the airport at once.

Some time later Ramon was dropped at the airport. My goodness, how time passed slowly when you wanted to be somewhere fast, he thought. Why had he made the trip just at this time when it wasn't absolutely essential? Why hadn't he waited? And why had it never occurred to him, when Nena refused that glass of champagne at lunch, that there might be a reason for her refusal?

In the first class departure lounge he quickly dialled his father's mobile phone.

'What's happening?' he asked anxiously. 'Is she all right?'

'We don't know yet. She's with the doctor now, but don't worry—we'll be here with her, never fear.'

'Thank you,' Ramon murmured gratefully, trying to combat the sudden wave of nausea that gripped him at the thought of Nena lying there in the hospital, perhaps losing the baby. Their baby. A baby conceived in one of those torrid moments of—

For a moment Ramon swallowed. He'd never realised it until this very moment, but it was love he felt for Nena. A feeling different from any other he'd ever experienced for any other woman. He shook his head and let out a long sigh, stunned by what he'd just become aware of. He loved her—loved this girl whom he'd known for such a short time, who'd entered his life and taken over in a way that would have been inconceivable to him a very short while ago.

'British Airways flight—' That was his flight.

Grabbing his briefcase, Ramon followed the other passengers and made his way to the plane.

It could not reach London fast enough.

The car was waiting for him at Heathrow to take him to the Chelsea and Westminster Hospital, where he found his mother and father waiting in the corridor outside Nena's room.

'She's been sedated, poor child,' Doña Augusta told him.

'But is she all right? And the baby?' he asked, trying to quell the overwhelming anxiety he'd been suffering all night.

'I'm afraid she's lost it,' his mother answered sadly.

Ramon said nothing, just shoved his hands in his pockets and turned and stared doggedly out of the window. It was his fault all this had occurred. His fault that she'd lived through this horrendous experience alone and unhappy when he should have been next to her. And worse was that it was all because of that dreadful day with Luisa. Had that not occurred, none of this would have happened. It was probably all the anxiety and nervous stress she'd been subjected to that had caused the miscarriage in the first place.

He turned. 'Can I go in and see her?' he asked his mother.

'I think you'd better wait to see the doctor first. He should be here in a few minutes,' his mother demurred.

'Yes,' Don Pedro seconded. 'Wait to speak with the doctor, Ramon. And see to it in the future that you take proper care of your wife,' he added sternly. 'You are not a bachelor any longer, my son. You have duties. Make sure you see to them properly.'

Ramon said nothing, just nodded. His father was right to chastise him. There was no excuse for his absence, only Nena's rejection of him to hang his hat on. But he should have insisted, not allowed her to get the better of him with her arguments. He should have taken charge, as he always did with every other damn aspect of his life, and simply told her how things were going to be—insisted instead of deferring, being gentlemanly and giving way to her wishes. Damn her wishes. He was her husband, after all, and it was his duty and his right to make sure she was properly taken care of.

Several minutes later the doctor put in an appearance.

'Ah! Mr Villalba.'

'Is she all right?' Ramon enquired, features tense.

'Yes. She'll be fine. She's young and in excellent health. But of course a miscarriage is never an easy thing for a woman to go through, no matter how early in the pregnancy it occurs.' He lowered his voice and the two men walked along the corridor. 'She's very upset emotionally. It will require a lot of patience and care on your part to help her through this. Of course the best solution is another baby.'

'Right away?' Ramon looked at him steadily.

'No. Not immediately. She will need a few weeks to get over this, both physically and emotionally.'

Ramon nodded. 'I blame myself for not being here.'

'Don't. These things happen. We don't know why they do, but they do. And it has in no way affected her ability to bear children. Still, once a woman knows she's expecting a baby, has absorbed the fact and has lived even for a few days with the knowledge of another being growing inside her, the sense of loss can be tremendous.'

'I understand.' Ramon nodded. 'May I go in and see her now?'

'Yes. I don't know if she'll be awake yet, but you may stay with her. Don't get into long discussions about all this until she's better, though. There is always a sense of guilt accompanying these things.'

'Thank you, Doctor.' Ramon mustered a smile and shook his hand. 'I'm grateful for all you've done for my wife.'

'I'm afraid I didn't do anything except take care of the problem. The rest will be up to you.' He squeezed Ramon's shoulder, then, after a goodbye and a handshake to Don Pedro and Doña Augusta, he left down the corridor as Ramon prepared to enter Nena's room.

'We'll be leaving now, *querido.* Your father is very tired and must get some rest. If the doctor lets Nena out later today bring her back to Eaton Square. Enough of this being on her own.'

'Of course I will. Go home, Papá, and get some sleep,' Ramon said, touching his father's arm. 'And thank you both for all you've done. I—' There was a catch in his voice.

'It's nothing. We think of her as a daughter,' Doña Augusta said gently. 'See that you mend this breach between you, Ramon, and *don't,*' she begged earnestly, 'let pride and stupidity get in your way, my son.' She reached up and kissed his tense bronzed cheek. 'You will see. God willing, all will be well.'

Ramon quietly opened the door and stared across the bleak hospital room at Nena, lying motionless, like a doll in the centre of the bed. Her hands lay on the white coverlet, and as Ramon approached the bed he reached for one of them, touching it tenderly, a wave of emotion gripping him as he thought of all she'd been through. How scared she must have been, waking up to such a horrible experience in the middle of the night alone, obliged to telephone his parents. And what might have happened if she hadn't phoned? What if she'd been too embarrassed and had stayed there bleeding until morning? What then?

He shuddered and perched on the side of the bed, gazing down at her lovely pale face, her hair lying tidily to each side of it, as though she hadn't stirred. He drew his hand away from hers, afraid of disturbing her, and a rush of tenderness overwhelmed him. She looked like a little girl, lying there so quietly. Yet she was a woman.

His woman.

And in that instant Ramon determined that he would never let her go.

* * *

Nena woke to a painful sensation in her lower tummy. Eyes still closed, she winced. Then little by little the events of the previous night shaped themselves in her sedated brain and slowly she opened her eyes.

'Nena, *mia*.'

She heard Ramon's voice, blinked, and stared up at him, her lips parting in an 'oh'. He had come, after all. He was here, had not abandoned her and stayed in New York as she'd feared, but was by her side.

Ramon slipped his hand over hers, then leaned down and softly grazed her lips with his.

'You're here,' she said blurrily.

'Yes, I'm here. And I have no intention of going anywhere.'

Nena registered his words silently, and let him take her hand in his, feeling the soothing movement of his fingers as he stroked her palm.

'I'm so sorry about the baby,' she said finally, battling a sudden new wave of emotion. 'I shouldn't have—'

'Nena, none of this is your fault.'

'But it is. If I'd—'

'No. I will not permit you to assume any responsibility for this. If anyone is to blame it is I,' he answered bitterly. 'I must have been blind not to recognise that something was different that day in the restaurant. Perhaps you were even going to tell me and it just didn't register.'

'Well, it doesn't matter any more,' she said in a small voice. 'It's too late.'

'Shush. You mustn't get upset. There is time enough to talk of all this once you are better and well again. Now, I am going to see if the doctor will allow you to leave the hospital later today.'

She nodded and closed her eyes, not really caring what happened any more, feeling a great wave of unhappiness for the baby she would never hold in her arms, that tiny piece of life that she'd already pictured alive and kicking, with Ramon's dark eyes and her nose. He—because she was certain it had been a boy—would have looked just like his father…

Silent tears seeped through her tightly closed lids and coursed down her cheeks.

Ramon watched her, helpless. All he could do was wipe the tears away gently with his thumb. There was little else he could do but double his resolve that never again would he allow her to be on her own to suffer.

Later that afternoon Nena was allowed to leave. She felt tender and fragile, and grateful for Ramon's assistance as together they walked out of the hospital and entered the car. When it pulled up at Eaton Square she looked out of the car window, surprised.

'But I thought I was going home,' she said.

'This is home, Nena.'

'But—'

'No buts,' he said firmly, clasping her hand, and the set of his jaw left her in little doubt of his determination to keep her by him. 'You are staying here with me and that is an end to it.'

'I—' Nena was about to protest, then, too tired to argue, she gave in.

Minutes later she was being taken upstairs and

helped into bed by Doña Augusta and one of the maids.

'You need lots of rest, Nena dear. I remember when this happened to me,' Doña Augusta said, sitting on the side of the bed. 'It takes a lot out of you. Emotionally and physically.'

'I hope I'm not being a nuisance,' Nena murmured, the force of habit taking over.

'Rubbish. You are a part of this family now. It is only natural that we should care for you.' She leaned down and dropped a kiss on Nena's forehead. 'Now, try and get some sleep, *querida,* and don't worry there will be many more babies in the future.'

Nena swallowed the knot in her throat and tried to hold back the tears that were never far from the sur face. She nodded.

'No more worrying,' Doña Augusta insisted, patting the coverlet. 'Everything will take care of itself.'

CHAPTER NINE

'How about a trip to Agapos?' Ramon enquired, three weeks later. Nena still seemed very down, lethargic and uninterested in life. Ramon was seriously worried about her. He'd tried to talk about what had happened, but she didn't seem to want to. He'd insisted she see a psychologist, but Nena hadn't derived much benefit from the visits.

'Agapos?' she said, remembering the beautiful island where they'd first made love, where maybe their baby had been conceived.

'Yes. It would do you good to have a break—get away from here and be in the sun. It's lovely in early autumn over there. We would be all by ourselves.'

He reached across and took her hand. Lately she neither accepted or rejected him. It was as though she was living in another world, a place of her own where she didn't allow any intrusions. But Ramon knew—sensed—that either he got through to her emotionally very soon or he might lose her for ever.

'I think we should go down there,' he insisted. 'I shall have the plane ready to take us the day after tomorrow.'

Nena shrugged. She really didn't care what she did any longer. The loss of the baby seemed so tremendous, so incredibly painful. And, although Ramon had been attentive and caring, she just couldn't overcome that little inkling of mistrust that lingered, surfacing every time she was about to let down her guard and let him in.

Would it ever leave her? she wondered. Or would it persist, looming over their marriage, making it impossible for them ever to really come together, for her to trust him fully? After all, what would happen when all this had passed? Say she agreed to live with him and take up a normal life—would she ever be free of the fear of walking into another restaurant and seeing him with another woman? Maybe now he'd be more careful, but she'd learn it from some other source, or simply know instinctively that he was making love to someone else.

Nena sighed. They might as well go to Agapos as be here in London, where it rained all the time and she felt so bleak. Her girlfriends had called, but she had no desire to see them. Or anyone else for that matter. It was as though she'd shored herself up in her own little cocoon, and was loath to leave it in case another nasty surprise caught her off guard.

Ramon, though she didn't know it, had taken heed of the doctor's words and was sleeping in the room next to hers. But as the days went by he was determined that soon they would be sleeping together once again.

Two days later the helicopter was once more hovering over the island, different now in the early autumn light, a soft glow etching the white houses, making them stand out. The blue waters of the Aegean shimmered, the bright coloured fishing boats shining brightly in the lingering sun.

Soon they were up at the house. Nena changed, donning a comfortable white kaftan, then walked barefoot over the terrace and stared out at the sea, at the late-afternoon sun dipping on the horizon, at more fishing boats returning to port with the day's catch.

It all seemed so peaceful, so distant from London and the mental turmoil of the past weeks. Ramon had been busy the last few days, had seemed to spend a lot of time at the office. She hadn't questioned him about it. Or maybe he was fed up and was beginning another affair with some other woman, she reflected sadly.

Sitting on the balustrade, Nena told herself she must stop being paranoid. It was one thing to realise that the possibility existed, another to assume, with no real reason, that his absence was caused by some new attractive female he'd come across. Still, however hard she tried she was unable to banish that image of Luisa, glancing up at him over her shoulder, of her intimate smile.

Perhaps all the attention Ramon was devoting to her now was just part of his sense of duty, of the obligation he'd undertaken, the promise he'd made to her grandfather. But she didn't want to be considered part of a contractual obligation. She wanted to be wanted for *her,* for who she was.

And that was an unlikely scenario.

At no time had Ramon ever said more than the murmured words spoken in the heat of passion. And those, she realised sadly, meant very little. They were part of a vocabulary he had probably used frequently with every woman he'd bedded.

'Nena?' Ramon stepped out onto the terrace and came to join her on the balustrade. He wore a pair of Bermuda shorts and a T-shirt.

Nena looked at him, surprised. She'd never seen him quite so casual before. And she liked it. She swallowed despite herself at the sight of his strong muscles, still tanned from their previous stay. The overpowering masculine aura still surrounded him, but she'd been less conscious of it over the past few weeks, too tied up with her emotions. Now, as he sat opposite her, his dark hair stirring in the early-evening breeze, his strong arms uncovered, she experienced a charge of desire like nothing she'd felt since before the miscarriage.

She pulled herself up with a jolt.

It was fundamental to remember all the reasons for which a long-term relationship with this man really couldn't work out, all the doubt and the knowledge that he might betray her at any given time. She would have to be firm, she realised with an inner sigh, make a final decision about what she was going to do with her life. It wasn't fair to either of them to linger on in this vacuum of uncertainty.

But it was hard to contemplate life without him at her side. She'd become so used to his presence over the past few weeks—to him popping by in the morning before he left for the office, kissing her tenderly goodbye, ringing her in the late morning to suggest a spontaneous lunch.

It was in the early evening that doubts took hold,

when he rang in to say he'd be late because of a meeting or the occasional 'business dinner'. It was then that she asked herself if he was telling her the truth or merely covering tactfully while all the time being ensconced in the arms of some woman or other.

And there was the fact that she hadn't been sleeping with him herself to contend with too.

He was hardly a monk, she recognised, and could hardly be expected to live an entirely celibate life. And if she wasn't sleeping with him, then who was?

It was all so terribly difficult, and Nena gave a deep sigh, wishing things could be different.

'Something wrong, *querida?*' Ramon asked, leaning forward and taking her fingers in his.

The touch of his hand, which for the past few weeks she'd accepted as tenderness and care for her wellbeing, turned suddenly to fire. Nena caught her breath imperceptibly, wanting to draw back, yet staying all the same. Ramon was somehow different here. Not radically. But there was a subtle change. He looked more rugged, more determined, and his eyes held a gleam that she hadn't seen in the past few weeks. She swallowed, felt her body tingle. Was it this place that made her feel so suddenly altered? Was it the gentle breeze blowing in from the sea that was dissipating the pain and unhappiness leaving the way open for the new, unexpected feelings surging through her being?

Ramon drew closer. Night was falling fast, stars peeking in the inky sky. She rose quickly and turned towards the sea, unable to face him.

* * *

It had been too long, Ramon decided. He had waited the time she'd needed to recover from the miscarriage, but now he wanted her. Rising, he moved behind her and slipped his hands around her, caressing her ribcage, stopping just below her breast and nuzzling her neck.

Nena gasped, unable to control the rush of desire searing through her like a white-hot arrow. Her breasts ached, and she could feel the soft, moist surrender between her thighs. Then Ramon's thumbs grazed her taut, swollen nipples, very lightly, taunting them through the thin kaftan, slowly, lazily, until she let out a gasp of pleasure. His body pressed against her back, her bottom, and she could feel the full length of him.

Then just as quickly he turned her around and she stood facing him, reading the hunger and determination in his eyes, in the unyielding line of his lips, and knew that he was not going to give in. He would take her. What she wanted was immaterial.

His mouth came down upon hers, and Nena knew a hot rush of exaltation. At first his mouth was tender, as though afraid of hurting her, then all at once she could bear it no longer, knew a raw, primal need for him, could no more control the rampant hunger gnawing at every inch of her body. And as she brought her arms up around his neck and cleaved to him Ramon let drop all barriers, let go the fears he'd had of frightening or hurting her and allowed his mouth to ravage, his tongue to play havoc. He pressed his hand into the small of her back, bringing her closer to him, forcing her to feel the extent of his desire, revelling in her hair, the soft feel of her skin, her scent, her being.

Then, when he could bear it no longer, he did what he'd done once before, and lifting her into his arms carried her masterfully through to the bedroom.

Nena sighed as he laid her on the bed, unable to protest, her whole being pining for him, for his hands on her body, for the feel of him inside her aching core.

And Ramon was quick to satisfy. In one swift movement he lifted her kaftan and threw it aside. Somehow his own clothes were quickly strewn on the floor and he stood naked.

'My *linda,* my beautiful, lovely Nena,' he murmured hoarsely. 'How I've wanted you, how I've missed you.' Then he was on the bed and his hands were all over her as she writhed, unable to control the spasms of delight overtaking her body as stealthily his fingers ventured within her, easing that delectable yet unbearable pain until she was gorged, filled with the same delicious saturation he'd shown her already, and that, though she hadn't admitted it, she'd missed like the devil.

Ramon crushed his own need, mastered his feelings, delighting in her moans, triumphant when she let go a raw cry of completion when he brought her to a peak.

But this time he didn't wait for her to recover. Instead he thrust deep inside her. For a single instant he experienced a wave of fear that he might be harming her. But Nena's immediate breathless reaction, and her legs curling about him, drove him on and on, dispelling any and all doubt. And once more they travelled as one on an ever-rising journey that ended in a rush of such unadulterated joy that neither could do more than lie gasping, limp in each other's arms.

The next few days were spent in a glorious lazy haze. They spoke little, unwilling to allow anything to obliterate the blissful atmosphere created on their first night, only too ready to let it last for as long as possible. Together they investigated the island in an old army Jeep kept for the purpose. They had picnics up on the rocks overlooking the sea, spent long hours idling away the time, kissing, fondling one another, unable to resist the urgent sexual tug that was present from dawn until dusk.

Nena knew she was deluding herself, that soon she would have to wake up and make up her mind. But for now she didn't care. She was too busy absorbing the whole of Ramon's seductive being—the scent of him, the feel of him, the delicious hours spent trailing her nails over his back, his arms, through his hair. Then suddenly, when she least expected it, he would turn around and with a wolfish grin bring her on top of him, and the whole thing would begin all over again.

Each time they made love he taught her more. Sometimes Nena experienced a stab of shock when they became more experimental, and Ramon positioned her in ways she would never have thought of. But that too excited her, gave her new and exhilarating confidence. She felt truly a woman now, baptised for ever into the art of lovemaking by a man so expert he would be very hard to replace, she realised ruefully, smiling at her own daring.

One day they went out fishing with the villagers. They were friendly and open, and she enjoyed seeing Ramon help heave in the heavy nets. Such a different Ramon, she reflected, from the severe, well-dressed businessman back in London and Buenos Aires. He was getting browner by the day, as she was herself, the soft autumnal sun streaking her hair and seeping into her tanned skin.

Gradually the events of the previous month, the deep sense of loss and fragmentation that she'd experienced faded. She could laugh again, often giggling at Ramon's jokes, amazed at how relaxed he'd become since their arrival on the island. And she was secretly afraid of the day when they would have to leave it. She wished that they could stay on and on, stowed away like luxury castaways, not having to face the ordeals of an everyday life, of the business waiting for him back in London, or the possibility of another woman popping out of the woodwork to destroy the status quo.

In the evenings they sat on the terrace, sipping ouzo or retsina, then sitting down to a late dinner prepared by Efi, the cook, delighting in her melting *moussakas* or delicious *aranaki*—lamb. Occasionally they would take the motor boat and ride over to the nearest island to eat in one of the tavernas by the waterside, where large squid were hung up to dry like washing, then squirted with lemon and cooked on the grill.

Sometimes they would stay there for several hours, and Ramon would play a game or two of backgammon with some of the older villagers, old Petros or Taki, who sat all day, their backs to the warm wall, smoking their strong Turkish tobacco and drinking *cafedaki*—small cups of thick, lethally strong, sweet, black coffee.

When Nena had drunk hers, Maria, the wife of the taverna's owner, would sit down heavily on a creaking wooden chair and turn Nena's cup upside down, allowing the grains to take their course. Then several minutes later—usually after a lengthy conversation with her husband that sounded like a quarrel but that Ramon assured her was not— she would turn back to Nena with a smile and begin telling her fortune, which her grandson of thirteen, Janis, translated into surprisingly fluent English.

'She says you are married to a good man but you don't trust him,' he said one day, as his grandmother placed the cup back in the saucer and looked at her understandingly. 'She says it is normal. Kirios Ramon is a very handsome man. His cup says he had many women. But not any more.'

'Right. Well, thanks,' Nena said hastily, looking up uneasily, hoping his words had been drowned by the lapping of the water and the *sirtaki* music playing on the radio, and that Ramon, seated two tables away, hadn't heard.

'Want a game, Nena?' he called. 'I've just been beaten by Petros. He's the best player on the island. But we still have time for one more before we get back.'

Then he glanced out to sea and said something to

Petros in Greek. The old man narrowed his eyes and peered across the water.

'Actually, I think we'd better go after all. Petros says there may well be a storm brewing. It's autumn now, and these things can whip up out of the blue at this time of year. I'll play you at home, *mi linda,* how's that?'

Nena could think of other games to play at home, but she agreed, picked up her basket and the straw hat that had become a part of her island uniform and, saying goodbye to the islanders, moved with Ramon towards the motor boat.

They were three-quarters of the way back when the storm struck. The sky turned purple and dark, heavy black clouds loomed, lightning flashed and the wind picked up. Huge waves heaved to and fro, making it difficult to steer the small motor boat.

'Hang on tight,' Ramon said, ploughing mercilessly through the rising waters. 'We'll be there soon. Are you okay?' He sent her a worried glance, then concentrated once more on steering.

'I'm fine,' Nena shouted, disguising her fear.

Then all at once an immense wave rocked the boat off balance, nearly sweeping them into the deep.

'Hold on!' Ramon shouted, as they clung, drenched, to the boat. 'Grab a life jacket.'

Nena did as she was told, and with difficulty pulled on the floatable life jacket. Ramon was just doing the same when a clap of thunder sounded and another huge wave rammed into them. Before Ramon could do anything they capsized.

Nena felt her body catapulted into the deep waters of the Aegean. Where was Ramon? Oh, God. She spluttered and tried desperately to hold on to the boat, that was still near enough to clutch.

'Ramon!' she shouted desperately as soon as she surfaced. 'Ramon, where are you? Answer me.' She could just distinguish Agapos and realised that they were not far from land. But would somebody see them? Would anybody be out in this weather and able to rescue them? And where was Ramon? Why didn't he reply?

A horrible vice-like fear gripped her as she tried desperately to fight her way around the capsized craft to see if she could find him. Maybe he'd been knocked out in the fall. Maybe— *Oh, God, no—please, dear God, make him be safe, make him be alive.*

She was finding it hard to stay afloat as the waves rushed at her, sweeping her and the boat in their wake. She could hardly breathe as water filled her lungs and she went under once more, before spluttering back to the surface, desperate to find him.

Then suddenly she heard the distant rumble of a motor and a wave of relief poured over her. Someone had sighted them. Thank goodness. If only she could reach Ramon.

But what if he'd been swept away and—? No—she mustn't think like that. He was here, close by, she was certain. He just couldn't call to her.

Then at last she saw men from the island leaning over the side of a small, sturdy fishing boat, undaunted by the turbulent sea. They came up close, then one threw her a cord with a lifesaver attached and urged her to hold on to it as he pulled her in.

Shivering, she climbed on board, oblivious of her cuts and bruises, her eyes searching the water for any sign of the man she loved.

She loved!

Suddenly the words sprang at her. How hadn't she recognised it fully before? Why had she not admitted to herself just how much he actually meant to her?

Then she heard a shout and watched frozen to the spot as one of the men, wearing a life jacket and secured by a rope, jumped in and swam towards an inert form floating nearby.

Nena gripped the side of the boat and gazed in terror as the man slipped his hand under Ramon's chin and brought him in the lifesaving position back to the fishing boat. There were shouts and exclamations as the men heaved him on board and Tasso began immediately to pump his lungs.

Nena stood by, terrified, fearing to interfere lest she get in the way. *Come on,* she begged silently. *Please, dear God, make him all right. Please don't let him die.*

After some thirty seconds she heard a cough, and watched, trembling, as Ramon spluttered and wretched.

'Oh, darling,' she cried, throwing herself on the deck and reaching for him.

Ramon spluttered again, and gulped, and tried to open his eyes. He'd been hit hard on the head and was reeling from the shock and pain.

'Breathe deeply, darling,' Nena urged as the boat

turned and ploughed steadily back towards Agapos and safety.

She held him in her arms, feeling him limp on her breast as he lay there, too exhausted to move, to do anything but try and breathe. Soon they were docking in the tiny harbour at Agapos, and men rushed aboard and lifted Ramon easily in their arms.

Nena followed close behind as they carried him into the nearest villager's home and laid him on a simple wooden bed, above which hung a large Greek cross and a picture of Hagios Stefanos—St Stephen—the patron saint of the area.

Women came in and began treating him. The owner of the house was named Elpida. Luckily her son, who was a doctor in Athens, was visiting for the weekend, and came hurrying in with his medical bag. He pulled out his stethoscope and carefully began listening to Ramon's heaving lungs while Nena stood by in agony, waiting for the verdict, wishing she could wave a magic wand and make him all right.

Slowly Ramon's breathing became easier. The doctor went about his business, and little by little he began to register what was going on around him.

'Nena?' he whispered hoarsely, his voice a thread. 'Where is she? Is she all right?'

'I'm here, darling, and I'm fine.' She sat down next to him on the bed and smoothed his brow, wincing at the sight of the cut on his cheek where the boat must have hit him. 'Darling, you're fine. Everything's all right now. You're going to be all right.'

Ramon's eyes met hers for a moment and he tried

to smile. 'I thought I'd lost you,' he whispered, the words obviously an effort.

'Don't talk, darling, just stay quiet,' Nena admonished, her fingers entwining his, watching as his head sank back on the pillow.

The doctor reassured her, 'He'll be much better in a few hours, once he's had some rest.'

'But I thought people who'd had concussion should stay awake,' Nena countered, looking at him uncertainly.

'Don't worry,' the doctor replied in excellent English, 'We'll keep an eye on him. Now, I recommend that you let me take a look at you. A few cuts and bruises as well, I see.'

Nena looked down at her arms and legs. It was true. There were a couple of bruises forming on her arm, and a cut just above her knee.

'Let me treat them,' the doctor said firmly, seeing how loath she was to leave Ramon's side even for a minute. 'Your husband will be fine now. All he needs is some rest.'

Reluctantly Nena rose and allowed him to disinfect her cut and put a bandage round it. But she never took her eyes off Ramon's sleeping figure.

They stayed there all night—Ramon sleeping peacefully in the little wooden bed, with Nena seated on a stool next to him, never taking her eyes off him, gently smoothing the hair from his brow from time to time. As dawn broke she saw how pale he was and her heart lurched once more with fear. Was he really all right? He had to be. She couldn't bear it if he wasn't.

There was no sign of yesterday's storm now. The day dawned bright and sunny, and soon the household was up and moving. Nena could hear Elpida's movements in the kitchen, could smell the scent of fresh coffee and baked bread and hear the low murmuring of voices.

Then Elpida peeked around the door.

'Ti kani?' she asked.

'Better, I think,' Nena answered in English, smiling.

'Eisai kourasmeni,' Elpida said, and Nena understood enough to realise she was telling her she must be tired.

Only then did she become aware of the stiffness in her limbs, and a mild throbbing in her leg. Elpida was indicating to her that she must go and rest. But first she gave Nena a cup of steaming coffee, which she drank thankfully. She had refused all food the night before, unable to stomach anything. But now, seeing Ramon pale but better, and certain that he was on the road to recovery, she relaxed a little and realised that she was in fact quite hungry.

Elpida pointed to the kitchen and insisted she join the family for a breakfast of thick hunks of bread spread with home-made butter and fresh honey. It tasted glorious, and as she bit into it Nena sent up thanks for their timely delivery from what could have been a fatal accident.

Then she returned to Ramon's bedside, watching him tenderly, hoping that soon he would open those wonderful chestnut eyes and smile at her as only he knew how.

* * *

'I can't believe we've been here three weeks,' Nena said one evening as they sat with jerseys slipped over their shoulders, for the nights were much cooler now. Ramon had made a surprisingly quick recovery but he still needed to rest.

'It has passed so quickly,' Ramon agreed, slipping his hand in hers and squeezing her fingers. 'Thank you, *mi amor,* for caring for me as you have. I couldn't ask for a better wife.' He grinned at her, the cut on his cheek practically healed now and the bruises barely visible.

'You aren't an altogether easy patient,' she chided, recalling the first few days after the accident, when Ramon had begun to recuperate, demanding to get up, impatient at being kept quiet when he wanted to be active. But Nena had insisted, and for some reason he could not put his finger on, Ramon had complied with her wishes.

'Another glass of wine?' he asked, leaning the bottle in the direction of her glass while glancing at his watch. 'I have a couple of calls to make in about twenty minutes—just time to sit here a little longer.'

'Okay.' Nena smiled. She loved these evenings spent on the terrace, sharing time together—moments that had become increasingly precious after the accident.

The latter had formed a silent bond between them. They didn't need to talk about it, or go over it time and again, but each knew how close they'd been to losing the other and the thought had left them both shaken.

'Ah, there's the phone,' Ramon remarked, getting

up from the wrought-iron chair and making his way inside.

Nena caught snatches of his voice through the open glass doors.

'Yes? When did you find out? Ah, I see. Well, it will have to be dealt with immediately. I was sure he was the one. I'm afraid so—no, that would be impossible. Fine. I'll be there tomorrow.'

Nena listened to his last words with a sinking heart. She knew the call must be from London, that something was going on in the office—either his or at Carvajal's—that would require his immediate presence. Now, finally, the dream was about to end.

'Nena, I'm afraid we shall have to leave tomorrow and go back to London. There are things I need to attend to at the office,' he said absently.

'I see,' she replied, masking the rush of fear and disappointment. Here everything was so perfect that she was loath to return to the real world. 'Is something wrong?' she asked, seeing his brows creased in a thick dark line above the ridge of his nose.

'I'm not entirely certain as yet, but I believe so. It's a bit difficult to explain right now.'

'Well, I don't see why,' Nena responded touchily. 'I'm not totally dense.'

'It has nothing to do with you being dense or otherwise. I'm just not sure of my facts and this involves others. I'm afraid you'll have to wait.' His tone was arbitrary and she experienced a flash of annoyance.

And pain.

It had already begun. The outside world was already insinuating itself into their little paradise, tainting it with the doubts and fears that for the past weeks she'd managed to exclude from their existence.

And now was reality check.

Nena said nothing, but she rose and went inside, all desire to sit out in the evening breeze suddenly gone. The magic interlude was over, she realised sadly, and the sooner she recognised the fact the better it would be.

CHAPTER TEN

SINCE their return home Nena had barely seen Ramon. He seemed inordinately busy, often returning to Eaton Square close upon ten o'clock. She didn't question his absences, but they hurt. Surely there couldn't be *that* much to do at the office that required him to stay so late? One night she actually telephoned him on his mobile phone, but she was given short shrift and never repeated the action

'I'm in a meeting,' he'd said impatiently. 'I'll call you as soon as I've finished.'

But it was past midnight when he reached home, and Nena had long since cried herself to sleep.

It was no use. It would always be the same. The few weeks away had been nothing but an illusion that they'd both bought into for a while. Now he was back in his own world—a world of business and possibly casual or less casual affairs—and all that went with it.

The other thing that worried her was that they'd hardly made love since their return. This fact, coupled with the late nights and Ramon's increasingly short temper, did nothing to allay her fears.

She must, she realised, make up her mind whether

or not she was going to continue with the marriage or bring it to an end once and for all.

The other matter that she'd left on hold was the applications to the universities she was interested in. But for some reason she didn't have the energy or the will to get on with them. Perhaps she would just have to let it go for another year.

Life was altogether not bright, and Nena felt herself slowly withering.

There seemed little light at the end of the tunnel.

As his investigation deepened Ramon became increasingly angry at the discrepancies he was coming across—not only in the Carvajal accounting, but in the way several big deals had been handled. It was a gruelling job to try and get to the bottom of the whole thing without alerting the principal suspects, and it had to be done carefully, mostly out of hours. He had enough to keep him busy during the day anyway, running not only his own businesses but seeing that Don Rodrigo's affairs were put back on track.

His days were long and his nights short. He wished he could explain to Nena, but felt it was impossible—the whole thing was just too tricky and too delicate to be broadcast before he had definite answers and proof of the double-dealing he suspected.

But when one weekend he suggested they go to Paris and take a break she seemed unenthusiastic. She didn't want to open up her grandfather's flat there, and said they might as well just go to a hotel.

Ramon agreed, and booked a suite at the Plaza Athénée.

They arrived in Paris on Friday evening and prepared to dine at the Relais Plaza attached to the hotel. Perhaps later they would go dancing or have a drink somewhere, he reflected as they sat down.

But Nena was strangely silent, unwilling even to make conversation.

'Nena, is something wrong?' he asked, irritated despite his desire to spend a nice time with her. She certainly wasn't making it easy. Hadn't he been at her entire disposal during three full weeks? Surely she must understand that he had a lot of work to catch up with now, as well as his other responsibilities?

'No, nothing's wrong—except everything,' she muttered, savagely spreading butter on her French roll.

'What do you mean, *querida?* I thought we were past all that now, that things were settling down between us.'

'Really?' she said, glaring at him across the table. 'Well, you thought wrong. Maybe you think you can just shove me into a convenient drawer the minute you have other priorities to deal with, but I think that I merit some consideration.'

Ramon sighed. This was not going to be easy. The investigations had reached a critical point where any kind of revelation might be fatal to the final outcome.

'Look, Nena, I know I've been out a lot—'

'A lot? Talk about an understatement?'

'Please,' he pleaded patiently, 'I can't explain everything that goes on at the office to you, but right now there are some fires to be put out.'

'I'm sure. Especially from six o'clock onwards.'

'Nena, what exactly are you saying?'

'That you seem to have an awful lot to do after hours, Ramon.'

He looked at her haughtily. 'As a matter of fact, I do.'

'Great. Well, that tells me all I need to know, doesn't it?'

'What are you implying?' he asked carefully, lowering his glass, his eyes narrowing dangerously and his mouth forming a thin, angry line.

'That you obviously have a mistress. Which is why I think the best thing would be if we finally brought this whole rigmarole to an end.'

'You want to end our marriage?' he said bitingly.

'Yes. I think that this time I've really reached the end of my tether, Ramon. First it was Luisa, and now— Well, I don't know who it is now, but I can only deduce there must be someone for you to spend every night out with as you're doing.' Her eyes were bright, her smile fixed and brittle, but she kept it in place, damned if she was going to make a fool of herself again.

'This is absurd,' he threw, putting his napkin down on the table angrily.

'No, it's not. You think that you can handle me as if I was a piece of personal property that you can pick up or put back on the shelf whenever you feel like it. Well, I'm not. And the sooner you realise it the better. The problem is that I don't think you're capable of seeing it any other way, so the sooner we get divorced and get on with our respective lives, the better it will be for both of us.'

'I don't believe I'm hearing this,' he muttered, hot rage simmering below his cool exterior.

'Don't you? Well, that's because you're too used to getting your own way, I suppose.' Nena made a show of sipping her champagne.

'Okay, that's it.' Ramon's face was dark and forbidding now and Nena swallowed, wondering if she'd gone too far. But it served him right. He had no right to treat her the way he had, in that autocratic manner.

'Waiter.' Ramon signalled the young man. 'We won't be dining after all. Put it on my bill.' He made to rise.

'But we've just ordered!' Nena exclaimed.

'Get up, Nena, and come with me.'

Nena hesitated, about to refuse, then realised that she could hardly make a scene in the middle of the Relais and obediently followed him.

Ramon marched her out of the restaurant and down the corridor back into the hotel. There he called the elevator. They rode it in chilled silence that could be cut with a knife. Nena held her head high and pretended not to give a damn, but she couldn't help peeking at his furious face. What did he plan to do? Pack up and leave for London again at once?

Ramon unlocked the door of their suite and pulled off the jacket of his suit. Then he turned and eyed her, his eyes hard. 'I've had just about enough of these games.'

'What games? I'm not playing games. If anyone does that it's you,' she threw, standing her ground.

'Really? You think I play games? That I spend the

better part of my time with some woman instead of with you, is that it?' he asked, voice menacing.

Nena took a deep breath determined not to cower as he moved towards her.

'I—yes. I think that—'

'What exactly do you think, Nena? Tell me,' he said, looming over her now, his dark eyes gleaming with anger.

'That you're—well, that—'

'Yes? Say it. Go on—or are you afraid?'

'Of course I'm not afraid,' she spluttered, forcing herself to look him in the eye. 'It's just that—'

'What?'

'This whole thing was wrong right from the start,' she muttered, looking away.

'Really? Well, let me show you just how wrong I think it is.'

Before she could react his arms were about her, his body ramming hers. His hand slipped to the crook of her neck and he pulled her hair back, forcing her to look into his face. 'I'll show you once and for all what is right and what is wrong, *señora mia,*' he muttered hoarsely, practically throwing her onto the bed.

Then he was kissing her, stripping her of her garments and laying her naked before him.

'Don't, Ramon,' she whispered, feeling that inevitable tug of desire pulling somewhere deep within her and trying desperately to resist it. 'Don't, please—we must be reasonable.'

'Reasonable? Ha!' With a few quick movements he stripped off his clothes and was back on the bed, his mouth ravaging her breasts, causing her to cry out.

Then his lips sought further, descending until they reached her most vulnerable spot, that tiny nub of flesh, which he laved, taunted, leaving her moaning, the indescribable pleasure more intense than anything she'd ever felt, even in their most ardent lovemaking on Agapos.

And he didn't stop, but continued relentlessly until she climaxed over and over, unable to prevent the thrilling rush of pleasure and fulfilment.

Nena could do nothing to stop the ardent onslaught, all thoughts forgotten as her plundered being surrendered to Ramon's merciless siege of her body. When finally he thrust inside her, not gently, but hard and fast, as though determined to possess every inch of her, she curled around him, basked in the delight of him, breathless, responding now kiss for kiss, arching to receive him, all reason forgotten.

When it was over at last, and they lay spent among the rumpled linen sheets, Ramon on one side of the bed and Nena on the other, he turned and looked at her hard. 'Is that what you call wrong, Nena? Would you be able to conceive doing that with another man?'

'Of course I wouldn't dream of making love with another man,' she threw at him witheringly, wishing he would take her in his arms as he usually did, not leave her abandoned and alone on the far side of this very large bed.

'I see. And you think that I would find it perfectly natural to make love in the same manner as I do with you with another woman? Is that it?'

'It had occurred to me,' she mumbled, feeling

rather foolish under his intense scrutiny. 'After all, you were out with Luisa.'

'Luisa! Always damn Luisa. Can't we forget her? I certainly have. She's nothing but a friend now.'

'That's not what it looked like to me,' Nena muttered, curling into the pillow, her tired limbs aching.

'So you're jealous?' he said thoughtfully, sitting up and eyeing her closely.

'Of course I'm not jealous,' she snapped, sitting up as well and pulling her knees under her chin. 'I'm realistic, that's all. You had an affair with the woman for two years. I suppose it's normal that you wouldn't just break up with her because of a marriage of convenience that was thrust upon you when you least expected it.'

'Hmm.' His gaze was speculative. 'And just out of interest, *querida,* how did you find out about Luisa and I?'

'I read an article,' she replied defensively. 'In *Hola!* magazine. You were splattered all over it.'

'I see. And so you believe that now I must be either continuing my affair with Luisa—an interesting thought, since she's several thousand miles away—or out every evening making passionate love to someone else?'

'I didn't say that.'

'Not in so many words,' he said, his lips twitching, 'but you implied it.'

'Well, you have to admit you spend more time out than in,' she threw, eyeing him crossly from under her thick lashes, unaware of how lovely and young and vulnerable she looked, huddled against the pillows, her lips pouting.

'Then perhaps it is time, *mi amor,* that I explain to you exactly why I have been spending an unusual amount of time away from you. It is not by desire, I assure you.'

'No? Then why is it?' she challenged, wondering what sort of excuse he'd come up with—though she was feeling less certain about her former theory by the moment.

'Perhaps we should get up first, have a shower, and I'll order Room Service,' Ramon replied, reaching over and helping her up. 'Then I promise to give you a full account of why I've been so tied up.'

'But—'

'Shush,' he ordered. 'For once just do as you're told, and don't get me annoyed again or this time I'll lay you over my knee and give you the spanking you deserve for being so suspicious of your husband,' he said, laughing before he leaned down and kissed her brow. 'Now, off with you into the shower.'

He slapped her bottom lightly, and Nena felt her face breaking into a smile in spite of the doubts that still lingered.

Later, once they'd both showered, Nena joined Ramon at the table brought up by Room Service, piled with scrambled eggs and bacon, toast and tea. They sat wrapped in the thick terry towel robes provided by the hotel and Nena realised that she was hungry now—and for just what he'd ordered. Forget wine and fine cuisine, she was delighted to dig her teeth into something wholesome.

'I hope this suits you,' Ramon said, passing the butter. 'Personally, I'm rather hungry.'

'Me, too,' Nena agreed, lifting the silver dome covering her scrambled eggs and bacon and delighting in the delicious aroma wafting to her nostrils.

This she realised wistfully, was another aspect of her husband that she so enjoyed. The fact that he could be fun, casual and relaxed. That she didn't need to be on show the whole time, like some wives appeared to be, that she could be herself.

But she still hadn't heard what he had to say, and she was determined that before she allowed herself any more breaks she simply must know what Ramon had been doing for the past few weeks. Even though she had her own ideas, the least she could do was listen to his version of the story before passing final judgement.

She looked across the crisp white tablecloth at his handsome features, his bronzed face and neck appearing from inside the white terry robe, and sighed.

How she loved him!

Nena took some toast from the basket and absently spread it with butter. For, although she recognised her feelings, she knew that unless his excuse was a very good one she could never live happily with a man whom she believed was betraying her at every turn—however handsome, however wonderful he might be.

'Are—are you going to tell me?' she said finally, biting the bullet. Better to get it over with right away than spend the whole meal conjecturing.

'I told you I would tell you, Nena, and I will. It may come as a surprise, and be somewhat upsetting, but I'm afraid it's the truth and must be faced.'

Nena nodded. Her heart quailed. So it was a woman after all.

'Ever since your grandfather died,' Ramon said, stirring some sugar into his tea, 'I have been dealing with the Carvajal affairs, as you know.'

She nodded, gulped down her tea and listened.

'After several days of studying files, and meeting with members of the board and the staff, I became aware of certain discrepancies. Or what I assumed might be discrepancies. One file in particular caught my attention. I won't bore you with a lot of detail that is really unimportant at this stage—suffice it to say that I became increasingly suspicious of several people, and principally, I'm sorry to say, Sir Wilfred.'

'Sir Wilfred?' Nena exclaimed, shocked. 'But he was Grandfather's most trusted person.'

'I know. Which makes what I've discovered doubly bad.'

'What have you discovered?' Nena asked, caught between shock at his revelation and delight that the reason he'd been spending time away was so far removed from what her fertile imagination had been creating that it left her feeling stupid and guilty for having falsely accused Ramon.

'I'm afraid he's been siphoning funds from the company ever since your grandfather became ill. But it'll be difficult to prove, and I would hesitate to take the matter to court. It will only cause a scandal, and would probably affect the market value of the company as a whole. I feel we should deal with this as discreetly as possible. Sir Wilfred is, after all, getting on. It would be no surprise to anyone if he decided to retire.'

'But that's awful!' Nena exclaimed, horrified that such a trusted member of her grandfather's entourage could have stooped to this level. 'How could he have done this to Grandfather when he knew how much he was trusted? It's awful, Ramon. He shouldn't get away with it.'

He shrugged. 'I know he shouldn't, but believe me, Nena, this is the best way to deal with the matter. It'll avoid an uproar, and the company has not suffered very much from his devious behaviour. Mercifully, he hasn't had time to do much damage.'

'No—thanks to you,' she said, her eyes meeting his across the table.

'I did nothing but my duty. This sort of thing is precisely why your grandfather wanted someone responsible at the helm. I was merely doing my job.'

Nena smiled tentatively. 'Perhaps that's true, but—well, I feel awful that I imagined so many things about you.'

'You aren't entirely to blame,' he responded ruefully, reaching for her hand and stroking her fingers. 'I did nothing to alleviate those doubts. I couldn't, you see. I didn't want to upset you unnecessarily, and I didn't feel I could voice my opinion until I had absolute proof of what Sir Wilfred was doing.'

'I understand. How stupid I've been.'

'Not at all. I rather like that my wife is jealous of me. I would be just the same about you.'

'Would you?' she asked, colouring, suddenly curious.

'Yes. Don't even think about having any good-looking young men hanging around.'

'I wouldn't dream of it,' Nena said, smiling at him. 'I'm quite happy with what I've got.'

'Are you? I certainly hope so. Because I am. More than happy.' He rose, came around the table and, slipping his hands around her neck from behind, firmly kissed the top of her head.

'You're sure this marriage isn't just an obligation for you?' she queried once again, needing to be certain, to feel absolutely sure before she committed.

'Tell me, what does it look like to you, *mi amor?* Do I seem bored to you? Unhappy? Not forthcoming in bed?'

'No, of course not.'

'Then what are you worried about?'

'I don't know. Nothing any more, I suppose. It just seemed so—so imposed, so businesslike.'

'Let's face the truth of the matter, Nena. My parents and your grandfather were right. Despite this be ing a totally intolerable situation by today's standards they've proved us wrong.' He pulled her up and they faced one another. 'Frankly, all I want to do is take you back into bed and see if together we can't make another baby as soon as possible.'

'Oh.' Nena stared at his chest and swallowed, the thought of the baby sending a shaft of pain searing through her.

'Nena, the miscarriage happened because the time wasn't right. We weren't completely sure of one another, and somehow nature understood that and took care of things in its own fashion. But not any more. This time I will be here, next to you, making sure nothing happens to you ever again.'

'And Luisa?' she asked in a small voice, needing to cover every piece of terrain.

'I explained to her that day at the restaurant. That's why I met with her. To tell her once and for all that it was over between us, that I had found the woman of my dreams and that there was no possibility of us having any kind of relationship except friendship.'

'Really?' Nena raised her face to his, a rush of relief and warmth coursing through her at the gleam in his bright chestnut eyes, at the possessive look he sent her and the delicious feel of his hands caressing her back.

'Let's get one thing clear, Nena,' he said, drawing away from her and posing his hands on her shoulders. 'I will never lie to you. Either you trust me and I trust you or this relationship makes no sense. Do you trust me?'

She looked at him for a long moment, drinking in his words. Then she smiled, looked straight into his eyes.

'Yes, I do.'

'For as long as we live?'

'Until death do us part,' she whispered in response.

'Then there's very little left to say,' he murmured, drawing her close, 'that can't be said in other ways.'

Scooping her into his arms as though she were a feather, he held her a moment, gazing into her eyes.

'You are mine,' he declared, 'all mine. And I shall never, ever let you go.'

'Ditto,' she murmured, letting her head sink onto his strong shoulder.

Ramon took her to the bed and laid her in the middle of it. 'Now, it's time to get down to augmenting our small family, *señora mía*,' he said, a wolfish grin spreading over his features.

'And I'll be only too happy to oblige, kind sir,' she whispered, pulling him down onto the bed, where he landed on top of her.

'Then let's get to it.'

'Wait—hadn't we better put the "do not disturb" sign out?' Nena asked suddenly.

'Forget it,' he growled. 'They'll get the message soon enough when there's no answer. Now, can we please forget about anything that isn't just us, Nena?'

'Anything you say, my love,' she replied demurely, smothering the gurgle of love and laughter bubbling inside. 'Anything you say.'

Unlimited access to all your favourite Mills & Boon romances!

Start your free trial now

Available at

weloveromance.com

JOIN THE MILLS & BOON BOOKCLUB

- **FREE** delivery direct to your door
- **EXCLUSIVE** offers every month
- **EXCITING** rewards programme

Join today at

Millsandboon.co.uk/Bookclub

MILLS & BOON

MODERN

Power and Passion

Prepare to be swept off your feet by sophisticated, sexy and seductive heroes, in some of the world's most glamourous and romantic locations, where power and passion collide.

Eight Modern stories published every month, find them a

millsandboon.co.uk/Modern

LET'S TALK

Romance

For exclusive extracts, competitions and special offers, find us online:

facebook.com/millsandboon

@MillsandBoon

@MillsandBoonUK

Get in touch on 01413 063232

For all the latest titles coming soon, visit

millsandboon.co.uk/nextmonth

WANT EVEN MORE

ROMANCE?

SUBSCRIBE AND SAVE TODAY!

'Mills & Boon books, the perfect way to escape for an hour or so.'

MISS W. DYER

'Excellent service, promptly delivered and very good subscription choices.'

MISS A. PEARSON

'You get fantastic special offers and the chance to get books before they hit the shops.'

MRS V. HALL

Visit millsandboon.co.uk/Subscribe and save on brand new books.

MILLS & BOON
A ROMANCE FOR EVERY READER

FREE delivery direct to your door

EXCLUSIVE offers every month

SAVE up to 25% on pre-paid subscriptions

SUBSCRIBE AND SAVE

millsandboon.co.uk/Subscribe

MILLS & BOON

THE HEART OF ROMANCE

A ROMANCE FOR EVERY READER

MODERN Prepare to be swept off your feet by sophisticated, sexy and seductive heroes, in some of the world's most glamourous and roma locations, where power and passion collide.

HISTORICAL Escape with historical heroes from time gone by. Whether your passi for wicked Regency Rakes, muscled Vikings or rugged Highlanders, the romance of the past.

MEDICAL Set your pulse racing with dedicated, delectable doctors in the high- sure world of medicine, where emotions run high and passion, comf love are the best medicine.

True Love Celebrate true love with tender stories of heartfelt romance, from th rush of falling in love to the joy a new baby can bring, and a focus c emotional heart of a relationship.

Desire Indulge in secrets and scandal, intense drama and plenty of sizzling action with powerful and passionate heroes who have it all: wealth, s good looks...everything but the right woman.

HEROES Experience all the excitement of a gripping thriller, with an intense mance at its heart. Resourceful, true-to-life women and strong, fearl face danger and desire - a killer combination!

To see which titles are coming soon, please visit

millsandboon.co.uk/nextmonth